BEAST
OF
BURDEN

BEAST

OF

PEDER CARLSSON
DAN GLIMNE

BURDEN

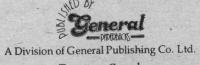

PUBLISHED BY

General
— PAPERBACKS —

A Division of General Publishing Co. Ltd.

Published by Bra Spänning, Höganäs Sweden
in 1982: Swedish title: *Lastdjuret*

General Paperbacks edition published in 1983

ISBN 0-7736-7051-3

Cover design: Brant Cowie and
            Bruce Westerby

Illustration: D. Zacropolis

Printed and bound in Canada

For our friends the drivers, and especially for Lasse and Christer. For all the rides, for all the meals, for all your hospitality, this is our way of saying "Thank You."

For invaluable information and assistance during the writing of this book, we would like to thank:

Mark & Barbro Lippold
Tommy Ljungberg
Lars-Olof Sjögren
Mikael Bar-Zohar
Sten & Monica Henning
Scaniabilar, Malmö
Hugh Ashton
Kristine Singh, SAS
John Rodney
The Institute of Semitic Languages, University of Lund;

1

SUMMER CHANGED SLOWLY INTO WINTER and day into night around the six-hundred-metre level. In the distance, the snowcapped peaks of the high Taurus Mountains rose in the evening-dun sky, catching the rays of the setting sun. The pines and larch trees cast long shadows across the narrow, winding road, blurring its edges. Down in the ravines the first patches of snow showed among the trees. Inside the big Swedish Scania 141, the cassette stereo was playing ABBA at full blast, while the V-8 diesel laboured on the uphill stretches into the mountains.

The road was steep and rough, and even though the semitrailer was empty, it took the driver a lot of shifting to keep the engine pulling strongly. He had raised the bogie for a softer ride, but still every pothole jarred the truck to the core.

He had bought some oranges from the last roadside vendor on the green lowland, some kilometres back. Now, on one of the rare stretches of straight road, he drove with his elbows on the steering wheel, savouring the last taste of summer as the seasons turned. On the other side of the mountains was the wintry Turkish highland; summer and the Syrian desert lay less than twenty-four hours behind.

The high snows were losing their last glow. A chill was stealing into the cab, and he reached for the air-conditioner controls in the ceiling. The Kysor was run-

ning at low speed, a soft whine drowning in the deeper
song of the diesel. He turned it off.

Brake lights flashed ahead in the dusk; in front was
Hugh Ashton in his Volvo F89 with the yellow and
violet Funston Transport logo on the tarpaulin sides of
the semitrailer.

Normally, the Scania would have taken the ferry from
Tartous in Syria to Vólos in Greece, but with Christmas
only nine days off the trucks queuing for passage
stretched for kilometres. The driver was in a hurry to
get to Austria, pick up his return load, and get back
home, so he had chosen the route through Turkey. But
nobody in his right mind liked doing the 1400-odd kilometres from Cilvegözu to Kapikule alone, and having
met Hugh, who had opted for the same alternative, was
a stroke of luck—for both of them. They had met half
a year before, going down the H4 from Haditha to Dammam; it was one of those quickly developed, easy-going
friendships of the road, born without any great ceremony out of the camaraderie among the drivers on the
Middle East run.

The lights ahead were a comfort, an extension of the
snugness within his own cab. He finished off the last
of the orange, rolled the side window down and threw
the peels out, then got a cigarette out from the pack
of Prince that was bouncing around on the dashboard
and lit it. ABBA had run out and reversed for the third
time.

Music was necessary. It kept the drivers awake on
long, monotonous journeys, but variety was equally
necessary. He pressed the eject button, and fumbled for
another cassette without taking his eyes off the winding
road. Then Shirley Bassey filled the cab. That, too, was
good music. All disliked tapes had eventually fallen by
the roadside as the kilometres had accumulated, been
traded one for one to other drivers during long waits

in customs, or surreptitiously slipped to agents in order to get the papers processed a little faster.

The clock on the dashboard said a quarter to six; he ought to be rolling into Aksaray a little before nine, depending on traffic and the weather on the other side. A few scattered stationary lights showed further up the road; all the illumination offered to the world by Tekir, the village at the top of the ascent. This was as high as he would climb into the mountains. Now came the worst part of the road, the long, winding downhill stretch to the highland.

As the Scania rolled into the village, its headlights cast a bright glare across a motley collection of buildings that clung to the slopes by the roadside, illuminating animal carcasses hanging skinned by their hind legs outside the houses, and briefly catching locals going about in their inevitable cloth caps, with ancient but efficacious rifles slung over their backs, making vague footprints in the wet, muddy snow that filled the ruts between trees and houses. Through this godforsaken place most of the Middle East traffic was once channelled, and people here were still used to the sight of the big vehicles. But whatever the trucks carried, love was a commodity not lost between drivers and locals and never had been in the two decades during which the flow had swelled from nothing to a river and then dwindled to a trickle. Tekir was quickly negotiated; a few bends, and the village fell behind.

North of the village the road began to drop in a long lefthander that eventually doubled back in a tight righthand bend. The Scania had fallen a little behind the Volvo, and Hugh's taillights disappeared around the hillside. For a moment the driver feared that Hugh had at last misjudged the turn and had taken the "hotel" with him. The "hotel" was a cherished phenomenon, one of the oddest of landmarks on this run—a deserted, wooden ramshackle building right in the middle of the left-

hander, which hung over the precipice a metre or so
from the edge of the road, precariously propped up from
underneath and on its side bearing a quite nicely painted
sign with the legend "Hotel Toros." It was all thor-
oughly mystifying, since there wasn't a hotel around
for tens of kilometres. It was a miracle that some skidding semitrailer hadn't taken a swipe at it long ago and
knocked it, sign and all, from its perch into the valley
far below.

The Scania picked it up in the high beam, intact, and
rumbled by. The sign was lost in darkness, and further
down the road Hugh's taillights glowed as he slowly
took the Volvo through a tight righthander.

Another set of lights suddenly appeared; a collection
of garish running lights seemed to hover in his left mirror above two blazing headlights. Turkish, he thought.
Must be one of those decrepit tankers from Mersin. And
it was coming downhill fast, very fast, closing the gap
quickly, at the same time pulling out into the oncoming
lane to pass.

The Scania was doing over sixty-five; there seemed
to be no chance the Turk could squeeze in ahead of
him before the bend. But the Turk kept coming, flashing
his high beam, pulling up alongside, red cab, silhouetted
driver crouched in grim concentration. The tanker's engine was revving near its limit, without doubt aided and
abetted by some fifteen tons of petrol pushing downhill.
Now the tank was beside the cab of the Scania, and
slowly cleared it, filling the left half of the windshield,
displaying the sign with the Turkish words *Tehlikele
madde*, "Inflammable goods." And the tanker and semi
were nearly into the bend. The Turk cut in sharply in
front of the Scania.

"Dammit!" exploded the driver as he hit the trailer
brake handle on the steering wheel column, at the same
time stomping hard on the foot-brakes. The artic arched
itself in a giddy motion. The Turk was well into the

bend, braking, the rear end of the tanker swivelling sickeningly and threatening to break loose at any moment; close behind was the big artic, still behaving abominably with the brakes desperately applied.

"Bastard! *Jävla svin*! Did Santa Claus give you your driver's licence?"

Adrenalin flooded his body as he mentally heaped profanity upon the head of the driver of the red tanker in front. Kill yourself if you want! I don't mind, but what if I had had thirty tons pushing back there instead of only six? Would've jackknifed and carved right into your arse, and the two of us would have gone bouncing down the hillside in a nice fireball.

"Hey!" he yelled out. "How about having a look yourself at what it says back there, dammit. Christ! Driving like that with a full load of petrol."

The profanity came steadily, as if from an opened safety valve, while Shirley Bassey kept on singing, unperturbed; he felt the tires slipping in the mixture of mud and half-melted snow that covered the tarmac as he released the brakes and took the artic through the bend. The Turk had regained control of his vehicle but had made it through with no margins to spare. The distance between them was some thirty metres and growing.

The driver in the blue 141 clamped his teeth down, the profanity ceased, and his right foot grew fractionally heavier. The gap ceased to grow, kept steady for a moment, then began to lessen. The two vehicles began to close in on Hugh's F89, the tanker sandwiched in between the two European artics. The road wound along the mountainside, with enough oncoming traffic to make anyone think twice, but at times the tanker pulled out a little to size up the situation.

The Turk jumped at the chance on a straight, fairly long downhill stretch and pulled clear out of his own lane. The Scania immediately closed the gap, flashing its headlights twice. The tanker came abreast of the

Volvo—and kept on hanging there as the F89 gathered speed. The Turkish truck was locked in the oncoming lane while the Scania kept the back door closed.

The Scania's speedometer needle was climbing steadily, past seventy, eighty, nearing ninety kph. The gap between the two artics was still closed. The thought of the increasing nervousness of the Turkish driver brought a slow smile of grim satisfaction to the mouth of the 141 driver. He caught a glimpse in the darkness of the cliffside falling from the road into the ravine below. This was a foolish game to be playing, a deadly game. They were nearing the end of the straight stretch. The *Tehlikele madde* sign seemed to hang stationary on Hugh's left.

Two quick flashes of the Volvo's taillights; oncoming traffic on its way. The road was curving left, and the side of the mountain hid whatever was coming up to meet them. But trees further down reflected the glare of approaching headlights, and he knew that the Turk could also see it and that he must be close to panic.

Abruptly the oncoming vehicle swept into view, less than one hundred and fifty metres ahead; big headlights, a yellow-lit roof sign high above—another European TIR truck. The Turkish driver and the driver of the Swedish Scania hit their brakes almost simultaneously, and the gap immediately yawned wide. The headlights were rushing on to meet them. The empty 141 kept on braking, losing speed much faster than the heavily laden tanker, and suddenly the desperate Turk realized it and yanked the tanker right and back into his own lane. A second later the oncoming truck rushed by, followed by another; the Scania driver barely had time to register the Austrian roof sign and teeth flashing whitely. The Austrians had seen and understood and would have a story to tell when they paused in Adana.

The driver in the 141 was suddenly aware that he had been holding his breath. Slowly he let the air out of his lungs, feeling a faint film of sweat along his back.

That had been a little too close for comfort; the Turk must have been scared witless. That braking had deposited twenty-five dollars' worth of rubber in black strips on the tarmac, and quite possibly five liras' worth of processed lunch inside the Turk's baggy pants.

The tanker behaved very sedately the rest of the way down to the highland and seemed content with its position. The road finally levelled out, swung left along the foothills, then straightened out. After a while Hugh slowed down a little and blinked his right turn indicator. The Turk hesitated, but then pulled out and crept past. The Volvo and the Scania let him accelerate away, and the tanker had soon gathered a huge lead over the two artics.

They were on the highland proper. The night sky was clear, with a myriad of stars shedding a weak light that was reflected by the snow covering the plain. The serenity, as well as the vehicles, were jarred only by the numerous potholes in the road. In the Scania's cab Shirley Bassey was succeeded by Ray Charles. The driver lit another cigarette, slouching over the wheel.

The Turkish tanker was nowhere to be seen when they reached the longest straight stretch on the entire run: forty kilometres of slightly undulating road slashing across the snowy highland. Traffic was light. Hugh slowly let his F89 gather speed until he was clipping along at a merry hundred kph with the Scania pacing him. In the darkness, on this long, straight road, the likelihood of their being stopped by the police was small. The driver felt relaxed, leaning back in his seat, scratching his beard, looking forward to a hot meal and a cool beer in Aksaray.

*   *   *

In the beginning was the camel, and the camel ambled its unperturbed way on wide soft pads across the desert

sand, carrying what modest commodities that needed
to be carried. Underneath the sand, as unperturbed in
its way, lurked the fossilized remains of algae and other
organisms which had fallen millions of years ago to forgotten ocean beds, been sedimented over and eventually transmogrified into the black gold: petroleum, oil.
Allah saw that it was good and smiled upon the deserts
of Arabia, and apart from a prophet named Muhammed,
who rose to prominence in the seventh century, and
whose followers became rulers of the Middle East,
Northern Africa and, for a period, most of Spain, the
desert and its peoples remained unchanged for millenia.

But all things must pass—or at least suffer change.
In another part of the world, under the smile of another
deity, other men rose to prominence, men who thought
differently and displayed a fabulous inventiveness and
energy in devising ways of having things done for them.
One of the major triumphs of this way of thinking was
the internal combustion engine, which was powered by
a refined variety of the black goo these men had learned
to pump from the world's innards at various places
around the Gulf of Mexico.

The black goo itself, which could be turned into every
kind of energy for virtually every purpose, into motion,
heat, and electricity, made life—and warfare—change.
It saw man—Western man—become used to a life with
pliable energy available on a heretofore unheard-of scale.
And, as usual, Western man wasn't satisfied with what
he had himself; he craved more. A war came and went,
a war that was called the Great War; and it showed
beyond a shadow of doubt the consequences of the new
way of life. Oil was power, and more oil was more power.

The opening up of the Middle East was, in many ways,
like the opening up of the American West, two hundred
years before, except that now the hunger was for the
black gold beneath the sand; and this time, incidentally,

the natives were to come out of it a good deal better off.

The richest oil fields in history were found on the Arabian peninsula where the Kingdom of Saudi Arabia had only recently emerged as a nation under King Abdul Aziz bin Abdul Rahman al-Saud. King Abdul al-Saud's attempts to introduce order, structure, and administration into this traditional hotbed of tribal warfare and family rivalry required money; and this was to come from the exploitation, with the help of Americans, of the oil resources.

The arrival of oil men in Saudi Arabia was remarkable in two respects: the Americans had gained a foothold in a country which in time would show itself to have the largest oil reserves in the world, and it was also the Arabian peninsula's first great clash with another wholly different kind of culture and way of thinking. To a country which for millenia had slept under the sun, where for untold generations the desert nomads had roamed, where the ways of life had remained unchanged by the passage of time, came men from the West with their machines and strange contraptions to probe the interior of the earth for that precious and desirable black fluid without which their kind of civilization could not function.

Another war came and went, greater even than the preceding one. And again it served to hammer in the lesson that oil was power.

But new oil reserves were found quicker than the old ones could be emptied, and as a result consumption boomed in a stunning way. People bought more and more energy-consuming products; they bought all the electrified paraphernalia of modern life. The automobile industry boomed as never before. The West came to regard cheap oil to be as natural as cheap water. So much oil flooded the market that prices were forced down, and yet down again, and the royalties of the oil-

producing countries were depressed. They decided to
stand up and fight for what was, after all, their oil,
although others controlled it. So OPEC was born.

As all things must change, so what has changed once
must change again. OPEC, initially organizationally weak,
found its real strength with the first signs that the oil
wouldn't last forever, as everybody in their innocence
had tacitly surmised. Suddenly those who had the oil,
rather than those who used it, called the shots.

By the mid-'70s OPEC had shown itself to be the
biggest financial power in the history of the world. Again
it had been shown, and this time as never before, that
oil was power—and if the West, for one reason or another, had to go without it, it would simply collapse.
And Saudi Arabia, which sat on one-fifth of the world's
oil, with greater reserves than the United States and the
Soviet Union combined, had become a world power.

And what did this world power do with its fabulous
wealth, which it had accumulated in a mere matter of
decades? For Saudi Arabia it bought an unprecedented
leap through the centuries. It bought a modern society,
it bought administration, hospitals, schools—among them
the first girls' school, which wasn't compulsory but which
was there to cater to those heads of families who cared
to have their daughters educated. Money bought contacts with foreign countries and foreign cultures—and
more education on a higher level at the best British
and American schools for those bright young Saudis who
were to become the new technocrats of the emerging
economic superpower. It bought London deluxe hotels
and London super-discos. It bought whatever Marks &
Spencer had to offer, and it bought Rolls Royce motorcars
in which one could sit impassively in Edgeware Road
while the harem did its thing in the nearby boutiques.
Money was the "open sesame" to a new world, and at
the same time it was the fertilizer to make this new
world blossom.

The new world blossomed at home as it did abroad; like the mountain that came to Muhammed, the new world came to Saudi Arabia. The same thing happened to the other Middle East countries with petroleum beneath the sand: Iran, Iraq, Kuwait, Oman, Qatar, the Arab Emirates. First came the foreign labour and the experts on administration, communications, construction work; there were Westerners planning and leading the technical and material modernization of the country, South Koreans building the roads which began to span the desert, Pakistanis working in harbours and customs, and a considerable number of well-educated Palestinians working in administration or as teachers, while the Saudis themselves, their livelihood guaranteed by the oil, went about supervising.

Certainly, as many of the old ways were swept into oblivion while the new and strange world grew up around the one-time Bedouin, so the cry "Cast out the foreigners!" was raised here and there, but without much success. The most it accomplished was that the Saudis, while enjoying the benefits of the new life, warily kept the new life itself at arm's length.

The development called not only for labour, but for tools, equipment, raw materials and—for gracious living—a comprehensive range of consumer goods which the oil countries were in no position to manufacture themselves. And there were countries more than eager to sell . . .

The only question was how to get the wanted goods to where they were needed. The capacity for air freight on the necessary scale wasn't there, and harbours . . . well, one of the first large-scale projects *was* the building of a modern port in Jeddah, but already that called for a lot of stuff being there in the first place. And even with the port half finished, ships might still have to wait for up to six months to unload.

But one thing that was easy to build with the avail-

able resources was roads. Straight and well-built ribbons
of tarmac began webbing the desert, and down these,
on their way to Baghdad and Teheran, to Riyadh, Jeddah, Abha, Kuwait, Dammam, Doha, Dhubai, Muscat,
Aden, and so on, rolled the international juggernauts,
the TIR—*Transports International Routiéres*—trucks. The
English, with old interests in the area and Lawrence for
inspiration, were the first in the early sixties, but they
were soon followed by other nationalities: along with
British Leylands and Fords rolled German Mercedeses
and MANs, Swedish Scanias and Volvos, Dutch DAFs,
Italian Fiats and French Berliets and Saviems.

The loads they carried were mainly machinery of various kinds and spare parts, material for construction work,
special equipment and supplies, but also such pedestrian
commodities as fridges, freezers, and televisions—the
cinema was odious in the sight of Allah, but no measure
of Islamic zeal had been able to keep television out of
the country. Foodstuffs also went down in great quantities, and now and then something quite out of the
ordinary was shipped, which caused no end of administrative confusion—like the time Hugh from Funston
Transport rolled into Halat Ammar on the Saudi border
with a complete chicken farm in his semitrailer—well,
almost complete; you had to add chickens.

The Saudis went through the papers accompanying
the load and immediately charged him 26,000 riyals in
dues. They were adamant in the face of his protests that
it was *their* government which had ordered the chicken
farm, and *he* shouldn't have to pay dues on it. In the
end he parked his truck, hitched a ride with another
driver into Tabuk, ninety kilometres away, caught a plane
to Riyadh, located, after a search that lasted for some
days, someone in the Ministry of Agriculture who would
listen to his problems, and returned, finally, by way of
Tabuk, to Halat Ammar in the passenger seat of another
truck, with an officially signed and sealed paper which

stated that the chicken farm was exempt from all dues. This had taken three weeks, so the ever alert customs officials charged him 1,000 Riyals for overtime parking.

But apart from things like that, formalities mostly went comparatively smoothly. Certain difficulties were considered part of a driver's job—something one had to suffer. The Arab's shrug and his "Maybe tomorrow" had to be taken in one's stride. Although Hugh, who had done the Spain run and knew the same phenomenon from there, remarked: "*Mañana* at least *sounds* better."

Were the truckers then the "Saudi pilots"? The true adventurers of the twentieth century? Yes and no. Like chartered accountants they came in all shapes and sizes. Unlike chartered accountants, they were all somewhat adventurous, but apart from that they were, as a lot, quite normal men, ranging from those in their early twenties to the grizzled veterans who were said to donate their blood at the diesel filling-stations, neither more neurotic, nor much better adjusted to life than most of us. They were merely original enough to undertake month-long trips, across all of Europe and then as far again and more into Asia to deliver their loads at various destinations in the Middle East. Had circumstances been different, some of them might have become airline pilots instead, some might have become sailors, some oilriggers in the North Sea or the Arabian Gulf, some salesmen, and some might even had stayed at home and had normal jobs.

But all Middle East drivers fell into one of two categories: either the this-is-positively-my-last-run-did-I-say-that-the-last-time? -well-you-know-my-hauler-talked-me-into-it type that you still met at Londra or in Halat Ammar on your next run; or the I-couldn't-ever-imagine-having-another-job-no-boss-breathing-down-my-neck type that became a fixture in the international brotherhood of truck drivers.

And in and around this brotherhood a subculture evolved, with its own code of behaviour and honour, its own concepts and ideas, its own jargon and its own anecdotes and legends, some of which were quite truthful in spite of their fantastic contents while others were altogether mendacious in spite of their reasonable tone. It had its own heroes and villains—the latter mostly crooked bar owners, and less than honest agents, cops, and customs officials.

Those watering-holes that cared for the drivers grew rich; establishments like Anna's Café in Czecho, Humphrey Bogart's in Jordan, Helmuth's in Austria.

The drivers were in essence loners, the modern cowboys some said, whose horses had been replaced with eighteen-wheel steel monsters on which they lavished their attention whether or not they actually owned them; they decorated them inside out with paint, pictures, badges, and souvenirs picked up in a dozen or more countries.

Cowboys or not, the Middle East pilots had their special togetherness, their sense of loyalty; what bound them together was not the fierce *esprit-de-corps* of a tightly knit, well-trained military unit, but a kind of self-evident decency which dictated that one should care for one's brother-in-the-trade. Somebody needed help to change a trailer wheel: you put on your coveralls and lent him a hand. Or somebody temporarily ran out of the local currency: the next round was on you. Among the brotherhood of the Middle East drivers, it all evened out in the long run, somewhere down that road.

*   *   *

The clock said ten to nine when lights showed ahead on his left; Aksaray, with one of the few TIR parks in Turkey, one of the few places in the country where truck drivers could sleep in relative safety inside their cabs. The park was situated on the northern outskirts of the town—or village—as the case might be. The drivers didn't care which, all they were interested in was the park itself, the comparatively modern restaurant and the vanilla pudding served there.

Hugh blinked right and braked; so did the Scania, and the two vehicles rolled off the road and into the TIR park. The Scania driver nosed his 141 forward until it was less than a metre behind the Volvo and the glare from his headlights in the dirtstreaked tarpaulin was almost intolerable. He hit the parking brake handle and heard the *whoosh* of compressed air from the hoses and valves in the undercarriage, then switched off the headlights and cassette player. Only the yellow glow of his position lights outlined the length of his vehicle. In the relative silence he listened to the big V-8 diesel engine idly ticking over.

His back ached; he raised his arms above his head and arched his body against the seat, feeling the tiredness in his limbs. Always the same thing, no matter how often you promised yourself to take it easy on the way home, you always slept too little and drove long hours, sometimes around the clock. He thought for a moment of what it was like being home, able to shower every day and sleeping in a made bed, then abruptly slid back into the seat and shook his head. Sweden was still a long way off. He pulled out his log and made some entries, then remembered to empty the pockets of his jeans and jacket, sorting out the coins of various Arab countries. The curse of the Saudi truckers, he reflected, as he reached down under the passenger seat and fished out the small jar in which he kept loose change.

Hugh came up to the cab and knocked lightly on the door. The driver swung it open and pulled the compression release. The engine died. Then he took his jacket from its hook behind him, pulled his keys off the dashboard and jumped stiffly to the ground. The air was bitingly cold, and Hugh's breath came in puffs of white smoke. "Shit, I'm freezing my ass off."

The Scania driver gave him a half-amused smile. "Yeah. Sitting all day in a nice, warm cab makes you soft." He slammed the door shut and made sure it had locked. "Let's get inside and have something to eat."

Hands deep in their jacket pockets, they made their way across the narrow TIR park, which in reality was nothing more than a wide stretch of asphalt that branched off from the road and continued up past the restaurant and some other buildings, to rejoin the highway further up. Their boots thudded loudly in the silence, and their eyes roved over the other three trucks parked there. The place was almost deserted.

The Scania driver singled out the lone southbound truck parked right outside the restaurant, another Volvo F89 painted in a white-and-green striped pattern, "Well, well," he muttered under his breath and veered closer to check the licence plate. He stopped for a few seconds, looked the truck over, saw the crudely painted Arabic calligraphy above the grille and the band of yellow tassels hanging down inside the windshield, illuminated by light from the windows of the brightly lit restaurant. Behind him, on the dark road, another big truck rumbled by in the night towards Ankara.

Inside the door they exchanged nods with the two middle-aged men near the entrance, the drivers of the other two northbound trucks. Seated in the far left corner, hunched over a small bowl of brown and yellow vanilla pudding, absentmindedly thumbing through a magazine, was a burly figure with dark, close-cropped hair. The Scania driver tiptoed up behind him and gave him a resounding whack across the shoulders.

"Going the wrong way, aren't you, Lennart?"

Lennart dropped his spoon with a clatter, but as he looked up the expression of surprise on his face changed to one of delight inside of a second.

"Leif Wallman! *Fan, vilken överraskning!* Hell, what a surprise! It's been a long time. Sit down!" He half rose and heartily shook hands with the Scania driver, a grin revealing uneven teeth in a slightly pockmarked face with a black, drooping moustache.

Leif returned the smile, indicating Hugh with a wave of his left hand. "Have you met Hugh? Drives for Funston Transport in Cambridge. We're convoying up to Istanbul together." He changed from Swedish to English. "Hugh, this is Lennart. Old friend of mine. We used to drive for the same hauler once, back in Sweden." Lennart and Hugh shook hands, smiled.

"We'll just have something to eat before we starve to death," Leif went on. "Be right back, OK?"

The drivers liked the restaurant for its good food, its vanilla pudding, considered to be the best in Turkey, and for the fact that it was fairly clean—or at least had been; it was nearly half a year since Leif had passed by the last time.

They opted for the same fare: large meatballs swimming around in a dark red sauce, with rice, vanilla pudding and cool beer; they jiggled out a few Turkish bills from their pockets, paid and returned to the table where Lennart had finished his meal.

"Getting kind of long haired, aren't you?" he said, looking at Leif's blond mane which fell over the collar of his dark red jacket. "A little longer and you'll be looking like Jesus with that beard."

"I know," Leif said. "But I'll be damned if I do anything about it down here. I wouldn't trust a barber not to cut everything off at shoulder level." He pulled out the chair opposite Lennart and sat down, unzipping his jacket. Hugh settled in beside him. Between mouthfuls, Leif picked up the conversation again.

"It's certainly been a long time, Lennart. Hell, must be seven or eight months since we last saw each other."

"More, I think. Wasn't it at the Steps in Bulgaria?"

Leif brightened. "Yeah, I remember! Sometime in March—you and me and Affe and that Norwegian guy with the scar finished off your bottle of Bell's in your cab."

"Right. I have a new bottle."

Leif shook his head. "Thanks. Another time. Got to stay awake till we hit Ankara tonight."

"You've come far today?"

"Started from Tartous this morning."

Lennart raised his eyebrows. "That's a good distance . . . you can't have slept very much last night."

"No." Leif speared another meatball. "But I'm all right. What have you been doing since March, then? You haven't been on the Middle East run, I haven't seen you or heard anything about you."

"Actually, I've been off driving for a while. Got fed up and worked as a longshoreman in Gothenburg. But then Charlie called me up and . . . well, here I am again." Lennart grinned sheepishly.

"So you're still driving for him, eh? How's my old employer?"

"He's all right, still the same old Charlie. He's recovered from his heart attack now. He was glad to have me again, even let me have my old F89 back."

"So I noticed. Seems he talked you into going south, too. I thought you'd want to spend Christmas and New Year's at home."

Lennart rocked back in his chair, stroking his moustache. "Doesn't really matter to me right now. Jerre had a rush load for LME in Baghdad and somebody had to take it down. Besides, it's a cash bonus job and I can use the extra money. Linda and I got divorced in May."

Leif looked up, and their eyes met. Then he reached out and briefly touched Lennart's hand. "I didn't know that, mate. Sorry to hear it. Hope things aren't too bad for you."

"Oh, it's all right. We're still friends and see each

other now and then." Lennart stroked his moustache again and shrugged half-heartedly. "That's why I quit chewing road dust for a while."

Leif made no reply.

"Wouldn't you know," Lennart went on. "I had to drive down around Christmas time last year, too. Remember? Got stuck in Humphrey Bogart's on Christmas Eve, together with a few other drivers, and we had one hell of a party. You remember Robban?"

Leif swallowed, waving his fork in the air. "You mean that crazy little guy who drove for PIE and carried a stiletto? Sure."

"Well, he was there. Got stinking drunk and woke up Christmas Day with one hell of a hangover and somehow got it into his head that he was in 'West Berlin' in Istanbul and had forgotten to pay his bill, so he tried to escape through the service hatch and stepped right on Humphrey himself who was sleeping on the kitchen floor."

Leif laughed uproariously. "How did Humphrey take it?" he asked weakly, finally.

"Yelled like a pig. Made us all wake up in one hell of a hurry. But he was fairly gracious about it afterwards, even offered Robban a beer."

Hugh looked puzzled, and Leif translated the whole thing for him and watched his features split in a wide grin.

"Poor Humphrey," Hugh said. "Almost worth missing Christmas for."

"Just don't mention it too often to him," Lennart cautioned.

"Someone told me," Leif said, "that Teddy from Eastern Trailer got stuck in Rözske on the Hungarian side on New Year's Eve when they closed the border. The customs people had a sex party going on in Hungarocamion's office, and felt sorry for him and invited him in . . ."

Lennart whistled softly. "The son of a bitch! That won't happen in Halat Ammar."

"You probably didn't miss anything . . . I was told the Hungarian girls were all fat and had hairy legs."

"Wouldn't mind all the same; anything beats sitting alone in your rig on New Year's Eve. Teddy, is he a steady on the Saudi run now?"

"No. Austria and France mostly, just odd trips to the Middle East. Oh, I met the Sheriff on the ferry on my last trip, and he told me Teddy had taken a load down to Albania."

"Albania?" Lennart looked thoughtful. "First time I heard of anyone going there. What was it like?"

"Rough, apparently. Bad roads, diesel bad and hard to find, tough customs." Leif grinned. "They wouldn't let him through until he had trimmed his hair and beard."

"A run for you."

"The hell it is." Leif was silent for a moment. "If you're bound for Baghdad, how come you're going via Turkey? The border is open, and the ferry is almost empty going down this time of the year."

"Oh, saw in the newspapers that the Syrians and the Iraqis were quarrelling over something again, so I thought I'd play it safe."

Hugh looked up from his second bowl of vanilla pudding and put in, "What's it like up north?"

"Good, right now," Lennart answered in singsong but otherwise good English. "The weather's been clear for the last few days, so they've had time to scrape the snow and ice off the roads. Even the stretch between Ankara and Istanbul is OK, except for a few fresh wrecks."

Hugh nodded, satisfied. Whenever drivers going in opposite directions met they exchanged information—on the weather, the roads, the traffic, what it was like at the borders. The "asphalt vine" could turn out to be a cheap life insurance, and at the very least it helped them steer clear of trouble and to shave hours and perhaps days off their schedules.

"How's the border? Kapikule?"

"A bit worse—lots of rigs heading home now. Probably take you anywhere between five and ten hours to get through. Easy going down, though; the compound was almost empty when I came through." He snorted. "What's it like where you came from?"

"Bit of slush up on Tarsus." Hugh used the drivers' name of the Taurus Mountains. "No problem, really. I haven't heard anything about how the Baghdad route is beyond Adana."

"I'm lucky going there, anyway. At Londra I met a couple of guys coming back from Teheran, and they told me Erzincan and eastwards is white hell right now. The military are barely able to keep the roads open."

Leif had finished his meal and held out his pack of cigarettes to Lennart. "I suppose you still don't smoke?"

"No, thanks. And you still haven't quit?"

"No, but I've got to one of these days. Annika's bitching at me about it whenever I'm home."

"Home? I didn't know you had any. This is what—your thirteenth trip?"

"Fifteenth." Leif put a cigarette in his mouth and lit it. Can't quit as long as I drive this run, he thought. A way to fight the boredom of long, long kilometres. Music and cigarettes, a shot of liquor now and then. And vanilla pudding in Turkey.

He remembered something. "Oh yeah, one thing. A warning. The Mobil TIR park in Adana is out."

Lennart raised his head. "Why?"

"Three West Germans and a Swede—Milan, you know, bound for Kuwait—were robbed there a week ago. Woke up in the afternoon with their cabs stripped of everything except dirty laundry. All the rest gone; money, papers, clothes, watches. One of the Germans had a wedding ring that was so tight they skinned his finger when they pulled it off." Leif blew a stream of smoke roofwards.

"How did they do it?"

"They're not sure, but the four of them had tea together the night before in that restaurant nearby. Probably drugged."

Lennart shook his head, incredulously. "Shit. How could anyone be so dumb? They won't have any drivers parking there for the next goddam year."

"Serves them right. The other TIR park by the airbase road is still open, though."

Lennart looked very serious when he went on in a slow voice. "It's things like that I hate about the Middle East run. You and me, Leif, we both drive trucks because we like working without a boss hanging over us, but things like that make me want to quit once and for all. One day I'm going to be tired of bribing customs officials and greasing the palm of every little fart of a cop who gets it into his head to pull me over and hand me some phony charge, and waiting for the moment when some crazy bus driver who can't find his arse with both hands pulls right out in front of me and takes me with him—you've seen all those wrecks too, every year some of us get it—and then I'm going to quit, get a quiet job back home and stay put. I hate being screwed all the time by every bastard in every country I pass through."

He looked up, and there was something in his eyes that Leif had never seen before in all the years he had known him, an almost frightening hardness.

"You know what happened on my last trip down?" Lennart said. "I was carrying a max load up Tarsus, couldn't stop and couldn't go faster than ten kilometres an hour on the uphill stretches, and a bunch of Turk kids came running up from behind and tore all my position lights off both sides. What the hell could I do about it? If I'd swung out and run them over, the cops would've got me before the border and murdered me. But I've made damn sure it won't happen again. I suppose you didn't look that close at my rig outside?''

''No. Why?''

''I've taped razor blades on the back of all my position lights this time.''

Leif shuddered. Is that what this run does to us? he wondered. God, it's getting to be a war between them and us, with casualties on both sides. We're getting more cynical with every trip. This isn't the Lennart I used to know, the guy who always joked about everything and always had a helping hand for everybody. I should get out.

A memory surfaced in his mind: a red tanker desperately slewing right, ducking in before him only metres from approaching headlights. Why had he done it? Why had he risked three or maybe more lives and trucks, even his own?

He became aware of the cigarette almost burning his fingers, and quickly stubbed it out. ''Matter of fact,'' he said, ''I've been thinking about quitting, sometimes I feel about it the way you do. Annika's been talking about it for a year. She gets to see me a couple of days every four or five weeks, and that isn't the way she wants it.'' And to be truthful, he added silently, that isn't the way I want it either. She's a good kid, and I'd hate to lose her.

As if he had read Leif's mind, Lennart spoke up. ''If you want to keep Annika, think it over. Look what happened to me—not to mention to just about everybody else.''

Their eyes met across the table, before Leif looked away. Hugh broke the silence.

''Time we hit the road again, Leif. Still a long way to Ankara.''

The others looked at their watches and nodded. Nobody spoke. Hugh rose, stretched and yawned, Leif put his pack of Prince and his lighter back into his jacket pocket, Lennart picked up his magazine and the jacket he had thrown across the next chair, and together they walked through the restaurant. The other two drivers were still sitting at the table by the entrance, engaged in a vigorous discussion in French. They stopped for a moment to exchange nods and the rather awkward *ça va*, then left.

The cold met them outside. In silence they went over to Lennart's green-and-white striped F89 and waited while he unlocked the door. The glare from the restaurant illuminated their faces.

Lennart reached out his hand. "Well, so long, Leif. Hope I'll run into you again. If you're ever in Gothenburg, come and see me."

"I will. Have a merry Christmas and all that, and take care." Leif shook his hand almost solemnly.

"Same to you, mate. Give my best to Annika. See you next trip, perhaps."

"Maybe. I might decide to quit."

"In that case, good luck. Take it easy." Lennart turned to Hugh, shook hands, exchanged goodbyes, then grabbed the handrail and swung himself up into the cab. He raised his hand, winked at them.

"Keep your fingers crossed that the party at Humphrey's will be a good one."

Leif and Hugh grinned, waved and then walked back towards their own trucks. They heard the door slam behind them and the Volvo diesel thunder into life.

Leif said to Hugh, "Hope you didn't mind all that Swedish talk, but it's been a while since I last saw Lennart."

"Come on, Leif, it's all right."

They reached the Scania. Hell, it's cold, Leif thought. "Just have to take a piss, and we can start."

Hugh nodded. "Me too." He went forward towards his own cab.

Leif took a step towards a cluster of leafless shrubs near his left front wheel and unzipped while he raised his head to the stars which shone with incredible brightness in the crystal-clear night sky. From the other side of the Scania he heard gears engage as Lennart's Volvo rumbled away and slowly gathered speed as it disappeared southward.

He finished, zipped up, but remained standing with his face turned up, watching the infinity of the heavens, listening to the faint night wind around his ears. He thought again of quitting and finding some other job in Sweden, one that got him home to Annika every night.

He turned to look at his big truck. Hell of a life, he thought. Most of the people you associated with were other drivers, and most of the conversation was about trucks, roads, loads, customs, and what had happened to whom since the last time you met. And you lived in a kind of symbiosis with the truck you drove. No wonder; you spent something like three-quarters of your time inside that cab, working, eating, sleeping, cooking, reading, and sometimes masturbating in your loneliness. A one-wheel apartment, Annika had once called it.

It was a way of life that in time changed you and in a curious way made your world both greater and smaller. It gave you a restlessness; a couple of days in the same place, whether at home or waiting at some border station, and you felt irritated and wanted to be on the move again. The drivers had a name for it: they called it whiteline fever.

Perhaps he really ought to quit.

He shook his head to clear it. Better think of the long road ahead. Plug in some music, smoke, eat another orange.

He heard Hugh's Volvo cough once and fire up front; in a moment he had his keys out, unlocked the door and climbed up. The dark, silent cab was still warm and he was grateful for it. He found the right key, inserted it, turned it. Instruments lit up. His fingers found the starter button and pressed it, and the truck sprang to life.

He was Leif Wallman, twenty-nine years old, from Kävlinge outside Lund in southern Sweden. He had driven over three thousand two hundred kilometres from Riyadh in little more than three days; he was halfway home.

*   *   *

And the brightly painted trucks rolled on, bringing all the riches that the petrodollar was able to buy to Saudi Arabia and to the rest of the Middle East. As they rolled down the roads, the camel, which was still an excellent beast of burden when it came to carrying various modest commodities across the desert dunes, stood ruminating by the roadside and impassively, as if he had been a sheikh in a Rolls Royce, watched them go by. And Allah saw it all and smiled upon it, because all in all it was a satisfactory state of affairs.

But certain people had other ideas.

2

Senior Lieutenant Andrei Nikolaievich Starshinov, commander of Kolyma One Six, a MAZ-543/SCUD-B launcher/missile unit attached to the 14th Soviet Motor Rifle Division of the Red Army, stationed at Leninakan, Armenian SSR, Transcaucasian MD, was, to his immense chagrin, not related to the legendary ice hockey player.

But he was a competent officer who had risen from his *kolkhozy* background through diligence and dedication, which was also the reason he was sitting in the righthand cab of the missile launcher, on the third day of the manoeuvre, when instead he should have been in bed nursing a head-splitting cold.

At the moment Starshinov was grateful that he could just sit in his seat while the MAZ-543 rushed along the narrow, uneven gravel road towards the position it was due to take up by midmorning, south of Lake Paravani. The unit was running slightly behind schedule, and Sergeant Markov in the driver's seat in the lefthand cab was pushing the launcher close to its top speed, trying to make up for the delay.

Starshinov's joints felt stiff and sent protesting stabs of pain with every jolt. He braced himself against the seat harness with the map spread across his thighs, its left edge wedged between his leg and his Kalashnikov carbine. His throat was sore and his ears felt as though they were swathed in wool. Gennadi, who sat behind

Markov in the other cab, was doing the map reading;
with his cold and the roar of the V-12 diesel engine,
Starshinov was barely able to catch the brief exchanges
between the two in his earphones over the vehicle intercom. Yuri, the engineer and fourth crew member,
sat behind him.

With its two cabs separated by the wide, flat engine
cowling, the launcher resembled a huge toad with protruding, unblinking eyes and a curious cylinder on its
back. Starshinov looked across at the other cab, studying Markov.

Markov had joined the crew two months ago, re-
placing Misha. Starshinov missed the talkative little
Ukrainian. In contrast, Markov was quiet and never
seemed to speak except to give orders to his subordinates or confirm orders from his superiors. He hadn't
assumed any of the liberties that any member of a highly
trained, close-knit crew eventually begins to take in his
conduct towards his officers.

A particularly vicious jolt threw Starshinov against
the harness and made him wince. The engine's growl
fell and then rose sharply as Markov let the MAZ-543
drop out of overdrive and into a lower gear with a crunch,
and then Starshinov had to hold on to the grab-handle
in the ceiling as the launcher swung right along what
was little better than a cattle path. A small tree had
fallen across the path, and his ribbed helmet hit the side
window with a crack as the eight wheels climbed over
it. In the back Yuri cursed. Snow-laden branches whipped
against the cab, then the path widened and they were
rumbling along through the deep, wintry forest.

He glanced again at the map, trying for a moment to
locate their position before giving up. It didn't matter,
he knew the spot where they would eventually arrive.
He pulled back the sleeve of his black coveralls to check
the time. A little less than forty-five minutes to rendezvous.

Funny, Starshinov reflected, how Markov's correctness and deference towards his superiors made it appear as if he were making a game out of sticking meticulously to the rules. He had his own private opinion of Markov, but it was one he did not care to voice around the barracks; Markov was almost certainly from the KGB Armed Forces Directorate, and his title of Sergeant was as phony as a seven-rouble note. Captain would be closer to the truth. Ah well, that was only to be expected on a launcher unit carrying a real missile with a live nuclear warhead on a major military manoeuvre within forty kilometres of NATO territory. Not that the security people really· had anything to worry about; one didn't defect with a thirty-five-ton launcher/missile rig and a crew of four like one did with a MIG-25.

Outside the snowfall had thickened further. Starshinov studied the darkening sky between the treetops. They were getting a bit of wind, and if it continued they'd have a proper blizzard soon. He swore aloud, a sound that was lost in the rumble of the engine but carried over the intercom. There was a noise like a stifled snicker.

When they reached their destination they would have to go through the motions of arming the warhead and elevating the SCUD-B missile to launching position. A lot of trouble and hard work, he thought sourly, for the sake of delivering a 50-by-25-centimetre 93-kilo cylinder of plutonium, high explosives, steel, lead, and assorted electronics. Hell of a job at any time, worse when having to go outside in a blizzard to do it, and an absolute bitch when his body felt worse than after a three-day drinking bout.

He blinked, abruptly coming out of his reveries.. The MAZ-543 was slowing down. He pulled at his sleeve, confused, to check the time again. They still had over twenty minutes to go before they reached their position.

He looked around. He could see nothing barring their

way. Almost gently, the vehicle came to a standstill; the
V-12 settled down to a slow idle. He could hear Yuri
shift in his seat and turned his head to look at Markov,
who was vaguely outlined behind a shifting curtain of
snow as he bent over the dashboard.

"Why have we stopped?" Starshinov asked over the
intercom. His voice came raspingly. The throat microphone itched against his skin.

"One of the rear tires seems to be losing pressure,
comrade Lieutenant." Markov's voice was dry and matter-
of-fact. "Requesting permission for myself and comrade
Karamzin to go outside and check."

Starshinov swore under his breath. The central tire
pressure regulating system was malfunctioning again.
The workers at the Minsk Motor Vehicle Plant probably
put the sealing gaskets on backwards in their haste to
fill the end-of-the-month quotas. *Chort vozmi.* They
could manage fair enough with one wheel out, but it
meant they would be running late. Starshinov had an
orderly soul and disliked small failures under normal
conditions; in his present state he hated them.

"Permission granted. Will it take long?"

"Not more than a minute or two, comrade Lieutenant."

There was a click from behind as the vehicle engineer
unfastened his seat harness. As he opened his door it
let in a rush of cold air and snowflakes. Starshinov shivered and felt miserable. Then the door slammed shut,
and in his rear-view mirror he could see the coverall-
clad figure descend the small metal ladder and walk
towards the rear of the launcher.

Starshinov longed for a cigarette, but he knew it would
taste like wet cotton. Perhaps he should have gone outside with Markov and Yuri; in a strict sense it was his
duty as vehicle commander. Well, it was probably only
a trifling matter. He might as well wait inside.

A minute passed while the engine idled evenly. He

looked left again and frowned. Was Gennadi stepping outside as well?

Masses of snowflakes danced across the ribbed engine cowling with a strong gust, nearly blocking the view. Starshinov leaned sideways against the cold glass, peering intently through it. Yes, the other cab was empty.

He frowned again, with an uneasy feeling. Things weren't going the way they should. He unplugged his headset and clicked open his seat harness, and then opened his door.

The cold air hurt his sore throat and made it difficult to breathe. His bare fingers already felt numb from touching the cold metal as he climbed down.

The snow was coming down in thick shreds. He bent into the wind and bunched up his shoulders. His boots sank into the snow as he walked around the front of the launcher. He turned the corner, looked along the vehicle, and the shock jarred him like an electrical charge.

Markov was bending over the prostrate form of Gennadi by one of the front wheels. He was tugging at the bayonet that protruded from Gennadi's back, trying to wrench it free. Dark red spots had stained the fresh snow.

Starshinov turned, the taste of fear mixing with the sour taste in his mouth. He had gone outside without his weapon; in the launcher he didn't even carry the usual sidearm. He ran back, slipping and nearly falling, and frantically groped for the door handle. He had to get his Kalashnikov.

Something heavy slammed into his back. He felt brief surprise, then realized it was Markov. The impact nearly numbed his right arm. He twisted around, saw Markov's face and threw a punch at it. It was a bad blow, but he could feel it connect. Then something exploded near his temple, and the world was black, hazy pain.

Slowly his awareness returned. He was lying with his face in the snow, and his bruised right shoulder and head throbbed in agony. Sluggishly he raised himself to a half sitting position. He could taste vomit in his mouth.

The world swam into focus again. The snow was still coming down, racing along the idling MAZ-543. A figure in black coveralls stood in front of him, six paces away. Markov, poised in a wide-legged stance, was holding a gun with both hands raised to eye level. Starshinov stared into its muzzle.

He didn't feel fear any longer, only a peculiar mental numbness. There was a strange quality of unreality about the situation. The eerie midmorning light demarcated a sphere beyond which the swirling snow wasn't snow any longer, only greyness. Inside the sphere a deadly drama was being acted out.

Starshinov opened his mouth, closed it again. There was a tiny trickle of blood running from Markov's nose. They were both breathing heavily.

"Is this part of the manoeuvre?" Starshinov knew the question was stupid; Markov had no right to do this.

"No." Markov's gun did not waver. His voice seemed to come from further away than he actually was. "But part of something else."

"You've murdered Gennadi and Yuri." Starshinov's throat hurt from speaking.

"It was necessary. Obstacles to be swept aside." A sneer crept into Markov's voice. "You were easy to take. You're soft, just like the fools in the Politburo. *Nachalstvo*, all of them. Fat cats content to sit on their behinds and pray for the downfall of the Western imperialists. Too concerned with their reputation abroad to do anything about it."

Starshinov raised one hand and wiped phlegm off his nose and upper lip. "What do you want?" he asked.

"Don't be a fool."

And suddenly he knew the answer: Mount Ararat, the American communications nerve centre was less than two hundred kilometres away, well within reach of the SCUD-B they carried. The sudden realization, the palpable insight as opposed to his previous academic knowledge of what the tactical missile was capable of, made him try to get to his feet.

"You can't do that!" he blurted out. As a protest it was feeble and not very original, but he had at least tried.

"No, *tovarich*?" Markov dropped his gun a fraction, his arms almost straight like in competition shooting, and fired.

The bullet hit Andrei Nikolaievich Starshinov squarely in the chest, just a little to the left. He felt surprisingly little pain, only a hard blow which knocked him backwards against one of the huge front wheels of the launcher vehicle. Then he started to go under in a dark, reddish haze, and his mind slipped. At that moment he had a sensation that this wasn't really happening to him, that this was a delusion. In reality he was in the Moscow Ice Stadium, watching the final, decisive match of the Ice Hockey World Championship, and Balderis, brilliant Balderis, had just scored. Three to two for the USSR against Czechoslovakia with fifty-two seconds to go; the Moscow crowd was delirious, the cheering wouldn't cease, it rose and became a clamour that broke all boundaries and engulfed everything in a roar of darkness.

*   *   *

There was no obvious trace of disturbance in the Operations Room of Command HQ at Leninakan. Everything continued to be carried out in an orderly fashion; messages were received, decoded, relayed to their proper destinations, new messages sent out; symbols were moved across a large, illuminated screen at one end of the room as the better part of two Motor Rifle Regiments moved in to establish control over the main highway and rail-

way between Leninakan and Kirovan, and two Main
Battle Tank Battalions passed Akhuryan to intercept the
advancing enemy. Close to the lower edge, barely over
on the Turkish side, three widely spaced white dots were
slowly moved along—American SR-71 spy planes, flying
in the clear high air above the raging snowstorm, their
electronic ears listening, their IR eyes straining to see.

Several higher-ranking officers moved about in the
dim areas between the sharp lights. A large manoeuvre
like this one had many observers: there were the usual
senior officers from Military District Command and
higher; there were those with the green piping on their
uniforms, which denoted the Chief Border Guards
Directorate. Military movements close to NATO territory
were always of particular interest to the Directorate, and
some of its units participated in the manoeuvre.

Finally, there was a third category of observers, the
KGB. Officers from the KGB Third Directorate (Armed
Forces Directorate) held positions everywhere in the
Soviet Armed Forces. Although they held their assigned
positions in the military hierarchy, they might at any
moment choose to stand outside it, answerable only to
their own superiors within the Directorate.

Officers of all categories moved in the room or stood
on the observers' balcony that ran along three of its
walls. Although everything seemed to be running
smoothly, the first hint of unease was spreading, and
Lieutenant-General Shevchenko could sense it.

He glanced again at the large screen. Well to the north
of the theatre, on the south shore of Lake Paravani,
were three identical yellow symbols grouped closely together. They represented three MAZ-543/SCUD-B units
already in position. There should have been four.

The fourth one was missing. Its crew had failed to
keep its assigned rendezvous or report in to explain the
failure.

Shevchenko clamped his jaws together and looked at

the clock on the wall, painfully aware of the presence of the KGB. The missing unit was twelve minutes overdue, but he did not want to cause an unseemly panic by suggesting that something was wrong; after all, the commander of the missing unit might still show up with a perfectly logical explanation. On the other hand, he didn't want to delay too long in taking steps to find out what was wrong and do something about it, to avoid the Scylla and Charybdis of what the paranoid KGB mind might interpret as anti-Soviet activity on the one hand, and sabotage on the other.

Shevchenko, walking with measured paces, made his way across the room to the bank of radio transceivers, his face carefully neutral. The operator who monitored the SCUD-B units sensed him coming and answered, even before Shevchenko had time to formulate the question.

"Kolyma One Six is still missing, comrade Lieutenant-General. Both Kolyma One Seven and Kolyma One are trying to contact them."

Shevchenko frowned. Where the hell were they? If their vehicle had broken down and prevented them from keeping their rendezvous, why hadn't they radioed in to report it? And even if they had had a fire in the main electrical system, surely both transmitters couldn't have been knocked out?

How much should he interfere with the manoeuvre?

He was aware of the seconds ticking by. Scylla and Charybdis. He wanted to turn his head, wanted to see whose eyes were watching him, but ingrained instinct held him back.

"Try to raise them on the emergency channels," he said finally. "Inform Kolyma One, and have Kolyma One Seven through Nine stand by to await marching orders."

The clock on the wall said 0933.

*   *   *

The snow was a curtain borne by strong gusts. Markov drove almost recklessly, pushing the MAZ-543 to its limits. The tach needle hovered in the red on the short straights of the winding, narrow lane, and at times he could feel the tires slipping in the slush of fresh snow and gravel as he braked before turns.

He was alone in the lefthand cab. The bodies of the other crew members had turned out to be sickeningly difficult to handle, but with a strength born out of near desperation he had managed to lift them into the other cab, Yuri and Gennadi in the back, Andrei in front, occupying his rightful place as vehicle commander even in death. His body in the stained black coveralls was sprawled sideways across the seat, jerking obscenely as the launcher negotiated the potholes in the road.

Markov lifted the map almost to his chin with his left hand, his eyes flickering from the road to the map and back. Damn it, *chort vozmi*, where was that junction? Or had he already passed it in the snowstorm?

The radio receiver crackled in his earphones, repeating the call signal five times in the same monotonous voice, and was followed by silence. He ignored it. He had decided against sending any false messages in an attempt to buy time. It would be all too easy for them to wonder why he and not Starshinov answered, and then they would know that something was seriously wrong. He had already had his bad luck when he had crossed the main road and found too late that he had done so right in front of an approaching convoy. His only hope was that they wouldn't have any reason to radio that information in before they were specifically asked for it.

His jaw muscles tightened. The search would soon start, and he knew how precariously small the margin of time might be.

From the other cab the dead face of Senior Lieutenant Starshinov stared at him through the racing snow.

* * *

In Command HQ at Leninakan, Shevchenko watched the minute hand of the clock on the wall creep forward another fraction. 0940. Twenty minutes overdue and still no sign of the missing unit. He was aware that some of the high-ranking officers behind him now stood in larger groups, whispering and nodding towards the large screen.

The radio operator was glancing up at him. There was perspiration on his brow, and he was clearly ill at ease.

"Ask Kolyma One if the exact route of Kolyma One Six is known," Shevchenko ordered. Some seconds passed while the inquiry went out.

"Kolyma One says affirmative, comrade Lieutenant-General."

"Have Kolyma One Seven and One Nine backtrack along the route of Kolyma One Six with instructions to report immediately if they have any information." Shevchenko looked up at the screen. "Kolyma One Eight is to remain on standby. Yana Two is to report to Kolyma One and send two NAMI-076 units along the route of Kolyma One Six, starting from point oh-four-one five-five-three. Emergency code Saturn. Confirm."

* * *

In the driving snow that obscured the road, Markov overshot it. He hit the brakes, slid to a sideways stop and slammed the gearbox into reverse. The launcher jerked backwards with a complaining whine from the cog wheels, and then he slammed it into forward again and turned the steering wheel full lock as he accelerated among the sparse trees, away from the road. This was virgin terrain, and he had to hold on tightly to the steer-

ing wheel while the MAZ-543 rushed forward, bucking
and shaking, bouncing him against the seat harness. He
watched the last digits of the odometer roll by, four
hundred metres, five hundred, and suddenly the launcher
rolled into a small clearing. He stopped close to an outcrop of rock, crowned with a cluster of dark conifers.
On the other side were more trees, forming a copse, so
that the launcher stood as if guarded by rock and wood.
Markov shut off the diesel engine.

He reached out and flipped the high-beam switch,
three quick flashes, pause, two more flashes, longer pause,
one single long flash.

The wind rushed the snow along with a muted wail
as it funnelled between the cabs and against the body
of the launcher. The seat springs creaked as he shifted
his position to unfasten the harness. In the relative silence of the cab he heard the soft crackle of static from
the radio and the ticking of cooling metal. He un-
strapped his helmet and looked at his watch and sat,
waiting tensely, balling his hands into fists, trying to
peer through the white curtain outside.

There was movement at the edge of the copse. Three,
no, four armed men in heavy white anoraks and face
masks were emerging from the firs. Four quick flashes
in succession, from the flashlight held by the tall figure
in the lead. He felt a surge of relief.

They had made it.

He opened the door and slid down the metal ladder,
then trudged through the snow to meet the group.

The man in front stopped and raised his left hand to
pull off his mask. Markov stared into his face; it was
paler than he remembered after all this time, but still
carried the brand on the left cheek. They nodded to
each other, almost hesitantly, but wasted no time on
handshakes or further greetings.

"We must hurry," Markov said in English with surprisingly few traces of a Slavic accent. "I met a small

northbound convoy about ten minutes ago. A search for the launcher has already started. When the general alarm is raised they'll know where the launcher has been seen."

The other man nodded.

"First of all, those two in the rear of the right-hand cab must be transferred to the other cab. Don't bother being artistic about it. Hand me my clothes."

The man with the brand turned and barked orders in a staccato language. Two men immediately set off for the launcher while the remaining man handed Markov a white canvas bag.

Markov wormed out of his black coveralls, got his uniform tunic off and threw all of it in the snow. From the bag he took out a thick sweater, a white parka identical to those worn by the others, a face mask, and a pair of medium heavy boots of the kind used for terrain skiing. He put everything on and went over to the right-hand cab and threw the abandoned garments into the back. By the time the others had taken care of the dead crew, he looked like one of them except for his olive-green army trousers.

He motioned to the man with the brand and one of the others to follow him and began to climb onto the top of the MAZ. The other two went back to where they had left the rest of their gear among the trees.

Markov had memorized the stolen photostats of the manual carefully before burning them, but the ice-cold metal and the gusts of thick snow made the work slow and difficult. The calipers which served to secure the SCUD-B missile to its launching cradle was swung aside, and then he had to take off his gloves and work with numbed, aching fingers as he opened the first hatch and started to run through the steps in the disconnecting procedure. From time to time the other men with him gave him a helping hand, but mostly they crowded in closely, trying to give him as much protection from the wind as possible.

The other two men returned, carrying five pairs of skis and ski poles. In addition to the skis they brought a small wooden sleigh, 120 by 60 centimetres, padded and fitted with a system of straps. They brought the sleigh up to the launcher and then went back to fetch four compact light-weight rucksacks, a tent, aluminum shovels, and a large black plastic bag. Markov hardly shot them a glance as they flung the bag and the shovels on top of the ribbed cowling. The bag came to rest just below the tip of the launching cradle. He knew what it contained—carefully collected trash, all the remaining evidence of a four-day bivouac while they had waited for him to find the right moment to make his move.

The tall man with the brand had put his face mask back on and shouted an order to the men on the ground. One of them immediately opened one of the rucksacks and brought out three short, carefully coiled lengths of thin and flexible orange nylon rope which he flung up to the men on the MAZ-543.

Minutes later Markov threw one rope end to the men on the ground and shouted instructions. One of the men began pulling at the rope while the other adjusted the position of the sleigh.

A cylinder appeared over the edge; grey-painted, steel-coated, with Cyrillic script stencilled in white on the side. It was slowly lowered on two lengths of rope tied around the ends of the cylinder while a third held it away from the side of the launcher. With care it was manoeuvred into position over the wooden sleigh until it finally came to rest on it. Markov and the tall man looked down at the cylinder for a moment, then their eyes met. There was no mistaking the expression of triumph.

On the ground one man cast off the lines while the other handed one of the rucksacks up to Markov. The two men who had assisted him climbed down and to-gether began to secure the cylinder with the straps, tying the tent down on top of it. They worked purposefully, efficiently, exchanging a minimum of words.

From the rucksack Markov brought out a flat, thick, dark green disc and a plastic pack. He weighed the disc in his hand for a moment and then pressed it to the fuselage of the missile, where it stuck with a muted clang. He unscrewed a small cap a little off-centre in the disc, broke open the plastic pack, looked at his watch, selected a thin glass tube from the pack, inserted it into the hole, and screwed the cap back on. As he gave it the final twist there was an almost inaudible sound of breaking glass from inside the disc. In roughly fifteen minutes the acid in the glass tube would have finished its job and the limpet mine would detonate and ignite the liquid fuel inside the missile, and scatter the launcher and its three crew members all over the forest. Markov was satisfied. The elapsed time since he had stopped by the outcrop of rock was nineteen minutes, forty-five seconds.

He slung the rucksack onto his back and climbed down. The others had already put their skis on and were wait-ing for him. Quickly he adjusted the bindings of his skis and snapped them on, gripped the ski poles held out to him and nodded.

One minute later they had left the clearing and were skiing in a westerly direction into the foothills north of the Akbaba Dagh massif towards Turkey, led by a short, broad man; second was the tall man, followed by the others, one of whom was towing the loaded sleigh from a harness around his waist. Markov was bringing up the rear.

Alone in the clearing between the rock and the copse, waiting for the explosion which would shatter the bowl of snow and midmorning light, stood the deserted launcher. Its three dead crew members sat grotesquely in their seats, while small ridges and deposits of snow formed along the windshield wipers and inside the rims of the wheels.

Presently the hijacking party felt the ground tremble slightly and heard a concussion reverberate among the trees like distant thunder, dulled by the snow, but long and drawn out. Markov muttered to himself in Russian: "Well, that ought to give them something to puzzle about. Will take them a long time to find out what is missing and what isn't."

*   *   *

In the Operations Room of Command HQ at Leninakan, Lieutenant-General Shevchenko stared uncomprehendingly at the slip of paper in his hand. It had just been brought to him by a uniformed aide and stated that a MAZ-543/SCUD-B launcher/missile unit driving in a southwesterly direction at high speed had been observed by a transport unit at approximately 1003 hours crossing the main road near Bogdanovka. Vehicle unit designation and possible damage unknown, due to bad sighting conditions.

He lifted his head and stared at the screen. Near Bogdanovka ... no SCUD-B units should be there! What were they trying to do?

He could feel the precious seconds ticking away. He had to act, and act fast. Confer with other senior officers in the room. Maybe stop part of the manoeuvre and send search units into the area. Alert the border guards.

Shevchenko swore silently, cursing the lost missile carrier, the eyes he knew were watching him, the raging blizzard which made it impossible to send up helicopters from the air base at Aparan. Something was very, very wrong.

*   *   *

The snowfall had eased a little and the wind had dropped

when they came upon it. Sergeant Litvak looked past the swishing windshield wipers of the GMZ. The driver, Private Vereshchagin, hit the brakes and brought the tracked, armoured vehicle to a stop on the narrow road.

Something had thrown earth and gravel and blackened pieces of shrubbery over the road as far as they could see. Litvak gazed among the trees for any sign of the origin of an explosion.

"In there," he said to his driver, pointing right. Vereshchagin put the GMZ in gear again, and then steered it in among the trees, the tracks slipping a little in the snow.

Debris was scattered everywhere, and patches of sooty discoloured snow grew larger as they proceeded; a twisted scrap of metal had gouged a long, black furrow in the snow and had finally stuck in the stump of a fallen tree. Litvak looked at it, open-mouthed; then they rounded a rocky outcrop, and a holocaust emerged from the snow.

Litvak had seen MAZ-543s before, but he had difficulty recognizing this one. The hefty launcher/missile unit had been reduced to something skeletal, except that the colour was wrong: nothing of the remains was anything but soot-black. Like some broken prehistoric monster, it seemed to have perished in a desperate attempt to crawl out of its own grave. The cabs had been blown open like eggshells and the engine cowling was twisted like a discarded serviette, but they still clung together over the edge of an oblong crater. There was no sign of the missile; the only thing to indicate that it had ever been there were pieces of hydraulics which dangled grotesquely here and there. Behind the engine the launcher had been split along the middle by the rearward blast, but still it stood upright, resting on the rims of its eight wheels. The tires had melted from the heat of the explosion and formed large puddles of something black, sticky, and stinking on the ground, while the wheels remained enmeshed in a web of clinging steel cord.

A great number of trees had been felled and several more unfoliated by the blast. Several dark streaks ran across the rocky surface of the outcrop, roughly radiating from the wrecked launcher. The heat had left its imprint with a vertical crack about twenty centimetres wide, running from the top of the outcrop almost all the way to the ground. Some of the conifers near the edge had been burnt more or less completely, and the remains of one tree hung precariously over the precipice. For something like fifty metres in every direction the snow was melted away and blackened. The darkness continued among the jumble of felled trees and even seemed to discolour the falling snow itself. There was a curious soft-focus quality to the entire scene, and if Litvak and Vereshchagin had stepped outside they might have been able to catch a soft sizzling sound. The thing that had once been a MAZ-543 launcher was still so hot that the snow which fell upon it was instantly vaporized and the black hulk was surrounded by a soft mist.

"Oh, my sweet God," Sergeant Litvak breathed softly. And then a thought filled him with panic. The warhead: it might lie broken somewhere, spilling out kilos of poisonous, deadly plutonium.

"Back up!" he screamed at Vereshchagin. "Back up, for God's sake! We've got to get out of here!"

Private Vereshchagin stared dumbly at him and then suddenly understood. He threw the GMZ into reverse with a crunch, the tracks throwing up clouds of sooty snow while Litvak frantically reached for the microphone.

*   *   *

It was late afternoon when the man at the head of the

group of skiers called a halt. They were in deep forest. The snow was still falling, but softly now. The wind had almost died.

The man's name was Abel Gavarian. He was Armenian and born in the town of Tbilisi, in the Georgian SSR of the Soviet Union. He had lived there for over twenty-five years before he availed himself of a propitious moment to move over to the "right" side of the border and settled in Erzurum. He knew the terrain like the back of his hand, and occasionally made an excursion into the old country on behalf of those who paid him well, as these men did.

He did not know any of them and he had no wish to. He had read the Cyrillic script on the steel cylinder and had a strong suspicion as to what it was, and he only wanted to part from these men with the rest of the money they owed him.

He had fulfilled his part of the deal and guided them back into Turkey to the place from where they had started. With the money he would leave Erzurum. He would be richer than ever before in his life.

The man with the brand had taken off his skis and planted the poles in the snow, and was taking a small parcel from his rucksack. He handed it over to Gavarian.

"The rest of the money, as we agreed."

Gavarian took off his gloves and opened the parcel and riffled through the stacks of notes. Dollar bills and more dollar bills. He quickly wrapped it up again and put the parcel into one of his parka pockets.

"Thank you for your help. We wish you good luck." The man held out his right hand. Gavarian felt surprise at the gesture, but automatically reached out his own hand.

The other man gripped it, and jerked sharply. Gavarian's head shot back; for a fraction of a second he looked at the treetops, and then the knife sliced through the skin under his jawbone, through the roof of his mouth and into his brain. There was an explosion of light, and then nothing.

Slowly the body of Gavarian collapsed, crumpling slightly sideways into the snow. The man with the brand bent forward to retrieve his knife, wiping it off on Gavarian's white parka before returning it to its sheath. Then he took the parcel from Gavarian's pocket and returned it to his rucksack, and nodded to his companions.

Soon a curtain of silently falling snow separated the departing skiers and the dead body they had left behind.

3

THE DOG HADN'T MOVED. Annika crawled forward another inch, slowly and cautiously, her body taut with tension. Another inch. The big, black dog lay still on his belly in the snow, fixedly staring at her.

"Good doggie," she crooned soothingly. She moved her hands forward again, trying to dig her toes firmly into the snow. The dog lifted its head a fraction. Their eyes locked across the three metres separating them.

She crept forward again, very slowly this time. The dog curled its upper lip, tensing itself for the attack. She flung herself forward with her arm outstretched, but the dog was faster. It exploded out of its crouch, and its jaws closed on the wooden stick a fraction of a second before her fingers groped where it had been; the dog jumped sideways in among the trees, flopped down and started chewing on the stick while it watched her. She lay flat in the snow, and behind her she heard Leif laugh.

"You'll never beat Sammy at that game, Annika. You're no match for those reflexes of his."

"I will, dammit!"

He came over and helped her up, brushed the snow away; then he adjusted her red cap and parka hood and kissed the tip of her nose. She pushed him away.

"Well, all right," he said, "maybe if you practise hard for the next five years . . ."

She hit him in the chest with her left hand rolled

into a fist inside her mitten. He took a surprised step backwards with flailing arms, staggered and fell. At once she was on top of him, straddling his stomach and rubbing snow into his face. "Apologize!" she commanded with glittering eyes.

"I apologize, I apologize—a thousand times," he said. "Please stop."

"Why should I?"

Leif's face was flushed red. "Because I love you."

She hesitated. "Just like that?"

"Well, isn't that enough?"

She said nothing, and a slight frown spread across her brow. Suddenly she stopped and her arms fell to her sides. Leif regarded her for a moment and then cupped her face in his hands and pulled her down and kissed her.

For a long while they lay in the snow in a kind of desperate embrace, kissing with eyes open as if trying to gauge each other's reactions. Finally Sammy dropped the stick and came up to them, sniffed at them, stuck his nose between their faces and licked Leif across the cheek until he was forced to let go of Annika and wriggle away. Annika giggled, and the tension suddenly broke.

It was New Year's Day. Five days of continuous snowfall had come to an end during the night; the world around them was blanketed in white. They walked clumsily in the deep snow, while Sammy, Annika's big Labrador, leaped among the trees in heavy bounds, sometimes sinking to his belly in the drifts. The whisper of the wind among the firs was muted, and high cirrocumulus clouds hung in the intensely blue sky; already the short afternoon was coming to an end, and dusk was deepening among the trees. The dark green branches of the firs hung low, weighted down by the snow.

"It's getting late," she said. "Let's get back to the house, OK?"

"OK. Know what I'd like? A cup of hot chocolate."

She smiled and pulled off her mitten, then stuck two fingers in her mouth, and a piercing whistle rang out among the trees.

"Sammy! Sa-a-ammy!"

Leif looked at her where she stood with eyes darting back and forth, looking for the big dog. She had a pretty face with a smallish nose and a small but full mouth. Only the tiny white scar on her chin and the slight unevenness of her teeth prevented her from being called a beauty in the classical sense. Her hair, hidden beneath her cap, was shoulder length, a sparkling dark brown colour matching her lively eyes. She was small and very lovely, and he felt a pang of pain as he looked at her and wondered if he would be able to bear it if she tired of it all and left him.

He carried a picture of her in the cab of his Scania, a small colour photograph which he had taped to the back of the sun visor. It showed her standing on the beach wearing a red bikini, hands on her hips, smiling straight into the camera. It was a reminder that some-body was waiting for him when he came home.

Sammy came out from among the trees, jumping in long heavy strides towards Annika. She bent down and rubbed his ears affectionately, and together they turned and plodded towards him, breaking his gloomy chain of thoughts. He pulled his mitten off and ran a finger along her cheek.

"You know, you could do with a tan."

She sighed. "Don't rub it in. Not everybody has your fringe benefits."

"Maybe you should take a HGV certificate and start driving on the Saudi run."

"The Arab customs officials would be delighted, no doubt."

"Oh, they would. Or you could come along with me, just for one trip."

She shook her head. "That's impossible, and besides, it's no place for a girl."

"Well, you *could* do with a tan," he said lamely.

She shrugged and took his arm. With her other hand she reached up and tousled his beard. It was much shorter now, along with his hair, after having met with a pair of scissors in Annika's deft hands. "Come on, let's get home. It's all right, you know. Super tans aren't good for you, anyway."

He nodded and pulled his parka sleeve back to check the time. A little past three. He would have to call up his hauler soon.

*   *   *

In the evening he sat in front of the TV, smoking a cigarette. The sound was turned down; he took no real interest in the shapes which blurred back and forth across the screen. Sammy lay snoring on the rug in front of the fireplace where the logs had burnt to embers. From the kitchen he could hear the scraping and shuffling as Annika put things in order after their dinner. She appeared in the kitchen doorway, wiping her hands on a towel.

"Would you like a glass of Madeira?"

"Eh? Yeah, that would be nice." He uncrossed his legs, stretching in the big leather armchair. "That was a very good dinner, by the way."

"Glad you noticed we ate," she called back over her shoulder.

She came back with a bottle and two small glasses and sat down in the chair beside him.

"What's on television?"

"Oh, just some old movie. Wasn't really paying attention to it."

There was silence, and they sipped the dark red liquid. He stubbed out his cigarette, stubbornly looking at the TV screen while she watched him.

"What is it, Leif?" she asked. "What did your hauler say?"

"He wants me to go out the day after tomorrow provided he can get all the papers cleared with Jerre in Stockholm. He wished us a happy New Year, too."

She looked serious. "That soon?"

"Yeah. The load is building material for ABV in Riyadh—insulating material, cans of Rugasol, that kind of thing. Seems they're running short of the stuff and need it down there in a hurry."

"Do you really think you'll be going out on the third?"

"No." He smiled weakly. "Bert is always a bit optimistic about those things. The roads may not even be open. Probably the fifth, maybe the fourth if things go quicker than usual."

"I see," she said in a small voice. "I was hoping we'd have more time together."

He knew only too well what was coming. This time they had so far avoided the subject that always cropped up when he was at home: the long trips which kept them from having any real kind of life together and at times made them feel like strangers when he came back. Then, sooner or later, they returned to the same discussion, repeating the same arguments. He would say that he *liked* the job, and remind her of the money he made, and she would retort by pointing out how few friends they had and that this wasn't what she wanted out of her life, and besides, she had a job of her own and was independent. The last time she had said that he had seen the look in her eyes and realized that no matter how much she loved him, some day she would leave him if he went on doing the Middle East run.

Then, as now, he had felt himself caught in a desperately mute tangle of conflicting emotions. Hell, he didn't want to quit, at least he didn't think he wanted to. Why should he have to choose when it still was much easier to show his love by saying a noncommittal

"I love you" and then make physical love to her? "Isn't that enough?" he had asked, and immediately silenced her with a kiss before she had a chance to voice her doubts.

It was at this point somewhere that their arguments turned into a downright fight that often lasted well into the early hours of morning, when they still ended up making love because that was the only way they knew to end it. He knew he couldn't have it both ways forever, but as long as there was nothing on a gut level telling him he couldn't, he knew he'd go on trying.

"God, Annika, let's not have another fight," he sighed. "We've been through all that I don't know how many times."

"And why shouldn't we have another fight?" she replied hotly. "How many times will it take to get you to understand? Maybe this time, maybe next?"

"You know we never get anywhere . . ."

"Except into bed, which is a lot easier, isn't it?"

"Oh, come off it. You don't mind getting laid."

"Don't be so conceited. I mind it a lot as a way of putting a stop to unpleasant discussions, and you know it."

He was silent, regarding her glittering eyes and set mouth while the knot inside him tightened a little more.

"All right, Leif," she said in a suddenly reasonable tone. "We won't have another argument. You're right, it doesn't get us anywhere. I'm just going to tell you something. You can go on driving for as long as you like, but one day when you get back home I won't be here."

He had wanted something on a gut level, but he had never expected her to be able to say those words in such a cool, detached way.

"I'm not blackmailing you, Leif," she went on. "I'm not saying I'll leave you if you go out again. I may still be there in a year's time, I may be gone when you get back next month. I'm just saying I won't be able to take it forever, and then it's for you to decide."

"A sort of Arabian roulette, eh?"

"You might call it that if you want to," she said in a level voice.

"Hell, it's not fair!" he flared up. "Why should I be the one to decide?"

"And why not?" For a moment there was fire in her voice again. "Leif, there is no way I can accommodate myself to your life, except to stay at home and accept seeing you a couple of days now and then, and I won't do that. I can't follow you, I can't share your life, I can't do anything. Our life together depends on you, so why shouldn't it be fair if you have to decide something for a change? I've given you the alternatives. For God's sake, decide something, even if you decide not to decide! I'm just not going to accept being made love to and told 'I love you' as a substitute. I refuse to be taken for granted!"

He said nothing, just looked at the greyish-blue figures that chased across the TV screen to a faint, unintelligible murmur. He had tried, several times, to describe how he felt, had shown her the photos he had taken, but she had not understood, not *really*. The thrill of crossing the Bosporus Bridge in Istanbul, the famous cities he drove through—Budapest, Damascus, Ankara, Vienna—the desert sunsets, snow-capped mountains in the distance, the exhilaration of firing up the big diesel engine and moving the lumbering truck back up onto the road, the hypnotic sound of eighteen tires against asphalt and the endless white line unwinding beneath him; meeting colleagues and friends along the way, feeling pride in knowing that he and he alone was responsible for the truck and its load—how could she know? She had never been there.

But then, how could he understand the comforts of a regular life, the security of a home and someone to come home to? He had never been there, at least not since he had left his parents' home and started to fend for himself.

"I may not be able to stand it," he said quietly.

"That," Annika replied, "is something you will never know until you've tried it."

"You know, lately I've thought I'd quit. When I've been on the road, that is, and seen the new wrecks and talked to the other pilots. Did you know that Lennart, from Gothenburg, I met him in Aksaray on the way back, that he's divorced? And then, when I'm at home I want to go out there again."

She said nothing.

"If I make this my last run, and after that we'll have a go at it, will you be here when I come back?"

He could always get a job as a driver in Sweden—or maybe haul cargo on the Austria run; he wouldn't be gone more than five or six days. If it worked out with Annika that would be good; if not, well, it wouldn't have worked out at any time, and there would always be a demand for experienced Middle East pilots.

"Yes," Annika said. "I'll be waiting."

"All right," he said and looked directly at her for the first time in a long while. "I'll call Bert first thing tomorrow morning and tell him. Maybe he can spread the word among the haulers at home that I'm out for a job."

"What's he going to say?"

"Oh, he won't like it. He considers me his top pilot. Never failed to deliver a load, never ditched a trailer—reasonably sober. He'll just have to get used to it."

Annika set her glass down, then laughed and climbed across the armrests into his lap. "You know what?" she said and unbuttoned his top shirt button. "I'm very happy you want to try this, Leif." Second button. "And you know another thing?" Third button. "You're right, I don't mind being laid, just as long as it's for the right reason.''

"And this reason is right?"

"Not because you're quitting. I can't be bought. Because I want to and because it's good, that's all." The shirt was completely unbuttoned, her hands were moving across his chest, her fingers circling his nipples.

He felt the dryness in his throat and his tightening groin as he unzipped her jeans and pulled up her sweater, baring her small, rounded breasts. Their eyes met in the semi-darkness. He leaned forward to kiss her breasts and he felt her soft skin. With Annika in his arms he rose and carried her up the narrow stairs.

"I love you, Leif," she whispered in his ear a little later.

For once he had sense enough not to reply.

* * *

Afterwards, he slept uneasily. He was in his truck and in bed with Annika at the same time. Somehow he was able to walk directly from the cab into the trailer, where goods of all kinds were piled. He was looking for a special item on the load sheet, but since he couldn't read the load sheet he had no idea what he was looking for and couldn't check if it really was in the trailer. While he searched, other drivers whom he told about his problems joined him; Annika came too, with Sammy, and curiously looked all over the truck, while the big Scania rushed along with empty cab, bucking and shaking on an endless line of asphalt.

He forced himself awake, but it was a while before he was fully convinced that he wasn't inside the trailer, only in a bed with Annika's warm back against his chest and his arms around her. He listened uneasily to the sounds of the house: the quiet whine of the refrigerator and the ticking of the kitchen clock from downstairs, the soft creaking of the walls as the cold was at work outside.

Eventually he calmed down, and other thoughts and images began to grow while he slowly tumbled into the darkness, and the house became quiet around him . . .

He slept.

4

WINTER IN MOSCOW had been severe. Snow had been bountiful, and by early January it had turned the city into one vast wintry fortress. Banks of snow lined the streets and avenues like parapets, and made squares and open places into massive white strongholds. Buildings had sprouted roof crenellations which balaclava-helmeted attackers armed with shovels were tumbling down onto the streets, where others added the new snow to the old fortifications. The siege showed every sign of being an extended one.

The ramparts of Dzerzhinsky Square glittered with painful brilliance in the sun. It was one of those bitterly cold days with a completely cloudless sky. The time was ten o'clock in the morning; most people were at work. Those who were not and had cause to go somewhere by way of Dzerzhinsky Square did their best not to look at No. 2, from where they were watched by General Yakov Mikhailovich Ladygin, Director of the First Chief Directorate of the KGB, the Committee for State Security.

Ladygin was standing by the window of his office on the fourth floor, musing about watchers and the watched as he gazed down at the square and Marx Prospect beyond. Ladygin had long ago come to recognize the contradiction in the ordinary Russian's unwillingness to look at the Centre of that organization under whose scrutiny he was virtually all of the time. It was as though the commoner imagined that if he pretended that the KGB didn't exist, the KGB would pretend that he didn't exist.

The amusing fact was that the Russian's feigned indifference made him all the more conspicuous. If somebody just once stopped in the middle of the square and openly scrutinized No. 2, he would suddenly become eminently overlookable and at the same time he might see things more clearly. He might even see me, Ladygin thought, despite being protected by his position at the deeply sunken window, and the darkness of his office and the brilliance outside made difficult work for prying eyes. But above all he was protected by the fact that *he* was one of the watchers. If he went out there he would still be one of the watchers, and therefore invisible. The watched ones would safeguard his invisibility with their own timidity. If one of them dared to look at him he would be seen and in his turn not see so well.

It was a paradox that never ceased to intrigue General Yakov Mikhailovich Ladygin. It was also merely a private device for his own amusement and, to a certain degree, his own illumination.

Ladygin himself was a bit of a paradox, like so many of the Soviet ruling cadre. He was a trim man in his early fifties, a little under medium height, with thinning blond hair, light blue eyes, and a rather broad Slav face which revealed his peasant origin. However, his education was quite cosmopolitan; his language tuition had been given by the best teachers the Soviet Union could muster and had left him fluent in English, French, and Spanish, and during his career in the KGB he had picked up considerable knowledge of science, economics and the arts, as well as lots of specialized knowledge which wasn't that easily categorized but very useful in his profession.

His career had risen steadily; ruthless ambition coupled with circumspectness and matter-of-factness, which had stood him in good stead as KGB resident in Madrid and subsequently as Chief of the Third Geographical Department (UK, Australia, NZ and Scandinavia), had also kept him out of the major power shifts in the Soviet hierarchy, and he was now one of the youngest Directorate heads in the history of the KGB.

There was a knock on the office door. "Come in," he called, without turning away from the window.

The door opened and a female voice cheerfully said, "Good morning, Yakov Mikhailovich."

Ladygin turned and regarded Lydia Markovina Popova. Officially she was his personal secretary, but in reality she served as his assistant and *aide-de-camp.* Ladygin had met her during his tour of duty in Madrid and had been immensely impressed by her intelligence and sound judgement. She was then the wife of the third secretary of the Soviet Embassy, and Ladygin had quickly co-opted her for intelligence work. She had also, for a period of time, been his mistress.

Having returned to Moscow, she and her husband had split up, and when Ladygin was promoted to head of the First Chief Directorate he had offered Lydia Markovina the position as his personal secretary. Realizing her potential, he had used the KGB "old boy network" as a shortcut to get her a higher security clearance than anybody else in a similar position and turned her into an extremely efficient assistant. Everybody knew Lydia Markovina to be Ladygin's extension, and although she was a woman in what was very much a male preserve, she was treated accordingly.

"Good morning, Lydia." He smiled at her and pointed at the thick dossier she carried under her arm. "You've been through it?"

"Yes. Took me the better part of last night."

"Have you found out why Special Investigations sent that thing via us and not directly to Viktor Anatoli?" The investigation of the Leninakan affair had been or-

dered by Viktor Anatoli Chernyshov himself, KGB
Chairman and member of the Politburo.

"No, but I suppose Zhernov has his own reasons for
wanting us to have a look at it before further steps are
taken. Did you have time to read it?"

"No, I only browsed through it before I turned it over
to you. Sit down, Lydia, and give me a breakdown."

The KGB chain of command was strictly hierarchical.
Intelligence material went directly to the heads of the
various departments, in some cases directly to Chernyshov, in a crude, undigested form, and much of the
chief's time had to be devoted to breaking down, sifting
through, and interpreting information to be able to make
decisions, which were passed back down the chain. The
Americans had review boards and panels of experts at
all levels, and virtually all information that reached the
decision-makers had already been digested for quick decisions. Ladygin thought the Americans overdid it a bit,
but he realized the advantages of the system and had
made Lydia Markovina his one-woman review board.
She gave him power, the power to handle many things,
and that meant a lot in the KGB bureaucracy.

"You want it all from the beginning?" Lydia sat down
and opened the dossier, which was stamped *Top Secret*,
the highest KGB security classification. The desk between them was a heavy, wooden, pre-war article. On
the wall behind the desk was the standard Lenin portrait, in which the great leader was looking, with slightly
lifted chin and clear brow, at something beyond, above
and a little to the left of the viewer, probably the so-
cialistic future. On the desk itself, Ladygin had a portrait
of his wife, a plump, somewhat drab woman in her late
forties, and his two children. They were looking directly
into the camera. Within easy reach from behind the
desk stood an old, dented, but well-polished *samovar*;
Ladygin consumed prodigious quantities of tea. He poured
a cup for Lydia, saying:

"No, take it from the point when the wreck was discovered. I want the technical details, the background that Zhernov's been digging up." Ladygin's information, in the typical KGB manner, had been incomplete and on certain points hazy; but for over a fortnight he had been heading a frantic search throughout the Middle East with the object of finding an eighteen-kiloton Soviet nuclear warhead, abducted from Soviet territory by a party of unknown hijackers. For some reason Zhernov wanted him to be more illuminated, and Ladygin wasn't going to disappoint him.

"Well," Lydia said, "here we are. The wrecked launcher was discovered at 1055 local time by a GMZ unit which had been diverted to search for it. I suppose you've seen the photographs?"

"Yes. What a damned *mokroe delo!*" *Mokroe delo* or "wet affair" was a euphemism for a clandestine affair involving bloodshed.

"Then you know what it looked like. There was debris scattered all over the place. Sergeant Litvak in the GMZ unit radioed into HQ with a request for a sanitation crew to go in there first in case there was free plutonium about from the warhead."

"Can't say I blame him. And this crew arrived when?"

Lydia Markovina was riffling through the dossier to keep pace with Ladygin's questions. "They were set down by helicopter at 1123. Took them some twenty minutes to reach the wreck itself, and another fifteen minutes to make sure there was no significant radioactivity. After that HQ sent in a Motor Rifle Regiment to cordon off the area and start sorting through it. A number of experts arrived in the hours that followed."

"Didn't anybody suspect at that time that the warhead was missing? Wasn't the lack of radioactivity any indication?"

"The report says no. These warheads are built to take a lot of punishment. The idea is that they should be impossible to set off by accident." She sipped her tea and looked up.

"All right, I'm suitably impressed. Go on."

"Well, the first thing was to find the warhead. It took forty-five minutes before they started to suspect it wasn't there. Then they came across faint, nearly covered ski tracks leading in a westerly direction, towards the Turkish border, plus what might have been a bivouac."

Ladygin frowned as he added up the delays; the compounded time lag came out disturbingly high. He had not known this in detail. "*Chort vozmi!* Damn! Well, that had them hopping, I suppose."

"Yes, the border guards had the border sealed off by 1345, and special patrols were organized to cover the most inaccessible parts in the mountains."

"1345," Ladygin repeated as he turned and looked down into Dzerzhinsky Square once more. "So they had at least three hours in which to get across the border. The blizzard probably gave them an extra hour. So the warhead went over. With a bit of fancy climbing, eh?"

"Yes, the tracks indicated four or possibly five men with a sleigh. Closer to the border the search party lost the tracks due to the blizzard, but their probable crossing point is in very difficult terrain, considered well-nigh impossible to penetrate. From the top there is a steep descent on the Turkish side, but with modern climbing techniques it's said to be negotiable, even with a heavy load."

"I don't imagine the Turkish border guards gave them any trouble," Ladygin said bitterly. "And we know they had a good guide." That was where all the traces of the hijackers had ended in Turkey: in the woods at a dead Armenian that the KGB knew well. It was admirable: a brilliant plan, thorough preparation, audacity, and faultless execution—plus ruthless covering up. It was done by professionals. A thought suddenly struck him.

"How come that SCUD unit was alone? I thought those things operated in batteries of three or four."

"They usually do, but certain tacticians have criticized this as affording the enemy too good a target. One aim of the manoeuvre was to test a new procedure whereby the SCUD units arrive separately at their positions by different routes, regroup, fire and scoot away again separately."

Ladygin groaned. "Hell! That many factors working together for one purpose could make you religious. All right, it happened. And we haven't come up with anything in two weeks, except Gavarian—dead. So now we hope this report will turn out to contain something useful, eh? Right, let's start with the launcher. What did the experts find out except that the warhead was missing?"

Lydia Markovina held up a quarter-inch section of the dossier between thumb and forefinger. "This. They've been through virtually every scrap of it. As for the missile, it was probably exploded with the use of a limpet mine with a time fuse. Origin of mine impossible to ascertain."

"How did they find out that Markov was missing?"

"By sorting through charred human remains, examining twisted identity discs, analyzing pieces of metal from badges and stripes and so on," Lydia said dispassionately. "Detective work; not enough pieces to fit four people together, and conspicuously few traces of Markov, so they're 99 percent sure he's the one who's missing. Do you want the grisly details?"

"I think I can do without them. So Captain Markov of the KGB Armed Forces Directorate is missing." For all its professionalism, for all its planning and audacity, the scheme had called for one indispensable factor to succeed: an insider. Ladygin cursed himself for having been so incredibly, irresponsibly blind as to have overlooked the possibility that a KGB rep might be a renegade as he had been when he first had sat with the dossiers of the four crew members on his desk. It was exactly the kind of KGB thinking he despised as being counterproductive, inhibiting, and smug. "Repeat his background briefly, it might tell us something."

Into Dzerzhinsky Square an old flatbed lorry rumbled with a dozen foot soldiers in the Winter War, who jumped down and fell upon a section of the white fortress in the middle of the square. What a simple war, Ladygin thought. Behind his back Lydia was turning pages in the dossier.

"Thirty-four years old," she began. "Comes from Chelyabinsk. Father and mother working at one of the local factories, dedicated Party members since before the war. Markov got into the Komsomol at fifteen. Ideologically sound and zealous, you might say. Applied for training as an officer at eighteen, was accepted, did well, was co-opted as an informer for the KGB. Recruited as staff officer at twenty-five. Served as small arms instructor in one of our foreign guerilla training camps near Odessa from '76 to '77, before he was transferred to the Third Directorate. Generally considered to be reliable, competent, unimaginative, and politically rigid."

"A zealot, eh? Did he get to where he was solely on ideological merits?" Ladygin sounded disapproving.

"You could say he did. He wasn't what you'd call New Class." In the relative privacy of Ladygin's office— he made regular checks to neutralize any bugs placed there by other KGB departments—Lydia Markovina could mention what officially didn't exist; the "New Class" was the party aristocracy which had access to the best education and enjoyed material privileges denied to the ordinary citizen. Virtually all KGB staff officers were recruited from this class.

"But one of Markov's best friends in Chelyabinsk," Lydia went on, "was the son of Fedor Noskov in the

Administrative Organs Department of the Central Committee."

"Ah," Ladygin said. "So." Ideological merits alone usually didn't go far towards ensuring a KGB career. You had to have some sort of connection. Markov had had that, too; someone in the very department that sanctioned all assignments and promotions of KGB personnel abroad as well as within the Soviet Union. "Well, now we know how he was assigned to the SCUD unit. Does Special Investigations say anything about responsibilities?"

Whenever there was a defection or a penetration by some foreign intelligence service, it was Special Investigations that went in and fixed the circumstances, assessed the damage and, lastly, judged who held the responsibility. Zhernov, Head of Special Investigations, was a powerful man. The fact that he was sending the report by way of Ladygin instead of directly to Chernyshov meant that Zhernov in this manner was trying to influence the steps to be taken.

"Nothing definite. It seems more like a series of unhappy circumstances. They do suggest certain measures, though."

"Yeah, unhappy is the word. Still, it's likely that Noskov's next position will be as head of a power plant in Siberia or a wool mill in Azerbaidzhan—if he's lucky. Poor devil, probably thought he was just doing a friend of his son's a good turn. In any case, I want to be kept up to date on the investigation of Markov that Zhernov is running."

Down in the square the battle against the snow went on. The platform of the lorry was filling steadily. Ladygin turned away from the white carnage.

"By the way," Lydia Markovina said, "who knows about this? I think *we* have put the blanket on it rather effectively, but do the Americans know anything—provided of course that they aren't behind it?"

"They probably do, although they may not be aware of it. You know how they are. They're sure to have recorded every bit of radio communication during the manoeuvre, and now it's all being processed by their computers. When that's done the information is sorted, categorized, screened by panels of experts, digested and presented to the brass. Unless they're really in a hurry to know something, things like that take time. Information overload." He shrugged.

"Satellite pictures?"

"In a snowstorm? Well, they ought to have something on their IR pictures, but I doubt that they know what it is they've got. Still, they must be curious. Unless . . . well, Lydia, *was* he working for the Americans?"

Lydia Markovina shook her head. "What would they want with only the warhead?" They'd be more interested in the missile and the launcher. And in any case, they wouldn't go about it that way. A SCUD launcher isn't a MIG-25."

"No," he said. "That's exactly what I've been thinking. And the same goes for the other major Western powers. China? No. If it had happened on the Sinkiang border I'd have bought it. And Markov doesn't sound like a defector to me. More like some fanatical renegade. I just wonder what the hell his motives are. And his plans."

Actually, he thought, the Soviet leadership might well approve of Markov's plans *as such*, just as long as they *weren't* accomplished with the use of unaccounted-for Soviet nuclear warheads. That was the crux of the situation. Even if the Soviet Union might profit from Markov's doings, it was something they couldn't afford on those conditions, what with SALT negotiations, US-Chinese rapprochement, the off again-on again Iranian-Iraqi war, the Middle East . . . The possible repercussions were too vast.

"I hate to say it again," Ladygin went on, "but the

only thing we're left with is terrorists. Which in a way is worse than if the Americans or the Chinese had got the warhead, because they would merely take it apart, not use it. All right, if Markov had terrorist connections, where did he get them? It must have been the training camp where he worked. What sort of people were being trained there?''

"Africans mostly, plus some Cubans, I think. MPLA troops, Ethiopians, Rhodesians, the odd Tanzanian, very hush-hush. You know.''

"Doesn't sound right. What else? Any Palestinians?''

"You're being paranoid." Lydia Markovina smiled. "I'll have a look." Again she turned pages in the dossier. "Well, what do you know. We did have a group of Palestinians in the camp at that time, training to become instructors in their turn in the PLO training camps in Syria. Interesting.''

"Very. So Markov may have had Palestinian contacts." Ladygin sighed and looked out. The snow-laden lorry was just turning into Marx Prospect while the assault party trundled off in the opposite direction in search of tea, *pirogs*, the Russian pastry, and vodka. "Location, method, everything speaks for Palestinians. Some of them would be mad enough to pull a stunt like this. We'll let that be our starting point. I want you to try and find the names of all the Palestinians who were in that camp while Markov worked there. It'll give us a short list. Then the question is, where will they use it?''

"That goes without saying," Lydia Markovina observed. "Israel would be the first alternative. Lebanon would be next. Anybody there with a nuclear warhead could more or less dictate his own conditions. Iran isn't very likely, in spite of the unrest there. The Palestinians have a chance of getting in there legally.''

"I tell you some of them would. But on the whole I agree with you. Don't forget the oil, though.''

"Saudi Arabia and the Gulf States?''

"A possibility. Actually, I don't think anybody could move the Saudi government. I remember we tried to organize a Saudi Liberation Front in the early seventies. It was a complete failure. Internal security is effective and the government stable. But blow up a major pipeline or Raz Tanura where all the oil goes out to the world . . . or just sit and flaunt it at the Hormuz Strait. And by all means, let's not forget Egypt. Even with Sadat gone, there's no love lost between many Palestinians and the Egyptian government. Well, Lydia, we've been at it for two weeks getting nowhere. Those people have managed to cover up everything, or we would have heard at least some sort of whisper by now. We've had our chance to peek at this report before it goes directly to Viktor Anatoli. Any bright new ideas?"

"Nothing that you haven't thought about already. You must have been at it all morning."

"For what it's been worth. All right, routine measures. Send out additional instructions to our residents in Ankara, Damascus, Baghdad, Tripoli, Amman, Beirut, Kuwait, Bahrein, Aden, and Muscat to pay special attention to Palestinian activity and report directly to me. When we get the names of those Palestinians we trained at that time I want a special agent to go through them and check on what they're doing now." Trespassing on Zhernov's territory, but that couldn't be helped, he thought. He made a long pause. "Then, Lydia, I want the Americans to know what has happened."

She stared at him. "Why?"

"Why? Lydia Markovina, come now. That warhead might accomplish something we've been trying to bring about for years. Who knows? But if so we'll be on the spot because it will appear as if we had provided it. We have, after all, signed the Non-Proliferation Treaty and can't afford even the slightest suspicion that we were in any way behind it. No, we must make ablutions. Just having lost the bloody thing is bad enough." Ladygin spoke with unusual emphasis.

Lydia Markovina looked thoughtful for a while, then nodded. "There's just one catch. What you're proposing is policy-making. You'll have to clear it with the Politburo first."

"I'll have to bloody well clear it with Andropov himself. That means selling it to Chernyshov to begin with."

She nodded again. "How is it going to be done?" What Ladygin was suggesting was highly unorthodox, of course, but once she had come to the realization that he was right, the efficient assistant took over.

He smiled and walked over to the desk. "Just like that, eh? That's what I like about you. I think we've got somebody in Ankara. A double. His code name is . . . wait . . ."

"Alphonse."

"Alphonse, yes. Your memory is astounding. Who's directing him? The Eighth Department?"

"He's an Army officer. No, I think it's the GRU through the Military Attaché in Ankara."

Alphonse existed in an odd equilibrium between the CIA and the KGB. His well-being depended on his not upsetting that precarious balance, and he never did anything that was even remotely likely to jeopardize his own position. As a spy he wasn't worth a thing to any of the organizations, but he was discreet and both of them found him a useful interface when the intelligence business at times deviated into a semblance of diplomacy. As the Ankara resident had once remarked to Ladygin, "Alphonse is no bloody use in intelligence work, but he's an absolute whiz if you want to send Season's Greetings to Colby."

"All right," Ladygin said. "Alphonse is our man. He'll handle something substantial for once. Further instructions to our Ankara resident. Set up Alphonse for a drop, say, two or three days from now. By that time it ought to have been cleared with the Politburo. I'll get in touch with Viktor Anatoli at once. After you've seen to it that the instructions are dispatched, I want you to devote yourself to the message. The Americans must know what has happened, what we're missing, that it was done with the help of a renegade—no need to mention that he was from us—and that we had nothing to do with it. You can mention that we suspect some unknown Palestinian group. They can draw their own conclusions. And I'm aware they'll tell the Israelis. We'll have to keep a close tab on the Israeli security services, which means having to activate a couple of sleepers, but that can't be helped. Their boys at Dimona would just love a chance of taking one of our nuclear warheads apart piece by piece. But if they can lead us to it we might beat them to the punch. Right, back to Alphonse. Make absolutely certain that it comes across that this derives directly from us, that it isn't anything that Alphonse stumbled onto, and to the extent that it is possible, that this isn't any fancy *dezinformatsiya* stunt we're trying to pull. They'll want their own confirmation, of course. And impress upon Alphonse that this information is to go directly to his American contact and to nobody else, or he won't be a glorified errand boy any longer but occupying a prominent place on our nasty short list. Got it all?''

''Got it.'' Lydia Markovina rose and started towards the door.

Ladygin had seated himself behind his desk and had his hand on the special telephone which would connect him directly with KGB Chairman Chernyshov, who had his office on the floor below, when Lydia Markovina reached the door. Without opening it she turned and looked hard at Ladygin. He met her glance, and for the first time in several years some of their old intimacy had entered into that look of mutual respect.

Finally she said. "Yakov Mikhailovich, what happens if the Politburo doesn't approve this plan?"

Ladygin smiled a minute smile. "Then I shall have to think very hard whether I should jeopardize my position, even my life—and yours too, for that matter, my dearest Lydia—and leak this information without authorization."

5

LEIF WENT OUT on January 4. Annika rode with him from Kävlinge to the ferry landing at Ystad in the passenger seat of the blue Scania, stockinged feet propped on the dashboard in the warm defroster airstream, enjoying the half-light in the cab and the panoramic view of the road as dusk fell outside. Now and then Leif reached out and touched her; he was glad to have her along in his great, rumbling beast of burden.

The day before he had gone out to Bert Nilsson's place and had inspected the entire vehicle before the trip. The semi-trailer had been loaded and delivered from Jerre's Malmö terminal a little before noon, and he had spent the entire afternoon methodically running down his private checklist: he vacuumed the interior of the cab and wiped down the dashboard before arranging all loose articles neatly; then, despite the cold, he washed down the whole truck until it shone in the pale winter sun. He rummaged through the large storage boxes on each side of the semi-trailer, checking tools, spares, and other equipment; changed the engine oil; tested the light and brake systems, and the fuel-feed system. Lastly, he stowed his bag containing his clothes and sleeping bag, and replenished his supplies; a new LPG bottle, tinned food and bread in the trailer boxes, fresh provisions that went into the small refrigerator underneath the bottom bunk, and an assortment of new cassettes on the shelf above the windshield.

Bert Nilsson, a short but powerfully built man in his fifties, came out now and then to give him a hand; in the evening, when Leif's arms and back ached but his mind was satisfied, Bert and his wife invited him in for dinner.

Leif and Annika arrived at the ferry well ahead of time, and were met by Bert who had driven via Sturup Airport to collect the necessary papers which had been sent down from the Jerre head office on the afternoon flight.

Leif cut the engine and Annika scampered over into the bottom bunk as Bert climbed into the passenger seat. He said hello and opened his briefcase, which contained load sheets, customs declarations, and Leif's passport stamped with a string of new visas from another round of the capital's embassies. Leif thumbed through them, smoking a cigarette and quietly humming to himself. He noted that his entry papers into Saudi Arabia were not written over Haditha but over Halat Ammar where the ABV agent was. Then he saw the telex copy confirming his reservation with the ferry from Greece to Syria.

"You've got me booked for the tenth, Bert. That doesn't give me a hell of a lot of time, especially at this time of year."

Bert looked worried and scratched his ear lobe. "I know. But you have a rush load in the back. ABV Riyadh are out of Rugasol and part of their shop is at a standstill. I'm counting on you. That's why I took a chance on the tenth."

Leif grimaced. "Fastest pilot in the business, eh? All right, I'll see what I can do." He stuffed the papers into his own black attaché case and they climbed down and went to square their business with the ferry company and the Swedish customs. Then he shook hands with Bert, who excused himself and waited in the Volvo 245 while Leif and Annika said their farewells.

*   *   *

He missed the ferry from Vólos by less than two hours.
The trip through a snow-covered Europe was uneventful, but slow. He stopped at some of the traditional truck
stops and felt a bit foolish making a ritual of his last
Middle East run. There was Orbis in Zielona Gora; Anna's Café just south of the Czechoslovak border, where
Anna herself hugged him goodbye; Budapest, where he
lazed in the incredible mosaic-decorated baths at the
back of Hotel Gellert.

Outside Belgrade the snow came—large, soft flakes at
first, but then the wind came and the snow began to
lash down. Visibility was nil beyond fifteen metres, and
it finally got so bad that he was forced to stop for the
night.

The blizzard had almost ceased when he crossed the
border into Greece in the early morning hours of the
tenth. The Yugoslavs went through their usual routine
of probing his diesel tanks for contraband liquor while
he stood beside the cab and tried not to show his im-
patience. Then the Greeks went through their usual
routine of sending him running back and forth, paying
road taxes and collecting the number of stamps offi-
cialdom demanded, before he could curse them all, slam
his door and drive off. Outside Yefira the weather turned
to sun and blue skies, and along the coast road he let
the Scania have its head while he kept one eye glued
to the clock and did time-and-distance arithmetic in his
head.

He rolled into the fishing town of Vólos at 1545, hoping that something, anything, had delayed the departure
of the ferry. But when he reached the port the berth
was empty. Not even a trace of smoke on the horizon
revealed the position of the *M.S. Falster.*

He parked the Scania on the quay and cursed aloud
in frustration.

Grabbing his attaché case and smoking a cigarette to calm himself, he took a taxi into the centre of the town to the offices of the Greece-Syria Express Line. A talk with one of the clerks confirmed his worst fears. Both the passages of the twelfth and fourteenth were fully booked. He could either be put on the standby list, taking a chance that somebody else would miss the ferry, or book for the sixteenth.

Leif sighed and asked if he could borrow the phone. He gave the number of Jerre's Stockholm office to the operator and asked for the charge to be reversed. Two minutes later she called back with the OK; Leif put his finger in his other ear to shut out the clatter of the telex machine in the corner.

"Lars Persson? Leif Wallman here. I'm in Vólos and I just missed the ferry."

"Leif Wallman? Oh yes, I remember. You're carrying that rush load to ABV in Riyadh. What happened?"

Leif explained briefly. Lars was silent for a moment or two, while Leif waited patiently. Standard procedure. The agent was responsible for transporting the goods; if anything went seriously wrong, the driver had to get in touch and inform him.

"Leif?"

"Still here."

"Look, Leif, I hate to say this, but that rush load of yours is important. ABV even considered flying it down. With every day costing them thousands, I just can't advise you to chance a free slot on a ferry. I want you to go by way of Turkey."

Leif almost choked and then started to argue. Lars was sympathetic but insistent. In the end Leif grudgingly agreed before slamming the handset down and cursing.

He checked his watch. Almost half past four, no use doing anything today. He lit another cigarette and made his way down to the street.

One of the favourite watering holes for drivers waiting for the ferry was the Joker Bar. Leif went there,
flopped down on one of the sofas at the far end of the
room and ordered a beer. Two heavily painted girls sitting at the bar eyed him speculatively, but made no
move.

The beer arrived, and he sipped it slowly, thoughtfully.

There were footsteps, and he turned his head. Somebody was coming down the spiral staircase from the
toilets upstairs, somebody impressively big. Leif observed the blue jeans and the heavy, tattoed forearms
sticking out from the rolled-up sleeves of a checkered
shirt, and the immense black beard. The man was huge,
so tall that his curly black hair almost touched the ceiling, and seemed as wide as the side of a semi-trailer.

"Preben!" Leif shouted, rising from the sofa.

"Leif Wallman! *Før fanden, hvad laver du her?* Hell,
what are you doing here?" Both of them grinned and
shook hands.

Preben Sørensen was a Danish ex-sailor who had taken
to navigating the roads. His appearance had earned him
the respectful name "the Pirate"; indeed, with a wooden
leg and a cutlass in his big hand the buccaneer image
would have been flawless.

"How come you're here and not aboard the *Falster*?"
Leif asked after they had ordered another round of beer.
The two girls at the bar turned their backs on them.

"Me? Been here for two days. Goddamn trailer bogie
broke down outside Larisa and I'm having it welded.
Hope to pick up my rig tomorrow morning."

While Preben dealt decisively with his beer, Leif told
him about his own bad luck. The Dane slowly scratched
his beard.

"Turkey, huh? Sounds like you'd need somebody riding shotgun for you."

"Or someone to convoy with."

"Hmm. Maybe. You know, I'm in the same predicament."

They discussed the matter for a while. Preben had a dual destination load, foodstuffs for Jeddah and Riyadh. Finally he said, "What the hell, I might as well join you. You need somebody to look after you, like I said." He winked.

* * *

Late in the evening, the Turkish Army officer whose code name was Alphonse received a phone call in his flat in a residential area on the western outskirts of Ankara.

"Excuse me, could I speak to your uncle Hakim please?" said a male voice which Alphonse recognized although he had never seen its owner.

"I'm sorry," he answered. "Uncle Hakim just went out. Can I take a message for him?" His KGB contact had given his identifying line and Alphonse had replied with the right phrase.

"We had a date to meet on the morning of the thirteenth in order to discuss the new carpets he is buying for the living room. Could you tell him I'll be there?"

"I will do that," Alphonse said. "Goodbye."

"Goodbye," the voice said and hung up.

* * *

The Pirate joined Leif at the docks early next morning in his red Scania 141. Leif climbed into his passenger seat, and Preben made coffee while Leif scratched the contentedly purring Nick, Preben's big tomcat, between the ears.

Then they walked over to the customs office to square the paperwork. Their passports and trip-tickets were valid for any route, but the *carnet*, the papers accompanying a load, needed new stamps and more paperwork when they were altering their route to go via Turkey. The officials were in a good mood and proceeded to put things in order with unusual haste. Leif and Preben in their turn radiated cheerfulness and handed out packs of cigarettes.

They had a quick breakfast and were on the coast road before noon, heading north. Their progress over the uneven asphalt was slow, and towards evening they stopped at Xanthi. They reached the border crossing at Kipi at noon the following day; it was a sleepy little place, and they were cleared and rolling towards Istanbul again in the afternoon.

They clicked off the 200 kilometres effortlessly, sticking fairly close to the 70 kph limit, and at sundown they rolled in the thickening traffic along the four-lane highway which cut through the western suburbs of Istanbul. In the dusk, with the array of service stations and billboards, they tended to look like the suburbs of any other big city, harsh and anonymous. About sixteen kilometres before the city centre they turned right into the camping park that had once been the number one stop of the journey: Londra.

They deposited their passports at the gate and were assigned slots in the lower half of the main yard, rolled down the narrow ramp and backed up alongside a yellow, Liechtenstein-registered DAF. They killed their engines, and the Pirate and Nick climbed into Leif's passenger seat. Together they sat in silence, looking out through the dusty windshield. The asphalted main yard was not even quarter full. Lights shone in some of the trucks, and here and there in the dusk small groups of drivers stood talking. The arc lights in the steel lattice masts threw hard shadows.

"Shit." Preben slowly shook his head. "Only guys on the Hell Run here now. Things ain't what they used to be. I can remember when the place was so packed that every time you came you had to back your rig into a slot tighter than a virgin's asshole."

Preben let Nick out, and then he and Leif took the back stairs to the main building and the reception. They checked the drivers' bulletin board, found nothing of interest, and went downstairs to the restaurant.

The restaurant had more customers than they had expected. They saw a few familiar faces, exchanged greetings, fetched food and settled down at a long table with a group of other Scandinavians. The conversation gravitated around the usual subjects. A Finnish driver on his way back from Teheran related horror stories from the Turkish-Iranian border, where a strike before Christmas among the customs officials had caused three-week delays and had trucks queuing up for twenty kilometres; an English driver had been killed by bandits in Eastern Turkey; the Syrians were repaving another section of road, which meant a new detour around the outskirts of Damascus. The asphalt vine was at work.

"Did you hear that, Leif?" Preben tapped him lightly on the shoulder.

"No, what?" Leif raised his beer bottle. Glasses were a luxury not provided in this establishment.

"West Berlin is open for business again. If you want a piece of pussy better grab it tonight before they raid the place again."

Leif made a grimace. "West Berlin" was a row of bars less than half a kilometre up the road. Inside the bars one found the usual assortment of bad beer, loud music, and professional ladies.

"Ah, the hell with it, I don't care. Too tired."

Preben argued but Leif shook his head, and a few minutes later managed to leave the company. He'd just get a bad conscience or a bad headache, or both.

The night air was cool. Passing the gate, he suddenly remembered his first trip, when he and Cannonball Jack had come back from West Berlin after a couple of hours

of drinking beer and about half a moment with a girl
in a dirty back room. No drawn-out romantic affair there,
no sir, you paid your four hundred liras and were allowed as much fucking as you could manage in five
minutes. He and Jack returned to their trucks, drunk
and unsteady, when their minds were sicklied over with
the pale hue of afterthought; they had got out a bottle
Leif had bought in the tax-free shop at Kapikule, and
with their pants down, holding on to the front tire for
support, they washed their cocks in VSOP Napoleon
Brandy. The approach to preventive hygiene had been
optimistic, the waste of good liquor shocking.

Leif was still smiling to himself when he reached his
Scania. Ignoring the armed guard shuffling past, he unlocked and climbed in,. and within two minutes was
wrapped up in his sleeping bag.

*   *   *

In the cold night air the faintest sounds carried clearly,
and he heard the car before he could see its headlights.
With unhurried movements he unslung the AKM
Kalashnikov and removed his thick outer gloves. The
quarter moon had long since set, but the starlight provided enough light for him to glimpse his wristwatch.
It was nearly the end of his watch. He felt cold.

The car was closer now. Its driver shifted down and
the engine growled as it negotiated the steep hill. A
diffuse spot of reflected light moved further down, and
then the dimmed headlights swung into view.

He adjusted his parka hood and slid into position behind the rocks. The sound of the car was familiar, but
they had not come this far by taking unnecessary risks.
He thumbed the safety catch back. Getting into firing
position, he raised the barrel of the Kalashnikov and
let it rest in a crack between two smaller rocks.

The car was close, slowly creeping forward in the fresh

snow before it stopped, twenty metres away. He shifted the barrel a fraction until it pointed at the spot where the driver's chest would be.

The headlights of the car went out, followed by a single flash from the left turn indicator. Then the door to the dark hut opened and a figure stepped out, also wearing a white parka and white trousers.

The engine was switched off; two men stepped out. He thumbed the safety catch forward again before he rose and brushed the snow from his clothes.

The man who had been driving spoke. "Is everything ready?"

"Everything is ready," answered the man who had come out of the hut.

* * *

Leif overslept and awoke a little before eight to a light drizzle. The taste of cigarettes and Turkish beer was sour in his mouth. He lifted a corner of the curtains to look out. A few of the trucks from last night were gone, and one or two had arrived in their stead. He scampered over to the other side, lifted another curtain corner. Preben's red Scania stood silent, its curtains drawn. He let the curtain fall back and unenthusiastically started to gather his clothes up.

Twenty minutes later he had sprinted back across the yard after his shower and had breakfast going inside the cab. A rather morose Preben showed up presently, accompanied by Nick. For once the Pirate was in no mood for conversation, so they finished their breakfast in silence. The yard was slowly emptying as vehicle after vehicle started up and lumbered away.

The Dane offered gruff thanks and returned to his own Scania. Leif cleaned up, then fired up the engine and lit the first cigarette of the day.

He heard Preben's truck roar into life; presently he

put his 141 in low and led the small convoy up the
ramp to the gate. They paid and got their passports back,
and almost exactly at nine o'clock the two trucks rolled
through the gate and were swallowed up by the dense
stream of traffic heading into Istanbul.

The four-lane highway cutting through the northern
parts of the city rose gradually. The giant twin steel
towers of the nearside bridge abutment appeared in the
rainy mist, and then they were rolling across the Bosporus Bridge. On a clear day the view would be stu-
pendous, with sunlight streaming over Usküdar and the
Golden Horn, and the lofty spires of the Haga Sofia mosque rising in the distance.

The entrance fee to the new continent was 400 lira,
and then they were rolling into Asia proper. Leif felt
the rhythm of the road flow into his hands and feet,
felt his awareness grow to merge with the vehicle around
him, transforming it into an extension of himself. He
glanced in his rear-view mirrors and saw Preben some
hundred metres back, keeping pace.

                    *   *   *

Early in the morning Alphonse went to a carpetseller's
stall in the bazaar and made a show of shopping, haggling over the price of some carpets that interested him.
He was invited inside and offered tea. The seller presently excused himself, and while he was away Alphonse
slid his hand under the frame of the table and removed
a flat metal container which was taped underneath.
Slipping the container into his inside pocket, he quickly
left the stall and walked from the bazaar.

Once outside, he took a taxi south and then a bus
west, getting off at a stop three blocks from his flat; he
walked the rest of the way, carefully surveying the cars
which were parked alongside the street. With contraband on his person, he had to be wary of the Turkish

internal security service. But everything was as it should be, and he entered his flat without being accosted.

Inside, he lowered all the blinds and then pried one of the tiles in the seedy kitchen loose, exposing a hollow behind, from which he took a small black book. He brought the book and the container over to the living-room table, opened the container and started to check its contents, a slip of paper, against the book. It took him the better part of an hour, and after that he sat for another ten minutes, just staring emptily ahead.

Then he burnt the slip of paper and his transcription of it and made a phone call, speaking briefly for a moment or two. He replaced the code book behind the tile and fixed it into position with a homemade mixture of glue and grit, which made the joint look untampered with, and went out to buy a newspaper which he brought back to the flat. This time he took another, very similar book from under a loose floorboard in the living room and set about recoding the decoded message which he had memorized. In the process he underlined, with a 3H pencil, a series of letters in an article on page three. The pencil left thin, hardly discernible marks. When he had finished he replaced the second code book.

At 10:47 he was sitting on a bench in Genclic Park in central Ankara, reading the newspaper he had bought. He didn't look up when a youngish, European-looking man strolled by, softly whistling "Colonel Bogey." When the young man stopped at a stand a little way off to buy a Mars bar, Alphonse folded the newspaper and deposited it in the wastepaper basket behind the bench. Then he rose and walked away.

The young man got his Mars bar and walked back the way he had come, not whistling any longer, and sat down on the bench where Alphonse had been sitting. Unhurriedly, he finished his chocolate bar and dropped the wrapper in the wastepaper basket, at the same time retrieving the discarded newspaper, which he put inside his light windbreaker before he left.

6

ART HOLSTON rose on one arm, suddenly unsure of his surroundings. Then awareness returned and his eyes focussed on the red, luminous digits of the clock-radio beside his bed: 4:49. He had slept less than two hours.

The telephone rang again. He swore silently, threw the bed covers aside and started for the desk. His bad left leg refused to support him, and he would have fallen had he not managed to grab the edge of the desk. He lifted the receiver in the middle of another ring.

"Hello?" His voice positively grated.

"Art?"

Dan Morris's calm, efficient voice. Holston pulled out the chair and sank into it.

"Yeah, it's me. What's the matter?"

"Something's come up, Art. You'd better get out here right away."

"And it's so serious it can't wait a couple of hours?"

Morris hesitated for a fraction of a second before he answered. "No. It's serious."

"OK, I'll be there. Forty-five minutes." He hung up without waiting for a reply.

He got up and hobbled around the desk to the window. From his twelfth-floor apartment the city of Washington looked dead, closed down for the night. The streetlights were reflected in the rain-wet asphalt.

He stood for a moment and shivered in his thin pyjamas before he turned to look again at the clock-radio:

4:54. He tested his left leg, found that its weak muscles would support him again, and hobbled off to the bathroom.

The ice-cold water made him feel more awake. He leaned forward and scrutinized himself in the mirror. The grey and slightly bloodshot eyes of James Arthur Holston, head of the Near East Division under the Directorate of Clandestine Services, Central Intelligence Agency, stared back at him. Thank God he was a light drinker: only those faint red lines in his eyes revealed that he had arrived home about two hours ago.

He returned to the bedroom and rummaged through the closet before shrugging and taking out a rumpled suit. He dressed quickly and had taken the elevator down to the garage within minutes.

In an uneasy mood he sped west through nearly deserted downtown Washington, ignoring the speed limit. He felt unwilling to face the news Morris had in store for him, and unconsciously eased his foot off the accelerator. Then he clamped his teeth together and his foot came down; the automatic transmission kicked down into second and the Ford LTD leapt forward.

Once he had wanted to become a language teacher. World War II had given him a career in intelligence instead, and the intelligence career had given him a busted leg and a busted marriage. Once, too, he had imagined that by working for the CIA he would do his share in keeping the Free World free. Thirty years with the agency had stripped him of all those delusions. Holston had adjusted, hardened himself, but never to the point of forgetting the reality of what he did.

The large, sprawling building that was the CIA headquarters appeared among the sparse trees. He slowed down, unbuckling his seat belt to grope for the plastic identity badge that would allow him inside the place. He rolled the window down as he let the car crawl forward into the pool of bright light in front of the gates and then braked to a halt. One of the armed guards came forward to take his badge. He bent slightly forward to peer into the car, then let his impassive eyes travel from Art Holston's face back to the plastic card. The night air was cold, and his breath came in puffs of white smoke. Holston felt bored. He knew that while the guard studied his badge another was checking the colour, make, and licence plate of his car against the approved list.

The guard was finally satisfied. He returned the badge, stepped back and offered a slow salute. Holston nodded and waited while the gate swung open, then gunned the engine and drove the car through. He nosed it into an empty slot near the main entrance; not his own designated spot—he couldn't care less even if he parked in the Director's slot.

At the main entrance he was subjected to another scrutiny before he was waved through. He stopped in the lobby to fasten the badge on his jacket; and looked up at the inscription on the marble wall: AND YE SHALL KNOW THE TRUTH, AND THE TRUTH SHALL MAKE YOU FREE. Twenty years ago, the biblical quotation never failed to impart some semblance of grandeur to the intelligence work. Now it seemed merely ironical and singularly ill chosen: it would have suited the walls of a public library better.

The system of elevators and corridors took him up three floors. The guard inside the glass cage recognized him and nodded, and pressed the button that allowed him through the big turnstile. He barely threw a glance at the framed red letters lining the edge of Holston's badge. A minor security breach. Holston nodded back and stepped through, hobbling down corridors to reach his own department. Morris's tall, gaunt frame appeared from one of the doorways. His black features showed relief. He was in shirt-sleeves and clutched a paper in his right hand.

"Morning, Art. Sorry to drag you out of bed like this, but it was absolutely necessary."

"That's all right, Dan. What's happening?"

"Tell you in a moment. Let's go into my office—I've had coffee and sandwiches sent up from the main lounge."

"Good." Morris's office smelled pleasantly of coffee, and Holston suddenly felt hungry. He sat down and accepted a cup from Morris, then leaned back and closed his eyes as he sipped the hot liquid. "All right, Dan, let's have it."

Morris put his cup down and picked up the paper. It was from one of the teletype decoding machines in the Communications Department. Automatically Holston reached inside his jacket and got out his glasses.

"This came through from Ankara station at 0440 tonight. It carries a max security, top priority coding." Morris half-rose and handed it over to Holston. "What it in essence says is this: Somebody, probably a Palestinian group, stole a nuclear warhead from the Russians during that Christmas manoeuvre of theirs, managed to get it across the border into Turkey, and hasn't been heard from since."

"Somebody did *what*?"

"Read it."

Holston sank back in his chair. He read. Finally he looked up at Morris. "A deliberate leak from the KGB?"

"That's what it says."

"Great . . . just great," he said slowly.

Holston read the text twice more. Finally he replaced the paper on the desk. "I just can't believe it. If that piece of info is on the level, Dan, I'd hate to think about what might happen."

"It seems the KGB have taken great pains to assure us they're not spreading disinformation for once. On the other hand—"

"—we can't trust those bastards as a matter of principle," Holston finished. "Why the leak? I don't see how they'd actually admit somebody managed to hijack one of their nukes."

"I might have an answer to that. The Russians are scared shitless that they'll be blamed for what happens with that device. It's a fair guess that the leak carries approval all the way from the top—it's their way of keeping their back clear and telling us they're not responsible."

"Yes," Holston said, "and that's exactly what leaves me with this suspicion that it could have been staged by the KGB. They hand a nuke over to some friends and then arrange to be able to shrug off any responsibility."

Morris looked doubtful. "I think you're being overly suspicious, Art. If this is disinformation it's an all-out effort. The KGB have been up to some pretty hectic activity in the Middle East for the past two weeks; it's been in the reports on your desk, remember?"

Holston stared. "I'm sorry Dan," he said then in a tired voice. "It had completely slipped my mind."

Morris shrugged. "They've been combing the whole of the Middle East without finding what they're looking for, and now they're turning to us for help."

"Help?" Holston said. "If we sniff up any leads they're going to do their damndest to get in on the action ahead of us. And they're not going to thank us either. Is there any more coffee? Dammit, I've got to wake up some time." He held his cup out.

Morris poured Holston more coffee and said, "Odds are they're telling the truth for once."

Holston took a good swig and shrugged. "I'll want my own confirmation. Get back to Ankara and check out if this really is what it's purported to be."

"I already did," Morris replied quietly.

"What?"

"I've already relayed a message back to Ankara station, requesting exactly that information. It was the logical thing to do."

"Indeed." Holston regarded his subordinate with approval. Dan Morris was a major in the United States Marine Corps, "on loan" for serving a tour of duty with the CIA. "Well, good. Then we need hardcore info from our own organizations. The Russians have given us a good fix on the time and the place—I want the corresponding satellite photos, and I want them fast. Call up the boys at the DST, outline the situation, and have them get on the backs of the NRO. Crash priority. Then there must be records of all the radio traffic during that manoeuvre. Get on to the NSA; I want a complete report, with all relevant transcripts, translated wherever possible, within twenty-four hours. That's also crash priority whether they like it or not."

"That may take some doing," Morris remarked.

"Lean on them if you have to. I mean to have it. Turner will have to sort it out afterwards if necessary. Then we have the Soviet Bloc Division; I'll have to call up van Henck and set his department on the trail—they might know something."

"They ought to be very interested in getting their hands on that Red Army defector, or whatever he is," Morris said.

"They can have him and be welcome to it, just as long as I get the nuke," Holston said irritably and scratched the stubble on his chin.

Morris shrugged. "We'd need some information on that warhead. What it can and can't do. We'd . . ."

Holston interrupted him. "Dan—that fat professor-type who sat in on the panels on terrorism last year—what was his name? Silvermann?"

"Silverstein."

"Right, that's the one we want. Get him here on the double. Throw your weight around if you have to, but get him here. I seem to remember he gave a very thorough lecture on nuclear terrorism—I read extracts from his paper. I want him to give us a rush lesson and then draw up a brief preliminary report we can submit to the IRAC and the USIB."

"Shouldn't be any problem, he lives in Langley."

"Good. Get him and brief him on the situation, then bring him into my office. You'd better get going on that phone. I have to locate Turner and then organize a few reports to set things in motion. Keep me posted."

Holston picked up his coat and rose, and for the first time that morning he smiled a bleak smile.

"Hell of a way to start a weekend, Dan."

*   *   *

The minute hand of Holston's office clock jumped another notch: 0650. He sat at his own desk, sweating over the drafts of several reports, cursing the bureaucratic ways of the intelligence profession.

He had managed to reach Stansfield Turner, the Director of the CIA, in New York; he would be on his way with the first morning flight. Van Henck had gone with his family for a weekend of skiing in Colorado. Holston had put out a max priority tracing order via Communications. Morris had called him twice, first to inform him that the satellite photos and the radio traffic transcripts had been promised within twenty-four hours, and later to say that Silverstein had arrived and would be up shortly.

Meanwhile, those damned reports, raw and unfinished, were staring at him from his desk.

Holston glumly stared back. A spy's life held neither glamour, nor romance, just drab existence, either as a mousy, schizophrenic being in the field, or as a nine-to-five desk jockey or file carrier trying to keep up with a stream of memos, dispatches, and reports.

He looked at his notepad. He had written down the

known facts, provided that they *were* facts; they were
an all-too-meagre collection. Underneath he had added
a few remarks and observations.

Far back in his mind something stirred. He was dimly
conscious of missing out on something. He tried to rearrange the data to find some hidden pattern, but had
to give up. He picked up the drafts again.

The report to the President—that took priority. He
had already called the President's personal security adviser and given him a short briefing. With luck, he could
have a first report in time for the President's *Daily Brief*,
the special publication prepared by the Intelligence Directorate and put on the President's table at 0800 every
morning.

That took care of the nation's first consumer of intelligence, but he still had a long list to run through;
a longer and more detailed report for the eyes only of
the Secretary of State, and another to be distributed to
the members of the United States Intelligence Board.
The USIB met every Thursday morning in a conference
room on the seventh floor of the CIA headquarters;
Stansfield Turner would be sure to call an emergency
meeting within hours of his arrival. Then there was the
report for the Forty Committee. And the . . .

A knock on the door interrupted him. "Come in!"
he shouted. The door opened and Morris entered with
Silverstein in his wake. Holston rose and limped out
from behind the desk with his hand outstretched in
greeting.

Silverstein was in his early forties, tall but fat, the
kind that results from letting a well-muscled body fall
into disuse. In spite of the early hour, he was well dressed
in a blue suit and looked remarkably alert. He introduced himself in a pleasant, fruity baritone.

Holston motioned to a chair. "Sorry to have to order
you out here in this way, ah . . . Professor?"

"Doctor, actually—but do we need the formalities?"

Holston shook his head and Silverstein went on: "As for the early hour, it's quite all right. Your assistant here has briefed me on the gravity of the situation."

"Good. Care for some coffee?"

"I'd rather have tea if it can be arranged."

"It can." Holston spoke briefly into the intercom. "You know what we're facing, so I can get right down to brass tacks. You're an expert on nuclear terrorism. We want to know"—he raised his hand and ticked off the items—"first, what exactly those people have got; second, what it can do; and third, your opinion on how it might be used."

Silverstein nodded and opened his briefcase. "Mind if I smoke?"

Holston caught a sideways glance from Morris. "Go right ahead." Holston shrugged and brought out his emergency ashtray from a drawer in his desk.

"Thank you." Silverstein beamed and fished out a worn pipe and an old-fashioned leather tobacco pouch; unhurriedly, he proceeded to fill his pipe and light it. Finally he leaned back in his chair, crossed his thick legs, and spoke from behind a bluish cloud.

"The first two, no problem. The answers consist of more or less solid facts. As for the third, you will appreciate that all I can give you will be conjecture based on various probabilities and a very limited number of known facts."

"I'm aware of that," Holston said drily.

"Well, then. The Russians haven't specified what sort of warhead they've lost, so we'll have to make an assumption or two. I'm sorry Soviet armoury isn't a specialty of mine; I had to dig into our archives to get hold of these."

He reached into his briefcase and brought out two thin sheaves of photocopies, stapled together and covered with a sheet bearing the CIA seal, a rundown of contents, filing authority, and access security clearance.

He handed one each to Holston and Morris. Holston raised an eyebrow as he saw the security code. He had no idea Silverstein would have such a high clearance. He saw Morris hesitate and shot him an impatient glance to tell him to forget that his own clearance wasn't sufficient for this material, then started to leaf through it. It consisted of drawings of various shapes, mostly cylindrical, with measurements stencilled in and a short list of data at the bottom of each sheet.

"Since it was taken in a hijacking operation during a land manoeuvre," Silverstein went on, "we can assume that the warhead comes from one of their army vehicles, either from a rocket launcher or from shell-firing artillery. If you wish I can get pictures and information on those."

Holston thought of the satellite photos he had requested. "Yes, we might find them useful."

"I'll see to it. It won't make a lot of difference, though. We must remember that a hijacking party who intends to take their prize on a very hazardous border crossing, as I understand was the case, wouldn't want to burden themselves with something too bulky or too heavy. Consequently we can narrow the choice down to a few possibilities."

He paused to draw smoke from his pipe. "So the actual object would be roughly cylindrical in shape; in size anything from 15 by 10 inches to 25 by 20, with the weight in the 100- to 300-pound range. No more than can be transported with reasonable ease."

Holston jotted down a note to check the weather reports on the hijacking days, then picked up the thread. "That's not a lot. I seem to remember that the Hiroshima bomb weighed several tons."

"The new generation nuclear warheads compare *very* favourably with their ancestors," Silverstein answered. "Nuclear weapons technology has come a long way in four decades. Apart from being a very crude construction by today's engineering standards, the thing we dropped on Hiroshima carried a heavy streamlined outer shell, plus other gear these warheads don't lug around— an altitude sensing system, firing systems, and backups for—"

Holston interrupted him. "Hold on. You say these warheads are not equipped with any firing systems?"

"That's correct."

"Then whoever has it can't set it off?"

"I did not imply that. I merely stated that the warheads themselves are not equipped with such systems. In actual use, the warhead is connected with an outside firing system set for impact detonation or detonation at a certain height in the case of a shell. In a missile the warhead is hooked up to the on-board nagivation-and-target-seeking computer, which can be programmed to trigger the warhead when a preset number of conditions are fulfilled: height, geographical location, impact."

"But if you only had the warhead, how would you set it off?"

"Anyone with a sound knowledge of physics could do it, if he was willing to accept the risks of 'wrong' constructions and accidents. You would merely have to build a device which on a given command would send the right signal into the warhead. 'Command' in this sense could be liberally interpreted: a radio signal or an old-fashioned timing mechanism. Or even a push-button, if you're the suicidal type."

"You make it sound so easy." Morris's voice was devoid of emotion.

"It is. But we're a bit uncertain about Russian construction principles. It could be that it takes a special signal to arm the warhead, or it could be self-destructing if violently tampered with, say the HE charge would scatter the fissionable material, or some such detail."

"I'm afraid my physics is a bit rusty," Holston said. "How exactly does this warhead work?"

Silverstein struck a match and calmly went through the ritual of rekindling the light in his pipe before he answered.

"In principle, it's a fairly simple construction; in practice, it's considerably more complicated.

"In order to achieve an atomic explosion you need two things: enough fissionable material and enough free neutrons to initiate and sustain the chain reaction. If you collect enough fissionable material in one place, the relatively few free neutrons present will be enough to set it off; that is what we call critical mass. Below critical mass the material loses escaping neutrons faster than new ones are produced. No explosion." He paused briefly to suck at his pipe.

"So naturally you would have to keep the critical mass separated in two or more parts and only bring it together when you want the explosion to take part. For an efficient, working nuclear bomb you have to shoot the parts together with high explosives, going from under-critical to over-critical within milliseconds. You also have to take geometrical considerations into account; it's best to have the fissionable material in a spherical shape, partly because it has the most efficient volume-to-surface ratio. Finally, you can get by with less fissionable mass if you, simply put, add more neutrons. This is done with what we call a 'tamper.'

"To relate all this to the Russian warhead, it might be described as a container of roughly cylindrical shape with a hemisphere of plutonium backed by high explosives at each end. The plutonium will be weapons grade, that is plutonium 239, about 90 to 95 percent pure and in a suitably crystalline state—about twenty to fifty pounds of the stuff altogether. In the middle of the cylinder, right at the point where the plutonium halves come together, is a tamper. When the warhead is triggered, the HE smack the plutonium together, the tamper saturates it with neutrons, and a chain reaction commences.

"This is of course a generalized description in the absence of specific data. Several design refinements are possible." Silverstein took the pipe from his mouth and eyed Holston with an expression not unlike that of an owl while he blew a stream of smoke roofwards.

The silence which followed was broken by a knock on the door. Morris quickly went to open it and took a laden tray out of the hands of a sullen-faced young man, then closed the door with his foot and placed the tray on the desk. There was a steaming pot of tea for Silverstein, coffee for Holston and Morris.

Morris served them, then sat down again and sipped at his coffee, leafing through the photostats while the fingers of his left hand slowly drummed a complex rhythm against the armrest.

"All right," Holston said. "How much destruction can it accomplish?"

"That, as usual, depends. It can for example, knock down any building or structure. It would in fact nearly vaporize it. But contrary to what most people think, it can't raze an entire city to the ground; that requires something further up the kiloton scale. The Hiroshima bomb actually destroyed less of the city itself than people imagine. The death toll of close to two hundred thousand was mostly due to burns and radiation and its after-effects."

Two hundred thousand, Holston repeated silently to himself.

"I can supply a few figures." Silverstein's voice was dry, without any hint of emotion. "Assuming a nuclear device of Hiroshima capacity, it will level the houses for a distance of well over half a mile from zero point— the centre of the explosion—in the blast itself. The shockwave and the firestorms that follow will reach considerably further. The radiation is more or less in-

stantly lethal for about three-quarters of a mile and will
cause severe bodily damage for much greater distances.
Afterwards you'd have to evacuate about 1500 square
miles." He smiled minutely. "All these figures are of
course heavily dependent on detonation height, as well
as weather conditions and local geography."

There was a pause, and then Holston said, tonelessly,
"They have to be stopped."

"Perhaps you won't have to," Silverstein said.

Holston looked at him, frowning. "Why not?"

"Because they may not intend to detonate it." Silverstein paused to sip his tea for a moment. "You two
gentlemen may have overlooked a few important facts.

"First of all, why detonate a nuclear bomb? What
would it accomplish apart from indiscriminate mass
destruction? If you look at the records you will find
that terrorist actions intending to kill a large number
of people or inflict great damages are quite rare. The
Lod incident was actually something of an exception.
What terrorists want is usually lots of publicity, a way
of plugging their cause or putting pressure on a government in order, for example, to secure the release of
political prisoners. Mostly they want both. It does not
take a great deal of imagination to see that with this
warhead they are assured of getting it.

"But if they went ahead and used their bomb, it would
be like playing their trump card right at the beginning
of the game. I consider it unlikely that the hijackers
would actually go as far as to do that. It's not impossible—I can think of situations where the bomb might
be used with specific goals in mind—but as I said, it is
unlikely.

"Now, using it for blackmail is quite another matter.
The publicity would be beyond their wildest expectations: the news would make the headlines of every
newspaper, you'd have TV specials, the works. This, then,

must be considered the most probable alternative." Silverstein drew a long puff on his pipe.

"What's to prevent the terrorists from posing more demands once their first demands have been satisfied?" Morris asked.

"To put it bluntly—nothing." Silverstein shrugged. "The crux is that sooner or later the warhead *must* be recovered. Meanwhile, the good news is that they probably aren't prepared to detonate it for a while."

"Hell of a consolation," Morris muttered.

Holston leaned across the desk. "But the possibility remains that sooner or later they might use it?"

"Yes."

"So where do we look for it?"

Silverstein twitched his nose. "Frankly, it could be anywhere in the world. The hijackers have had at least two weeks, time enough to get it where they want it. A complicating factor is that it could have been done by one organization for the benefit of another. However, I consider it an unlikely, but again not entirely impossible, alternative.

"The point is that a modern, tactical warhead is a small enough object to be transported with reasonable ease—even across borders—in the trunk of a car, maybe disguised as something similar in shape and size, just as an example. But if you want my opinion, the thing is still somewhere in the general area where it was taken."

"The Middle East," Holston said heavily. "Yes, you're probably right. Hell of a place to have a rogue nuke."

"The Russians suspect a Palestinian group, don't they?" Silverstein looked at Morris.

"Yes, but they did not say why."

"They don't have to," Silverstein remarked. "A lot speaks for Palestinians. Plus, of course, that they hold the biggest grudge of anybody in the business."

"Israel." Holston made a statement, not a question.

"Yes."

"If," Holston insisted, "we're not dealing with Palestinians; if Israel isn't the target, what is?"

Silverstein threw up his hands in exasperation, and for the first time there was a hint of irritation in his voice. "Look, if you want targets for terrorism, just look around. You have wars, revolutions, political tension, and groups, factions, fanatics everywhere, even right here in the United States. If you want to get anywhere you'll have to concentrate on the most likely alternatives. These hijackers have kept out of sight for over two weeks; that doesn't mean they won't make their demands public today."

Holston almost had it then. He could feel it stir just below his conscious threshold, and opened his mouth to speak; and inside him it turned back and disappeared into the depths.

"I just want to know what other alternatives there are," he said finally, doggedly.

"Well," Silverstein said, "the idea of nuclear terrorism isn't a bolt out of the blue. The Directorate of Intelligence has been running conflict simulations on this theme for years, so we have some pretty good ideas about where and how it's likely to take place.

"Offhand, however, I can't recall any scenario assuming a nuke hijacked from the Russians. The odds against it were considered rather astronomical, I think."

"Jackpot," Morris murmured.

"I can't see that it matters that much," Holston remarked. "Are there any alternatives to terrorists?"

"Not really. Some nation? What's one single device to a nation? It wouldn't win any wars. One alternative would be a purely criminal organization. But criminal organizations are more interested in adapting themselves to work more or less within the social structure, they have no wish to disrupt it."

"Any other alternatives?" Holston asked.

"Yes," Silverstein said thoughtfully. "It is conceivable

that they could dismantle the warhead in order to hawk the plutonium on the black market. Black market plutonium would be even more profitable than heroin.''

Holston raised his eyebrows. Morris frowned, scratching his chin. Silverstein had taken his pipe out of his mouth, and both hands were resting on his knees.

''Two years ago the RAND Corporation in Santa Monica provided the government with a classified study on the security risks in the nuclear trade. The report showed that nearly one percent of the annual nuclear reactor fuel turnover in this country is unaccounted for—enough for several hundred bombs.''

''Interesting,'' Holston said. ''But it doesn't help us any.''

''Well, no. I digressed. But I meant to emphasize the fact that outright nuclear terrorism has long been considered only a matter of time.''

Holston was silent, toying with his coffee mug. ''Israel, then,'' he finally said.

Silverstein nodded. ''With a wide margin. I hesitate a little about number two. It might be Lebanon, but it might also be Egypt. Perhaps Iran or one of the smaller Gulf states. I'll have to get my department going on it if you want good, up-to-date, well worked out answers. You'll find most of the answers are going to place it somewhere in the Middle East.''

Holston nodded glumly and realized that the lecture had come to an end. He glanced at the clock on the wall: about thirty minutes had passed since Silverstein had entered the room.

''Thank you very much for the briefing,'' he began. ''In view of the short notice, it was excellent.'' Silverstein made a slight gesture with his hand in reply. ''Now, I need a few preliminary reports from you to add to my own. First of all, one for the President. Just sum up the facts you've given me, and keep it short. After that, a few others with more data in them—I'll send down a list within the hour."

He rose unsteadily. His leg ached again, and he had to support himself as he reached out to shake hands.

"My pleasure," Silverstein said and began to collect his pipe and papers. "I'll do my best. You'll probably have an extensive report by tonight, once I get most of my colleagues in the department here. Just one thing."

"Yes?"

"When you find them, Mr. Holston, give them hell."

Holston stared, then he understood and smiled a minute smile.

"We will, doctor, we will."

Silverstein closed his briefcase, then Morris escorted him to the door and shook hands with him. Holston sat down again and regarded Morris.

"Well?" Holston said at last.

"He seems to know what he's talking about. I wonder how good his predictions are?"

"They'd better be good. We'll have to go by them."

"Yeah. Are you going to initiate any action right now, or are you going to wait for the Admiral?"

Holston glanced at his notepad. "There are some things I have to get around to immediately, apart from those damned reports. Our Israeli friends have to get the word right away. Contact our Tel Aviv station and give them a rundown of the bad news; ask them to set up a special meeting with the Mossad. We'll send a man out as soon as we can. The usual facilities, and empowered. You'll handle it?"

Morris nodded.

"Next: we have to inform all our other stations in the Middle East. Get them to shake up their nets of agents, see if they can come up with any scrap of info, anything. That goes especially for Turkey." He looked up at Morris. "Got it?"

"Yes."

Holston leaned back and thoughtfully tapped his pen against the desk.

"Art," Morris said, "what do we do when we find the warhead?"

"What?"

"I said, what do we do when we find it?"

Holston stopped tapping his pen and straightened up in his chair.

"They sure aren't going to surrender just like that," Morris pressed on. "We'll probably have to hit them with an assault force of at least platoon strength."

Holston frowned. "The Israelis will be able to take care of that. They can equal the best force we can field. Besides, they'd never allow us to station a military assault force there. Or were you thinking of our Delta Team?"

Morris shook his head. "Any movements there would be as conspicuous as a brass band. No, this has to be done in the dark. And I was considering the possibility that the warhead hasn't gone to Israel. Once we get wind of where that damned device is, *somebody* will have to go in and take it away from them."

"So what do you suggest?" Holston sounded faintly disapproving.

"A task force stationed at one of our air bases in Turkey. That way we'll be close to the beginning of the trail and can regroup them later at very short notice, should it turn out to be necessary. We'd need a backup force too, also within striking distance of most of the Middle East. Both groups to be thoroughly briefed on the situation, at full combat alert and ready to be airlifted or parachuted." He paused. "Art, we need troops that can go in there and *fight*."

Holston took off his glasses and slowly twisted them around. "You realize the kind of political stink that could raise?"

"I'd rather face that than having to fly over a dozen

C-5s with field hospitals and radiation sanitization crews—afterwards."

"That would have to be a job for the 'animals,' " Holston said slowly.

For "special ops," which were by definition crude, violent, brutal—and highly illegal—the CIA had its own armed forces, the Special Operations Division, also known as the "agency's animals": a strange mixture of adventurers, ex-military men, mercenaries, and military "advisers."

Although he admitted the necessity of its existence, Holston wasn't happy about the SOD. He turned Morris's proposal over in his mind. He disliked it; but as Morris so succinctly had put it, somebody had to do the job.

"All right," he said finally, "I'll put it before Turner. If he goes along with it, I'll want the best men, even if they have to pull them off other assignments. We can't afford any slip-ups. Also, it wouldn't surprise me if the KGB has thought of the same idea."

"We'll have to live with that."

"Not much choice," Holston admitted. "Oh yes, we'll tell the Turks to smarten up their check at the border stations, in case the thing hasn't left Turkey yet. Anything else?"

"Nothing that I can think of right now."

"OK. Then it's noses back to the grindstone. See that you handle the Israeli side before anything else. And keep me posted."

Holston removed his glasses again, closed his eyes and rubbed them. God, he was tired. He put his glasses back on and looked out through the window. Dawn was breaking, a grey, dreary dawn that promised neither joy nor rest.

*   *   *

The outskirts of Istanbul fell behind Leif and Preben,

disappeared in the rain and the rooster tails from the trailer wheels. The four-lane highway came to an end, changing into an ordinary road among grey-green, sparsely clad hills.

The traffic thinned out a little, but twice they had to grind to a halt where fresh accidents blocked the road; Leif gave the second crash a long look as he crept past: a medium-sized truck had carved into the rear of an old bus; the seats in the back of the bus and the front end of the truck were crumpled beyond recognition. A large group of people stood by the roadside, huddling close together against the rain. Several shapeless things lay on the ground covered with blankets.

Leif shivered as he accelerated away, a thin needle of icy fear touching his back. His cheerful mood from earlier in the morning was gone.

Thirty kilometres before Bolu the rain ceased and the terrain grew wilder. The hills were covered with snow. The road rose in a steep, winding stretch, slippery with mud and diesel, and the Scania strained and slid as it crawled upwards with heavily labouring engine. Halfway up Leif and Preben passed two French TIR trucks who had given up and stopped to put on snow chains.

They stopped at the restaurant near the top of the hill for some food. It was dark when they came back outside, and a light snowfall had begun. The water level warning light in Leif's 141 had shone with a steady glow for the last hundred kilometres, and he took the opportunity to top up the radiator. The leak seemed to be a small but constant one.

The snowfall increased. There was very little traffic, and the pines pressed in close to the road. Several times Leif felt the Scania slide out a little in the turns; conditions were rapidly deteriorating. With a hundred and fifty kilometres to go to Ankara, Leif signalled and they swung into a parking place for a quick conference. Stay where they were for the night or press on? In the end they decided to continue.

The top of the infamous "Four-Mile Hill" was approaching. Leif was apprehensive as he put the truck in a low gear and started the long downhill roll, taking care not to let his vehicle gather speed. The hill was deceptive, a long stretch of road that grew gradually steeper as it wound down. Three years ago, it had claimed the life of an Englishman whose brakes had failed near the top of the hill; he had burst his gearbox in a frantic attempt to slow the juggernaut down as it had relentlessly slewed down the hill. The Englishman had been good; he had made it almost all the way down when the truck finally went off the road and forty tons mowed down trees and rocks as it tumbled over and over until it smashed into the side of the ravine below. The wreck had lain there for a year and a half.

After the hill they passed another bus wreck in the darkness, blue rotating police lights throwing eerie shadows among the debris. Shortly before ten the snow ceased and they could see the lights of Ankara in the distance. Less than half an hour later they rolled into the TIR park on the outskirts of the city, just in time to park and make it into the restaurant before it closed for the night. Warm food worked wonders with their well-being, and they joked light-heartedly about the day's incidents, but Leif felt his hands tremble from fatigue, and Preben's blue eyes had a curious lacklustre quality.

Soon they had returned to their cabs, undressed, and fallen into heavy sleep.

*   *   *

Darkness had long since fallen outside his office windows, and Holston sat massaging his hurting left leg, waiting for the painkiller to dissolve in the glass of water on his desk.

Saturday had been much as he had expected: a jumble of meetings, report writing, and telephone calls. Turner had stormed into the CIA headquarters a little after nine and taken charge as if he had been on the bridge of a battleship. He had received a thorough briefing and immediately called an emergency meeting of the USIB. Holston had, much to his surprise, been put in charge of following up the affair, while another agent temporarily filled in for him in his normal duties. He had picked Morris as his second-in-command.

Morris's proposal about two special strike forces had been passed with a minimum of discussion; obviously the USIB, too, felt the need for the capacity of swift, decisive measures. A special agent had been flown out to Israel, and later in the afternoon yet another. Every CIA station in the Middle East had been put on red alert status, and a number of Western intelligence services had been notified. And so on. Slowly, the CIA was gearing itself to the task at hand.

Towards early evening, van Henck had turned up, and a little later the satellite photos and the radio transcripts arrived. Now Holston sat with them spread out over his desk.

The radio transcripts in themselves had been inconclusive. The bulk of them was in undeciphered code, accompanied by a note from the NSA which in essence explained that cryptology was a highly refined business and that most of the high-order cipher systems were, if not in theory, then at least in practice, unbreakable. However, the length of the messages and the intensity of the traffic might provide clues; and in this case they did. Radio traffic had suddenly peaked around 1055 hours local time, then fallen off sharply after about half an hour, and later risen to its regular level. Obviously something out of the ordinary had happened. Holston swore silently. Why hadn't he been notified? All right, he knew the answer: Soviet Bloc intelligence was not his department. Chalk up another one to compartmentalization.

But some of the radio traffic was in clear, or had been deciphered: requests for a helicopter and a radiak sanitation crew, some other odds and ends, no more than could be passed off in the context of a military manoeuvre. But with what he knew, it screamed at him.

The satellite photos were a different matter. They were accompanied by a thin, blond man with a sad face, a drooping moustache and an incredibly high security clearance, who provided the necessary interpretation for one who was not accustomed to picking out the telltale details.

One of the US Big Bird spy satellites had passed over the area at 1038 local time. The photos taken in visible light showed only swirling masses of clouds, but when Sad-face pulled out those taken with infrared sensitive detectors, and Holston muttered "Bingo!" They clearly marked out an immense heat source on the ground. Although the outlines were vague there was no doubt as to what it was, the thin man said: a very large vehicle, gutted by fire. Holston asked whether the type of vehicle could be positively identified, and got the answer that they probably could narrow it down to just a few alternatives, basing it on estimates of its dimensions.

The photos from the following day, the twenty-seventh, were perfect: it had been a completely clear, cloudless winter's day, and the resolution was everything anyone could wish for. Sad-face spread out several photos before Holston, explaining and pointing out details with long, bony fingers. Most of the vehicle and the debris had apparently been carted away before the cloud cover had broken up at dawn. A wide, shallow crater in the middle of a clearing among the trees was clearly identifiable, along with trees that had toppled from the blast. Several people were moving about in the area, guarding it or sorting through the remaining debris. Holston marvelled at the clarity of the blowups; he could actually distinguish between those who were dressed in uniform and the others. In the end he wrote down a number of questions and handed them to the thin man, who promised more data.

Holston watched the last bubbles rise to the surface in the glass. He drained it in two long gulps, then forced his body to relax while he waited for the painkiller to take effect. With a little luck he might be able to grab a few hours of sleep later tonight. His eyes felt puffy, and his stubble had grown considerably.

There was a knock on the door, and Morris entered without waiting for a reply. He put a sheaf of new papers on Holston's desk but remained standing. When he spoke his voice sounded tired and coarse.

"Thought you'd like to know—Special Ops are flying out two assault forces sometime tomorrow night. The main force will be stationed at our air base outside Adana in Turkey, and will arrive around noon local time on Monday." Holston nodded.

"The second group," Morris went on, "will be stationed aboard our aircraft carrier *Midway* in the Arabian Sea. You'll find all the details in there." He indicated the papers. "Each group contains at least two who speak fluent Arabic. They will be equipped with a full detachment of weapons, and backed by airborne transport and 'copters."

Holston nodded again. "Good. What about our Tel Aviv connections?"

"Still only the preliminary reports. You've already got them."

"Anything from our other stations?"

"Nothing. All blanks so far."

"Well, let's hope that's good news."

Morris shrugged. "We sure could use a break. Don't forget that the Russians have had well over two weeks to look all over the place, and they've got nowhere. It's literally as if the warhead and those hijackers have vanished off the face of the earth—without leaving one single damned clue.''

Again something stirred inside Holston. He watched Morris leave and then looked down at the collection of photos and papers on his desk, dimly aware that somewhere in the confusion was the lead he was looking for.

7

THE ARAB in the dusty white dress was sweating profusely. The day was quite cool, even in the lowlands of the Jordan valley, but the Arab was sweating from an inner terror which radiated from him and seemed to bounce from the whitewashed walls.

David Bar-Sharon felt like a frozen meatball in a microwave oven, feeling heat where there was no heat. He shifted on his wooden chair to unstick his damp shirt from his back. He glanced at the Israeli *Zahal* major and saw that his khaki shirt, too, had dark stains under the arms and in patches across the stomach. The corporal and the private standing impassively to one side were similarly stained. Everybody was sweating.

The Arab had been caught trying to pass across the Allenby Bridge from Jordan into the Israeli-occupied West Bank without the proper documents on the morning of Sunday, January 14. David Bar-Sharon had been sent from the Shin Beth—the Israeli internal security service—to assist in the interrogation. The interrogation had turned out to be a singularly pointless way of starting a new week.

The man was in his forties, thin, with a slightly bent back. His story that he wanted to visit relatives in Aquabat, a small village south of Jericho, had a plausible ring to it. He claimed to have lived there before 1967 and seemed to know the area well enough. And he had tried openly to cross the bridge with incomplete documents. No, he was merely a simpleton. David rose and shrugged.

"I don't think we'll have anything to say about this man," he said in Hebrew. The Arab, who was by no means fluent in the language, still got the gist of what David was saying; he smiled a little timidly, with shining eyes. "There are the irregularities in his papers, but . . . I suppose you'll just have to put him back on the bridge and point to the other side, eh?"

The major rose from his chair behind the battered wooden desk, collected his papers and nodded. "I wanted to do that right away, but regulations . . . you know."

"I know. Well, Shmuel, I'd better be getting back to Tel Aviv, now that we've sorted this thing out." David used the first name, as was customary in Israel, regardless of rank.

"Care for a *gazoz* before you go, David?" The major looked younger than he actually was, neat, clean-shaven, trim. Shmuel was a nice enough fellow, but the last thing David wanted at the moment was a *gazoz* with a neat, clean-shaven, trim military man. It would be the crowning pointlessness of an altogether pointless day.

"Thanks, Shmuel, but I'm afraid I don't have the time. The next time maybe."

They shook hands, and David quickly stepped outside, while the corporal motioned the Arab to his feet.

David lit a cigarette and got into his car, a light-brown Ford Escort from the Shin Beth car pool. He leaned back and regarded the scene. To his left ran the verdant gash of the river Jordan through the arid lowlands. Traffic across the Allenby Bridge was light: a few lorries in either direction, carrying vegetables and building materials. There were almost no pedestrians. All traffic was carefully checked by Israeli troops. A tour bus which had just been cleared across was discharging its load of American tourists, who went for a photograph of the river or in search of soft drinks armed with traveller's checks and dollar bills. The nearby stands did a good business.

On the other side of the river, some ten kilometres away, the Jordanian highland rose in the haze in various shades of brown and ochre with occasional green patches. David turned the ignition key, put the car in gear, and swung out onto the main road towards Jerusalem.

Outside the gates of the military camp down the road, an Israeli private stood waving to show he wanted a ride. David pulled over and opened the door for him; it was bad form not to pick up a tramping soldier.

The soldier poked his head inside the door and asked, "Going past Rehovot?"

"Almost. Tel Aviv. Jump in."

"*Yohfee.* Thanks." He settled into the passenger seat, and David put the car in gear.

"Well," David said, "you're lucky you won't have to stand around freezing somewhere on the highland. There was frost in Jerusalem this morning. You on leave?"

"Yeah, it's my kid brother's Bar Mitzvah tonight. I'm off till noon tomorrow. Mind you, I had to be on duty during the Sabbath to get away."

David smiled. "I see." He regarded the soldier sideways. A young lad, hardly past twenty. Mediterranean good looks. Most likely a *sabra*. David, himself a first-generation *sabra*, suspected that the family of the young soldier had lived in Palestine for generations. "So how long have you been in the *Zahal*?"

"Two years and three months. Nine months to go."

"So? In my time you would have been through by now."

"When was that?"

"Sixty-five to sixty-seven."

"You fought in the Six-Day War, then?"

"Yes. The Golani Brigade."

The soldier whistled. The Golani Brigade was the

prestigious crack unit of the *Zahal*, the Israeli Defence Forces.

"How was it?" he asked eagerly.

David looked at him. "Brief, I'm glad to say." He didn't mention the Syrian bullet that had gone clean through him and penetrated his right lung on the fourth day and put him out of commission for the rest of the war and for two months after that.

The young soldier began to prattle. "Brief but glorious. Look at what it gave us." He indicated the landscape with an inclusive triumphant gesture. "Sinai, the Gaza strip, the West Bank, the Golan. The territories."

"Gave us?" David said. "We took them."

"Of course we took them. And about time it was, too. They belong to us, don't they?"

David groaned inwardly. Aloud, he said, "We've already given the last of the Sinai back to Egypt."

The boy scowled. "But we'll never give Samaria and Judea back," he said defiantly.

The road was climbing towards Jerusalem. The young soldier pointed to a cluster of whitewashed houses mixed with military-style tents, situated high on one of the hills a little off the road: Maleth Domin, one of the Israeli settlements of the Gush Emunim sect.

"There," he said. "The Gush Emunim will see to it that the West Bank becomes a rightful part of Israel."

"And what about peace?"

"We'll have peace when we have *Eretz Yisrael*."

"So?" David shrugged. For him the idea of *Eretz Yisrael*, Greater Israel, was no road to peace, only to more desperation and bloodshed.

The soldier fell silent and remained silent the rest of the way to Jerusalem. The main road passed through the northern outskirts of the city. David pointed to his left.

"There's a suburb down there called Kfar Sha'ul," he said. "Do you know it?"

"No. I don't know Jerusalem very well. Why? Does your family live there?"

David smiled minutely. "No. But you may have heard of it under another name. It used to be called Deir Yassin."

"Ah, yes. I *have* heard about Deir Yassin."

"Good."

"Yes, it was one of Menachem Begin's greatest victories in the fight for freedom, wasn't it?"

"I don't know. There are those who hold a different view, who say that 254 Arabs, women, and children included, were slaughtered in a combined *Irgun* and *Stern* attack against a peaceful village."

"Are you saying the attack on Deir Yassin was wrong?"

"I'm saying," David replied quietly, "that there have been black moments in recent Jewish history in Palestine, and that Deir Yassin by any standard is one of the blackest."

"I don't get it, how can anyone who fought in the Six-Day War think that way?" the soldier exclaimed.

"Maybe it's because I did fight in the war that I think like that," David replied. "Tell you what, these days I'm working for the government. I'm a realist."

David dropped the soldier off at Ramla. Before he had lost him from sight in his rear-view mirror, another car had stopped to pick him up.

The soldier hadn't improved David's bad mood. He thought about quitting, about getting out before he started to be regarded as a security risk. He might even quit Israel altogether, and go back to teaching somewhere.

David's father, James Davidsohn, had been a Jewish textile worker from Carlisle in England, who found himself working for British Army Intelligence in the Middle East during World War II. Having taken to Zionist ideals, he stayed in Palestine after the war and began to work for the *Shai*, the intelligence organization of the Jewish *Haganah* Army. He took a Hebrew name and called himself Yaacov Bar-Sharon; Sharon had been his mother's name. Then, in 1947, his son David was born, and became a citizen of the new state of Israel and a genuine *sabra.*

Young David grew up in a community of mainly British Jews in an area that had been predominantly Arab for centuries. When he went to England in the autumn of 1967, having recovered from his war wound, he spoke Arabic like a native of Tiberias, English fluently with a slightly out-of-place northern accent, and Hebrew perfectly, although with a certain self-conscious restraint. He returned to Israel in 1971 with a degree in History, specifically Middle Eastern, Sociology, and Arabic, for which there was little demand in pioneer-minded Israel. For a time he taught in Tel Aviv, and then, through the intervention of his father, he found himself at one of the Shin Beth's recruitment courses.

It wasn't one of those incredibly demanding, downright dangerous training courses for Mossad field operatives, but in its way it was tough enough. He ended up with a desk job in the Shin Beth. He had never really managed to overcome his surprise.

Gradually, to his further surprise, he grew to be an expert on Palestinians in general and Palestinian terrorists in particular. He came to be regarded as a good agent. But the good agent was beginning to have second thoughts; ironically, the second thoughts were a consequence of his profession more than anything else.

*   *   *

The Israeli Secret Service is located in the Hakirya district of eastern Tel Aviv. Within a ten-block mixed complex of flats, shops, and office buildings between the Derech Petah Tikva and the Leonardo da Vinci is David's Eye, the military and civilian intelligence services.

It was a little after one when David Bar-Sharon parked

in the garage below the modern, undistinguished office block off the Sderot Shaul Hemelech which housed, among other enterprises, the offices of the Shabak, the Shin Beth counterintelligence service. There was nothing about the building to indicate that anything of a clandestine nature ever went on there. The shops and the majority of the businesses were quite genuine. There was an armed guard in khaki uniform and a beret stationed outside the entrance, but that was a common enough sight in Israel.

But below ground, where the garage ramp swung out of sight, two armed soldiers in a bulletproof glass cubicle and TV cameras monitored every vehicle before it was allowed into the garage.

The porter in the entrance hall was actually a very competent security officer, whose business it was to discourage questions from casual visitors about the firm which was the cover for the Shabak, and to see that only those who had any business to do reached the special lift which deposited its occupants on the floor below the Shabak, where the final security check took place. In a stark, white room that could, within seconds, be hermetically sealed off and turned into a death trap, visitors had to identify themselves once more and were liable to be searched for weapons and other contraband. In an adjoining room, four people were monitoring the six TV cameras which covered the building: the two at the garage entrance, one in the entrance hall, two hidden ones in the building opposite covering the street outside, and one covering the back. Direct, protected phone lines connected all the security points with one another and with a number of outside security centres in the area.

Although he had been working for the Shabak for years, David had to be cleared through the checkpoints before he could take the last flight of stairs up to his office, and again he marvelled at the invisibility of the system. The net spread over ten city blocks, and yet, if one had legitimate business in the area or in any of the buildings, one had to look hard and with an experienced eye for any tell-tale signs.

David had expected a number of files to have been passed on to his desk during his absence, but he found only a memo telling him to report at once to his boss, Colonel Saul Shaltiel, head of the Shabak Anti-Terrorist Section. On entering Shaltiel's office, David found his superior standing with his back towards the window of the spartan, businesslike room.

"Hello, Saul," David began informally. "You wanted to see me?"

Shaltiel nodded. "I had expected you sooner. Did the interrogation take long?"

"It dragged on a bit."

"Anything in it?"

"Nothing except a frightened and ill-advised Arab."

"I see," Shaltiel said and sat down behind his desk, toying with a green plastic ruler. "Well, as of now, you're on special assignment as liaison officer to the Mossad."

"The Mossad? Why?"

Saul Shaltiel laid the ruler down, carefully aligning it with the top edge of the blotter.

"You'll help locate a tactical nuclear warhead that the Russians have lost and which might be in the hands of Palestinian terrorists."

"You're joking!" David exclaimed.

"I wish I were," Shaltiel said slowly.

"Oh, Lord."

"You'll report to Aaron Ofer at the Mossad Arab Affairs Section. He'll brief you fully." David nodded.

"In view of the extraordinary situation," Shaltiel said, "the Memuneh has decided to set up a group, directly under himself, to coordinate all the incoming information. The group consists of Ari Ofer, an Aman representative, a CIA liaison, and you."

"Why the CIA?"

"The Russians apparently leaked this info to the CIA.
I know it sounds crazy, but that's their stake in it. You're
relieved of all other duties until further notice. If you
need specified information, all resources will be open
to you. Ofer will take care of the reports to the Memuneh,
and you will report directly to me. Got it?"

"Got it," David replied automatically. He half opened
his mouth again, but Shaltiel cut him off.

"If you have questions, save them for Ofer. Now
move."

*   *   *

Ten minutes later David Bar-Sharon identified himself
to the porter of another office building off Dizengoff,
in many ways similar to the one that housed the Shabak,
and was directed to the trading firm that was the front
for the Mossad.

Left to himself in the elevator, David reflected on the
strange penchant of intelligence outfits, real as well as
fictitious, to hide behind import-export firms. He decided that it must be because that way they could send
inane coded telegrams all over the world in the guise
of orders, offers, requests, and price quotations with lots
of figures. Not to mention that such firms would be
expected to have widespread international contacts.

After another thorough security check, a girl in uniform led David to Aaron Ofer's room, which overlooked
the courtyard at the back of the building.

David regarded the three men in the room. He knew
Ari, a tall, rangy man with a huge hook of a nose set
in a lugubrious face under a shock of unruly black hair,
but the other two he had never seen before. One of
them was dressed in the rather plain uniform of a *Zahal*
major; that would be the Aman rep. The other man
was dressed in too formal a manner to be an Israeli:

brownish herring-bone sports coat, beige shirt, and maroon tie. He was tall and had a blond, well-scrubbed look. The American from the CIA.

"Ah, David, there you are at last." Ari Ofer rose, shook hands with David and immediately started to perform the introductions.

"Dov Kultz from the Aman." The Aman was the intelligence-gathering section of the Directorate of Military Intelligence. David had heard about Dov Kultz. He was reputed as having one of the sharpest minds in the intelligence community, and the joke had it that the Aman wasn't certain whether to put his pay down as salary or computer upkeep. Kultz was a fairly short man with almost startlingly everyday looks.

"And," Ofer went on, changing to English, "this is Bill Herman from the CIA Near East Division." David shook hands with the American, too. "And David Bar-Sharon here is from the Shabak."

A brief pause, during which they regarded each other in the awkward way newly introduced people do; then Ari Ofer said:

"All right, David, take a seat. We'll keep this in English since our friend Bill here doesn't have the Hebrew."

"Not much," the American said in broken Hebrew and smiled apologetically.

"See?" Ofer said. "Well, I take it Shaltiel informed you before you came here."

"Yes. I don't suppose there is any mistake about this?"

"We received final confirmation from Washington just two hours ago," Bill Herman said. "They've been through transcripts of Soviet radio communication, satellite photos, the works. It happened."

"So," Ofer said, "we work on the assumption that it's Palestinians who have the warhead, and we're the target. We have to decide what to look for in the available information. This will be a rather informal talk. What we say here, by the way, is of course classified as top secret." He leaned back in his chair, silently inviting comment.

David looked at the others. "Tell me exactly how this happened."

"Sure," Bill Herman volunteered and gave a brief account of what was known about the hijacking. David listened intently while Ari Ofer silently regarded two flies that were buzzing around the light fixture and the still fan in the ceiling. Kultz of the Aman was writing in his notebook.

When the American finished, Ari Ofer shook his head. "And until today we couldn't even figure out why the Russians have been so busy these last weeks."

"Hell," David said, "if they've been that silent it may mean we'll have to sit around and just wait for them to make a move."

"Unless we can come up with the necessary wisp of a clue. Yes, that's the situation."

Bill Herman smiled a frail smile. "You guys know more about the Palestinians than anybody else, including the KGB. You might be able to—you know—listen to the sounds of what's going down among the Palestinians."

David regarded him thoughtfully for a long moment, then said, in a level but emphatic voice, "Bloody hell, man, with anything this size you listen to the bloody silence."

Ari Ofer looked at David. "You know," he said, "David's got a point there."

"Yeah," David said, "and it scares me. Any ordinary terrorist group with a nuclear warhead in its possession would never keep it a secret. The last thing they'd do would be to hide it from the world. But we have complete silence. Our agents among the Palestinians haven't heard anything?"

Ari Ofer shook his head and received a puzzled stare

from Bill Herman. He shrugged. "No reports that can be directly tied in with this."

"They may not even be Palestinians," David said, "they may not even have given us a thought. The damned thing may show up anywhere in the world."

"Granted," Ofer said, "but we're not going to gamble on that."

"How about Egypt?"

"It's been thought of," Ofer replied. "The Americans have a couple of operatives there already. Bill will be in touch with them. And we've activated our own contacts. But the basic assumption is that we're the ones who are on the spot."

There was silence in the room. Outside, clouds were darkening and the first raindrops began a soft patter on the windowpane. It was January in Tel Aviv.

"Whatever the case, they must have left some traces," Ari Ofer went on. "A job like this demands training, financing, logistics. They must have trained somewhere, someone must be paying, there must be some sort of organization behind it. Why haven't we heard a thing?" He let the question hang like a reproachful odour in the room.

"We may have," Dov Kultz said in his heavily accented English, "without putting the parts together."

"The lunatic fringe," David said. "A splinter group. No official backing from the big factions. Money from heaven knows where, or perhaps from you-know-where. I suggest we run through the list and see if there are any likely candidates that are unaccounted for."

"Suppose it's people we've never even heard of?"

"Possible, but not likely. You don't try anything this big the first time out. The name of the group will probably be new to us, but I doubt that the leaders will. *If* it is Palestinians. This is a completely different style, though, and I'll tell you again that's what's disturbing me. Somebody has had new ideas . . ."

"Let's hope they stick to their new ideas and keep quiet for a few more days, and we might find out something about them. How long will it take for you to have that list, David?"

"We update it continuously. I ought to be able to have a short list this evening. The lunatic fringe isn't all that big."

"Good," Ofer said. "Through Dov we've access to the DMI's computers, and ought to be able to cover the financing and logistics angle fully, check all the usual suspected accounts in Switzerland, Liechtenstein, Belgium, the Bahamas, Beirut. Somewhere there must be or has been a trickle of money, and if there is we'll find it."

"We have two CIA computer guys coming over late tonight or early tomorrow," Bill Herman ventured and went on, in the face of Ofer's and Kultz's skeptical expressions. "That way you'll at least have an interface with our data."

"Fair enough," Ofer admitted. "And you'll keep us informed about what the CIA is doing?"

"Sure."

"And who," Dov Kultz asked, "will keep us informed about what the KGB is doing?"

"Hasn't anybody thought about that already?" Ari Ofer turned his eyes to the ceiling. "I'll include it in my report to the Memuneh and recommend that he instructs the Shabak to have every known Soviet agent in the country neutralized one way or the other. It's going to cause some political hullabaloo, I'm sure, but he'll just have to get the necessary clearance from the Cabinet."

"He'll get it," David said. "No toes are holy." He half snickered at the deliberately clumsy metaphor. "Is that all for now?"

"I suppose it is. I suggest we meet again tonight for a further run-through, and again tomorrow morning."

"Right," David said. "I'm going to eat. I'll take Bill with me and see if I can get any more out of him. And he could probably do with something to eat, too."

"As a matter of fact I could," the American admitted.

"Sure." Ari Ofer nodded rather absentmindedly.

"All right, Bill, care for a *kosher* meal? It's about all you'll get in this country anyway."

The CIA man smiled again, in patient acceptance of a world full of imperfections.

They took the elevator down to the underground garage, and Bill Herman said, "Jesus, the way you guys work together. If we had anything like that in the States we'd be . . ." He let the unfinished sentence hang in the air and sighed.

"If you had someone at your front door with a nuclear warhead you'd probably find it a lot easier," David observed.

"Yeah, maybe. I wondered, you all seemed too casual about it. Almost fatalistic. Me, I'm really worried sick."

They had reached David's car, stood on either side of it and regarded each other across the roof. David glanced around, at the rough concrete of the walls, at the cars, at the dim, damp daylight that penetrated beyond the neon light at the exit ramp. Nobody moved in the garage. In the stillness he instinctively lowered his voice.

"Don't ever think we're not, Bill," he said. "It's just that worrying doesn't get us very far. We do what we can do, and that's usually one hell of a lot. We're good and we know it. What you've seen today is only a small part of it all. I have no idea of how many agents here and abroad have been mobilized in this search, but they are many. A number of them will be blown away or lost in the bargain, and work that has taken us years will be disrupted at best and ruined at worst. Then there's the brass. They're already making plans to be able to act as soon as we—or somebody else—come up with anything worthwhile. The rest will sort itself out, *in'ish Allah*, as the Arabs say, God willing.''

He unlocked the door on his side, got into the car and leaned over to unlock the other door. As the American got in, David went on without looking up. ''You know, Bill, I may not be a very representative Jew, but I feel that what makes all this fighting so tragic is that we have more things in common with the Arabs than most Jews care to admit.''

*   *   *

Leif awoke at half past seven to a cloudless blue sky and a pale winter sun. Shortly Preben and Nick turned out, and once more they all gathered for breakfast in Leif's cab, talking optimistically of reaching the Syrian border sometime in the late evening or during the night. Nick sat on the engine tunnel while Preben fed him large pieces of bread and liver pâté. The sunlight streaming through the windshield warmed them.

Shortly after eight they fired up their trucks and rolled out onto the ring road around Ankara and were soon at the crossroads: left for Iran, right for Iraq and Saudi Arabia.

They followed the four-laner cutting through the southwestern suburbs. Thirty kilometres outside the city, when the road had changed into its usual self and wound among the hills, they turned into a service station to take on diesel. It was more out of convenience than necessity; both trucks were fitted with long-range tanks and fuel-feed systems from the trailer tanks to the main tractor tanks. The total fuel capacity of Leif's rig was well over 2,000 litres; with an average load he could go from Sweden to Damascus before having to start looking for service stations.

Twenty minutes later the trucks were on the road again, and presently they were out on the Turkish high-

land, a vast, white desert of snow that glittered under
the immense blue sky. Its beauty was breathtaking; its
sheer expanse seemed to dwarf the big vehicles, made
them shrink into insignificant specks. Distant mountains
rose with sharp, jagged features, wavering in the far
haze.

The diesel engines droned past the great inland lake
and a few scattered villages. Traffic was unusually light,
and sometimes it would be several kilometres between
oncoming vehicles. Shortly after noon they stopped in
Aksaray for lunch—and vanilla pudding. The restaurant
was almost deserted, and hounded by the clock and the
distances yet to cover, they were soon on the road again.

Leif drove up front, as the truck with the heaviest
load always headed a convoy. His good mood from the
morning had persisted, and he felt warm and secure in
the cab of his Scania in the middle of the immense,
cold plain. No police patrols had so far appeared to ruffle
his placid mind. He drove briskly; the speed limit for
trucks was 70 kph and the Scania's capacity a good 120,
even fully laden, so he had picked a compromise, the
philosophy of which was that if the cops stopped you,
you were going to be fined no matter what. You might
as well get what you paid for.

He reached behind him and fished out the thermos
flask which contained the rest of the coffee he had made
for their breakfast. He got out his green plastic mug and
poured the still hot coffee. Glancing at his wristwatch,
he suddenly realized that today was Sunday. What was
Annika doing back home? Perhaps out walking with
Sammy. He put a lump of sugar in the coffee and reached
for the small screwdriver he kept on the dash by the
edge of the windshield and started to stir his coffee with
it, steering with his elbows. Sunday or Wednesday, on
the Middle East run the days seemed to merge into one
continuous, anonymous stream that flowed along with
the vehicle. He replaced the screwdriver and sipped the

coffee. He had put on a tape of his favourite Swedish singer and he hummed along under his breath.

The Taurus range rose in the distance above the white and barren plain, and the black line of asphalt lost itself in the foothills. Preben's Scania 141 hung in his rear-view mirrors, well back and pacing him. The small, frozen sun was low above the horizon. and soon the short afternoon would be drawing to an end.

8

KERIM IPEKCI felt miserable. The cold wind from the mountains dug relentlessly into his back, finding its way inside his worn blue-grey uniform and thin shirt. The pale winter's sun had passed out of sight behind the snow-covered stone massif.

He nearly regretted having accepted the deal.

What if he failed? He tried to look at things from a fatalistic point of view. *Sula bula*. Like this, like that. If he failed, he failed.

But he knew he had no wish to go back tonight and face the two strangers and tell them that he had failed. He stroked his grey moustache, then looked at his wrist-watch. He still had over three hours to go.

He dug his hands into his pockets and walked from the car, carefully measuring one hundred paces, then turned and walked back. He felt a little warmer from the exercise. Aziz sat in the passenger seat of the Murat, smoking and sourly eyeing him. Ipekci ignored him.

He reached the battered car, lifted the binoculars and rested his elbows on the roof. He adjusted the focus and scanned the road, from the sharp turn at the base of the jutting rocks, and right along the straight ribbon of asphalt. He froze for a second as a bright red spot swam into view, but then he identified it as another tanker going down to Mersin. The binoculars continued their slow sweep to the north, until the road was lost in the distance. He sighed and lowered them.

He ran a loving finger over the cold, black-anodized metal. They were good, Zeiss 10×45, far better than those issued with his post as chief of police in Ulukisla. He had bought them in Istanbul; they had been expensive, nearly half a month's salary.

Money bought things. His younger brother worked in Germany, drove a BMW—second-hand, or maybe third-hand, but still—and sent money home every month, and Kerim Ipekci's wife never let him forget it.

Behind him a car came around the bend at good speed, then braked violently as the driver caught sight of the blue-grey car and the policeman beside it. Ipekci turned and looked the driver straight in the face, then the car was past and cautiously starting to accelerate again.

Fifteen minutes before, suddenly despairing and tired of the cold wait, he had stopped a French-registered Berliet, even though he knew that it didn't satisfy the conditions of the deal. He had thumbed through its papers and to his relief found that it was bound for Iraq He had pocketed a pack of Gauloises lying on the dashboard, climbed down, and waved the two baffled chauffeurs on their way.

He walked away from the car again, stomping his feet and flailing his arms to fight the wind and the cold.

Four, no, five days ago there had been a knock at his door. His wife had answered it and come back to tell him that two persons wished to see him privately. Puzzled, he had escorted the two men into his study. One was of medium height, in his thirties, well built, with brown, short-cut hair, and carried himself in a way that suggested that he had served a long time in some military force. The other man was taller, sinewy, with quick movements. On his left cheek was a prominent area of scar tissue. Ipekci thought him to be an Arab Both of them were dressed in nondescript European clothes.

They declined his offer of tea, and came directly to

the point. They would like to do a business deal. The deal was unusual. They explained in detail.

He hesitated; they put forth reassurances. Of course, his side of things would have to be performed with a minimum of talk and a maximum of discretion. Then they mentioned the money he'd be paid.

Allah Buyuk! For that kind of money he'd agree to bring an airplane down from the sky. He had agreed without much hesitation, convinced that everything would go smoothly. He was, after all, chief of police; nobody would ask embarrassing questions, nobody would challenge his authority.

But out here on the road he felt cold, miserable, and out of luck.

He had wondered several times what they were up to—it was probably smuggling. But for the money they were offering him he was happy to ask no questions. He returned to the car, leaned against the roof and raised the binoculars again. The first hints of dusk were beginning to show, smoothing out features in the distance. He scanned the road.

The car that had passed was still visible on the snowy plain. He let the binoculars sweep past it, then stopped. Something big, had to be a TIR truck. There was no mistaking the size and outline. With trembling fingers he adjusted the focus. As he looked another truck appeared behind the first one. He stood without moving, no longer aware of the wind in his back, watching them.

*   *   *

The Taurus range filled Leif's windshield, dwarfing the big Scania 141. Jutting, bare rock-faces, here and there spotted with pines and evergreens, but mostly snow-patched and of brownish grey stone, stretched into the distance in a disorderly array of cliffs, crevasses, and deep gorges.

The sun had disappeared. He was driving in the mountain shadow, and around him the late afternoon grew darker. He could see the end of the long straight, a sharp lefthander at the foot of the rising massif.

Time for a change of cassettes and another cigarette before the climb began. As the turn drew nearer, he decided on an old Rolling Stones tape, pushed it into the deck, then braked hard and shifted down three times in succession. The Scania strained and groaned, and then he was around the bend. He shot a glance out the side window, saw that Preben was still pacing him, and pushed the accelerator down. The V-8 diesel rumbled as it slowly picked up speed.

The water level warning light flickered briefly; well, that could wait until the TIR park in Adana. Less than three hours, and he would have the windows down and feel the warm night air with its smell of palm trees and summer. Funny how eighty kilometres could make that much difference. Then he looked further up the road, and cursed.

Helvetes jävlar! Two Turkish cops, one crossing over to his side of the road, the other getting out of the car. Bloody hell! He'd be stopped, have a fine slapped on him, and probably be robbed of the new pack of cigarettes on the dash. He had an impulse to steer his truck over, crush the police car, and drive on. Cool it, he told himself. Don't argue, just say yes sir and please sir and smile and cough up the fine, and you might be away again in a couple of minutes.

He took the cigarette from his mouth and stubbed it out, shut off the cassette player and flashed his turn indicators. A fat police officer with binoculars around his neck was waving vigorously at him. He eased the Scania out onto the edge of the road and braked to a halt.

He pulled the compression release and hit the parking brake, checking his mirrors: Preben's red Scania was

gliding up behind him. Then he tried to arrange his face
into something resembling friendly neutrality before he
reached across the passenger seat to unlock the door.

The door swung open, and the fat police officer with
a large star-and-crescent metal badge on his left breast
and a leaf-shaped disc on his right climbed up and settled into the passenger seat. He took off his peaked cap
and placed it on the dash.

He reached out his hand. "Papers?"

At least he didn't start by asking for whisky or cigarettes or *sex magazin*. And he seemed sober. Leif turned
in his seat and grabbed his battered black attaché case.
He placed it in his lap and opened it a crack, aware of
the Turk's staring eyes and the big revolver at his side.
The cold air coming in made him shiver.

He got out the TIR papers for the load and his vehicle,
and silently handed them over. The Turk flipped the
pages, barely looking at them.

"You going where?" he finally said.

"Saudi Arabia," Leif answered, pronouncing it the
Arab way, with short a's.

"Riyadh?"

"Yes, yes, Riyadh."

The police officer turned his head so quickly that Leif
was surprised. Then he turned back and flipped pages
again before he put his cap back on and jumped down,
still with the papers clutched in his hand.

Leif cursed again. He could sense trouble in the
policeman's manner. He grabbed his jacket, opened his
door and jumped down. If a cop decided to inspect your
rig, the safest way to get him all worked up was to wait
in the cab and look bored.

The police officer walked along the right side of the
semi-trailer, now and then bending down to peer at the
undercarriage or reaching out to test the plastic-covered
wire that secured the tarpaulin cover to the folding trailer
sides. Leif paced him at a proper respectful distance and

shot a glance over his shoulder at the other Turk, who still stood in front of the truck, looking back with a scowl.

They came to the rear end of the semi-trailer. Preben had cut his engine and was sitting in his cab, both elbows on the steering wheel, watching them.

"What is load?"

"Building material." Leif saw the policeman frown. "To make houses." *Can't you read, you bastard?*

"Ah."

They turned and walked back to the front of the truck. The police officer looked at the TIR papers with renewed interest, turning the pages.

"Riyadh?" He asked again, looking up at Leif.

Yes, dammit! "Yes, yes," Leif replied, nodding for emphasis. He felt cold and nervous, and only wanted to pay the fine on whatever charge was going to be thought up, and be rolling again.

The police officer closed the paper folder with an audible snap.

"Papers," he pointed at them with his free hand, "papers not in order. You must come with us."

"What?" Leif exclaimed. "What's wrong with them?"

The policeman shrugged, an infuriating, arrogant gesture. "Papers not in order," he repeated. "You come with us to Ulukisla."

Leif felt his pulse starting to race. "What for? Which papers are not in order?"

He heard a door slam and footsteps approach. Preben came up, while putting on his jacket. He towered over the others. The Turk hesitated for a moment, taking half a step backwards.

"What's going on?" Preben asked in Danish. "What's the bastard trying to pull?"

"Don't know, but it stinks," Leif answered in Swedish. He understood Danish well enough and knew that Preben had no difficulty with Swedish, so between them they didn't bother with any mixed *lingua scandia*. "He claims my papers aren't in order; wants me to go with them to Ulukisla."

The fat policeman looked from Preben to Leif and back again, trying to get the gist of the conversation. The other Turk hovered in the background, looking worried.

Preben stroked his beard. "You know your papers are OK?"

"Of course they are, dammit! I always check them out myself before going down."

"Maybe this one sees it differently."

"Maybe. Maybe he's angling for more money than just a fine. I don't know, but this stinks. I think . . ."

The policeman interrupted them. "No more talk! You come with us, we check papers."

Leif turned to him, trying with an effort to sound friendly. "To check papers—how much time?"

The Turk shrugged again. "Finish, maybe tonight, maybe tomorrow."

Frustration welled up inside Leif. "Maybe tomorrow"—a meaningless phrase in the Muslim world. "This is going to cost me at least a day!" he complained to Preben. "Hell, they might even be planning to steal my rig!"

Preben slowly shook his head. "Not likely with your load. I'll be damned if I can figure out what he wants. Maybe he really has got it into his head that your papers don't seem all right and wants to check them out."

Leif snorted; the policeman pointed at him and barked, "I say no more talk! You come with us to Ulukisla!" He indicated Preben. "Finish here—you go!" His hand came down to rest on the butt of his revolver.

"He means business," Preben muttered.

The Turk turned to his colleague and spoke in a commanding tone. The smaller Turk nodded and shuffled off towards the open passenger door of the Scania. He passed close by them, grinning at Leif with bad, brown-stained teeth.

Leif felt enraged, desperate, helpless. They were actually going to more or less *arrest* him, for Chrissakes, on some idiotic, trumped-up charge. Probably put him in a cell for the night. What if he wasn't out by morning, or by next week? How could he notify Annika, or Bert, or his parents?

Preben reached out and grabbed Leif's left arm in a viselike grip.

"Look, mate, I'll be waiting in Adana, in the TIR park by the airbase road. If you haven't showed up by tomorrow evening, I'll raise absolute hell, I promise. OK?"

Leif nodded, gratefully squeezing Preben's muscular arm.

"Don't worry. The bastard is sucking wind, and you'll be free and clear tomorrow. I'll see you over a glass of beer in Adana."

Leif nodded again, and Preben gently boxed him on the shoulder and gave the police officer a contemptuous glare. Then he turned and started to walk back to his own truck, without looking back.

The other Turk had already climbed into the Scania's cab. The fat one, his superior, removed the binoculars from around his neck and motioned Leif to get in before he turned on his heel and crossed the road to the police car. Leif looked longingly at the TIR papers, which the policeman still clutched in his hand.

A green, beat-up Volkswagen whizzed by, and the sound of it died away in the distance. Leif clamped his jaws together and reached up to open the door and climb in.

The cab was icy cold. The pack of Prince cigarettes was gone from the dash, and a bulge in the left breast pocket of the Turk's uniform advertised its new whereabouts. The Turk grinned at him from behind a cloud of smoke.

"Nebu?" he asked.

Leif ignored him. The engine came to life with a rumble and settled into a steady idle. He switched on his lights and released the parking brake. Ahead, the police car pulled out, did a U-turn, and started rolling down the road. Leif put the Scania in low, and slowly the big truck climbed back onto the road and gathered speed. In his rear-view mirrors Leif could see Preben's Scania behind him.

"Musik?"

Leif glanced sideways in the twilight inside the cab and saw the Turk indicating the cassette player. He started to shake his head, then changed his mind and put the Stones cassette in. The Turk grinned and drummed his hand against the armrest in time to the music.

Might as well keep him happy, Leif thought. All the same he deeply resented having the other man riding in the passenger seat. The truck was his, the cab his personal living space. It was one thing inviting fellow drivers in for a beer and a chat and some music while customs officials and agents got off their lazy butts, another thing having it invaded by someone who stole his cigarettes.

He tried to concentrate. Think, he urged himself, *think!* What can I do? What will they do?

The answer to the first question was obvious: nothing. The fat policeman had his papers, and that settled it. All he could do was follow orders and hope for the best.

The second question worried him. The whole thing might turn out to be a simple misunderstanding, and he would be away again in the morning. If not ... he could think of several alternatives, each less alluring than the next. He felt a tiny twinge of panic, and fought it down.

He glanced at his speedo and saw that it had crept up to nearly 80 kph.

"Oh no, you don't," he muttered and throttled back until the truck was doing a steady 70 again. The distance to the Turkish police car increased until its driver noticed what was going on. Then it, too, slowed down.

Night fell and the stars came out, distant fires against the velvety darkness. They were in the foothills now; the road wound along the bottom of a valley, its sides now pressing in on them, now receding to form vast plains.

The tumult of thoughts died down and was replaced by a dull sensation in his solar plexus. Leif drove with his inner autopilot, unthinkingly following the rear lights in front, ignoring the Turk who had started to fiddle with the knobs of the cassette player and was jumping up and down in the passenger seat in delight over the soft hydraulic springing. Now and then Leif glanced in his mirrors and saw the familiar array of lights on Preben's Scania. He wished, not for the first time, that the trucks were equipped with communications radios. Few TIR trucks carried them; the normal route from Scandinavia was via the Eastern Bloc states, where border guards and police officers took an ungenerous view of any potential spying equipment.

The kilometres rolled by, and the lights of Ulukisla appeared on his left. The police car flashed its turn indicator left, and Leif flicked his own and pumped the brakes three times in quick succession. He was answered with two flashes from Preben's floodlights, and then he was turning off the main road, and the other Scania shot past and was gone in the night on its way to summer and Adana.

The road was bumpy. Leif drove slowly, zigzagging to avoid the worst potholes. The Stones burst out with a new rock number, and, suddenly irritated, he ejected the cassette. The relative silence was blissful. The Turk scowled at him. He scowled back.

Shortly they reached the first houses. The street lighting was spotty at best. Ulukisla was a large village, but the streets could barely accommodate the big truck. Leif carefully manoeuvred between the low, light-brown buildings, swearing at every turn.

At a large, open place the police car braked to a stop. The fat police officer jumped out and came up to the truck. Leif rolled the window down. The Turk pointed to a spot alongside some houses, and with gestures and a few words in English made it clear that he wanted Leif to park there. Leif eased the Scania past the car, then put it in reverse and backed up to the precise spot the policeman had indicated.

He pulled the parking brake handle and switched off all his lights. He let the engine idle while he looked around. A solitary lamp on a house wall angling away from him provided the only permanent illumination; most of the open area was in near-darkness. He could see nothing that resembled the entrance to a police station.

The Turk who had ridden with him opened his door and jumped down. Leif reached across to pull it shut and lock it, then cut the engine. In the silence he leaned back in his chair and tried to collect his thoughts and feelings.

The fat policeman came up to the truck again. "You come with us."

So now they would take him somewhere, most likely to a cell. What should he keep with him?

He turned and picked up his attaché case. That took precedence: it contained all his money, thousands of Deutsch-Marks for road taxes, customs dues, fines and so on, plus his passport and all the rest of his papers. He did not dare let it out of his sight.

What else? He opened the bag that he kept stashed in the upper bunk, got soap, toothbrush, toothpaste, a small towel, and some toilet paper. As an afterthought he took a thick, woollen sweater, and another pack of cigarettes.

Jumping stiffly to the ground, Leif closed and locked the door. He turned and found himself confronted by the policeman's outstretched hand.

"You give me keys."

He hesitated, then handed them over. He didn't have much choice.

The arrival of the Scania had attracted attention. Several Turks came out from the shadows among the houses. Leif swore under his breath. If he still had any mirrors or lights on the truck tomorrow it would be nothing less than a miracle.

The police officer turned and shouted, and the figures among the shadows seemed to shrink back. Then the two policemen started off for their car. Leif followed in their wake, clutching the attaché case under one arm and stuffing his jacket pocket with the rest of the stuff he had brought along.

He was placed in the back seat, and then they were off through the nearly dark streets of Ulukisla. The fat Turk was at the wheel, the binoculars back around his neck. Leif's one hundred and eighty-five centimetres were badly cramped, and a couple of broken springs forced him to lean to the left. Now and then the other Turk turned and grinned at him.

The narrow streets were nearly empty despite the relatively early hour. The houses seemed all alike, constructed of brownish grey material resembling cement, with small windows and wooden doors. Leif soon lost all sense of direction.

After a few minutes they pulled up sharply in front of a fairly big entrance. Leif recognized the sign outside with the official emblem of the Turkish police force, and above it crudely hand-painted letters in blue: POLIS. His mouth felt dry. The cops in most countries along the

Middle East route had a bad reputation; judging from
the asphalt vine, the Turks were the meanest of the lot.

They motioned at him to get out. He tried to hurry,
but his legs already felt stiff from the ride. They took
his arms and dragged him up the stairs, almost making
him drop his attaché case and his towel and sweater.

The entrance doors were pushed open, and he was
in a large room, with several desks and chairs, and various notices and bulletins littering the grey-green walls.
Two men in grey police uniform shirts were already
there. Through an open door to a back room he could
hear the sound of a radio playing Turkish music. The
air in the room was hot and sticky and reeked with
stale cigarette smoke.

The fat policeman gave him a rough shove and pointed
to a chair. Leif sat down on it, clutching his possessions.
The Turk, who was obviously the chief officer, uttered
a stream of Turkish words and gesticulated at Leif. Leif
caught one word he recognized—*Ishvetj*, Sweden.

For a minute the four Turks talked among themselves, now and then glancing at him. One policeman,
a thin, middle-aged man, gestured at him to step forward. Leif rose quickly and came up to the desk. The
man pulled out a large ledger and opened it. He eyed
Leif while he lit a cigarette; the smoke was thick and
acrid.

"Name?"

"Leif Wallman."

The policeman picked up a pen and wrote slowly.
"Leff . . . Vallmann." He cocked his head and examined
the orthography, apparently satisfied. "Country?"

"Sweden."

That also went down in the log. Then the Turk reached
out his hand. *"Pasaport?"*

Leif cursed silently. It was in his case, together with
the bundle of banknotes. He had to try and get it out

without arousing suspicions or revealing how much money he had.

"Moment," he said, trying to sound calm. He cradled the case in his left arm and with his right hand fumbled the latch open and raised the lid a crack. He was conscious of being watched as he slipped his hand inside and started to search for his passport. Where was the damned thing? He felt unbearably hot; a drop of sweat slid down his nose.

There! He pulled it out quickly and snapped the case shut, suddenly realizing that he had been holding his breath. Nobody seemed to have noticed. The Turk accepted the passport with its shiny black cover and the royal emblem in gold and flipped it open. He turned a few pages and examined the massive array of stamps, then found the page with the passport number and wrote it down.

The senior police officer started to speak. The fourth Turk came over and stared Leif in the face. He was young, about Leif's age, but shorter. He was unshaven, and his shirt was dirty. He grabbed Leif by the arm and tried to turn him around.

"Hey!" Leif shouted. "I want my passport back."

The Turk hit him in the side, a painful clip that made Leif grimace. *"Gel! Gel!"* he growled, grabbing Leif's arm again. The senior officer turned red in the face and screamed something at the younger man, who let go of Leif's arm.

The police officer pointed at Leif. "You go with him! You get passport back tomorrow."

Leif had no time to answer. He got a none too mild shove in the back, stumbled through a doorway and found himself in a corridor. The Turk led the way around a corner and then stopped before a sturdy-looking door to fish a heavy key-ring out of his pocket. He unlocked the door and gestured. Leif stepped inside and heard the key turn again in the lock.

He was in a small cell, about two metres by three, dimly lit by a naked lightbulb in the ceiling. A narrow cot with a folded blanket stood alongside one of the walls. In the far corner there was a dirty washbasin with a single tap, and in the floor a standard issue Turkish toilet: a hole and two diminutive boards for the feet. A small, barred window was set high in the wall opposite the cot.

The cell was cold and smelled of dirt and human excrement. He glanced up at the window and saw that the pane behind the bars was broken, with a large piece missing.

He put his attaché case and the towel and the sweater on the blanket; the red towel looked indecently bright against the drabness of the cell. Then he sat down and buried his face in his hands.

His tension slowly eased. He had steeled himself for the worst, but the thing had been over quickly, with a minimum of harassment. He was grateful for that. He didn't like to admit it, but he had been scared.

Suddenly he felt an overwhelming urge to urinate. He had been too keyed up to notice that the pressure of his bladder had been in the red zone for at least half an hour. He stepped over to the hole in the floor and unzipped his trousers.

Peeing seemed to make him start functioning again. His stomach rumbled impatiently. He hadn't had anything since Aksaray. Was it possible to get anything to eat?

He knocked on the door, listened. Silence. He gave it a few heavy blows, then stepped back. The seconds ticked away. He was debating with himself whether to give it another try or give up when a small hatch at about eye-height flew open and the unshaven face appeared.

"Food?" Leif inquired.

The face frowned.

"Essen? Manger?" he tried in German and French.

No reaction. The face in the hatch kept staring at him. He turned to sign language and went through the motion of eating and drinking.

The face crinkled up in anger. "No!" it stated. At least the Turk knew one word of English; too bad it was the wrong one. The face disappeared and the hatch slammed back. Leif's spirits fell flat.

"Förbannade idiot!" he shouted at the door.

The judas window flew open again. The face glared. *"Ipnay pesavek!"* the Turk spat back, then the hatch closed again.

Well, he thought, I suppose that means the Turkish ambassador has been recalled for consultations. But at least he had water, and cigarettes in his jacket. He got the plastic soapbox out, gingerly put it down on the cracked washbasin, and turned on the tap. The water was cold and tasted good. He washed his hands and face vigorously, then toweled himself dry. He put the attaché case on the floor and carefully spread the towel on top of it, then laid down on the cot using his sweater for a pillow.

He lit a cigarette, stared at the lightbulb which was swinging in the draft from the broken window, and tried to assess his situation. On the minus side: plenty. He was locked up in a cell, without his passport or other papers, and the cops had the keys to his truck. The chief of police had said that he would get his passport back tomorrow. Did that mean they would release him tomorrow?

A memory suddenly came to him: last summer he had met a guy at a party who had worked as a courier for a Swedish tour operator in Izmir. His view, which he had told Leif with some conviction, was that the Turks were a generous, charming people, possessed of a great hospitality and a fascinating culture. Leif, with equal conviction, had countered with stories of what drivers on the Middle East run had to suffer from cops, bandits, and Turks in general. The clash had been violent, the party had folded, and Annika had had to take a drunk and angry Leif home.

How could the same people appear so different to different persons?

Maybe the Turks in Izmir were different.

The mattress was lumpy. He shifted his position, tried to find one that was less rough on his body. The cigarette was almost finished; he ground it out against the side of the cot and flung the butt towards the toilet hole. It landed just a little bit short. He shrugged. The toilet, the mattress, everything was *turk-mali*—Turkish made. Turkish crap.

He tried to console himself with the only item on the plus side: Preben. The Pirate would see that the word got around that Leif was in the clink, and then the Swedish Foreign Office would get on the back of the Turkish authorities.

And if that didn't help?

Leif shivered. His beard itched.

Could he survive years in a Turkish prison, with their bad food, their beatings, their homosexuality?

He tried to put those thoughts from his mind. It *had* to be a stupid mistake; it would soon be cleared up, and he would be on his way again. After all, the police officer had promised him his passport back in the morning, hadn't he?

He yawned, blinked sleepily at the hypnotically swaying lightbulb. Tomorrow he'd be rolling into Adana to have a beer with Preben and laugh it all off.

Tomorrow . . .

Presently, he dozed off.

*   *   *

Lief awoke, disoriented, wondering what had stirred him

out of his sleep. The cell was dark; the feeble light was switched off. He raised his arm to look at the luminous dial of his watch. Ten to eleven. He hadn't slept long.

He swung his legs over the edge of the narrow cot and stood up. The window was a dark grey patch against the darker backdrop of the wall. The building was quiet. He strained to listen.

A sound drifted in from the broken window, the merest ghost of a whisper, so faint that he would not have recognized it, had he not lived with it for so long.

The sound of a big diesel engine.

Preben coming to rescue him? Someone stealing his truck? Or a truck passing by on the far highway, the sound carrying in the still night?

He listened again but couldn't hear it any longer. Had he just imagined that he had heard it?

The cell was cold and silent around him. He put his thick sweater on over the jacket, returned to the cot and crawled in under the blanket.

*   *   *

The arc light rigged in the ceiling of the garage threw a bright glare over the scene, while deep pools of shadow remained in the corners and under the truck where the light didn't reach. The big Scania tractor unit dominated the space inside. It towered almost to the overhead wooden beams, dwarfing the three men. The trailer, unhitched, stood outside, a fourth man guarding it.

All loose articles had been taken out of the cab and neatly placed on a large piece of cloth on the floor. Several papers lay beside them, with sketches and notes of how every single item should be put back inside. The cab itself had been tilted forward at the maximum angle, and secured.

Behind the cab, the large, crisscross-patterned metal sheet just ahead of the trailer coupling had been removed, giving access to the drive shaft and the insides of the heavy U-beams that made up the backbone of the chassis.

An array of tools had been laid out behind the Scania's right front wheel: crowbars, a sledge hammer, spanners, an acetylene torch, and a portable heavy-duty welding unit.

A precision-cut steel plate, seventy-five centimetres wide, had been carefully inserted between the U-beams. It rested flush on their lower edges, and had been welded into position above the drive shaft. Its forward edge was turned up to hide the six loop bolts attached to its top.

Lastly, a specially made PVC-coated nylon bag, sealed against dust and water and containing a grey steel cylinder encased in layers of shock-absorbent padding, had been lifted into place and secured to the six loop bolts with thin, flexible steel wires.

With the metal grill bolted back on to the frame, there would be nothing to reveal the extra cargo the Scania carried. The only way to detect any change would be to crawl under and glance up between the main frame beams—provided one knew exactly what a Scania 141 was supposed to look like. Otherwise, it was just another metal sheet, lost in a maze of tanks, brake lines, and bogie and chassis members.

The man stood beside the tractor unit and fingered the scar tissue on his left cheek. He glanced at his gold watch: nearly 0530. The operation had stretched dangerously close to their morning deadline, but now it was almost over. One man was gathering up the tools, while another lay on his back beneath the Scania, his face streaked with dirt, carefully applying a thick coat of mud to the shiny new steel plate. When it dried it would blend in exactly with the rest of the underside of the truck.

The man touched his scar again. He felt tired, but elated. Another forty-five minutes and the Scania would be back where the driver had parked it, trailer hooked up again, the truck looking untouched. The recording unit would reveal nothing; they had removed the discs before they started the vehicle and would put them back with a thin line added to cover the lost hours.

The only possible tell-tale detail was the odometer. It had added a kilometre and a half and would add the same distance again, but they had to take the gamble that the driver would be too preoccupied to notice it. The report from the chief of police, when he had met them at the truck to hand over the keys and collect his money, had been encouraging. The driver had seemed confused and nervous, and would probably be all too relieved to notice anything amiss when he was released in the morning.

The third man came up, smoking a cigarette, and pointed to the man under the truck. "He will soon be finished?"

"Yes. We'll be ready in time. Have you packed the other equipment?"

"*Da.* Almost."

"Good. Then you will drive it back."

The man nodded and went away. The other man remained, fingering his scar and turning things over in his mind.

The plan was extremely tenuous, of course, but it was the sheer tenuity of it that would serve to bring it off. So far it had worked extraordinarily well. The first critical part, the hijacking, had come off smoother than he had dared dream.

Now the second critical part was almost over. In a few hours the driver and the Scania would be on their unsuspecting way. Only the third and last stage of the operation remained.

He walked over to the small window and peeled loose a corner of the black, self-adhesive masking paper, and looked out. The window faced east. Above the jagged outline of the distant mountains, the sky held the promise of a new dawn.

He smoothed the paper back into place. No sleep yet. They had to be in Adana before noon, to send the two telegrams.

And then the wait.

*   *   *

Dan Morris turned around where he stood by his file cabinet. He hadn't heard the door open, just sensed it. Holston stood in the doorway, leaning tiredly against it. His eyes behind the spectacles were rimmed with red.

"You look like death warmed over, Art. I thought you'd gone home long ago to get some sleep."

Holston ignored the remark. "You were wrong, Dan," he said tonelessly. "And Silverstein too. You were both wrong."

Morris frowned. "What are you talking about?"

"You said the hijackers didn't leave a single clue, last night. You were wrong. They left one. It's been staring us in the face all the time, and we didn't see it."

"I don't follow you."

"The time factor, Dan. Silverstein touched on it, but he failed to see the important point."

Morris was silent. Holston took two limping steps into the room and went on: "Dan, you're a professional soldier. You've seen action. The two main requisites of battle—what are they?"

Morris automatically responded. "Fire and movement."

"Exactly. And?"

"I still don't follow you."

"Fire and movement," Holston repeated. "Those hijackers have got themselves the biggest goddamn firepower any single group ever had, but they haven't moved. Why?"

Comprehension began to dawn on Morris's face.

"Dan—if they wanted to blackmail somebody, why haven't they done so already? For every day they stay holed up the risk of being discovered and smoked out increases. They've been sitting on that warhead for over two weeks, and haven't given a single peep.

"They must have one hell of a good reason: they intend to use it for something very special, and they're waiting for that very special thing. Silverstein was wrong. I think they're going to detonate it, somewhere and without warning."

"God," Morris said softly. "They must be operating on a timetable . . ." His voice trailed off.

"What do they want?" Holston whispered. "What in hell's name do they want?"

9

AROUND ANOTHER BEND of the road, and the last buildings of Ulukisla were gone in his mirrors. Savagely, he yanked the wheel to the right and felt the Scania lurch as the righthand tires hit the shoulder and sank into the dirty brown slush. He braked hard and had to wrestle with the steering wheel as the truck tried to climb back up onto the road. Thirty-six tons of Scania and semi-trailer groaned to a stop to the *whoosh* of compressed air. He flicked the hazard switch, and orange lights fore and aft started flashing in a steady rhythm. No Turkish bastard was going to be handed an excuse to run right into his arse.

Leif's eyes raced from the mirrors to the dash, and on. Where should he start? The cab was as good a place as any.

He turned in his seat, got up on one knee and reached up to unhook the straps. The upper bunk came down to horizontal with a thud, and Leif lifted his large brown leather bag down onto the engine tunnel and tore it open.

Jeans, shirts, T-shirts, socks, underwear, a couple of books, his Instamatic camera . . . everything seemed to be there, untouched. He zipped up the bag, replaced it and folded the bunk up.

Reaching across the cab, he clicked open the glove compartment and encountered the usual jumble: packs of discs for the trip recorder, his spare sunglasses, a small packet of Brooke Bond tea bags, and a few other odds and ends. He slammed it shut again.

On impulse, he reached down under the passenger seat. The jar of coins was still there, wedged between the floor mat and the seat base.

The cassettes . . . He straightened and counted through his stock of taped music. No cassette was missing, not even the one with love songs in Farsi that he had bought on the Teheran trip.

What else? Oh yes. He took hold of the lower bunk and gave it a forceful tug. It came away and revealed the small refrigerator and its compressor housed underneath. Everything looked normal, no sinister packages stashed in any corners. To make sure, he unsnapped the lid of the fridge and peered down. Nothing there that he hadn't bought and put in himself. He replaced everything.

One last detail, but one that had worried him: his small stock of porn magazines, the great lubricant south of the Alps. Slipped into the right hands, they could have you ready and rolling again within a few hours; slipped into the wrong hands or found, and you faced a year in the slammer.

His fears had been allayed the moment he climbed into the Scania; tens of thousands of miles had taught him when his behind was snug upon an extra centimetre of glossy colour mags. Still, it didn't hurt to make sure. He slid over to sit on the engine tunnel and grasped the seat cover. It came away to reveal what looked like the seat itself but was in fact another cover. Working with precise movements, he wriggled it upwards and removed it.

The magazines lay wrapped in a small towel on the seat. He unfolded the towel, reflexively taking a look out through the windows, and counted them. A full dozen, exactly the number he had taken along.

He glanced at the mags again, and blood rushed to

his groin in an automatic response. For a second, he
felt an almost unbearable stab of loneliness and longing,
sensations that flowed hot and cold along his nerves
and veins.

God! No wonder hardcore porn mags were dynamite
for Arabs and Turks, some of whom had perhaps never
seen a member of the opposite sex undressed. Quickly
Leif wrapped the mags up, replaced both seat covers,
and slid back onto his seat.

The inside of the cab seemed untouched. Even the
thin film of road dust that had accumulated on the dash
seemed undisturbed, except for his own marks. He got
a cigarette out and lit it, blowing smoke through his
nostrils. Perhaps they hadn't touched his rig after all.

Well, he wasn't finished yet.

He pulled the keys from the dash, opened the door
and jumped down. The cold, wintry morning outside
greeted him, with a sun obscured by driving clouds. He
zipped up his jacket against the wind, slammed the door
shut, and walked to the nearest of the trailer boxes.

The pieces of rubber hosing he had cut to fit the padlocks were caked with dirt. He wiped it off, folded back
the hosing and unlocked the trailer box. His scrutiny
revealed nothing out of the ordinary. The box was full
of tools, an hydraulic jack, oil cans, heavy snow chains,
and a collection of other gear, all in fairly good order.
He hooked the lid back into place and locked it.

The rear one of the leftside trailer boxes proved untouched. It contained his camping cooker and a large
cut-down cardboard carton holding paper plates and cups,
cutlery, and rolls of toilet paper. The rest of the box
was filled with tinned food.

Walking around the back end of the trailer, he stopped
to inspect the cluster of customs seals. They were all
there, one from Sweden and one from every country
he had passed, all unbroken. He nodded to himself, more
relaxed.

The single trailer box on the righthand side also contained neither more nor less than it should—three camping chairs and more foodstuffs, plus two ten-litre cans filled with fresh water.

The cigarette was finished. He dropped the butt in the slush and ground it in with his boot.

Was he making mountains out of molehills?

Slowly, he made a complete circuit around the Scania, scrutinizing everything: lights, wheels, diesel tanks, air tanks for the brake system. Here and there he bent down and peered at the dirt-streaked underside of the trailer, inspecting the bogie and the cables and hoses carrying electricity, compressed air, and diesel. Nowhere could he see any signs of tampering. Nothing was missing.

He came back to the righthand trailer box, scratching his beard and frowning. Looking around, he saw a flat, bare rock, and sat down on it. He regarded the truck. The orange hazard lights flashed steadily.

He lit another cigarette, turning the events of the last hour over in his mind. He had been in a foul mood when the unshaven young cop had shaken him awake. A little later his jailer had returned with a tray with a bowl of thick soup and fresh bread, as well as a mug of tea. Leif had wolfed it down without any second thoughts; he had been hungry.

Just as he was finished, the fat police officer had entered and handed over the carnet, the TIR papers, his passport, and the keys to the Scania, curtly informing him that all his papers were OK, and he was free to go. Leif felt the proverbial stone fall from his heart. But it was not until he was taken back to the Scania that he really allowed himself to relax. The cab was ice-cold; still, it had never felt so good to climb into it. The police officer actually shook hands with him before leading the way out in his battered, blue-grey Murat, and then waved to him as he pulled over to let the Scania go by.

The sun came out from behind a cloud and warmed

him. He closed his eyes and lifted his face, felt his black
mood being dispersed by the sun and the fact that he
was free and clear and back on the road again. Just
some stupid mistake, he concluded. He was being overly
suspicious. Surely, he wasn't the first pilot to be stopped
and hauled in for a once-over with regard to the papers.

And the Scania appeared to be completely untouched,
though that in itself was not conclusive. Leif knew as
well as anyone else that there were any number of places
on or inside a truck where you could hide things.

The trip recorder! The one thing he hadn't checked.
He came out of his euphoria, quickly stubbed the cigarette out and was inside the cab in no time.

He selected the right key from his key-ring, inserted
it, and flipped up the speedometer. He took the pack
of discs out and checked them. Thin, squiggly black lines
that recorded the speed at every moment. Hairlines on
circular discs, twenty-four hours to every disc, seven
discs to a pack, one pack lasted a week. Leif changed
every Tuesday.

He found the last two sheets and scrutinized them.
A long, wavy line showed his progress down from
Ankara, steadily keeping between 80 and 90 kph. God,
if the Ulukisla cops had checked that! Two stops, one
for taking on diesel and one for eating at Aksaray. Then
the next stretch until he had been stopped by the police,
followed by the uneven line of his progress into Ulukisla. And then . . .

Nothing. The thin, black line ran along the zero kph
line. Nobody had moved the Scania during the night.
The line continued on the next disc, unbroken until the
moment he had put the truck in gear in Ulukisla this
morning.

Well, that settled it. He put the pack back and closed
the speedometer. Time to get a move on. Preben, a beer,
and summer were waiting on the other side of the
mountains.

* * *

Preben's truck was exactly where he had promised it would be, in the TIR park by the road to the American airbase on the northeastern outskirts of Adana. His was the only truck there.

Leif rolled up to the gate and started haggling with the surly guard. He had no intention of staying longer than necessary, and didn't feel like shelling out money just for entering and spending an hour or so talking to Preben. Eventually the old Turkish one-two took care of the matter: a pack of cigarettes and a wink, and the guard even managed a smile as he waved him through.

Leif made a wide U-turn and came up alongside the red Scania, then cut the engine and looked it over. Preben's large grey cat was eyeing him through the half-open window, but the Pirate himself was nowhere to be seen.

He opened the door to the sunshine and the warm air and thought he could detect a trace of salt in the air. The Tarsus crossing had been uneventful; he had marvelled again at winter changing into summer in two hours from Tekir as the vista of green fields and distant azure water unfolded before him.

A light breeze came in through the open door. On the other side of the barbed-wire fence ran the branch road to the airbase, and down the main road he could see the low buildings on the outskirts of the town. Gently rolling hills beyond rose up to the Taurus range in the distance. The time was a quarter to eleven, and he felt hungry.

He unhooked the upper bunk and took down his bag, and exchanged his check flannel shirt for a faded yellow T-shirt. It was summer for real.

Still no sign of Preben. He reached up and pulled the cable to the compressor horns on the roof, and a deafening blast rolled across the yard. Preben's cat appeared again like a flash at the window. The guard came out from his hut, scowling, and then a large, black-bearded face came into view beside the cat. It blinked sleepily, but brightened as it caught sight of Leif.

The door swung open. "Come on over!" Preben shouted.

Leif swung down onto the running board above the wheel well, then leapt across to the red Scania, pivoting himself into the passenger seat. The cat jumped over to the driver's seat to make room for him.

Preben was sitting up in the lower bunk, dressed only in oil-streaked blue jeans and running his fingers through his black, unruly hair. He grinned and thrust a giant paw forward and squeezed Leif's hand.

"Jesus, am I happy you're back! What happened? Did they fine you?"

Leif grinned back. "No. They just took me into Uluk-isla and put me in a cell, then let me out this morning." He managed to retrieve his hand and flexed it experimentally. Nothing seemed to be broken. "They just handed me my papers back and told me I was free to leave."

"How did they treat you?"

"Pretty OK, considering. No *falaka* sticks or anything. They left me alone. But last night I . . ."

"Hold on, mate." The giant put up a hand to check him. "Have you had any breakfast? I mean, are you hungry? I can fix up something, and you can tell me the story while we eat. OK?"

"Yeah, I could do with a bit of lunch right now."

Preben shot the clock on the dashboard a glance. "Right, I'll rustle up something. You know, I'm pretty curious."

"I imagine you are. I'll just go and take a leak first."

"OK. Can you get your cooker out, too? Takes less time that way."

"Sure."

Preben yawned, showing white, surprisingly even teeth in the black beard, and then scratched his belly. A tattoo of a square-rigged ship on a shy reach, done in Japan, almost hidden behind the mass of body hair, testified to his sailor background. "Good. I'll get started in the meantime."

Leif went to the rear end of his semi-trailer and had a quick piss. The sun felt good on his back. Then he unlocked the trailer box, got his camping stove and walked around to the sunny side of Preben's Scania. The Dane had put on a red T-shirt with "Londra Camping" in faded letters across the chest. It was stretched taut and barely covered his navel, leaving a hiatus of dark hair and tanned skin. The folded-down lid on one of Preben's trailer boxes served as kitchen table. Leif sat down on the camping chair Preben handed him.

The big, grey cat came up to Leif and rubbed himself against his leg. Leif picked him up and scratched him behind the ears. The cat purred.

"Looks as if even Nick's been missing me," he said.

They were interrupted by a low whine, growing into a deep, resonating roar. A big grey-green military aircraft was coming in for landing from the direction of the Mediterranean. Before their eyes it levelled out and kept losing altitude, while its landing gear unfolded from its belly. Its course would carry it straight over their heads.

The sound of its throttled-back jet engines pounded their eardrums with a thunderous rumble as it passed over them, and they could make out the American military markings. The ground vibrated as the aircraft disappeared out of sight behind some houses. Slowly, the sound died away.

Preben shrugged, muttering, and returned to his kitchen duties, preparing meatballs and macaroni. Simple, honest grub, the way the Middle East pilots did it when they acted as chef and *maitre d'*.

He heaped the food onto paper plates and handed one to Leif. A bottle of beer appeared, as well as ketchup and a couple of tomatoes. The beer was reasonably cool. It had been stashed between the wheels of the semi-trailer bogie, shaded from the sun. To Leif it was delicious.

Between mouthfuls, Leif told Preben the complete story of his first, and with any luck, last sojourn in a Turkish prison. By now it was possible even to take an amused view of the incident, and Leif embroidered it with a number of wry details that had been conspicuously lacking while he had been there, living it. He also told about the search of his truck. Now and then the Pirate asked a question, nodded at the answer and looked thoughtful.

"Hm!" he said eventually and then started to empty the remaining food in the pans onto his empty plate. He put it on the ground and whistled for Nick. The tomcat appeared from the cab where he had been lazing in the sun and wolfed the food down. Then Preben got a clean plate out and emptied his beer bottle on it. The cat started lapping it up.

"I didn't know he drank beer," Leif remarked, amused.

"Hell, he's a veteran—nine trips. He'll eat anything that doesn't eat him first. He'll even touch whisky if you hand it to him on a finger."

The cat was lying down on the ground, stretching, while his master gently stroked his fur.

"You're really fond of that cat, aren't you?"

"Sure am." Preben grinned. "Good company on the run, doesn't talk back, completely housebroken. The truck is his home. Good guard, too—left the cab unlocked for a minute in Ramtha once, and the Arab that tried to climb in got a faceful of claws. You know, I saved his life that time when I picked him up in Damascus. One day he might even pay me back." He laughed.

On the road beyond the fence two American military jeeps rushed past, stirring up clouds of dust. They could see two men in each, dressed in the fashion of American military personnel stationed abroad: green khaki shirts with rolled-up sleeves, dark sunglasses. Then the jeeps passed out of sight behind the houses, heading for the airbase.

"Pretty active today, aren't they?" Preben remarked.

"Probably just jittery because of some new computer error. If the war comes our way, we'll just tell them to wait till we're finished."

Preben rose, went to his cab, and returned with a box of Danish cigars. He offered Leif one, but for once Leif didn't feel like smoking. Leisurely Preben lit his.

"I don't mind telling you now, Leif," he said, "but I was scared when they nailed you. I thought they were going to shave your arse for sure."

"So did I. Anyway, it was good to know that you'd be there to yell if I didn't get out in time."

"Don't mention it. You would have done the same for me, right?"

He sat with his elbows on his knees, smoking his cigar, looking towards the distant Taurus range that seemed strangely serene and harmless from where they sat. The cloud from the jeeps slowly settled. Nobody was moving about. The nearby houses and the rolling brownish-green hills had taken on a hazy, dreamlike stillness. The intensely blue sky was broken only by a few scattered clouds in the west. Nick had returned to the driver's seat to doze again. Small motes of dust danced in the yard.

Leif leaned back against the trailer wheel and up-ended his beer bottle before putting it down and belching contentedly. He closed his eyes and turned his face to the sun.

"I just can't figure out why they stopped you," Preben

said almost as if to himself. "You're sure they didn't touch your rig?"

"Not as far as I can see." Leif opened his eyes, stretched, and yawned.

Preben shrugged. "Funny. Well, you know the way the Turks are, suspicious, the whole damn bunch of them. You got off easy."

Leif nodded and looked at his watch. Nearly eleven-forty, time to get the show on the road again. With a little luck they could be out and in Bab-el-Hawa on the Syrian side of the border before nightfall. And from then on no more speed limits, just turn on the air conditioner and put the pedal to the floor.

He stretched again and sniffed at his right armpit. Not exactly Chanel No. 5, but what the hell, maybe he could have a quick shower in Cilvegözu. Otherwise it would have to be Ramtha, but by then he would probably smell more like Camel No. 5.

"Let's move," Leif said. "And thanks for the meal, I needed that."

"That's all right. I'll just clean up, and we can be off. How's your radiator?"

"Still leaking. If it gets any worse I'll have to tilt the cab and see if I can fix it."

Preben rose and threw his cigar away. He grinned. "Right, Leif, let's get down to Halat Ammar and chew camel cocks."

*   *   *

East of Adana the country consists of flat grass steppe, interspersed with clusters of low shrubbery. The road is fairly straight, but bumpy, running more or less parallel to the Mediterranean. About one hour from the town is the second of the two crossroads of the Middle East route. It is simply a road branching off to the right, southwards, and a short distance before it stands a wooden, weatherbeaten sign saying right for Syria and Saudi Arabia, and straight on for Iraq.

The southbound road soon starts curving into the foothills of the Gavurdag Mountains. Time has eroded and dulled their sharp, jagged peaks, and left rounded hills with low vegetation. The road at times runs no more than a kilometre from the blue waters of the Mediterranean. It is another hour's drive to Iskenderun, a sprawling town with wide, palm-lined boulevards leading through its western outskirts.

Once past Iskenderun the potholed tarmac road begins its ascent in earnest: a long, steep climb, running in wide serpentine curves. For trucks hauling heavy loads, those are difficult miles. Past the village of Belen the road levels out and gives the drivers a breathtaking view of Lake Amik and the lowlands beyond; on clear days it is possible to see all the way into Syria and to where the green belt, the "fertile crescent," ends and the desert takes over.

At the top the road curves around the side of the mountains in a northeasterly direction, and a long downhill roll begins. It is another dangerous stretch that taxes gearboxes and brakes, and tires and drivers. In a few places they can see monuments to those who failed: trucks and trailers twisted into fantastic shapes that had bounced down the mountainside, and sometimes gutted when belly tanks were torn open and hundreds of litres of diesel were ignited. The drivers who pass waste no time praying for the dead; they are too busy staying alive.

Down on the plain, the land changes character once more. Here the road runs past fields and groves; this is cultivated land, lush and green, with a few small villages scattered here and there.

Past the last village, the road winds along a barbed-wire fence on the right; beyond it is no-man's-land, and beyond no-man's-land is Syria. It is only a gravel road now, deeply rutted and badly kept, and the trucks stir up great clouds of brownish dust.

One comes to the last righthand bend, and there is yet one more small village on the other side, set among low hills, no more than two dozen houses, a tiny mosque, and the customs station: Cilvegözu, the end of the long trek through Turkey.

*   *   *

They rolled into Cilvegözu at a quarter past four. The little village seemed to be asleep, and there were only six other trucks and a few cars queuing up behind the white iron bar across the road. Leif rolled right up to the British-registered Ford Transcontinental that was last in the line. In his mirror he could see Preben's left door open a crack, and a grey blur jump down and disappear among the houses. Preben and Nick had honed their routine to a fine art: before the border, out of sight of official eyes, the cat left the cab and came back on the other side. If Preben had to wait long, Nick sometimes returned to the Scania for food, but he always crossed the border on his own. It was simple, it was foolproof. Who could stop a cat from sneaking across?

The water level light shone again. He cut the engine and climbed out with his jacket and his attaché case. Clouds were coming up from the south, and a chilly breeze replaced the shimmering heat.

The big Dane was already out, locking his door and looking his truck over with a dissatisfied air. "Hell, it needs a washing down," he grunted. "Damn windshield is so dirty I've got to look in my passport to see where I am. Let's get inside. You think she's still there?"

Together they climbed the two steps to the agent's office and pushed open the door. The place was exactly the way Leif remembered it from the last time. Two large maps on the yellow walls, covering Europe and the Near East, and a row of chairs. There were only two drivers there as they entered. Leif recognized neither of them, but nodded in greeting.

He looked left. Behind a glass partition, at a desk, sat an incredibly beautiful girl. She looked up, smiled shyly and returned their nods. Leif took the cigarette from his mouth, knocked cautiously at the door in the partition, opened it and stuck his head inside.

"Excuse me, do you know where Mr. Bey is?"

The girl hesitated, then said, "He kom . . . soon. Pliss vait."

Leif nodded, closed the door and sat down beside Preben, regarding the girl out of the corner of his eye. Her long, dark hair was tied back with a pink ribbon in a ponytail down her back. She worked as the agent's secretary. None of the drivers knew her name, but her face was known to all of them. She had a gold ring on her left hand, and the shy smile and nod was as far as anybody got.

Preben and Leif sat quietly smoking. The clock on the wall ticked away, and fifteen minutes later the agent came in with a sheaf of papers in his hand. He was a fairly young man, moustachioed, and smartly dressed in a dark blue suit. They rose and shook hands with him. Bey was a good man, spoke excellent English and got things done in less time than the lazy lot at Kapikule at the other end of Turkey—and his secretary was a sight for road-sore eyes during the wait.

"How's everything?" Leif asked.

The agent threw his hands out. "Ah, not so good. Not many TIR trucks passing through, with the ferry operating. You know."

They managed to look sympathetic as they handed over their passports, carnets, and TIR papers. Bey riffled through them, checking the load statements, and said, "Probably finished sometime this evening, I hope. You go get something to eat, OK?" He smiled again and disappeared through his secretary's room and into his own office.

Leif and Preben went over to the small restaurant next door. It was only a large room, painted in pale blue and with scattered wooden chairs and tables. They bought beer and Turkish rice stew and sat down. They were alone except for a man in a sandy, grey-brown military uniform who reclined in one corner.

After their meal, they sat talking and smoking for over an hour. The uniformed man left. Leif and Preben remained, waiting for the border officials to get their thing together. What was handled in fifteen minutes in northern Europe took hours and days in these parts of the world. Patience was not a virtue, it was a necessity.

The sun had gone down when they came out again, and the chilly wind had increased. Golden-red clouds formed a magnificent epilogue to the sunset. Preben went to look for the agent, while Leif made a quick tour of his trailer boxes to fetch things. A few minutes later he had fresh coffee going in his cab.

The Pirate returned with his cat and another man in tow. The man turned out to be the driver of the white Ford Transcontinental; he was in his forties, short and wiry, wore a blue woolen cap and had a tattoo saying "Scotland forever" on the back of his left hand.

"A brother in need," Preben explained as they all piled into the cab. "Didn't have the heart to let him sit alone all evening."

The Scotsman's name was Jock. Leif shook hands with him, and Jock and the cat scampered into the bottom bunk while Preben hoisted his massive frame into the passenger seat and pulled the door shut.

"Well, what happened?" Leif asked as he got three plastic mugs out. "Or rather, is anything happening?"

"No," Preben admitted. "Doesn't seem to be any action at all in the customs building. Bey apologized and promised to investigate."

"Oh shit."

Jock appeared to have grasped the gist of the conversation. "Aye," he said in his strong accent, "mark me words, we'll be sitting here all night. Might as well have a wee dram." He grinned and pulled a bottle of Chivas Regal from his inside jacket pocket. "Just bought a drap from the wee tax-free across."

Leif and Preben whistled with delight, and laced their coffee heavily. Even Nick got his share from one of Preben's fingers. Leif plugged his Roger Whittaker cassette into the stereo, and the three of them sipped their steaming, reinforced coffee and talked. As always, the subject gravitated towards trucks and trucking.

Night fell while they talked, and the temperature in the cab dropped. Leif switched on the heater and then reached up to turn on the faint red light in the ceiling. The drivers called it the "ficki-ficki light," because it set the right mood when one happened to have consenting females in for a visit.

Leif poured more coffee and Chivas all around. It's moments like this I'll be missing, he thought, sitting in my cab far away from home, feeling mellow, talking to friends. On impulse, he leaned forward to look out. The hills were dark; the stars had come out, and only a few lights burned in the surrounding houses. The village seemed to be dead.

Jock started telling them the story of a serious accident he had had on the Rome run. With half-closed eyes Leif listened, leaning against the door and scratching a contentedly purring Nick behind the ears.

A knock on the door on the driver's side interrupted them. Leif turned the volume down and opened the door. The soft red light fell on the agent's upturned face.

"Hello," Leif said. "What's up?"

Bey gestured apologetically. "I just talked with the customs officers. They tell me that the border is closed. Tomorrow they will search all vehicles."

Leif slowly scratched his beard. "Why?"

Bey shrugged. "They don't know or they don't say. I don't know."

"Oh shit. Well, thanks for telling us."

"Sorry about it. Good night, anyway."

"Good night." Leif pulled the door shut.

"What did he say?" Preben enquired.

Leif related the news and added, "Typical; first a night in prison and now this." Maybe he really ought to ditch his porn mags if the Turks had a serious *kabinkontroll* coming up.

"Ah, hell." Preben held up the whisky bottle. "Then let's make a night of it, lads, and cops and customs officials be damned. Here's to the open road and no speed limits."

10

THE MORNING LIGHT filtered through the closed blinds and gave the room a soft, chariouscuro quality. Only faint noises from the street intruded and added to the atmosphere of unreality.

The man lay sprawled on the sofa, sandalled feet on the floor, his gaze flickering across the ceiling with its single chandelier. His chin and sunken cheeks were covered with thick, black stubble, and his strong Levantine features were a stark contrast to the pallor of his face. His eyes were puffy and dull from lack of sleep.

He had not been outside for over a month, except when they had changed hotels.

He raised his arm and looked at his wristwatch. Past nine. The telephone stood silent on the table. He reached out and found the crumpled pack of cigarettes, got one out, and lit it with unsteady hands. He smoked too much and slept too little, and there was a constriction across his chest.

Out of the corner of his eye, he was aware of Majio silently watching him from the adjacent room of the hotel suite. He did not turn his head. He seldom spoke to Majio or Abul anyway. It was enough that they were always there, one of them guarding the door in the corridor, and the other in here with him, always with their weapons at hand.

He knew that the guard outside the door did not go unnoticed. But in war-torn Beirut there was nothing extraordinary about it. He himself tried not to arouse suspicion or invite questions.

He lived in the perpetual twilight of hotel rooms with closed blinds. Now and then men came to see him and he would take them into the bedroom, away from Majio and Abul, where they would whisper bits and pieces of information before they would leave as stealthily as they had come.

As stationary coordinator and communications link, he was the only possibility for the others of being warned if anything went wrong. His outside contacts were a few slender threads, along which trickled erratic and sometimes uncertain information; but he did not dare to extend his net too far. Somewhere someone might sense a disturbance and trace it back to him, and he would be waiting there, like a rat in a trap.

But he knew what it was like outside, he knew that they were being hunted and had been hunted for weeks. It had been foreseen that they would be. What had not been foreseen was the demoralizing effect of sitting motionless in the midst of the raging hunt.

Another thing that had not been foreseen was that the Israelis should start a hunt of their own. He had not been able to determine for certain whether that had anything to do with them, but it was disturbing, as well as disrupting.

Slowly he sat up. His damp shirt hung loosely; he had lost some weight in the last weeks. He stubbed the cigarette out in the ashtray and rose. Through the doorway he could see Majio getting up, too, and going over to the door. Time to change guards.

The constriction across his chest started to blossom as sharp needles of pain radiated into his throat and left arm. The familiar giant fist reached out to squeeze his ribs. He opened his mouth and tried to suck in air. A steel ring seemed to clamp around his chest, relentlessly contracting, obscuring his vision with exploding stars.

Where is the jar? he thought desperately. He managed to force a hand into his trouser pocket, then remembered that it was in the green bag on the chair. The pain was building up, white fire exploding inside him, roaring in his ears. Frantically he dug into the bag, and found the small glass jar. The cold sweat stood out from his brow as he forced it open and placed two nitroglycerin tablets under his tongue.

He couldn't let his watchdogs see him like this; he had to get out of sight. On weak, rubbery legs he reached the bathroom and managed to close the door before he half collapsed on the floor, his right hand clutching the washbasin.

The agony seemed eternal. The pain came and went in waves, huge, paralyzing breakers crashing into his chest. He opened his mouth as if to scream, tried to draw breath between his sobs. Finally the pain lessened, and he was aware of having a heart, a wildly beating heart. He tried to get up and nearly slipped on something hard. Dumbly, he realized that it was the glass jar. He must have dropped it.

He dragged himself up on legs that could barely support him and held on to the washbasin, looking at his own reflection in the mirror: he looked revolting. His hair hung in damp, clotted strands across his forehead. His eyes bulged from his sickly grey face. With trembling fingers he turned on the cold water and splashed his face with it. He let it run a long time.

An insistent banging on the bathroom door interrupted him. He quickly turned off the water, grabbed a towel, and picked the jar up from the floor before opening the door.

Abul's dark, impassive stare met him. "*Telefon,*" he said simply.

The telephone was ringing with shrill signals. On shaky legs he pushed past Abul and picked up the receiver. "*Na'am*?"

"There is a call for you from abroad," said the operator at the Beirut exchange. To avoid the risk of having the calls go through the hotel switchboard, they had a direct line into the suite.

"*Shokran*. Please put it through." His tongue was swollen, stiff, his voice grating. He lifted the towel and started wiping his face. There was a series of clicks replaced by the hiss of a long distance connection, then the familiar voice he had not heard for almost three weeks.

"*Ana as-Saif.*"

His mouth was dry as he automatically replied, "*Ana at-Turs.*"

"Report."

No phrases of greeting, no expressions of emotion, just an order.

In the predetermined code phrases he told—uncertainly at first, but then with greater ease—of the KGB's shakedown of the Middle East area, and of the resulting confusion among the Palestinian organizations, adding the observation that so far the search seemed to have got them nowhere. Then, fitting it into the framework of the code as best he could, he told of the Zionists' recent, unexpected activity.

When he finished, the voice at the other end was silent. He listened to the hiss and faint crackle of static. Then, abruptly, "*Kuwayyis*. Good."

There was a click and the line went dead. Slowly he replaced the receiver.

He was alone in the room. Abul had left as soon as he had come out of the bathroom and was in the next room. He sank down on the sofa again, drained. His head was starting to ache, the inevitable side effect of the nitroglycerin tablets. The cold sweat was breaking out once more.

A small coronary; he knew what it meant. It was the

third since his heart attack two years ago. What if he had a massive one, here in the hotel room?

And what about Majio and Abul? They had seen his deterioration, although he had never told anybody about his bad heart. He was a link, but a chafed link.

He had to keep himself together for nine more days; but here, in the diffuse morning light of a Beirut hotel room, he saw with icy clarity all the things that could go wrong in that time.

In the street a car honked twice, but he did not hear it. He sat motionless, his uneven pulse pounding at his temples, and felt numb fear.

* * *

Leif stood by the open door of his Scania 141, with arms folded across his chest, a cigarette dangling in his mouth, and watched the Turkish customs officials search the trucks ahead.

He felt uncomfortable; he was next, and he felt sorry he hadn't quietly ditched his stock of porn mags in the night. The Turks were working in three teams, each consisting of three customs officers and an armed soldier accompanying them. They were brusque, efficient, thorough—and then some.

The drivers had been roughly awoken before seven. Leif had tumbled out of his cab in jeans and sandals only, still groggy with sleep. The customs officers had marched him to the rear end of the trailer where he had to be the witness as they cut the cluster of seals. Then they had told him in no uncertain terms to get his vehicle ready for the coming search before moving on to Preben's red Scania for a repeat performance.

Now he stood eyeing the proceedings which had already lasted for over two hours. He had folded the sides of the semi-trailer and rolled back the heavy tarpaulin, and taken the opportunity to inspect the load. Things were still in their places, undamaged, except for three cans of Rugasol which had banged into each other and started leaking. The thick, yellow goo covered a couple of square metres of trailer floor, sticking to the neighbouring wooden crates.

The big Dane came sauntering up behind him and stopped to lean against the cab. He, like Leif, wore only jeans and a T-shirt. The morning had dawned clear and warm, without wind.

"What do you make of it?"

Leif shrugged before answering. "Don't know. Probably just a crackdown to make us toe the line. Wish they would get on with it. The sooner we get to Babel-Hawa, the better."

"Yeah." Preben slowly scratched his beard. "Carrying any?"

"Sure." But now was hardly the time to attempt to speed things up with bribes of that kind. They would just have to hold on and be grateful if they weren't discovered.

"Trouble up ahead," Preben muttered, and then jerked his head to indicate the line behind them. "And more on its way."

Leif nodded. A West German driver was engaged in a heated argument with the customs official further up; a lot of arm-waving and pointing was going on to a chorus of angry voices.

A few more vehicles had added themselves to the line during the night, among them a Swedish-registered, battered old Volvo. They could be seen every now and then along the route: they came mostly from Britain or one of the Scandinavian countries and were packed with youngsters heading east for the adventure of their lives. He could see boys with hair down to their shoulders, and girls prancing about in cut-off jeans and T-shirts, no bras.

Bloody stupid kids, he thought. God only knew what

kind of stuff some of them might be carrying. Preben was right, they were in for trouble. The bus and the passengers would be searched thoroughly. Today every vehicle queueing up at the border was getting it, even the private cars. They had been searched first of all.

"Here they come," Preben said softly. "Good luck, mate. See you in Bab-el-Hawa—*in'ish Allah.*" He turned and walked back to his own rig.

One of the search teams was approaching. Leif felt his pulse race. The armed soldier and the three customs officers looked all business.

One of them carried a clipboard and a sheaf of papers. He stopped to pull out a fresh sheet, put it on top, and started making notes. With a brief exchange of words, the Turk with the clipboard and one other climbed into the cab. Leif saw them jerk the bottom bunk loose and start rummaging about.

The third customs officer touched Leif's arm for his attention, then pointed to the nearest of the left-hand trailer boxes. "*Açmak!*"

There was no misunderstanding him. Leif fished out the keys from his pocket, removed the padlock, and folded the lid down.

The soldier hung back, impassively, while the customs officer peered at the gear inside, hefted the hydraulic jack, opened the toolboxes. Now and then the Turk asked a question, bridging the communications gap with the usual assortment of international words and sign language, and Leif replied in kind.

Finally the customs officer was satisfied. While Leif locked up, the two who had searched his cab came over and joined the group. A short conversation took place. Leif grasped that it must be a description of the contents of the trailer-box. The Turk with the clipboard jotted down more notes. Leif tried to look neither nonchalant, nor scared, and heaved a quiet sigh of relief. Obviously they hadn't found his porn mags, unless they had pocketed them for themselves, knowing that the driver would be in no position to complain.

The foodstuffs and the camping gear in the other left-hand trailer-box and in the one on the right were quickly gone through. More notes, then Leif could lock them up again.

The inspection of the goods in the semi-trailer took much longer, almost half an hour, and at the end Leif was hot and grimy and sweating. He had to lift and shove and push and strain, clearing spaces and seeing that everything could be got at and scrutinized. The customs officers had produced his TIR papers and load sheets, and ticked off everything on the list. They were thorough and suspicious. He had to get tools to break the wooden crates open to show the contents and then hammer the lids back on. The cans of Rugasol were shoved and knocked on, to make sure that each and every one seemed to weigh and sound the same. The thick $1^{1}/_{2}$-metre by $4^{1}/_{4}$-metre sheets of white styrene foam caused the greatest consternation. Finally he had to cut the straps tying them together to show that there was nothing in between them.

The soldier stayed outside, carbine over his shoulder, the Turk with the clipboard beside him. Finally one of the Turks indicated that Leif could jump down again. He was in a foul mood as he looked at the disarray. He would have to get Preben to help him push everything back into place, distributing the weight evenly and tying some of the stuff down, before he could think of rolling the tarp back on.

He glanced back and saw that the Pirate had problems of his own. The team who had done Jock's Transcontinental had moved on to Preben's Scania and was busy throwing stuff around inside his cab. Not even the towering bulk and open displeasure of the Dane seemed to deter them.

And his own ordeal wasn't over. One of the customs

officers pointed to the diesel tanks, showing that he wanted them opened. Leif unscrewed the caps one by one and stood back while they prodded their interiors with a thin, flexible metal rod. More notes.

Meanwhile, another Turk had removed his cap and taken a flashlight from his pocket. Leif noticed the dust on his trouser knees and the streaks of dirt and diesel on his uniform shirt as he bent down and crawled under the semi-trailer to scrutinize its belly. The other three had broken out cigarettes and were smoking while they followed the progress of their colleague under the semi-trailer. He moved slowly on hands and knees, peering into all nooks and crannies, shining his flashlight. He knocked on the spare wheels in their metal brackets, listened to the resounding thump from hard-pumped tires, and crawled on.

He reached the forward end of the semi-trailer and crawled out to stretch his limbs. The customs officer with the clipboard gestured to him, said something, and he shrugged and went to ground again, this time on his back, and wriggled in under the tractor unit.

His gaze and the flashlight travelled from the front end, past the radiator and the huge diesel engine, to the rear. When he came to the bogie he stopped and seemed to reach up with his left hand and test something, then he shrugged and clicked his flashlight off. He wriggled out from under the truck, got on his feet. The others helped dust him off.

The officer with the clipboard scrawled a little more and nodded to Leif. "You OK," he said and turned to his colleagues. Together they moved off down the waiting line, heading for the next victim.

Leif was sweaty and dirty, but relieved. The search had been a tough one. He climbed into the cab and lit a long-needed cigarette. The inside was a mess. He sighed and started to tidy up.

Ten minutes later Preben came up and surveyed the disorder. "Did they find anything?"

"No, but they sure messed things up. How about you?"

"Nope." The Pirate grinned. "Had them stashed inside my Kysor this time. But the buggers took a box of my favourite cigars."

"No use complaining, mate." Leif grimaced and looked around. "Mind giving me a hand?"

*   *   *

He stood across the road from the customs house dressed in white *aba'a* and *keffiyeh*, the traditional flowing robe and headgear, looking down the row of trucks, fingering his scar, deep in ponderous thought.

That search. And the news from Beirut on the phone, less than an hour ago.

Something was very wrong.

Somewhere, somehow, a leak had occurred.

He felt no immediate concern for themselves. Their car had passed the search without difficulty; and now, as the uniformed men moved away from the Swedish Scania, he could not help but feel a surge of triumph. Their painstaking work had held up. He realized that those who had done the search could not, would not, be allowed to know the full truth. That was their final triumph: the searchers still had to play the game on their conditions.

He rubbed his scar again.

*   *   *

The white iron bar rose slowly, creaking, until it pointed straight up. Free to roll at last. Leif moved the gear lever into low, feeling the cogs engage in the gearbox. He let the clutch out, and the Scania rumbled forward, past the armed soldier in a sandy, grey-brown uniform and white helmet, and into the eight kilometres of no-man's-land that separated Turkey from Syria.

Preben was trailing him. They had helped each other rearrange and tie down their loads and roll the tarpaulins back on: a shitty job, with dried mud and road dust coming loose in great flakes. The agent seemed to have taken the day off, so they had gone into the customs house to repossess their papers, have their passports stamped and get seals at the backs of their semitrailers. It had cost them the usual *baksheesh*, a twenty-lira bribe. By then, Leif would gladly have paid fifty to get on the road again, and damn the shower he needed so badly.

In his mirrors he could see Preben slow down and disappear from sight behind a low hill as the road turned. Stopping for Nick. Leif grinned at his sudden vision of the cat sitting calmly by the roadside, waiting to be picked up, as if he had phoned for a bloody taxi.

The Scania rolled along past low, gentle, brown-green hills, past small fields with grazing sheep tended by ageing shepherds under a sun in a nearly cloudless sky. On the hills to his left were ruins: long abandoned buildings of reddish stone, crumbling, worn with time. Perhaps they were from the time of the Crusades.

The car startled him as it rushed past, a white Mazda cutting in sharply in front of him. He had a glimpse of the two men in the back seat, dressed in Arab fashion, before the dust blotted it out and the car disappeared around the bend.

He swore. Hell, they were all crazy down here.

He looked in his mirrors and made the truck slow down to a crawl, waiting for Preben to catch up.

11

ARI OFER'S OFFICE appeared like the eye of a tropical storm to David Bar-Sharon as the two of them met on the fifteenth. All around, the Eye of David was buzzing with activity. The meeting of the coordination group on the previous evening had been brief and rather inconclusive. It had been decided that Dov Kultz, assisted by Bill Herman, would spend the day introducing the two American computer experts to the DMI machines, while Ari and David handled the short list that the Shabak had distilled from the chaos.

The list consisted of eleven names; David and Ari were able to cross out five. The meeting ended with a decision to try and fill the remaining six names with further facts and detail.

The next day was a bright, untypically chilly day, and the meeting room seemed cold, expansive. Ofer motioned David, Dov and Bill, who now felt established enough to appear in blue jeans and gaudy sports shirts under light windbreakers, to sit down, and gave them a quick rundown on the Mossad activity during the past two days. Then he said with a wolfish grin:

"But the most promising line is the one David is going to tell us about. I can't say how much it will be worth, but it does form an interesting picture. David?"

"Right. What we've been doing is to check all known Palestinian leaders capable of handling anything of this nature. The leaders are the interesting persons; they're the ones that can't be easily replaced. Yesterday we had a list of eleven names that we hadn't been able to pinpoint. Ari and I were able to cut it down to six, to be checked further. Three of those survived till today as possible alternatives. Plus that a fourth name added itself, rather unexpectedly, to the list. I'll come to him shortly."

He fished out a pack of cigarettes, lit one and went on. "First candidates are Hashi Tabari and Ahmed Shefir. They've been working together in Habash's PFLP since the late sixties. There are facts to indicate that they, in their active time, were deeply involved in the Dawson's Field incident and subsequently in the killing of Wasfi Tel. Experienced lads. Since then they've moved up in the world. They don't go very near the dirty work these days, they just plan it and have others do it. After all, they have families, kids, good houses in Beirut—good salaries."

"They nearly got themselves on our death list," Ofer said, blowing a creditable smoke ring. "What makes them interesting this time?"

"Well," David said, "their relationship with Habash seems to have been somewhat unstable. There have been quarrels, about strategy, about tactics, about doctrine. In '75 they were virtually expelled from the PFLP, for instance, then in '77, after the Lebanese civil war, they were bosom pals again, that sort of stuff. Last November they were quarrelling again, reports say, and the upshot was that Tabari and Shefir went to Algiers in a hurry on December 7."

"Algiers? Hm."

"Yes, and since then they haven't been heard from. And we all know that a trip to Algiers is a common first step if you're getting a new identity or planning to go to ground."

"Quarrelling a cover?" Dov Kultz asked.

"Hard to say. Might well be."

"If those two have gone active again they'd definitely make a likely team," Ofer said. "But go on."

"Third on the list is Fayez Hijazi. He's never been known to take a direct part in any act of terrorism, or have any ideas of his own for terrorism. He's just the best damned back-up man in the business. If you want a coordinator to handle the logistics of the thing, or pull the right strings if anything goes wrong, then Hijazi is your man. And he has been gone since mid-November of last year. Nothing new about him has come up since yesterday."

"An intriguing puzzle," Ofer remarked, "that lacks one important piece. Someone for him to play back-up man to."

"I think," David said, "that I shall have to apologize to Bill. It wasn't all silence. We did hear something. Rumour has it, or rather the tiniest whisper has it, that el-Tha'ir is back."

Ari Ofer's jaw dropped slowly, then a wide, delighted grin spread across his visage. "El-Tha'ir, you say? Why, that's marvellous, that's simply bloody marvellous!" Ofer rocked back and slapped his thigh.

Dov Kultz said soberly, "I'm sorry, I'm not familiar with this one."

Ofer nodded and lit another cigarette, then said, "Mahmoud el-Tha'ir, meaning by the way"—he turned to Bill Herman—"Mahmoud the Avenger, our pet conundrum, you might say. He's one of the few and definitely the highest ranking terrorist whose true identity we haven't been able to determine. We know him only by his *nom de guerre*, and by his reputation. There wasn't one case of terrorism in the early seventies that he wasn't said to be mixed up in. Lots of it exaggerated, of course. But one thing we're certain of is that he was involved up to here in the OPEC raid in '75. It's curious, he seems to really have had it in for the conservative Arab states. Anyway, shortly after the Lebanon business broke out he disappeared. Some said he had been killed in the fighting in Beirut, others that he had gone to Russia. And we haven't heard a thing from or about him since. So maybe he did go to Russia. At least that possibility makes it all the more interesting."

"He can't have stayed in Russia all this time," David said.

Ofer shrugged. "Maybe not. Does your whisper say anything at all specific?"

"Not a thing. Just a vague, prophetic, el-Tha'ir is back. But it's insistent."

"Ah." Ofer looked thoughtfully at Bill Herman, Dov Kultz, and David Bar-Sharon before he said, "Well, I have something to add to that. There's been quite a substantial sum paid from the 'mystery' account in Zürich."

"Surprise," David said softly. "Where did it go?"

"The Kredietbank in Gent, Belgium. An account in the name of Esteban Breyten, a Bolivian businessman. Señor Breyten is a ski bum, apparently. Spent a lot of money in Austria. There have also been cheques drawn on various banks in Beirut."

David said, "The Belgian account was set up to finance this operation. The money spent in Austria could indicate that they trained there."

Ofer nodded. "It's a tempting picture, particularly considering that the Austrians always have been soft towards the Palestinians."

"I suppose you'll trace the money?" Bill Herman said.

"Of course," Ofer said without enthusiasm. "I doubt it will do us a lot of good, though. At the end we'll probably find some skiing instructor and mountaineer with a faulty memory or a fractured leg—or both. It's more important that we dig up more information about those four names we have."

"If Hijazi is in any way involved," David said almost

longingly, "then there must be a leader somewhere, and el-Tha'ir would fit the bill just beautifully."

"If Hijazi is el-Tha'ir's back-up man, what would he be doing right now, when they only seem to be waiting?" Dov Kultz asked.

"He'd be holed up somewhere," David replied, "with his ear to the ground to get the drift of the hue and cry, ready to warn el-Tha'ir if things get too hot. You don't have to be a strategic genius to see that."

"Where?"

"Beirut," Bill Herman said at once. "Money was paid to Beirut from that Belgian account, wasn't it? Haven't you tried Beirut?"

There was a moment of silence, then:

"Haven't we tried Beirut, the man says." Ari Ofer made a tired grimace. "Of course we've tried bloody Beirut. It's the first place we always try. Do you realize what Beirut is like? You've got two factions of right-wing Christians, you've got any number of Palestinian factions, Christian and Moslem, you've got left-wing militia, possibly Syrian troops, even Lebanese troops. And they're having a bloody round-robin tournament—you don't know who will be fighting whom on any given day. And the rumours, the suspicion . . ."

"You haven't heard anything, then?" Bill Herman asked.

"You've got it." Ofer shrugged eloquently. "Well, it's only been two days so far. The question is, how many more days will we get in which to try and find these people? Personally, I'm prepared to eat the *keffiyeh* off the head of the next *fedayeen* we catch if none of these four are involved. Should I suggest in my report that the search be specialized along those lines?"

Dov Kultz looked up from his perpetual note-making, gazed out the window for a moment, nodded, and went back to making notes.

"We'll have to gamble a little in any case," David said.

"All right," Ofer said. "Then I also think it's about time all good men came to the aid of the party."

"Eh?" Bill Herman said.

"Meaning we ask around at every intelligence and security service in Europe and the Middle East that we could reasonably contact, to hear if they have heard or seen anything lately of Tabari, Shefir, Hijazi, or el-Tha'ir. Right." He stubbed out the last in a series of cigarettes and rose abruptly. "Let's get busy."

*   *   *

Damascus fell behind, swallowed by the night. The traffic was the merest trickle, and the Scania's speedo needle was touching 110 kph on the well-paved but uneven road.

Leif, relaxed and cheerful again, leaned back in the driver's seat. He and Preben had traded cassettes at Bab-el-Hawa, and the music of Danish group Savage Rose was in his speakers. A bright orange light shone on the dashboard. He looked down and saw that the fuel gauge had climbed almost all the way to the 1/1 mark, and reached out to turn off the pumps that transferred diesel from the semi-trailer tanks to the main tractor unit tank. The orange light went out, and the only light in the cab was the soft glow of the gauges.

A phantom shape outlined in an incredible array of yellow, blue, red, and green lights swished by and receded in the mirrors: one of the local buses, decked out Arab style. The taste of auto decor in these parts was appalling. Just from looking at one of those things in the dark, you'd have a hard time guessing whether they were coming or going.

He flicked his floodlights back on, and the beam from his four Cibiés drilled a tunnel in the darkness. They had cleared Bab-el-Hawa in less than three hours, mostly due to the efforts of Mr. Lovely. That was the nickname among the pilots of the rotund, smiling agent, who offered them steaming hot, thick coffee while he sent his subordinates scurrying after the customs personnel.

Leif had spent five hours over the wheel, while the big Scania roared along the 350 uneventful kilometres down to Damascus. The city itself had been the usual shock. Daytime or nighttime, Damascus was a maelstrom of pedestrians, small lorries, bicycles, animals, and cars. No time for sight-seeing, you were too busy watching out that you didn't run down some skinny moped with three Arabs clinging to it or an old man on a donkey, all of them crossing without warning and going off hell-for-leather down the narrow lanes.

The time was almost eleven, time to park for the night and get some chow. Ten minutes later, he steered the truck to the right onto a stretch of new asphalt that ran in a big loop before rejoining the main road further down. He stopped where the loop was furthest from the road, hit the parking brake, turned the stereo off and the lights fore and aft, leaving only the orange position lights on, and let the diesel idle.

Preben came crawling up alongside before turning his lights down. The big tomcat moved over as the Pirate reached across the passenger seat to roll his window down. The night air was cool and fresh.

"It's only another eighty kilometres to Ramtha," Preben shouted over the idling engines.

"I know," Leif shouted back. "But I don't feel like driving any more tonight. Let's fix up some supper before we turn in."

"Right. Your place or mine?" Preben grinned.

"My turn. I'll just go and take a crap first."

Preben nodded and opened the door to let Nick out. Leif got out a roll of toilet paper and lit a cigarette before cutting the engine. He turned off his position lights but left the cab light on as he jumped down.

He walked off a bit before he stopped and dug a little hole with his foot in the hard-packed soil. Then he pulled his jeans and briefs down and squatted, Arab fashion, over the hole. He puffed on his cigarette and thoughtfully pinched his side. Hell, he reflected, I'm getting fat. No wonder, about the only exercise I get is beating time to the stereo. I'm going to need a little jogging, not to mention a crash course in etiquette, when I get back and out of this life. It's a wonder Annika can stand me.

He hadn't thought of Annika for a long time. Wonder what she's doing? Probably watching TV. And here I am, squatting in Syria with the wind caressing my arse.

Overhead, scattered stars shone from a partly clouded sky. He looked around. The landscape was completely dark, with not a single pinpoint of artificial light anywhere except the faint glow from the cab of his truck in the blackness.

*   *   *

Holston closed the door and walked over to the nearest leather armchair and sank down in it. He felt tired, and his leg ached. His watch read past midnight. He ought to go home and get some sleep.

The Director came around his desk and sat down in the sofa. He, too, looked tired, Holston reflected. The blue eyes under the greying eyebrows were heavy, and the tie, patterned with squares in various shades of brown and with a blue stripe, hung slightly askew.

"Care for some coffee, Art?" The Director regarded Holston.

"No thanks." For once Holston would have cared more for a stiff drink. But unfortunately one didn't put it that way to the teetotalling Director.

"I hope I didn't drag you away from anything important." Holston shook his head, and the Director went on, "I have spoken to the President and to the Security Adviser. They are worried . . ."

"They're worried?" Holston put in sourly. "Well, they're not alone."

"They're worried," the Director continued smoothly, "because they're beginning to feel a certain pressure from the State Department, which in its turn is being pestered by the press. You appreciate the situation?"

Holston nodded.

"There's no question of criticizing your way of handling this. You've been very discreet. It's just that the inevitable waves have been made, and the pressure is on for an explanation. Unfortunately, we've had some rather bad press recently. Jack Anderson . . ."

"The President," Holston interrupted and felt his mouth set in stubborn lines, "will have to tell the Security Adviser to tell State to tell inquisitive journalists something suitable to stall them. There's no question of the media having this one. Not yet."

"And how does one justify that standpoint? There's bound to be repercussions, you know."

"One doesn't. I still think it might well have been part of the terrorists' plans that only the Russians would know what had happened. They might do something really desperate if they find out that the world knows about their—plaything. For good or bad, it has to be played on their terms, silently."

There was silence, then, suddenly, the Director grinned. "All right, Art, that's what I've already told them. They agree, but they're still worried."

Holston nodded with a curious sense of relief. "We're all worried, Stan."

"Yeah. Well, actually I called you here to get your personal view of things. How's the operation going?"

"To be brief, we're treading water." Holston shrugged wearily. "None of our stations has come up with anything concrete. The Israelis are currently running down a list of Palestinian possibilities, probably our best line so far—provided they *are* Palestinians. It was the main item in Herman's report from Tel Aviv today."

The Director nodded. "Yes, I have read it."

"That's about it. You already know most of what little we know. The OSR has drawn up a variety of scenarios with a list of possible targets, persons—although I can't see how somebody would want to go after somebody else with a nuke—installations, military, industrial, civic, etcetera."

"Yes, I've read that, too." The Director pondered for a moment, then said, "Tell me, Art, what's your opinion of the target? Israel?"

"No."

"Why not?"

Holston hesitated before answering. "Let's say it's just a feeling I have. You might say that the target is right, but as I see it the facts simply don't tally." He looked at his watch again and realized resignedly that there wouldn't be any sleep for some time yet. The Director looked far too interested.

"If I can change my mind about that coffee, I'll try to explain . . ."

12

THE WATER WAS ICY COLD. He closed his eyes and splashed it liberally across his face and chest.

"Brrr!" he snorted and looked up at Nick, who sat on top of the red cab, licking his fur. The sun, hidden behind Preben's cab, was barely above the horizon. It looked like it was going to be a fine day.

Leif put the water-can away between the top of the diesel tank and the frame of the semi-trailer, and began towelling himself. "Let's see if we can't wake the big bastard," he muttered, climbing back into his own cab. He rummaged through his stock of cassettes until he found what he wanted, then plugged the cassette into the deck and turned the volume up to max. He grabbed a spray bottle of window cleaning fluid and a roll of toilet paper, jumped down and set about cleaning his dirty windshield.

From the speakers in the open doors came the first strains of "Anitra's Dance," strong and clear, rolling across the arid landscape. Leif kept spraying his windshield as he hummed along. Then he heard a curtain being pulled aside and a throaty voice rumble, "What the *shit*!?"

Leif finished spraying and shouted back, "Rise and shine, mate! What's the matter, don't you like classical music in the morning?"

"What?" Preben himself came into view.

Leif grinned and climbed into the cab to turn the volume down. "I said rise and shine, mate. Let's get rolling. With a bit of luck we can have a last one at Humphrey's tonight, and tomorrow you can have your camel cocks."

Preben blinked sleepily. His black, curly hair stood on end. "Yo. Sure. Guess you're right." His head disappeared.

Leif was busy wiping the glass to a sparkle when, a minute later, Preben's head reappeared in the window.

"What's that you're playing, by the way?"

"Grieg. From the 'Peer Gynt Suite.' Norwegian stuff."

The Dane scratched his hairy chest. "You don't say?"

* * *

Getting diesel before the border proved impossible. They tried a few stations and were met with cries of "*Ma'afi, ma'afi,*" "finish, nothing more."

Outside Meskine they were offered 200 litres for seventy Syrian pounds, an outrageous price that both of them turned down. The trouble in these parts was that you didn't just roll up at the next filling station and shout, "Fill 'er up, Charlie," or maybe Ahmed. The pumps were almost never equipped with counters showing the sum total, so you had to haggle first and be sure you were able to read Arab digits afterwards.

"What the hell," the Pirate muttered after their fifth try, "we have enough to make it into Jordan. We'll get diesel there."

Shortly after ten in the morning they rolled into Dara'a on the Syrian side of the border and handed in their papers at the station. As there were several TIR trucks ahead of them, they went across the road to the mini-sized café and gingerly sat down on the equally mini-sized wickerwork chairs under a sign that proudly proclaimed, "We hav everythink we hav sigaret," and ordered 7-Up and tea Arab style, hot and sweet.

Half an hour later a man came back with their papers,

all squared. Shaking their heads in disbelief they walked
back to their rigs to drive the six kilometres of no-man's-
land to Ramtha.

*   *   *

"How did it go?" Preben asked as Leif climbed into the
passenger seat of the red Scania.

"It's green," Leif replied. "He told us to go and have
a meal in the restaurant, and he will come in and tell
us when we can go down and have a shower."

The time was a quarter past one. They had handed
the Ramtha agent their papers and the money for the
dues, and had stood in line to fill in entry forms and
have their passports stamped in the big, white customs
building where Arabs in flowing robes rubbed elbows
with gentlemen in business suits and truck pilots in jeans
and colourful jackets while King Hussein benevolently
looked them over from his giant portrait on the wall
behind the full-length counter.

Preben had gone back to his truck to fix up some
coffee while Leif went in search of the restaurant owner
to arrange for the use of the staff shower. A friendship
which had grown with every trip had put Leif in this
privileged position.

"Good," Preben said and handed Leif a cup of hot,
steaming coffee. From the speakers came the cheerful,
English-speaking voice of the Israeli radio station an-
nouncer.

Leif emptied his cup. "All right, let's go. I'm hungry,
and do I need a shower. My jeans are about due for
an oil-change, too."

As they crossed the yard, a white car caught Leif's
attention; a white Mazda, with Lebanese license plates.
He slowed his step. Was it the same one that had passed
him between Cilvegözu and Bab-el-Hawa? Well, so what?
Only that the driver was a crazy bastard. He shrugged.

There were so many crazy bastards around it wasn't worth it to bother about them all.

In the restaurant several chairs and a few tables were broken. Preben raised his eyebrows. "Seems we missed a party."

Leif scratched his beard. "Yeah. The bastards never wait for us."

They found an intact table and ordered beer, decided to have the meal after the showers, and started to write postcards instead. Presently the owner appeared in the kitchen doorway and nodded to Leif.

"You go first," Preben said. "I've got some more cards to write."

"Right," Leif said and rose. He knew the way, through the kitchen and down into the basement. He stepped into the small cubicle, locked the door, and undressed. His dirty clothes went into a plastic bag. He took out soap and shampoo and turned on the taps.

One good thing about this life, you learned to appreciate the basic pleasures: good food, good friends, a good night's sleep, a good shower. He closed his eyes, feeling the hot water stream over his body, washing away the dirt, the miles, and the weariness.

*   *   *

General Yakov Mikhailovich Ladygin was in a foul mood as he stood by his office window and looked down into Dzerzhinsky Square, where the enemy was receiving massive reinforcements in the shape of a heavy snowfall. The bust of Feliks Dzerzhinsky, creator of the Cheka, revolutionary ancestor of the KGB, which had been recovered from the snow the same day, was getting it up to his ears and would probably be under cover again by morning.

Ladygin's foul mood had lasted almost a week and had initially been the echo of KGB Chairman Viktor

Anatoli Chernyshov's foul mood, which in its turn was the result of the debate in the Politburo on Ladygin's suggestion to leak the information about the hijacked nuclear warhead to the Americans. Most members had reluctantly recognized the political necessity of the step, but few had been prepared to support it wholeheartedly before they had sounded out the sentiments of the others. Rumour had it that the upshot had been an unnecessarily stormy meeting before the suggestion had been passed, and the bad feelings had spread down in the hierarchy. After all, if the idea of enlisting help from the West somehow backfired, it was important, in retrospect, to have balanced one's standpoint in a circumspect manner—meaning that it would have better "survival" potential to appear to have been persuaded against one's better judgement.

What had served to keep Ladygin in a foul mood was five names on a sheet of paper, accompanied by five personal dossiers, which Lydia Markovina had placed on his desk. The names and the dossiers belonged to the Palestinians who had been trained at the camp near Odessa in the Crimea while Markov had been an instructor there. They told an exasperating story. Two of them had been killed since, one in an Israeli air raid on a refugee camp outside Tyre, one in a skirmish with Christian Phalangists in southern Lebanon. Two more were alive and well-respected men in the PLO hierarchy; one head of the PLO Rome office, the other Press Officer at Baghdad. Both of them, furthermore, went about their duties and were easily found where they were supposed to be found, and were definitely not mixed up in any funny business.

Their accountability made the fifth name all the more galling. Mahmoud Nimiri. Ladygin recalled the photographs in the dossier. Nimiri was tall, for a Palestinian, with a lean, intense face. A taciturn, brooding character, with a flair for the enigmatic, the dossier said. He had wanted to enroll in the training program without re-vealing his true identity and instead use his code name el-Tha'ir, the Avenger. But as the KGB never accepted anybody for training unless he or she had been thor-oughly investigated, el-Tha'ir had eventually been pre-vailed upon to give up his identity. He had, however, insisted that it never was to go any further than the KGB files. And, Ladygin thought grimly, that's where it nearly stayed buried; in the KGB the right hand hardly even knew that the left hand existed.

Nimiri's training had consisted of the usual subjects: organizing, infiltration, explosives, firearms, close-com-bat fighting, sabotage, cryptology, with special emphasis on being able to teach others his skills. According to his instructors in the camp, he had completed the training with single-minded determination, speaking little, as if he had seen in his mind a goal far beyond the end of the course. The only incident during that time had been an incendiary bomb which had gone off at the wrong moment and left an area of fine, pale scar tissue on his left cheek. One hour after the accident he had been back in training with half of his face dressed in a skew-bald devil's mask.

In spite of being rather inaccessible, he had been con-sidered very good material to develop further, once he had taken up a position as teacher of young *fedayeen* or risen in the PLO. He had been spirited back late '80, using a number of false passports, by way of the Ger-man Democratic Republic and Holland and had reached Turkey, all according to plan.

And there he had suddenly, to all effect, ceased to exist.

The KGB had tried to locate him. A costly investment had unaccountably gone down the drain and the KGB wasn't going to allow that without an attempt at re-trieval, which had failed.

And, Ladygin thought bitterly, this ghost, this per-

ished nonentity, this whatever he was—and wherever—
was most probably the man behind snitching one of the
Red Army's nuclear warheads.

Well, el-Tha'ir would be their main target as of now,
even if he were a ghost.

Ladygin wasn't sure of what he resented most, the
atrocities anyone with a nuclear warhead was capable
of, or the disruption of everyday intelligence business.
The Israelis had already reacted to the KGB attempts to
keep tabs on their doings, and in neutralizing a number
of Soviet agents had shown that they knew the KGB
Middle East network better than anyone had expected.
This meant that Ladygin would have to send in new
agents, which was always a gamble, or activate the really
deeply embedded sleepers in the area, with the attendant risk of exposure. It was small comfort that the
Israelis were facing the same problems in their search.
They were better organized for that kind of job, had
greater flair for improvisation, and in a startlingly short
time were able to send in agents it would take years
for other agencies to develop. They would come out of
it better than their Soviet colleagues.

When it is all over, Ladygin thought, it's going to take
years to restore operations in the Middle East. And who's
going to benefit from that? The CIA, of course, and the
other West European intelligence agencies, those who
contributed nothing more valuable to the search than
a little information or perhaps a liaison officer. *Chort
vozmi!* Whatever el-Tha'ir—or whoever it was—intended to do with that infernal device, it had better be
good to be worth it.

Outside, the snow kept on blanketing the world, and
comrade Dzerzhinsky was having difficulty, as dusk fell,
to keep his nose above it all. The light from the few lit
lamps in the office was reflected faintly by the falling
snow, and the room was being turned into a softly illuminated aquarium with Lenin distortedly looking

through it and not noticing the goldfish Ladygin, who too was looking out.

*   *   *

"Yes, in Paris," Ari Ofer said into the phone with a satisfied chuckle. "Under lock and key, David. The DST have got Tabari and Shefir, have had them all the time. Came through from André Chalmel today."

He listened to David Bar-Sharon for a moment. "Yes, you're right about that. But you haven't heard the best part of the story yet. Listen to this. The PLO had—how shall I put it—browbeaten the Algerian government into giving them twenty-five blank, absolutely genuine Algerian passports. In the name of Arab unity, the world-wide fight against colonialism and Zionist aggression and so forth.

"Right, fill in everything, stick on well-resembling photograph, use cast of official stamp, sign on dotted line, and hey presto, you're a genuine Algerian.

"Yeah, sounds good, doesn't it? It only so happened that the Algerians marked the passports very neatly and sent off a list of the numbers to the French authorities.

"You would have liked to have seen their faces when they waved the nice new passports about—and wound up in the clink! Right?

"Well, seems they were going to France to organize a new network there. You know, activity in Europe has been flagging lately. The French internal security put them away and has been very quiet about it in order not to scare the other fish. They weren't all that happy about letting us have that piece of info. Luckily, I've fed André enough morsels for him to feel he owes us something. I don't know, he may have had some sort of OK from higher up, but the French have been a bit finicky since the Abu Daoud business in '77."

He listened while David's voice came tinnily over the line.

"El-Tha'ir?" Ofer said presently. "No, haven't heard anything about him either. But I've got one more thing for you, David. This may be the substantial item we've been waiting for. It seems to bear out the conclusions we reached yesterday.

"No, technically it's Mossad business to act upon it. Yeah. Well, we've had a tip that there's a man locked up with two bodyguards and his own telephone line in the Hotel Méditerranée in Beirut.

"Why we didn't know? Hard to say. It seems they've been doing the same thing in one hotel after another for a month. They just happened to be seen by a friend of ours when they changed hotels last week.

"I know, Bill will be very pleased. Anyway, nobody ever sees this man, food is taken in to him by one of the bodyguards, and so on. Our source got hold of somebody in the hotel who had seen him checking in, asked a few careful questions, and got a very crude description; it might be Hijazi.

"No, we're not sure yet. We'll have to arrange some sort of positive identification. I don't know exactly yet how it is going to be worked.

"If it is Hijazi?" Ofer grinned without mirth. "Then I think we'd better have a word with him."

*   *   *

Major-General Yitzak Hofi, head of the Mossad, looked up from the report he had received half an hour ago. He was thinking hard; the normally jovial expression was gone from his round, broad face under the high hairline.

Ofer's group had done a good job, and the Beirut tip had indeed proved the soundness of the suggestion in the previous report, that the search be concentrated on the four remaining unaccounted-for terrorist leaders. Further information from the evaluation branch of the

Mossad had continuously corroborated the contents of the reports from the coordinating group. Now the situation called for action.

The Mossad mostly used a special reconnaissance unit of the General Headquarters to handle the necessary dirty work. In April 1973 a number of Mossad operatives had prepared the way and supervised the landing in Beirut of eight commandos from the GHQ unit, who within two hours had located and shot dead three high-ranking Palestinian leaders, stolen the records from the PLO Beirut office and sent them off to Israel by helicopter, and escaped, without casualties, to the naval units waiting offshore.

Now another operation along the lines of the '73 Beirut raid seemed to be the only alternative. Ofer was right; they couldn't pay any heed to world opinion. As the Cabinet was already briefed as to the nature of the affair, there would be no trouble getting its sanction for such an operation.

What was worrying Major-General Yitzak Hofi was that the operation would have to be mounted at very short notice. In 1973 the Mossad had sent in agents under cover two weeks in advance to prepare the ground, and the military planning had been given commensurate time. Lack of planning in this case would make the mission much more risky, although its objective was simpler than those of the previous raid. Agents would have to be sent in at once, which meant that their covers would leave something to be desired.

It was clear that they would have to rely heavily on the experience gained in the earlier raid. They might even land in the same place. Hofi grinned briefly at this thought. One good thing was that the Hotel Méditerranée was situated conveniently close to the sea.

Major-General Hofi concluded his thoughts on Ofer's report by making three telephone calls. One was to the Special Operations Branch of the Mossad with instructions to identify, with the utmost speed, the man in room 417 of the Hotel Méditerranée in Beirut and to prepare, together with the GHQ unit and the Navy and the Air Force of the *Zahal*, a raid to kidnap said man and bring him to Tel Aviv.

The second phone call was to the commander of the GHQ unit, with similar instructions, plus that the men would have to be ready to go into action at any time within the next two to five days.

The third call was to the Chief of Staff.

After that Hofi called for his limousine, which was to bring him to Jerusalem and another meeting with the Cabinet Committee for Security and Foreign Affairs.

*   *   *

Dusk.

Sunrise, sunset. Leif had seen more of those through the windshield of his Scania than he could remember. Days accumulating with the miles rushing in under his eighteen wheels. Suns setting over snowclad plains and mountain ranges and vast expanses of desert.

Another day was coming to an end in distant, fading fires of yellow and violet beyond the darkening hills of Jordan. He felt tired, almost drowsy. The shower and a full meal afterwards contributed to his sense of well-being. He shook his head, then rolled the window down a crack to let the cool, refreshing night air in.

Two sets of lights hung in his mirrors, trailing him. The small convoy had enlisted another member at Ramtha. Tommy Edmundsson was a short, wiry man in his thirties, with a receding hairline and a wide smile under his incredible handlebar moustache. He drove a red-and-yellow Volvo F89 for PIE and was bound for Abha in Saudi with a load of door and window frames. He had walked into the restaurant while Preben had been taking his shower.

Leif glanced at the clock on the dash. Half past six. They had taken on enough diesel at El Husn to last them into Saudi where prices were rock-bottom and their tanks would be filled to the brim. He stubbed his cigarette out and turned the volume of the stereo up to fight his weariness.

*   *   *

Humphrey Bogart's bar in Ma'an in southern Jordan, with one hundred and fourteen kilometres of gravel desert separating it from the border point before Saudi Arabia, was an institution among the Middle East drivers. "The last outpost of civilization," some said, while others talked about "crossing the beer line."

In any other place, it would have been seen for what it really was: the village bar, in this case garishly decorated in red and with walls hung with ancient rifles, cracked mirrors, faded and dusty Christmas garlands, plus an impressive array of photos showing the owner in younger and more glorious days, when he had possessed and cultivated a remarkable likeness to the real Humphrey Bogart; this vanity explained his nickname, as well as his bar's. Nowadays he sported a goatee and a magnificent moustache and rather resembled a slightly shop-soiled Frank Zappa.

Humphrey cared wholeheartedly for the Saudi drivers, considered each his personal and very special friend, and knew most of them by name. The ten percent discount he gave them sometimes caused bad feelings among the local population, but what did he care, with a long line of trucks outside and a wallful of postcards behind the cash register?

But the *real* reason behind the booming business was neither the good atmosphere, nor the superb Petra beer, nor the fact that it was the drivers' own Piccadilly Circus South, where everybody passed through sooner or later, nor the extraordinary hospitality extended to the truckers; rather, it was a unique combination of political, geographical, social, and religious factors. Saudi Arabian law followed the Koran to the letter, which meant that absolutely no alcohol of any kind was permitted anywhere inside the country. Smuggling was a risky game, with a minimum of one year in Saudi jail for the losers, so most drivers had a few ritual last bottles of beer, and then went without it for the next week or two.

Humphrey Bogart's was the last place before the border.

*   *   *

They ducked under the low lintel, and stepped inside. The din that met them was deafening. Two drivers at a table in the centre of the room recognized them and waved them over. Leif saw several whose trucks he had recognized outside—Lasse and Olle from Trailertransport, the Hagen brothers, Judo John, and others. Greetings and whoops of delight cut through the noise of a dozen different languages and the heavy tobacco smoke.

"Well, if it ain't old Blackbeard himself!" one of the drivers exclaimed when they reached the table. "Almost thought you'd quit Circus Saudi. Where've you been?"

"Take it easy, boys," Preben said and grinned as he settled his two-metre frame on a creaking chair. "Man's got a right to celebrate Christmas in peace."

Leif knew the first speaker, Tore, who drove the brown-and-white DHK Scania parked outside. Now he recognized the second man at the table. "Cannonball Jack! I couldn't place you without the beard. Hey, what really happened in that crash you had in Belgrade? The asphalt vine has told me at least five different versions." They shook hands all around and unzipped their jackets. The room was hot, despite a few open windows up high.

"Oh, that." Jack smiled and sipped his beer. "Well, you know how the Yugoslavs drive. Can't even clench their fists without their fingers pointing in every direction."

They all laughed. "Let's get a waiter over, my throat's as dry as Saudi sand," Tommy said longingly.

"Don't worry, we'll get you a double camel crap on the rocks."

More laughter. Preben added, "Wouldn't mind some ham and eggs, either. Last chance, you know."

Tore managed to wave one of Humphrey's helpers over, and Leif and his convoy friends ordered beer and ham and eggs all around.

Jack entertained them with the story of his Belgrade incident. "You know the intersection just past the viaduct? I had twenty-two tons of drainpipes in the semi and the road was like fucking ice that early in the morning. I was about to take the turn when a car comes on my left, running right through the red light. Damn rig fucking jack-knifed when I braked, and continued straight on into that little street ahead. Stroked the arse of a guy bending down under his hood and mowed down about eight of those little Trabant things—you know, the ones with synchronized toolboxes and double overhead cardboard roofs. One of them was a fucking police car, too. All hell broke loose."

"Anybody hurt?" Tommy asked.

"No," Jack admitted. "But if you ask me, it was a fucking miracle."

The beer, deliciously cool, appeared, and they all drank.

The Pirate belched and put his glass down empty. "That, my friends," he announced, "may not have been Carlsberg, but it sure hit home all the same. I could hear that first sip fall all the way to the bottom."

"Right on," Leif said and grinned.

"So what's new?" Tore asked.

"Nothing much," Preben answered, "except brother Leif here got himself thrown in the clink in Turkey . . ."

"That's nothing," Cannonball Jack said lightly. "It's getting out that's the difficult part. How did you manage that?"

"Hell," Leif said, "I don't know. It wasn't very dramatic, probably just a stupid mistake. I'll tell you . . ."

*   *   *

The diesel sang its monotonous music, strong and steady. The tiredness was everywhere in Leif's body, and he felt a little bit drunk. The clock said two; they still had fifty kilometres to go before Muddawa'ara, the little collection of hutches in the middle of the desert that was the last outpost of Jordan.

A string of lights hung in his mirrors. He was riding lead truck in a seven-strong convoy that had left Humphrey's three-quarters of an hour ago. They had been sitting there far too long and had drunk too much beer. Now he only wanted to arrive and crawl into his sleeping bag.

The diesel engine sang.

The moon hung in front of him, four days past full, spreading a soft, silvery sheen across the desert. The road was straight as an arrow, the speedometer needle hovered just over 115, and his floodlights burned holes in the night as they raced towards Muddawa'ara, the end of the world.

13

THE PASSPORT OF THE STOCKY MAN with the close-cropped hair said he was Hans-Günther Dettmar of Remscheid, Federal Republic of Germany; the passport of the thin, sallow-faced man with the conspicuously dark-toned hair said that he was Willi Rudiger Schmidt of Hagen, also Federal Republic of Germany.

They were businessmen and had arrived at Beirut at five in the afternoon on Thursday January 18 on Middle East Airlines flight ME 216 from Frankfurt. At the airport and on the plane they had apparently consumed considerable quantities of Löwenbräu, and now they were turning their checking-in at the Hotel Méditerranée into a superciliously inconsiderate, solemnly Teutonic Laurel and Hardy act. The porter, from a distance, watched as they pestered the receptionist with extremely inept French once they had realized that she spoke no German; his only comfort was that he was probably in for a good tip in useful Deutsch-Marks.

The Germans finally settled on a twin-bedded room on the fourth floor, number 413, motioned to the porter for their luggage to be carried upstairs, spoke loudly in German and laughed in the lift on the way up, in the corridor, and in the room, and tipped the porter without ceasing their talk or even appearing to notice him. The tip was adequate, but not really up to expectations. When the door closed, the porter looked at the man sitting, as usual, outside the suite at the end of the corridor, shrugged eloquently, and shook his head at 413. He got no .reaction and sauntered off down the corridor in a peevish mood.

Alone in room 413, Herr Dettmar and Herr Schmidt went on talking loudly in German, and one of them told a racist joke about Semitic people in general and Arabs in particular, while they checked the room for possible bugs. When they were reasonably convinced that there were none, they began to speak in low, businesslike voices, but still in German.

The German passports were forged, but the German manner of Herr Dettmar and Herr Schmidt was not. Since 1974 the two of them had maintained identities as citizens of West Germany, but in reality they were Israeli illegals. Their forged passports, which they used in Beirut, were originally to enable them to work as Heth—or back-up members—of any Israeli hit team that might operate in Germany, without endangering their "genuine" deep covers. The real names of the two men were Samuel Limon and David Feinmann, but their employer only remembered them occasionally and they themselves seldom.

The taxi in which they had travelled from the airport to the hotel had been driven by a Mossad agent stationed in Beirut. He had slipped a thick manila envelope between the backrests, where it found its way, unopened, into the black briefcase of one of the "Germans." The envelope contained the plans of the electrical installations of the Hotel Méditerranée, together with the layout of the rooms and emergency exits. Earlier that day, dressed up in his best suit and armed with a peremptory manner and an impressive array of signed, sealed and apparently officially stamped documents, the taxi driver had paid a visit to the office of the contractor who had built the hotel and obtained the plans, copied them and returned them with suitably profuse thanks.

The two agents opened the envelope and spent the

better part of an hour poring over the plans, discussing various points before they finally settled on a plan of action. They then resealed the envelope with tape and placed it inside the removable lining of one of their suitcases. Half an hour later they redonned their bois- terous German mannerisms and left the hotel for a ren- dezvous in an office in southern Beirut, near the dividing line between the Muslim and the Christian sections of the city.

They returned to the hotel at a quarter past eight, had dinner, and retired to their room. At half past ten they went down for a drink in the hotel bar and left again for their room, by way of the stairs, twenty min- utes later. Three minutes past eleven there was a loud hiss and a flash from a fuse box on the second floor, and one wing of Hotel Méditerranée, housing among others suite 417 and room 413, was plunged into dark- ness. From his table at an outdoor café across the street, a man in dirty coveralls and with a toolbox watched the lights go out in the hotel, looked at his watch, and nodded.

The two Germans were first among the angry guests to call down to reception, which had also been hit, to complain about the blackout. The night porter had a busy time apologizing, promising to have candles brought up to the dark rooms and that the electricians who had been called were sure to be in at any moment to find the fault and fix it: "*Non, monsieur. Bien oui, mon- sieur, nous le regrettons. Immediatement, monsieur.*"

The electricians, two men in coveralls, arrived only ten minutes later in a small, badly dented Renault van, which they parked right outside the hotel entrance. They brought their toolboxes out from the back of the van and went into the hotel. Two minutes after that, the man who had been waiting across the road entered, nodded to the reception staff, visible only in candlelight, and made his way up the stairs to the fourth floor, guiding his steps with a flashlight.

The flashlight illuminated the corridor wall for half its length, and left vague shadows shot through with reflected light for the rest. In the murk down at the end of the corridor, a man stirred from his chair outside 417 and rose as if to challenge the electrician.

The man proceeded down the corridor, swearing to himself in Arabic, shining his light on each door as he passed it. He stopped outside 413, shrugged and knocked. The guard sat down again, watching him.

The door opened, the flashlight came up and illuminated the occupant, and a stream of angry German, mixed with the occasional French phrase, greeted the man.

"*Ja, ja,*" he said soothingly. "*Kaputt, ja.*" He entered the room, and a "*Ja, kontrollieren*" drifted out into the corridor. The man's German vocabulary was limited, to say the least, but the Germans seemed to be pacified. The door was left ajar, and from inside could be heard Arabic mutterings and some tool-rattling. A few minutes later the man reemerged in the corridor.

"*Ja, ja. Gut machen—in'ish Allah,*" he said before the door closed again and he made for the end of the corridor.

The guard rose again, but seemed to hesitate. The man in the coveralls pressed his advantage. "I regret very much that I shall have to check your electrical installations," he said in Levantine Arabic, in formal phrases shaped for extra emphasis. "There has been a short-circuit, and we shall surely have to go through all the rooms to find the fault."

The guard knocked on the door, and after a moment it was opened from the inside, a crack. "There's an electrician out here who wants to come in and check the electrical stuff."

"It is most important," the man put in.

There was hesitation inside the room, hurried words in low voices, then, "He can come in. But he shall have to be quick about it." The door opened fully, and the man entered.

Inside, he shone his light around the walls, locating electrical outlets and fixtures. A single candle burned on a table. There were two people in the room, a man half sitting on the sofa and another man, in posture and expression very like the man outside the door, who tried his best to stay between the man on the sofa and the electrician, who was crawling along the wainscoting in pursuit of electrical wire.

Having apparently found nothing amiss with the electrical installations in the first room, the man eventually gestured towards the bedroom. "I shall have to check there, too."

The inside guard nodded and then stood in the doorway while the inspection of the bedroom and the bathroom was carried through. The man in the coveralls finally straightened up, shrugged, and said, "Nothing in here either, I'm sure." Then he made for the door.

The guard stood aside to let him through, and the man walked briskly up to the man in the sofa and shone his light fully in his face, speaking apologetically in Arabic. "I regret very much having to disturb you like this, *Sidi*, especially as the fault with certainty is not in this room. We will check the unoccupied rooms as soon as the manager comes up with the master key, but I'm convinced . . ."

The man on the sofa was startled by the light, which cast his stubbled chin and sunken cheeks in hard contrasts of light and shadow. His eyes, unaccustomed to the brightness, narrowed as a reflex, blinked, and his hand came up as if to ward it off. Then the guard came up from behind the man in the coveralls and angrily knocked the flashlight aside.

"That's enough of that. If you haven't found anything

wrong in here you will get out at once and not bother us any longer." He got between the two men and urgently began to push the electrician towards the door.

"But I was only telling the worthy gentleman . . ." in obsequious tones.

"I said you will get out this very moment." The door was open now and the man in the coveralls was being shoved through it. "See that he leaves," to the outside guard. The door slammed shut.

The guard in the corridor rose. "So then, off you go," he growled at the terrified electrician, who was backing away, uttering apologies.

"Of course, at once. I will remove myself, begging your forgiveness. I was only . . ."

The guard grinned at the pathetic figure and sat down again. As the man passed 413, the door flew open and one of the Germans appeared, a spluttering candle in one hand.

"*Wann wird denn das alles in Ordnung sein? Verstehen Sie? Fix.*"

"*Ja, ja, alles in Ordnung, ja?*" The man backed faster, then abruptly turned and loped down the corridor at a half-trot.

"*Verdammte . . .*" said the German and slammed the door on the rest of the ejaculation.

Back in the reception hall, where the staff had put out more candles, the man in the coveralls waved his light about a little and nodded vaguely towards the van outside. Then he was out through the glass front door and down the outside steps.

Fifteen minutes later, the genuine electricians had located the fuse box which had caused all the trouble and repaired it, not finding anything peculiar about the breakdown. Light returned to the blacked-out wing of the Hotel Méditerranée.

By that time the third electrician had ditched his coveralls and toolbox, but had taken the thick manila envelope with him as he disappeared into the Beirut night.

*   *   *

If Muddawa'ara is the end of the world, then Halat Ammar is the beginning of another. They are separated by twenty kilometres of no-man's-land desert. A single tarmac strip winds past the dunes, bridging the two worlds.

As one part of the journey ends in Muddawa'ara, another begins in Halat Ammar, for here at last the Saudi pilots enter the country where their load will be delivered. No more rolling into the place and rushing about to get the proper amount of stamps on the proper documents before hitting the road again. In Halat Ammar you park and patiently await your turn to have your trailer opened, its contents checked, and pay the customs dues—a process which can last anywhere from an afternoon to over a month, depending on your load, the amount of traffic stacked up, the mood of the customs officials, Saudi holidays, and not least on your own behaviour and your own efforts.

Halat Ammar is a time of waiting. The drivers have learned, sometimes the hard way, that patience is more than a virtue, and have honed it to a fine art.

At one time, Halat Ammar was the sole point of entry if you came from the north. Now there is also Haditha further to the north, through which trucks bound for Kuwait, Qatar, Oman, the Emirates, Dammam and sometimes Riyadh pass on their way down the route known as the H4.

Not only trucks pass through Halat Ammar. Tourism is prohibited in Saudi Arabia, but personally imported luxury cars and cars driven by businessmen also queue up at the border. And then there are the pilgrims, a steady trickle during most of the year, a deluge at the season of the *hadj*, when they come in tens and hundreds of thousands, by every conceivable means, the white-clad faithful bound for the holy cities of Mecca and Medina.

The entrance to Halat Ammar is guarded by soldiers in dark green berets and uniforms. There is a small detachment in Halat Ammar itself; the main camp lies to the southwest, beyond the sandy hills.

The place is more of a small community than a mere border station; it's slightly reminiscent of an old Wild West one-street town. The asphalt road comes in from the desert, goes straight past the assortment of buildings, then curves left and disappears among the hills. To the right lies the military detachment, and then the big, square, walled-in area of the customs compound for the trucks, the offices of the agents, a mosque, a few houses, and an open curious building with a white roof supported by columns, which houses under it the slots for the cleared trucks and the cubicles for the Pakistani and Indian workers. To the left are the passport and customs buildings, a small bank and a post office, and, where the road starts to turn, a bakery, a little grocery shop, and an equally diminutive restaurant specializing in greasy chickens with a much better tomato salad. The elderly Arab who empties the trash cans inside the customs compound also works as the sole waiter in the restaurant in the evenings. His markedly protruding lower jaw has earned him the nickname "Balcony Johnny."

Such is the entrance to the new world, to Saudi Arabia, the "biggest sandbox in the world." But the drivers say it with an undertone of respect for the enormous, desolate distances that they have yet to cover. For although they have at last arrived in Saudi, the pilots bound for Riyadh or Abha or Yemen still have more than one-fourth of their journey before them.

*   *   *

Leif crouched in front of his Scania, and tearing off another length of black electrical tape, started to fix the paper plate to the fourth and last of his Cibié floodlights.

It was Halat Ammar routine, but he still swore. Traffic laws in Saudi made extra lights a definite out, so all the pilots covered theirs up in order to pass muster before they were let out of the customs compound and into Saudi Arabia proper. The law, naturally, was observed only in Halat Ammar itself. The pilots stopped behind the nearest dune and tore the paper plates off before they continued down the road.

He rose and sighed. One learned to live with lots of things.

Preben was coming back with two camel cocks and two bottles of Kaki-Cola. The day was still hot in spite of it being late afternoon. Preben's white T-shirt was stained with perspiration.

"Here's yours," he said and handed over half his load.

Leif took the sandwich and the bottle, nodding. The sandwiches were supplied by a short Arab with a pock-marked face, from a rickety stand strategically placed where all the drivers turned the corner on their way to their agents. The fare consisted of a piece of bread about a foot long, slit along the middle and stuffed with your choice of either goat's cheese and sweet marmalade, or sliced, hard-boiled eggs with Tabasco. From Teheran to Dublin they were known as "camel cocks" and consumed with relish by the drivers.

Leif and Preben ate and drank and regarded the compound, where a Syrian-registered Mercedes of late fifties vintage was trying to find a slot to back up in. Their own Scanias were near the southeast corner, with their noses pointing towards the middle of the compound. The number of TIR trucks was a little lower than usual. It had taken them less than six hours to get past the first hurdles, filling out entry cards, elbowing with the Arabs before the passport counter, having their certificates of vaccination checked by a doctor who seemed sorry that he had no excuse for giving them an extra shot or two.

Leif had seen times when the queue had stretched for two kilometres down the road towards Muddawa- 'ara, and it had taken him forty-eight hours just to get inside the compound.

"I spoke to the BM guys again," Preben said between mouthfuls. "They're in for more trouble."

"Oh no. Poor bastards. What's up this time?"

The Swedish Bolinder-Munktell Volvo bus had been there when they came in, parked outside the passport building. Its occupants were two senior mechanics and instructors, on their way to Jeddah to teach the Saudis how to repair trucks. The bus was fitted out like a class-room, and contained living quarters complete with a galley and a shower.

"It's the instruction films." The Pirate grinned. "The customs people want to sit through every one of them, just to make sure nobody's slipped in any tits and ass."

"How long is it going to take?"

"Two days." Preben took a swig from his Kaki-Cola. "They've got plenty of film aboard."

The shadows were lengthening with approaching eve-ning. Tommy and a Norwegian stood talking a little way off. Most of the drivers of the nearby trucks were either dozing in their cabs or off shopping or chasing agents.

"What do you think?" Leif said. "Any chance of mak-ing it to the loading ramp today?" He nodded towards the large, open-sided warehouse in the middle of the compound. There were trucks backed up against its eastern and western sides, their tarpaulins rolled back, and Pakistani workers shifting crates and boxes back and forth under the eyes of Saudi foremen.

"Probably not. Tomorrow morning, maybe."

"Muslim Sunday tomorrow."

"I know," Preben said. "But those Finns will probably be cleared tonight and get out tomorrow." He pointed to two white-and-blue Transcontinentals which stood side by side at the loading ramp. Large, wooden crates were being transferred from the ramp onto the trailers.

"Hope so. I'm running late as it is." He sighed and turned to look at his Scania. "And my damn radiator's still leaking, worse than ever."

"How much are you losing?"

"Over a litre for every hundred kilometres."

"Time you tried to fix it, then."

"Yeah." His watch was in the cab. He looked at the sinking sun. About two hours of daylight left. "I'd better crawl under and see if I can find anything."

"I'll give you a hand, mate."

"Good. Get your coveralls on, and we'll tilt the cab."

* * *

He sprinted back from the customs compound, his *tob* swishing around his legs. Slipping between the passport building and the little bank, he ducked out into the sun again, veered right and ran across towards the car that was parked behind the restaurant. Two men coming out from the grocery shop eyed him curiously, but he didn't care as he hurried by.

The men by the car had seen him coming, and the worry was clearly visible in their faces.

"The truck . . ." he said, catching his breath. "They have started some kind of work on it!"

The man with the brand on his left cheek took a step forward and gripped his shoulder in a painful grip. "*What?*"

"I don't know, they have started raising the cab, and they have taken out tools, perhaps they are trying to repair something, I don't know . . ."

The man with the scar said to the man with him, "Stay here." Then to the other man, "Lead the way back."

The man nodded and turned, walking briskly back the way he had come, past the grocery shop and the bank. The branded man was close behind him as they reached the entrance to the compound.

The guard eyed the two men for a moment without particular interest, and then looked away. The first man drew a deep breath, and looking down towards the far wall, he could see the cab already raised and the drivers piling in behind it.

He pressed his left arm against his side, checking that his knife was still in its sheath. Then he started slowly walking along the row of trucks.

14

LEIF GAVE THE LONG STEEL HANDLE a last downward push, then pulled it loose and placed it on the criss-crossed metal plate by the semi-trailer coupling. The cab of the Scania 141 was tilted all the way forward over the front bumper. Underneath was the turbocharged V-8 with its clutter of auxiliary components, dirty and caked, coated with a film of oil and dust from ten countries. Leif sighed. He flexed his fingers inside his work gloves, looking things over.

Tommy and Preben were beside him; from their trucks along the east wall, several Arabs watched with interest. They all gathered close to look the engine over. Leif bent forward to prod in a few places, pushing wires aside to get a better look.

"Can't see anything," he said. "No tell-tale puddle underneath."

"The thing could leak in a million places," Tommy said. He had stuck his head in close to the radiator, and the tips of his handlebar moustache brushed the metal. "But if you have a leak somewhere at the seams of the block itself, the water ought to have made streaks in the dust film. How much are you losing?"

"Over a litre for every hundred kilometres."

"Not the kind of volume that would just trickle out and evaporate. Do you have any sealant?"

"No," Leif admitted.

"I have some." The Pirate was holding on to the frame

with both gloved hands, trying to squeeze his massive body in under the tilted cab for a renewed scrutiny.

"Shit." Leif sighed again. "I'll crawl under and see if I can find anything." He started to bend down.

"Hold on," Preben said. "I have an idea. Bet it's a pressure leak. Start the engine."

Leif nodded and reached up to open the door, aided by Tommy, who held it so it didn't fall forward and break its hinges. He climbed onto the front tire, holding on to the leaning cab, and got the keys out. The diesel coughed as the starter turned it over, and then fired. Leif pulled the hand throttle out a fraction to let the V-8 settle down to a fast idle. The roar, without the muffling cab, was deafening.

"Watch the radiator and the water hoses," Preben shouted over the reverberating noise.

A minute passed while they strained their eyes, trying to discover tell-tale bubbles or drops of water. Got to cut the engine soon, Leif thought, or the guards will come rushing over.

"Hold!" Preben shouted. "I can see it. Kill the engine!"

Leif swung himself up and reached out to pull the compression release. Almost unwillingly, the V-8 revved down and came to rest. The sudden silence seemed as deafening as the noise before.

"Over here on the right side. You've got a bad hose clamp."

Leif and Tommy slammed the door shut and came over. Preben pointed, and they bent forward to look.

"I'll be . . ." Leif said and tugged at the metal clamp where the rubber hose entered the huge radiator at the bottom. It turned, far too easily, revealing a jagged crack that ran almost its entire width. "Damn thing's nearly broken." He gave it a hard pull, and the clamp tore free. A trickle of water started to flow onto the ground, splashing against the asphalt. Leif held the clamp up, then passed it around for inspection.

"Got another one?" Tommy asked.

"I think so."

He rummaged through one of his toolboxes. One compartment held a few hose clamps of different sizes. He selected one.

As he straightened up, he saw the Arab that slowly walked by, an unusually tall man, dressed in a clean white robe and headgear. There was an area of scar tissue on his left cheek. For a moment, their eyes met, then the Arab unhurriedly let his gaze travel over the Scania before he looked away and continued to walk along the trucks towards the entrance. Leif shot a glance after him, and then shrugged. Nosey Arabs.

A minute later he had tightened the hose clamp into place and was inspecting the other connecting hoses and clamps. Nothing else seemed broken or in need of replacement, so together they carefully lowered the cab back into place.

"Thanks, boys," Leif said and took off his work gloves. "You saved me a lot of trouble there."

"*Jä, jä.* Don't mention it. Just don't forget to replace the water you lost this time." Preben pointed at the spreading puddle beneath the truck before he and Tommy drifted off to their own rigs.

Leif nodded to himself, and as he peeled off his coveralls, made a mental note to add anti-freeze as well, for the trip back through Europe. Then he lit a cigarette and started to put all the stuff back in place. It took him almost twenty minutes.

Well, he might as well continue doing useful work. With the two plastic bags containing his dirty laundry, a packet of detergent, a clothes line, clothes pins, soap, shampoo, a clean T-shirt, clean underwear, a towel, and his last clean pair of blue jeans stuffed into a bright yellow plastic bucket, he locked his cab and left the compound on his way to the building where the Pakistani workers lived in their cramped cubicles. In the north end of the building were the large communal washrooms that the pilots used for showers and for doing their laundry.

There was only one other driver there when Leif entered. They exchanged nods as Leif went over to the trough along the wall and began to run cold water—the only kind you got—into the plastic bucket. The place looked naked, with white tiles. High on one wall was a colourful poster which gave graphic advice on how to use one's left hand, with water, after one had attended to the calls of nature.

Quickly he went through his dirty laundry, washing and rinsing it, then strung the line between two columns outside and hung the clothes up to dry. He would come back for them tomorrow. He had no worries that they would disappear overnight. Down here, thieves didn't get their wrists slapped, they got their hands cut off.

Even Westerners didn't always go free of traditional Islamic justice. "An eye for an eye" was literally the law. A British pilot had picked a fight with an Arab in Khamish Mushayt, and punched out two of his front teeth. The police had arrested him, and the next day he had been taken to a dentist, who had pulled two of his front teeth—without anaesthetic. He was put on the next flight out of the country.

So you didn't steal clothes down here.

He pinned the last sock to the clothes line and went back inside for a shower. He walked along the line of stalls that combined hole-in-the-floor toilets with a shower nozzle, found one where the walls were reasonably clean, and gingerly stepped inside. The water was ice-cold, and he gasped for breath.

Ten minutes later, in the growing darkness, he was

back inside the customs compound where Preben had the evening meal ready.

* * *

El Al flight 582 from Istanbul Yesilöy to Tel Aviv Ben-Gurion stood waiting at Gate 4, Larnaca Airport, Cyprus, rerouted. The time was drawing towards two o'clock Friday afternoon, and the plane had been waiting for almost exactly one hour. The passengers had not been allowed off the plane; instead, they had been placated with free drinks. The unscheduled diversion to Cyprus had been explained as a technical matter. Only the captain and one of the security guards had left the plane.

El Al is known as the world's most security-conscious airline, and those who fly El Al are aware of it, so the stop at Larnaca caused no great consternation. The passengers grumbled a bit; some vowed to risk being hijacked on another airline the next time they flew and instead get there on time, but that was the extent of it. Some drank their drinks, settled down in their seats, and fell asleep.

What most people do not know is that El Al is also part of the total Israeli security. The safest place for an Israeli agent to be outside Israel is aboard an El Al plane. It's safer even than being at an Israeli embassy, as the plane can be easily moved. El Al captains are under orders not to give up an Israeli agent aboard his plane under any circumstances. If necessary, an El Al captain will even desert his passengers and take off in violation of orders from airport control to fly an agent directly to Tel Aviv.

Those passengers aboard flight 582 who whispered about security were right in a way; flight 582 was waiting for a man who carried an important piece of a jigsaw puzzle which concerned the security of the state of Israel as a whole.

The captain of flight 582, hitched casually on the counter of the gate, and the security guard were smoking quietly, talking to the airport official whom had kept them company during the wait, when, a few minutes past two, the airport building reverberated with the sound of reversing jet engines and the PA system came on with a bing-bong.

"Middle East Airlines, Middle East Airlines, announces the arrival of flight ME 261 from Beirut."

The El Al captain nodded to the security guard and slid off the counter. Both of them turned and watched, through the plate-glass wall, the green-and-white 727 brake and stop at the end of the runway, and then come taxiing towards the airport building.

The plane came to a halt so near to where they stood that they could see the crew on the flight deck carry out the last post-landing checks, the co-pilot reaching up to throw a number of switches, and the captain making an OK sign to the ground crew. Boarding steps with the Cyprus Airways logo were rolled up to the plane, and the door swung open. A hostess showed in the doorway, securing it, then the passengers began to disembark. The third person to show at the top of the steps was a man in his late thirties, of a little less than medium height, with distinctly Levantine features. He threw a quick, incurious glance at the El Al liner and hurried down the steps, a briefcase in one hand.

In the arrival hall the man went directly to the transit reception, talked for a moment, and was then shown to the departure hall by another airport official. Once there, he made for the people waiting at Gate 4.

"I have a greeting for your friends," he said in Hebrew and shook hands with the captain, nodding to the security guard. The captain inclined his head, and the security guard accompanied the man aboard the plane while the captain spoke a few words to the airport official, who trotted off with a clearly relieved air. Then the captain boarded the plane and the waiting hostess swung the door shut and locked it.

Almost at once airport control came through over the radio with a slot for takeoff, and at seventeen minutes past two El Al flight 582 was hurtling down the runway to complete its interrupted journey to Tel Aviv.

*   *   *

According to the military records of the six men assembled in the Operations Room in Tel Aviv, two of them were convalescent after a serious illness, three were on leave of absence for studying abroad and one for family reasons. In reality they were serving in the top secret reconnaissance outfit of General Headquarters known simply as the GHQ unit, and those entries were the only traces this special tour of duty would leave in their records.

There were members of the GHQ unit on combat alert at all times. When the order from the Memuneh to prepare for a raid into Beirut had come through on Wednesday, six men had been detached for the mission and transferred to Tel Aviv for a preliminary briefing.

At the far end of the room was a table with four partially disassembled Colt XM 177E2 5.56 mm assault rifles. Beside it stood the leader of the task force, Paratroop Major Nathan Gehmer, a wiry man of medium height with pale blue eyes and light brownish hair, cut unusually short, even for a military man. He was a veteran, serving his second term with the GHQ unit.

Gehmer picked up one of the Colts. They had decided against using Israeli Uzi submachine guns, in order not to leave obvious evidence of their identity if they were captured or killed. But the Colts were a good second choice, shortened versions of the M16, reliable, excellent weapons for the kind of close-quarter fighting he hoped they would be able to avoid. He compressed its collapsible butt, felt it slide smoothly in, and then out again. He put the weapon down and wiped his oily fingers with a rag.

His second-in-command, Levi Cohen, a frogman veteran who had taken part in the Entebbe raid, was bending down over a curious-looking cube with two tiny holes and a lens in one side. Moshe Goren and Shmuel Ben-Zvi were running through a checklist of the rest of the equipment in low voices. The last two were Meir Shulsky and Shlomo Katz, the latter a medic who had served with the paratroops on the Sinai front in the Yom Kippur war and was now doing a stint with the GHQ unit.

Gehmer put the rag down and walked over to Cohen. "How are you doing with the taser?" he asked and pointed to the cube.

"Fine. Been practising with it all morning. Should save us some trouble if we can use it instead of the Colts."

"Good." Gehmer hoped Cohen was right. He was not too happy about pulling a raid inside a large hotel. Speed and silence would be of the utmost importance.

The time since Thursday morning, when the OK from the Cabinet had been received, had been filled with briefings and preparations. They had prepared their equipment and been issued with the necessary forged documents. A little after midnight, Thursday, a preliminary confirmation of the assumed identity of the target had been radioed in from Beirut, and by noon, Friday, the detachment was fully briefed as to the approach to Beirut, the movements in Beirut, the getaway. What was missing was the layout of the Hotel Méditerranée itself, a rundown on the kind of civilian and military resistance they were likely to encounter, and most important, a description of the suite, the two bodyguards, and the target itself.

*   *   *

El Al flight 582 from Istanbul landed at Ben-Gurion airport at ten to three. First off the plane was the man who had been picked up at Larnaca. He was quickly hustled past passport control and customs to a waiting Ford limousine outside. Fifteen minutes later the man was comfortably seated in a room in one of the Mossad buildings in Tel Aviv's Hakirya district.

Two tape recorders were rolling on a low table off to one side. A heavy-set man sat leaning his elbows on the desk. He was the officer from the Mossad Special Operations Branch who conducted the debriefing. Present were also Major Nathan Gehmer, and, in the background, silently smoking, Ari Ofer.

The Mossad officer wasted no time but rattled off a brief introduction, listing place, date, time, and subject for the benefit of the tape recorders. Then, in a more relaxed tone of voice, he addressed those present.

"I'm sorry we couldn't get Mike here brought over sooner, but we chose to do it discreetly in order not to give anything away. The regular flights out of Beirut didn't fit in too well with our schedule." He gestured a little deprecatingly.

Ari Ofer blew a small smoke-ring. He knew the identity of the agent. His name wasn't Mike.

"It has the benefit, however," the Mossad officer went on, "that if things go well, Mike will be back in Beirut next week after a brief vacation in Cyprus."

All present nodded, including Mike.

"On his way from the airport Mike has given us the identikit makeup on our three targets. I've ordered photocopies of them to be brought immediately. Meanwhile, let's get down to business. Mike, did . . ."

The door opened and a petite, darkish girl in uniform entered with a sheaf of photocopies, which she placed on the desk. Ari Ofer watched her legs as she left. Israeli "tigerettes"—girls in uniform—had a reputation for good looks, and she was no exception.

The Mossad officer handed the photocopies around, three each for Mike and Ofer, the rest to Nathan Gehmer.

Ari Ofer took out two photographs and compared them with the identikit picture of Fayez Hijazi. An identikit picture was a composite of individual ears, eyes, mouths, noses, etc., chosen from scores of alternatives and put together to form a complete portrait. The picture of Hijazi was an improvement on the rather unclear photographs in the Mossad files. There was no doubt that it was the same man.

"Well, then," said the Mossad officer, "that saved us a little time. Nathan, you will distribute your copies among your unit."

Gehmer nodded.

"The older man is the target. He has to be taken alive. The other two will have to be eliminated."

"That's clear."

"Good. Then we'll start the rundown on the hotel."

*   *   *

An hour later, the air in the room was thick with cigarette smoke, and Ari Ofer's shirt clung to his back. The debriefing was an affair primarily between the man identified as Mike and the Special Operations officer. Now and then they were interrupted by questions from Gehmer, who made notes as the three of them pored over the plans spread across the desk, going over the hotel from top to bottom.

What was the street like? The hotel foyer? Where were they likely to encounter people? How many? How many steps to each flight of stairs? What material? Where are the elevators? What colour and material are the walls and floors of the corridors? What kind of lighting? How efficient is it? How are the acoustics? Which way do the doors open? The emergency exits? Where? What are they made of? What kind of locks do they have? The dustbins at the back of the hotel, how many, and where? And so on, while Ari Ofer went on smoking with a preoccupied air.

Finally Gehmer straightened up. "All right, I'll need copies of these plans, too."

"Will do," the Mossad officer said. "And Mike will be present at your final briefing, if your men have any questions."

Gehmer checked his watch. "Five forty-five?" he asked Mike.

"No problem."

"You know where?"

"I'll escort him there," the Mossad officer said. "By the way, we've had confirmation from Beirut that all the necessary arrangements have been made."

"Good."

"Any further questions? Ari?"

Ari Ofer shifted on his chair and slowly ground his cigarette out in the ashtray.

"Mike," he finally said, "how did Hijazi look? I mean, how did his general condition appear?"

"He looked awful, just awful. You'd think he was about to crack at any moment." Mike shook his head.

* * *

"Excellent," said Mossad chief Yitzak Hofi into the phone. "You'll see to it that I get a report from the debriefing as soon as possible, will you? Good.

"No, considering everything, things have gone smoothly. We still have a couple of hours in hand." He glanced at his watch, then out through the window at the El Al building, which towered over the Tel Aviv skyline to the west with the Mediterranean behind. It was a fairly windy day with a thin overcast of alto-cumulus clouds.

"I suppose we can't hope for much better conditions when it comes to the weather. The wind will probably drop a little by tonight."

The Memuneh listened for a while longer.

"Yes, I've talked to the Chief-of-Staff. Everything's in order, the navy and air force units are ready and on standby. As our American friends say, the condition is *go*. Wish them luck."

15

LEIF AWOKE to a ululating, sing-song voice that he knew but at first couldn't place. He stared up at the blue, cloudless sky for a moment before he recognized the *muezzin* calling the faithful to prayer with his prerecorded excerpt from the Koran, broadcast from a hidden speaker in the minaret of the mosque in Halat Ammar. Leif was on the roof of his cab, where he had climbed with his sleeping bag and a pillow to get some sun and then fallen asleep. Slowly he sat up, scratching his chest, and looked out across the customs compound.

Most of the Arabs had gone off to the mosque. Those that remained were bringing out and unrolling their prayer mats, facing almost due south towards Mecca, and kneeled down on them. The few drivers he could see over by the European trucks studiously ignored the Arabs, keeping their voices low and avoiding direct stares. They knew better than to interfere with local religion.

Leif yawned and quietly gathered up his sleeping bag and pillow and climbed down. He opened the cab door and had to step back at the wave of heat that rolled out from the interior. He threw his gear onto the bottom bunk, got out a light blue T-shirt and put it on, then went around to Preben's Scania.

Nick was dozing on the cab, but there was no sign of his master. A few Scandinavian pilots had gathered by one of Cannonball Jack's open trailer boxes and were drinking coffee, making sandwiches, and talking. Lasse from Trailertransport was playing chess with a driver Leif didn't know. It was a typical Saudi Sunday.

"Anybody see the Pirate?" Leif asked.

"Sure," Lasse answered while his hand hovered over his remaining knight. "He and the Finns went to buy bread a couple of minutes ago. Should be back soon."

Leif nodded, and Jack handed him a cup of coffee.

The Arabs finished their prayer, rolled up their prayer mats and stuffed them back inside the cabs of their Mercedeses and Saviems. Cannonball Jack plugged a Manhattan Transfer cassette into the deck and turned the volume up with the cab door open. Leif drained his cup and had it refilled

Preben came back a few minutes later, accompanied by the two drivers from Finn Express. "So you're up and about," the Dane commented. "Thought I was going to have to wake you up."

"Hell, the *muezzin* took care of that."

"Good news," Preben said. "We just got ourselves free slots by the ramp. Jukka and Aalvar were cleared last night and will be rolling in a couple of minutes. We'd better make sure the Arabs don't beat us to it."

"Yo. Let us say half an hour," one of the Finns said in his half-singing accent. "We'll just get our things together and take a shower."

"Thanks," Leif said. He knew that the chances of getting through customs procedures were practically nil unless one stood with the ass of the truck kissing the ramp. There was no question of queueing up, so the pilots had invented their own "stick-together" system. "We appreciate it."

"And I've got some bread for tonight," Preben said, holding up a plastic bag nearly full of steaming, round, flat pieces of bread, delivered directly from the stone oven. Bread just didn't come any fresher.

"And rumour has it that Cannonball Jack has smuggled in a fifth of Scotland's finest," Preben added, grinning broadly.

"He's crazy!" Leif said.

"Well, it looks like there might be a little party tonight, anyway."

*   *   *

The missile attack craft *Kidon* made a slow turn, her four MTU diesels muttering as she sliced through the small waves made by the faint off-shore breeze. The six men in the black rubber tender paddled in silence, with long, steady strokes, as they covered the kilometre and a half to the rocky shoreline south of the Grotte aux Pigeons. Now and then the half moon appeared from behind the clouds, but the men were barely visible in their thin black stretch coveralls and facemasks.

The lights of Beirut shone ahead of them, presently obscured by rock as they closed in on the shore. The two men forward laid down their paddles and unslung their Colt assault rifles.

With a slight bump, the tender touched bottom. The two forward men jumped out and fanned out on each side, going down in a crouch, ready to open fire. But nobody seemed to have noticed their arrival. The other four dragged the tender across the sand and in between two rocks before they lifted out four battered, nondescript suitcases. Taking turns to cover the landing party, the men swiftly stripped off their coveralls and facemasks and put them in the suitcases. Underneath they wore ordinary business suits and crepe-soled shoes. The tender they covered with grey-mottled camouflage canvas.

Nathan Gehmer checked his watch: 2244 hours, running right on schedule. He motioned to the others, and with Levi Cohen covering the rear, they moved silently up among the rocks towards Boulevard de Chouran.

The van was already there. Gehmer motioned again, and the others fanned out with weapons at the ready. He took out a small flashlight, aimed it carefully and pressed the button, one single, long flash.

From inside the van came the answer, three quick flashes. One at a time, they sprinted in the darkness towards the now open rear doors of the van; a dark blue, battered Bedford, of uncertain vintage, its engine running. Gehmer was last in, then David Feinmann slammed the doors shut. A few seconds later the Bedford did a U-turn as it accelerated north along Boulevard de Chouran.

Phase one of the operation had come off without a hitch. The light in the ceiling was switched on, the suitcases opened and the assault rifles put inside, butts collapsed. The men hastily straightened ties and ran combs through their hair, looking at each other to check appearances.

The hatch between the cab and the back slid open, and Feinmann glanced at them over his shoulder. "The target is still in the hotel," he said. "We'll let the first group off in Rue el Hamra. Wait about ten minutes, then get a taxi to the Méditerranée. There are several hotels in the area, so you should have no problems. If needs be, the Méditerranée is within walking distance. Got it?"

"Got it." Gehmer nodded.

Cohen turned the light out, and the six men sat bouncing in darkness on the side benches as the Bedford sped through the city streets. Finally it made a sharp left turn and came to a halt. They waited in silence.

"Now," Feinmann said through the hatch.

Gehmer opened one of the rear doors, and carrying the four suitcases, Katz, Goren, and Ben-Zvi tumbled out after him into a narrow, dirty alley. The van raced off again, turning into Rue Makdisi and disappearing in the sparse late-night traffic. The four men in the alley waited for some minutes, then, carrying a suitcase each, they started walking.

The van drove westward, honking at intersections like any other Beirut vehicle, and finally reached the small back street at the rear of the Hotel Méditerranée. Limon parked the Bedford and cut the engine, and Feinmann brought out paper bags and three bottles of liquor, unscrewed the cap of a Johnny Walker "Red Label," and put it to his mouth. He took a sip, washed it around his mouth and then spit it out through the side window, and passed the bottle on to Limon, who repeated the performance before he passed the bottle through the hatch to Shulsky and Cohen. The bottle came back in a few seconds. They all rubbed their cheeks hard to redden them, and then left the Bedford.

The night porter wrinkled his nose in distaste at the party that entered the hotel foyer one minute later. Herr Dettmar and Herr Schmidt, accompanied by two other gentlemen, and all four of them had been drinking.

The man he knew as Hans-Günther Dettmar stepped forward, his tie slightly askew and a hint of unsteadiness in his gait. The night porter could smell the alcohol on his breath from four paces.

"*Nos collègues . . . à notre chambre pour une petite trinquée et un bout de causette, ja?*" With a clumsy movement he slid a fifty-mark note across the counter, winking broadly.

The night porter looked them over, taking in their mussed hair and the bags of bottles that Herr Schmidt carried, then shrugged almost imperceptibly and did a little vanishing trick with the banknote. As long as they didn't start singing. Fifty D-Marks was a lot on the black market.

"*D'accord . . . mais pas trop bruyamment, s'il vous plaît.*"

"*Ja, ja,*" Dettmar muttered. "*Nicht laut.*"

The four of them crowded into the nearest elevator.

The night porter shrugged again, and returned to the copy of *Penthouse* which an American journalist had left behind last week.

Ten minutes later a Mercedes taxi pulled up, and four men entered the hotel. They all carried suitcases, and two of them had light overcoats slung over their arms. They walked up to the reception desk, relaxedly talking among themselves.

"Good evening," the first man intoned as he produced his British passport and a business card. He wore his hair unusually short and sported one of those upswept moustaches London gents, in the opinion of the night porter, favoured. "Soames, Harlanne Machine Manufactures, London. I'm so sorry we're late, but we had to dine with some business associates. I believe you have our reservation by telex?"

The other three also produced their passports, and the four of them completed their registry cards and were assigned two adjoining twins on the third floor, 325 and 327.

"Would you like anything sent up, sir?" the night porter asked.

"No, thanks, we're fine," said the man who called himself Soames. "We're rather tired, so we'll just turn in. By the way, would you call us in the morning at 7:30, please?"

"Certainly, sir," the night porter replied and made a note of it. "Since I'm alone I'm sorry I can't leave the reception and help with the luggage. Could you . . .?"

"It's quite all right," Soames said. "We'll manage. Good night."

The night porter watched them disappear, and again went back to his *Penthouse*. A rather aloof lot, the British, but he'd sooner have them than hard-drinking Germans.

Once inside 327 Gehmer removed his itching moustache. Phase two was over, equally painlessly.

Shlomo Katz loosened his tie and lit a cigarette. "And now?" he asked, needlessly.

"Now," Nathan Gehmer said, "we wait."

*   *   *

The arc lights lit up most of the compound and bounced off the chrome and red lacquer of Cannonball Jack's Volvo F12. From the speaker in the open door came the first strains of Manhattan Transfer's "Tuxedo Junction." A dozen pilots were gathered alongside the trailer, sitting on camping chairs or standing in groups, talking, eating and drinking. Jack was making coffee, surreptitiously lacing every cup with golden liquid.

Leif smiled to himself as he watched. Damned if the thing didn't remind him of a high society party in one of those Fred Astaire movies on TV. He drained his mug and tilted his head backwards to look at the sky and the stars. The last drops of the coffee-whisky mixture trickled down his throat, but in spite of the warm beverage and his sweater he shivered. January nights were cold in Halat Ammar, with the desert on all sides.

Preben sidled up to him, a mug in one hand and one of his Danish cigars in the other. "Don't mind a shot of this, but God, what I'd give for a cool Carlsberg."

"Don't you think we're taking enough risks as it is?" Leif asked with a smile.

"I'll tell you something," Preben said. "One of the guys from Eastern Trailer smuggled in a few bottles last year. We were five trucks that stopped for the night north of Khaybar and had a roaring party. One of the guys passed out cold, so I put him back in his bunk, but turned his truck around. When he woke up next morning all the rest of us were gone, so he crawled into his seat and started driving like hell and had covered fifty k's before he discovered he was going in the wrong direction."

Preben took another swig, and Leif laughed.

"Maybe the Saudis do have the right idea," the Pirate said. "I'll drink to it. *Skål før aedrueligheden.* Here's to sobriety."

*   *   *

0025.

With a barely audible click, Gehmer locked the door behind them, and he, Katz, Ben-Zvi and Goren, the latter carrying one of the suitcases, made their way along the dimly lit corridor and up one flight of stairs, stopping around the corner from the corridor to rooms 413 and 417. They were wearing the black coveralls and facemasks, in their belts commando knives, hand grenades, and extra ammunition clips. Their Colt Commando assault rifles were unslung. Shlomo Katz carried a medikit over his shoulder. In Goren's suitcase were two more Colts for Cohen and Shulsky, with extra ammo clips, and two Polish-made M63 submachine guns with twenty-five-round magazines, light and compact weapons for Limon and Feinmann. Gehmer looked at his watch and tasted the metallic taste he always had in his mouth before going into combat.

0028.

To the sound of laughter and raucous German talk, the door of 413 swung open, and the guard outside 417 looked up for a disinterested moment. The door opened outwards, towards him, and obscured the people who were leaving. He shrugged and looked away. Those Germans were best ignored.

He looked hastily up again as footsteps came briskly towards him. His eyes widened; the man was wearing black combat coveralls and facemask. Then he noticed, and was almost hypnotized by, the cube with the shining lens that the man held in his hand, and started to get up, groping for his gun. His confusion gave Cohen the time needed to cover most of the distance between them, and at two metres he fired.

There was a dull *plop* from the taser as it spit out two needle-thin darts that went through the shirt into the Arab's chest, trailing thin, supple wires that sent their three-watt charge of electricity into the body. The Arab jerked, his features contorting in an involuntary spasm as his nervous system short-circuited and his knees buckled, and dropping the gun, he fell back in the chair.

Gehmer, Katz and Ben-Zvi were already beside Cohen, while Goren handed the suitcase in to the three in 413 before he took up position at the end of the corridor.

Cohen knocked at the door of 417, ready with the taser. There was silence for a few seconds, then the lock was turned. The door opened a crack, revealing one eye of the person inside. The eye took in the scene outside, and then the guard desperately tried to slam the door shut, without having opened it enough for Cohen's taser. Cohen viciously jerked the door open and kicked out at the Arab, then dived inside as the guard tumbled backwards, off balance. There was an explosion and a bullet whistled past his head and gouged a deep crater in the plaster of the opposite corridor wall. Gehmer held his fire for a fraction of a second until he was certain that this wasn't their target; then he pulled the trigger, and the Arab slewed half around as he went down, red flowers blossoming on his chest and belly and left side.

Gehmer swore as he and Ben-Zvi went in. Their cover of silence was gone, literally shot to pieces. The whole hotel would be on its feet within half a minute.

They threw open the next door, and the beam from the taser picked out a man half-sitting in his bed, his eyes wide, his sunken cheeks covered with stubble. Cohen fired the taser again, and the man convulsed, falling sideways over the edge of the bed.

Gehmer flicked on the light, his finger on the trigger,

but there was nobody else in the room. Just the man, whom he recognized: their target.

"Search the rooms!" he shouted. Katz pushed by, fished out a syringe, pulled the man's sleeve up and injected its contents. The stun effect of the taser was short-lived. Now their target would be out until they reached Tel Aviv. If they did.

Gehmer and Katz went over the room with lightning speed, jerking out drawers, upending the bed, lifting the carpet. Katz emptied the bag on the table while Gehmer tore out the innards of the bathroom cabinet. Nothing.

Ben-Zvi appeared from the other room. "Ready!" he said.

There was a burst of gunfire from the corridor, followed by another. Gehmer recognized the sharp reports of the Colt assault rifles.

Feinmann and Limon were in the room now, handing a Colt and an ammo belt to Cohen, who sprinted out to join Goren and Shulsky in the corridor.

"All right, let's go!" Gehmer shouted. "David and Samuel, get him!"

Carrying the unconscious man, whose head was lolling grotesquely, Feinmann and Limon followed Cohen into the corridor, while Ben Zvi, Katz and Gehmer brought up the rear. They ran towards the stairs. Gehmer threw a glance backwards, saw the door of 416 open a crack, and emptied the rest of his magazine along the corridor. He reached for a fresh clip from his belt and plugged it in as he ran to catch up with the others.

Third floor, second floor. Miraculously, no one appeared to fire at them. First floor, then they reached the ground floor, turned into the corridor out of sight from the foyer, running towards the back until they reached an unmarked door.

"Cover!" Cohen shouted. Ben-Zvi and Gehmer whirled about and went down flat, their rifles at eye level and ready to fire. There was a short burst as Cohen shot the lock to pieces and kicked the door open; then he tore a hand grenade from his belt, ripped out the firing pin and flung it through the opening. Three breathless seconds went by, then there was an explosion that moved the air and hurt their ears while debris rained on the wall across the corridor.

"Move!"

Gehmer saw a pale face peep around the corner to the lobby and fired. The Colt Commando bucked in his hands, and the head spattered blood and the body rolled over the floor as he and Ben-Zvi and Katz got to their feet again and ran.

The back door had nearly been twisted off its hinges. They rushed across the rubble, out into the cool night. The others were already turning into the alley where the Bedford was parked. They had made it out of the Hotel Méditerranée.

A burst of automatic fire from behind, and Shlomo Katz stumbled and fell, limply going down prostrate. Gehmer spun around, going down in a crouch, and caught a glimpse of movement in the ruined doorway. His Colt spewed fire, but the movement was already gone among the shadows.

"Take Shlomo!" he screamed at Ben-Zvi. "I'll give you cover!" Out of the corner of his eye, he saw Ben-Zvi bend down and pick up Katz's limp body. Running backwards, Gehmer fired again at the doorway, emptying the last of his clip as he turned into the dark alley.

He tore another clip from his belt and slammed it home as he ran, his footsteps echoing from the walls of the narrow alley. Damn, damn, damn. Shlomo wounded, no telling how badly. It seemed as if their luck was running out.

The others were piling into the Bedford as he reached it, Cohen covering the alley and the street. Two Arabs on the other side threw frightened looks over their shoulders as they scurried from the scene. The Bedford

coughed and fired, and Gehmer shouted at Cohen to
get in as he tore open the passenger door and jumped
up.

Limon gunned the engine, and with screaming tires
the van pulled into the street in a sharp turn, accelerating away. Gehmer twisted in his seat and slid aside
the hatch to the back. Somebody had turned the light
on: the scene was chaos, men holding onto grab rails
and assault rifles against the jolts and bounces of the
van. Feinmann had his left arm around the unconscious
kidnapped man, and Shulsky was bending over the
prostrate form of Katz on the floor, holding his head
up to protect it. Something darkly red was soaking the
throat and shoulder of Katz's coveralls.

"How is he?" Gehmer shouted over the roar of the
engine.

Ben-Zvi was closest. "Bad, I think," he shouted back.
"But he's still alive."

The gearbox crunched as Limon down-shifted and
turned right, into Avenue de Paris. Gehmer squeezed
the still warm barrel of his rifle; his commando knife
dug into his kidney, and he shifted in his seat to look
around. "Anybody following us?" he shouted to Limon.

Limon's eyes flew over the rear-view mirrors. "Don't
think so! Can't see any signs of it!" He pulled out to
overtake a battered Mercedes taxi, one of the few vehicles about, and Gehmer had a brief glimpse of a mouth
agape under a black moustache.

They were almost there. Gehmer leaned forward and
peered into the darkness towards the sea but could see
nothing. He checked his watch. Damn it, they were too
early, but there was nothing he could do about it now.

Limon braked hard, cutting the lights, and swerved
aside over the edge of the asphalt and onto the gravel
before he cut the engine and let the Bedford roll to a
halt.

Gehmer tore open his door and jumped out. The others were already getting out of the back.

"Levi and Moshe, give us cover!" he shouted. "The rest of you, follow me!"

He took the lead, sprinting down among the sand and rocks for a hundred metres, then he and Ben-Zvi went down behind the rocks, ready to open fire.

Feinmann and Limon came straggling in, carrying the limp form of their captive, then Cohen and Goren. Shulsky lay only a few metres away, panting hard from carrying Katz.

There was silence. Gehmer lay in the sand, squinting over the sights of his Colt Commando, listening to the sound of the surf below. He could see the Bedford silhouetted against the lights of Beirut, and he felt vulnerable. Things had gone seriously wrong. If the military or the police came in force, his squad would be dead ducks, hemmed in by the enemy in front and the sea at their backs.

A minute passed; an eternity ticking away.

Up on the road a car braked to a stop by their van, and he felt his pulse start to race. Then he heard the shout from Goren.

"The helicopters!"

He turned and strained his ears to pick up the faint sound of rotors; then he saw two dark shapes coming in low over the water, vaguely lit by the low half moon.

In a second he had his strong flashlight out and pressed the button. From the belly of the nearest helicopter a white searchlight flickered to life and then went out. They had been seen.

The sound of staccato gunfire came from up the road, and Gehmer swivelled around and saw fireflies of muzzle flames. Two more vehicles were coming to a stop. Jeeps, from which uniformed men jumped out and dived for cover.

"Fire!" he shouted. "Keep them down!" A series of

shots rang out as his group fired back. Gehmer touched
the smoke grenade in his belt, then changed his mind.
With the off-shore breeze, the smoke would drift back
and choke them.

The helicopters came rushing in, the roar of their engines growing. Two Bell UH-1D, painted flat black for
night reconnaissance and operations. The nearest one
was swinging in, hovering, its rotor whipping up a gale
that sent sand and gravel flying and tugged at their
coveralls. The door slid open, and Gehmer motioned to
Feinmann and Limon, screaming at the top of his voice
to make himself heard above the din.

"You first! Get in! The rest of you, *fire!*"

There was more heavy firing as Feinmann and Limon
got to their feet, carrying the prisoner, struggling against
the gale. Gehmer saw the other helicopter make a wide
swing to the right. There was a deafening crash as it
opened fire with a salvo of 70 mm rockets that turned
night into day for a moment.

"Run!" Gehmer shouted, but the others were already
on their feet, sprinting towards the door of the hovering
helicopter. Shulsky passed him, staggering under the
burden of Katz. More gunfire, and Goren twisted around
and fell, with his side red and wet, screaming. Gehmer
fired his last rounds towards the road as he ran to get
his hands around Goren and dragged him the last metres
to the helicopter. Strong hands seized them and pulled
them up. He stumbled and fell flat inside, the rear sight
of his rifle painfully digging into his ribs. The helicopter
lifted and swung right, and for a brief instant Gehmer
saw, through the open door, the other helicopter fire
another rocket salvo, hitting one of the jeeps and sending it bursting into a ball of flame. Then the hellish
vision swung out of sight and the door was pulled shut.
The floor started to tilt as the helicopter continued its
swing and began to climb. The roar inside was deafening.

Gehmer got unsteadily to his feet, holding on to a metal bar, and tried to take stock of the situation. Goren had fainted, and Cohen and one of the helicopter crew members were placing him across the seats alongside the right wall, strapping him in. The others were removing their facemasks, revealing drawn, dirt-streaked faces. The inside of the helicopter smelled of sweat and explosives and exhaust fumes.

Katz was lying on the floor with Shulsky kneeling beside him. The helicopter continued to climb, bucking and shaking. Gehmer got down on his hands and feet and crawled over to Katz.

"How is he?" he shouted in Shulsky's ear.

"Very bad." Shulsky shook his head, biting his lower lip.

"Isn't there anything we can do?"

"Nothing except get him to a hospital. He was hit in the throat."

"But, damn it . . ."

"Look, Nathan, what he needs is an operating theatre."

Gehmer fell silent and reached out to take over the task of holding Katz's head up away from the vibrating floor. He lifted his eyes and saw their half-naked, still unconscious prisoner, strapped into a seat with Feinmann by his side.

"Whoever you are, I hope you're worth all this," he whispered. Nobody heard him.

The roar of the Lycoming turbo-shaft engine reverberated through the metal as the helicopters went on climbing in the night on their way back to Tel Aviv.

Gehmer looked down and saw little air bubbles rising from the dark red sticky mess below Katz's chin. He sat on the floor, oblivious to the others who had died that night, and cradled Katz's head in his hands, poor little Shlomo Katz who was drowning in his own blood over the dark waters of the Mediterranean.

16

SLOWLY HE REPLACED THE RECEIVER and stared ahead with blind eyes.

"*Esh fik*? What is the matter?"

He jerked and turned his head, blinking and focusing his eyes. Reality returned: the squeaking fan that turned lazily in the ceiling, the bare walls of the post office where he stood in a corner, the rotund little man in *aba'a* and *keffiyeh* who was watching him anxiously. He suddenly realized how pale his face must look, and his hand, from habit, flew up to the brand on his left cheek.

"No ... no," he said. "It is ... it is just that I have received word about my brother. He is seriously ill."

There was genuine sympathy in the postmaster's fleshy face. "I am distressed to hear that. *Allah yishafih*. May God make him better."

"*Shokran*. He will get better, *in'ish Allah*."

The polite, formal phrase came automatically, while he tried to collect his wits. The postmaster appeared calmed.

He paid for his two calls and left the little post office, stopping on the stone steps outside. Halat Ammar lay before him, another busy working day under the hot morning sun, but he felt cold dread inside.

So they had somehow found Hijazi and taken him. He knew now that the silence he had relied on for their protection was broken. He held no illusions. The Israelis would break Hijazi in a matter of hours, and then they would have enough pieces to start fitting the puzzle together. For the first time since they had planned all this, he felt fear and the bitter taste of failure.

He still had two factors working in his favour. Fayez Hijazi had deliberately been kept in the dark as to their ultimate goal. Also, he did not know which particular truck carried the warhead. What he did not know, he could not tell, not even under torture. But Hijazi still knew enough to set the enemy on the right track. One thing would then lead to another.

He needed to buy time, five more days of it.

He looked across the alley at the recently white-washed entrance to the bank, and blinked. Perhaps there was still a way. But he had to move fast.

The familiar resolve was flowing back into him as he turned on the steps and reentered the post office. The postmaster sat at a table behind the counter and raised his head as he came in.

"I would like to make two more phone calls," he said.

* * *

Leif climbed the steps to the loading ramp and caught sight of Preben. The tarpaulin of the Dane's semi-trailer was rolled back, but Leif's semi was still covered and waiting for the customs officials to come and break the new cluster of seals he had collected since Cilvegözu.

As a rule, drivers were not allowed to handle any of their load during the customs clearance. But Preben didn't give a damn about that rule, and nobody seemed about to face up to his two metres and tell him otherwise.

The Pirate was on his trailer, dressed in jeans and work gloves. A long cold cigar butt dangled from the corner of his mouth, almost hidden in the black beard. With his hairy chest and arms he looked like a Kodiak bear hugging the packing crate he was slowly pushing aside. The Pakistanis were careful not to stand in his way.

Leif made his way over and stepped onto the trailer, ignoring the supervisor's startled look. Preben pushed the crate up to the side of the semi-trailer and looked up with a grin. He wiped the sweat off his forehead, then took the cigar butt out of his mouth and held it out to Leif.

"Got a light?"

"Sure." Leif fished out his lighter and handed it over. Preben lit his cigar and puffed out a cloud of blue smoke.

"How is it going?" he asked.

"Going back to my agent now. See if I can put their asses in gear. How about you?"

"Think I'll be through this afternoon." He grinned and winked at Leif. "With me growling at them, they sure can work in a hurry."

"Yeah, I noticed," Leif said. "Hectic, isn't it? Are you going out today?"

"Unless I'm cleared too late this evening. Yes, probably."

"Good. I'll be lucky if I can go out tomorrow."

Preben puffed at his cigar and stepped aside to make room for another crate being pushed in. "Talk any more with the guys in the BM Volvo bus?"

"Yeah. They're about halfway through."

"Any cuts?"

"Two so far. A sequence with a girl in a bikini, and one of the credits at the beginning of one film."

"In the credits?" Preben said.

"Guy's first name was Isak. I've got to go and see Yami. Come around and say goodbye before you leave."

"Will do." Preben grinned and put the cigar butt back in his mouth. "Isak!" he muttered and turned to another crate.

Leif left the compound and turned the corner by the

camel cock stand, then he ducked under the low lintel into one in a row of little offices.

There were two Arabs in the office, seated behind modern desks, busily rattling away at typewriters, the cylinders of which moved to the right instead of to the left as the papers filled with nice-looking, squiggly calligraphy. The desks and a small table and a filing cabinet were cluttered with papers. On the walls was an Air Saudia poster, a sign in neatly lettered Arabic, and the mandatory photographs of the late King Faysal and the present King Fahd. The left side of the filing cabinet was full of stickers for trucks and tires and various other firms, including a white-and-red Jerre sticker Leif had brought.

The nearest Arab looked up and beamed with his moustachioed face. "Aah, my friend Leif," he said in good English. "*La baes?*"

"Hello, Yami," Leif said amiably, "*La baes.*"

"*La baes*, Leif. *Alhamdullah.*" Yami touched his heart with his right hand. "You come to inquire about your papers, no?"

"Well, yes, just paying a visit to see how things are coming along."

"Please sit down! You would like some coffee?"

"Yes, please." He sat down on the nearest wooden chair and smiled back at the Arabs. This was their way of doing business, never getting down to things right away, but instead politely drinking coffee and passing the time of the day before homing in on the target. With time, Leif had actually learned to enjoy it—it was, after all, the only game in town.

As if by magic, a young boy appeared in the doorway. Yami spoke a string of words in Arabic, and the boy turned and disappeared.

"Your papers are almost finished," Yami said, beaming. "Maybe two hours, and I will go and tell the customs people your truck is ready for inspection, OK?"

"Good," Leif said and smiled again. This was better than he had hoped for. A large part of the job of the agents was translating the load sheets into Arabic for the benefit of the customs people, as well as doing all the paperwork for taxes and duties and so on. If trucks happened to be queueing up in large numbers, that could take time. "I'm ready, any time you say so."

The fan in the ceiling whirred softly while Yami and Leif talked on, waiting for the coffee to arrive.

*   *   *

The room had no windows, only a thick metal door at its far end. The walls were in semi-darkness, in sharp contrast to the brilliantly illuminated operating table at its centre. Metal clamps glittered in the harsh light, and black, thin cables trailed from them to a small instrument panel on a bench by one wall. The room smelled of antiseptics and sweat and fear.

The man on the table was naked, his hands, feet, chest and thighs strapped down. The black band of a blood-pressure meter was tied around his left biceps, and little silver discs were fastened to his chest, throat, and temples, connected by thin wires to inputs at the side of the operating table. The dark stubble of the man stood out against the pale skin, and his hair was plastered in wet stripes across his glistening forehead. His genitals were shrivelled up and wrinkled. He's very afraid, Ari Ofer suddenly thought.

He turned away from the man on the table and looked at the bespectacled, thin-haired man in a white coat who stood beside him.

"How is he?" he asked in a tired and gravelly voice. The tall, sallow-faced man at Ofer's side said nothing.

"In bad physical condition," the thin-haired man said. "Heart beat around 110, and erratic. Blood pressure low, blood sugar count low, body temperature down, though that's partially due to his lack of clothes. Basic reflexes slow. There is a trace of ventricular tachycardia, probably because he has been in shock. We just injected him with an adrenergic, which will get him out of it at the price of raising his heart beat further and putting further strain on his body." He nodded towards another set of instruments attended to by two male assistants. A series of green blips was travelling across an oscilloscope screen. "If you want my unsolicited professional opinion, this man is not fit for that kind of treatment."

"Don't you think I can see that?" Ari Ofer flared up. "Don't you think we've tried normal interrogation methods? Cajoling him, bribing him, threatening to beat him up?" He caught his breath, brought his temper under control again. "We're running out of time. We need information, and if we have to crush him to save maybe thousands of innocent people, then we'll crush him."

The thin-haired man shrugged. "All right."

"The tape recorders are running?"

"Yes." The man seemed suddenly indifferent. He spat out a curt order, and the two assistants started to fasten the metal clamps to the head and body of the man on the table, who squirmed in his straps, making a sound that was almost like the meowing of a cat.

Ari Ofer nodded to the tall, sallow-faced man, who slowly walked up to the table until he stood with his hips against its side. He looked into the naked man's eyes. "Fayez Hijazi, do you understand me?" he asked in Arabic.

Hijazi's eyes moved. He had heard.

"Fayez Hijazi, you force us to do this. But if you are willing to talk, I will have you released now. After you have talked you can rest and sleep for as long as you want."

The naked man mumbled something, and his eyes moved away again. Ari Ofer sighed and started for the door.

"Don't you wish to stay?" the thin-haired man asked.

Ofer reached the door, opened it, turned and met his gaze. He shook his head slowly.

A long moment went by, the silence interrupted only by Hijazi's mumbling.

"Look," the thin-haired man said vehemently, "I don't enjoy this any more than you do."

Ari Ofer did not reply; he just stared with expressionless eyes, then closed the door and was gone.

The thin-haired man turned, his jaw set and his cheeks hot, and nodded to the tall man by the operating table.

*   *   *

Leif was comfortably propped up in his bunk, composing his usual letter from Halat Ammar to Annika. The reading lamp behind his shoulder spread a soft sheen inside the cab and kept the deepening dusk outside his windows.

There was a knock on the door, and without reflecting Leif turned the Israeli radio station off before he opened. Preben climbed into the driver's seat, accompanied by his cat. The Pirate's damp black curls fell over the towel around his neck and smelled of soap and shampoo.

"All set to go," he said. "Coming along for a walk?"

"Sure. What's the time?"

"Quarter to six."

"How far are you going tonight?"

"Probably to Taima. About three hundred k's. Should make Jeddah tomorrow."

Leif put the letter aside, stretched and yawned. He slid into the passenger seat, found his sandals and grabbed his jacket before getting out and locking both doors.

Inside the compound things had settled down. Here and there the flames of camp stoves glowed, and faint music wafted along with the cool evening breeze. Preben's red Scania 141 was gone from the now dark and silent warehouse and replaced by Cannonball Jack's Volvo F12. The tarpaulin of Leif's semi-trailer was rolled back, and part of the load had been shifted onto the loading dock.

The stars had come out and they walked along in relaxed silence past the quiet mosque, as far as the building of the foreign workers at the far end of Halat Ammar. Three trucks stood parked, cabs facing inwards, in the slots among the columns. Preben's was the closest. The Indians and the Pakistanis were sitting outside their cubicles, smoking and talking among themselves, eyeing Leif and the Pirate with bland curiosity.

"You've got my address in Odense, haven't you?" Preben suddenly asked.

"Yeah, sure," Leif said. "I have it in my address book."

"Good. If you ever get there, drop in. If I'm not home, Ellen probably will be. She knows about you, has seen photos of you."

Leif suddenly realized what a peculiar kind of friendship the run created. Neither had ever been to visit the other, yet knew more about each other's lives than most next-door neighbours did at home.

"You're welcome at my place, too," Leif said. "But I'll probably have a new address when Annika and I move in together. I promise to send you a card, though."

"Aah, I'll probably see you next trip around. A couple of months of hauling timber and bread and milk and sticking to speed limits, and you'll be back chewing Saudi dust."

"Not this time. It's quits for certain, I've promised Annika." Leif bent down and patted the big grey tomcat affectionately.

"Be missing you too, Nick," he said. "Take good care of your boss now."

Preben grinned and reached up to unlock the door of his Scania. He gave a whistle, and the cat flashed into the cab, barely touching the steps. The Pirate grabbed the handrail and swung himself into the driver's seat. He rummaged around and then handed a cassette down to Leif.

"Here's the Tina Charles tape you liked."

"Come on, mate, I can't . . ."

"Aw, shut up. It's a present. You keep it."

Leif reached up and took the cassette. They regarded each other in silence, then they nodded and shook hands.

"Take it easy, Preben. Don't run over any camels."

"*I lige måde.* Same to you. Be seeing you." He winked at Leif, then closed the door and fired up the diesel.

Gears growled as Leif turned and started walking towards the compound, not looking back, whistling softly to himself.

*   *   *

From inside the white Mazda 929 behind the restaurant, the three men saw the big red truck slowly back out as the other driver returned on foot. The headlights and the roof sign came on. The truck started rolling forward, turning left around the building, gathering speed. They sat quietly and watched it pass and dwindle on the slow rise into the hills and the night.

The man in the front passenger seat fingered the brand on his cheek as his gaze followed the truck. When it could no longer be seen he nodded, and the man behind the wheel turned the key and started the engine.

*   *   *

The naked man fell back against the operating table, his body awash with sweat, his tongue between his teeth, blue and swollen. A trickle of vomit ran from one corner of his mouth; his eyes were bloodshot, dull, in a face drained of all colour.

The tall, sallow-faced man bent over the table with his face close to that of the naked man.

"Listen, Fayez," he said softly, "we can go on in this way, for as long as necessary, and we will. You're the only one who can stop the pain, do you understand? You can stop it right now by telling us what we want to know. What were you doing in the Hotel Méditerranée? Why were you hiding? What is el-Tha'ir up to? Tell us, Fayez, and there will be no more pain."

He stood back, impassively, then with an effort, Hijazi rolled his head from one side to another. The man pressed the switch in his hand once more and held it down for a full three seconds. Hijazi convulsed as the current shot through his battered body, but this time the shaking didn't stop. The whites of his eyes turned up, and his mouth silently worked the saliva into a blood-stained froth.

On the oscilloscope screen the steady blips changed to towering waves with little, irregular blips floating around the crests.

"He's having a heart attack!" one of the assistants whispered hoarsely.

The thin-haired, bespectacled man, who had kept in the background, monitoring instruments, rushed up and pushed the interrogator aside. He grabbed Hijazi's shoulders and held him down against the operating table.

"Quick!" he shouted. "Give him another shot of adrenergic, and get the shock equipment ready. You, start mouth-to-mouth resuscitation!"

While he gave orders he placed the heels of both his hands over Hijazi's heart and with straight arms pushed downwards with rib-crushing force, repeating the action with one-second intervals.

Hijazi opened his mouth as one of the assistants pinched his nose and bent down over him. A faint sound came from it.

"Hold it!" the interrogator cried. "He's trying to say something!"

Again Hijazi opened his mouth, parting cracked lips

to reveal bloodied teeth. With his hands poised over Hijazi's heart, the thin-haired man impotently watched the blips on the oscilloscope slow down as they recorded that life that was ebbing from the naked man, who was mumbling into the ear of his unwitting executioner.

*   *   *

"Damn, and damn again! I should have realized it!" Ari Ofer viciously threw the report down on his desk and went on to smite it with his fist. He held up his hand and with a kind of desperately restrained fury inspected the red edge of his hand, flexing his fingers. "Hell, the man had a heart condition he hadn't told anybody about, and we had to go and torture him!"

Dov Kultz turned away from the window. "There was no way we could have known. We have to accept that."

David Bar-Sharon was moodily lighting a cigarette; he nodded silently, while Bill Herman looked ill at ease and apologetic.

"Read the damned transcript," Ofer stormed. "Groans, moans, stifled cries, garbled refusals to speak, more groans, and so on *ad nauseam*—literally. Then suddenly he starts mumbling like a Catholic going to confession—*transport . . . police . . . Ulukisla . . . transport*— and then he expires. We have a corpse on our hands, a corpse we lost one man to get and which put another one in the critical ward. And newspapers everywhere are giving us hell about the raid!"

There was a moment's silence, then Bill Herman tentatively said, "Ulukisla—if that's the correct transcription? What's Ulukisla?"

"The interrogator was quite sure about the transcription," Ofer said in a more reasonable tone. "Hijazi spoke fairly clearly at the very end. They've checked it out; Ulukisla is a small place in Turkey, on the main road north of the Taurus Mountains."

"So when do we pull a raid into Turkey?" David Bar-Sharon said sourly.

"Hell, David, will you knock it off?" Ofer impatiently exclaimed.

"The information is tenuous, to say the least," Dov Kultz observed. "It is, however, what we will have to work on."

"You're damned right," Ofer said.

"Turkey," Bill Herman said in a curiously confident voice. "That's NATO territory. I think I might be able to make myself useful at last."

The others looked at him.

"I think," Bill Herman went on, "that I'll go over and arrange a few things with my people. Stay put. I'll be in touch and tell you the results as soon as I can."

17

BILL HERMAN, Arif Ofer, and David Bar-Sharon landed at the US air base at Adana in Turkey at 0845 Sunday morning. An Oldsmobile with American military plates, driven by a neat, youngish corporal, was already waiting to take them to Ulukisla. There were no formalities, no fuss, nothing about the arrival to make anyone take particular notice. The base commander came out to meet them and exchange a few words a little to one side with Bill Herman. He shook hands with the two Israelis and pointed out with some pride, as they were getting into the car, that they had the best driver the base was able to provide: he had been racing stock cars back in the States. The corporal grinned and proceeded to live up to his reputation.

Late the night before Bill Herman had visited the US Embassy in Hayarkon Street. Less than two hours later he had returned and cheerfully announced, "Got through to our people at Ankara Station. They'll handle the Turkish end of it, and promised to have a couple of reps accompanied by the correct number of Turkish brass to make it on the level out there first thing in the morning to have a word with the Ulukisla police. They're sending a company jet over so we can be there second thing in the morning."

Ofer had stared at him for a moment and then pounced on the phone. Less than a minute later he had been in touch with the Memuneh, explaining the new development. He had listened for a while and put the receiver down, grinning.

"All right, I'll be on that plane, and David, too. A little service abroad for you there. Dov will keep up this end of the operation. Damn it, we still may be getting somewhere."

* * *

The day was clear and the temperature was a few degrees centigrade below zero; the sun shone small and frozen and made the snow seem virgin, at least from a distance. When they reached Ulukisla a little after half past ten, David Bar-Sharon took a deep breath and started to relax. He had had no idea how any road, which they had seemed to touch in so few spots, could impart such jolts through the suspension of an American car.

The little Turkish town appeared abnormally busy. Slowly they picked their way through the narrow streets. Outside the police station several cars were parked, almost blocking the traffic. Two of them were big, black, official-looking limousines with Ankara plates; one of them had CD plates and small flags on the front fenders covered with black leather sheaths. There were also two large police cars, reasonably clean and with no damage either to paintwork or sheet metal; they looked as if they belonged in some more cosmopolitan place than Ulukisla. Some men in dark suits and topcoats were standing by the limousines, talking, while a number of policemen were keeping the locals, who seemed to have turned out to a man to gape at the spectacle, at a distance. Further up the street a private house was similarly cordoned off, with an ambulance waiting outside.

A police officer—of high rank, judging from the number and garishness of the badges of rank he wore on his right breast, and from the rake of his peaked cap—was coming out of the police station, saying something

over his shoulder in a clearly irritated manner. He gave
the Olds a long, hard stare, and the men by the limousines stopped talking and turned towards the new-
comers.

Getting out of the car, it took David a few seconds
before he could analyze the quality of the excitement
and place it. It was the excitement of a heavy-weight
title fight, the excitement of the bull fights, the excitement of an F-1 race, the excitement of a major accident.
It was the excitement of blood.

Bill Herman was already shaking hands with the
waiting men, Ari Ofer at his side, when David reached
the group.

Introductions were brief. James O'Neill, a tall sandy-
haired man with quick slate-grey eyes and a self-assured
drawl, first secretary at the US Embassy in Ankara, and,
David thought to himself, probably the CIA Chief-of-
Station. His assistant, Bob Kant, a man in his late fifties,
with thinning hair and a wrinkled outdoors complexion.
Nazim Karaman, a tall Turk with a military bearing, a
fine aquiline nose and a luxurious black moustache,
under-secretary of state in the Ministry of the Interior,
under the supervision of which the Turkish National
Police comes. Bülent Tahir, from the office of the Director-
General of Public Security, a man who could well have
been a championship wrestler in his youth. The police
officer was Kemal Hikmet, chief-of-police of Adana,
capital of the *vilayet*, or province.

There was a moment of silence, then O'Neill said,
with a grimness that was belied by his drawl, "You're
late, boys. The local chief-of-police is dead."

"Dead?" Arif Ofer echoed.

"Murdered," Karaman said in smooth English, almost
as if tasting the word in order to decide whether he
liked it or not. "Together with his wife." He pointed to
the house where the ambulance was waiting. "Maybe
you gentlemen will be able to provide a reason."

"Come and have a look," O'Neill offered.

The bodies of the chief-of-police and his wife were in a large, cluttered and rather threadbare living room on the ground floor of the house. They were covered, quite according to all conventions, with white sheets. There were dark stains of blood here and there on the floor and rugs. Apart from that there was little sign of disorder in the room. A bespectacled man in civilian clothes and a policeman were talking together over some forms to one side. Karaman bent and folded back the sheet covering the chief-of-police to expose the face; David sombrely studied it. The sunken cheeks were a translucent pale yellow-green colour. The beard had begun to show as the flesh had shrunk, and the grey moustache bristled almost defiantly in death.

Karaman drew the sheet across the face again and straightened up.

"Shot, six bullets, .22-calibre, probably a silenced gun. Bullets hit abdomen, four grouped closely together, two higher up and to the left. Wife with similar wounds. Professional work. A local doctor has estimated that they died sometime early this morning. They were found a little past nine, after Ipekci had failed to show up at the police station."

"Any witnesses?" Ofer asked.

Karaman snorted and pointed to the other lifeless form. "If there was, she's dead." He gazed at a big new Telefunken stereo radio with numerous knobs and switches and a built-in cassette deck, which stood on a low table by the sofa, and added, almost casually, "Ipekci seems to have been able to spend rather a lot of money lately."

Ofer nodded, and O'Neill remarked, "So this was the guy who had the answers to your questions. Pity somebody got to him first."

"Yes, it seems he had," Ofer said thoughtfully. "Could we go back to the police station? If there are any answers I think we'll find them there."

The police station had a barracks' smell of stale smoke, sweat, and inadequate ventilation. Two policemen who sat at the table rose to attention as the party entered, while two other men, who were already standing, drew themselves up. The latter had the better-fed, better-groomed look of bigger-city policemen.

They looked around, taking in the unwashed coffee cups on the table, the overflowing ashtrays, the notice-boards with papers of all sizes pinned to them, the desk with more papers, files, and ledgers, the bookshelf with a number of worn books to the left, the two filing cabinets beside it. The policemen regarded them a little apprehensively.

"All right," Ofer said, "so we'll have to find our answers elsewhere. I'd like to go through the documents."

Hikmet, who at the introduction had demonstrated a rather poor command of spoken English and therefore had left the talking to Karaman, started to say something in Turkish, apparently as a protest.

Karaman hastened to translate. "The chief says it's out of the question. Police documents are not official, and foreigners in particular are not allowed to read them . . ."

"I take it," Bill Herman said to O'Neill, "that our friends have been informed about the urgency and seriousness of this matter?"

"Certainly," O'Neill answered. "Mr. Karaman, could I have a word with you?"

Karaman nodded and accompanied the American outside, where they stood for a while, talking, before they returned.

"Well, this actually *is* police business," Karaman announced, "but considering the situation there is no need for the authorities to be unnecessarily inflexible and not let you follow our investigations closely." He coughed drily and talked to Hikmet in Turkish. The chief-of-police started to protest again, but was quickly silenced by Karaman.

"Good," Ari Ofer said. "Get me somebody who can speak English to go through the journals. David and Bill, get somebody to go through the files with you. Only those that are a month old or less. I don't know exactly what we're looking for except it will in some way have something to do with transport."

* * *

Leif came through the gate with easy, bouncing steps, showered and with his hair washed, a clean T-shirt on, and all his papers properly signed and stamped in his attaché case.

He had been to say goodbye to Cannonball Jack and found him hanging out the cab window, shaving before the rear-view mirror. Some of the other pilots had insisted that he stay for a little farewell lunch as it was his last run—on condition that he be the host the next time around. With a smile he had declined; he was cleared, ready to roll, and itching with whiteline fever after three days of getting nowhere.

He walked across to the bakery and bought four pieces of *chubz*, the local bread, and one of the few words of Arabic he knew and could pronounce correctly.

His blue Scania 141 stood ready in a slot under the white roof, where he had driven it one hour earlier. He felt a special thrill as he swung himself into his seat and reached into the plastic bag and broke off a piece of bread. The bread had come directly from the oven into his plastic bag, and was still so hot that it almost burned his fingers. He put the bread in his mouth and chewed. It smelled heavenly and tasted just as good.

He looked over his stock of cassettes and pushed Tina Charles into the deck. "Set My Heart on Fire" boomed out of the speakers with the volume turned up. He reached up and turned on the Kysor, put his sunglasses on and lit a Prince, then he turned the key and pressed the starter button. The V-8 roared into familiar, vibrating life. There was a slight crunch as he engaged reverse and, scanning his mirrors, started slowly backing out from the shadow under the roof and into the sunlight.

*   *   *

It was past noon when Ari Ofer, who had been assisted by Bülent Tahir, suddenly made an exclamation. "I think we may have found it. Listen, there's a notation here that a Swedish truck was stopped last Sunday—that was the fourteenth—and the driver held overnight and then released. The journal doesn't give any explanation."

David Bar-Sharon looked up from his stack of ledgers and files, which were spread across the desk where he sat. "Does it give the name of the driver?"

"Yes, but not much else."

Karaman came over and looked at the entry, nodded to himself and then barked an order in Turkish. The two local policemen, who had sat down again, looked at each other and then at Hikmet. When nothing more came of it Hikmet repeated the order, and one of the policemen stubbed out his cigarette and rose. He was a small, seedy man in his early middle age, doomed from all appearance never to rise any higher and compensating with an obsequious manner which, given the merest excuse, would turn to bullying.

Hikmet spoke again, and the policeman nodded. "Aziz here, on duty," Hikmet said in heavily accented English.

Aziz was palpably nervous; his eyes darted about, resting neither on Hikmet, nor on Karaman or any of the other outsiders, and his hands fluttered at his sides as if they longed for the comfort of the stubbed-out cigarette.

"Does he know anything about this incident?" Ofer asked and tapped the entry with his index finger.

Karaman repeated the question in Turkish, and Aziz began to talk, hesitatingly at first, and then with increasingly fluent eagerness, until Karaman stopped him. The under-secretary had an expression that was both pleased and perplexed.

"It appears," he said, "that he was not only on duty but actually present when this truck was stopped."

"So?" Ofer leaned back in his chair. "What happened?"

Aziz got going again after a word from Karaman, almost with apologetic zeal, and Karaman's face darkened visibly as he listened. When Aziz stopped for breath he translated.

"Ipekci took Aziz with him on a road patrol that day. Didn't tell him the purpose, but the only vehicles Ipekci took any interest in were southbound TIR trucks—what few there were. He would stop them, go through their papers and send them on their way. That is, until he stopped this Swedish truck, which Aziz says was travelling together with a similar red truck of some other nationality, Scandinavian at any rate, he believes. Ipekci said there was something the matter with the papers and told the driver to come along to Ulukisla while they checked it out. Aziz rode with the driver in the truck."

"What was the destination of that truck?" Ofer asked with a curious intensity in his voice.

Karaman relayed the question to Aziz and in reply received a stream of words which he had to dam with a peremptory movement of his hand.

"Aziz doesn't know. Ipekci took the papers and didn't let anybody else see them. Must have been somewhere in the Middle East."

"He says he rode in the truck. Can he describe the driver? And what happened to the other truck?"

The procedure of translation and retranslation repeated itself. Aziz threw longing glances at the pack of cigarettes on the table, but didn't dare make any move to get at it.

"The driver was tall, over one hundred and eighty centimetres. Fairly normal build, blond hair and beard. As for the other truck, it went on its way. Ipekci more or less had to order the driver to move on. This other driver was a very big fellow, bigger than the first, and with a huge black beard. Aziz says he looked like a pirate. When they got back here they booked the Swedish driver and put him in a cell for the night."

"What happened to the truck?"

"It was left on the outskirts of the town, and the driver was brought here in the police car."

"Why?"

"Why?" Karaman said without consulting Aziz. "You've seen the streets, haven't you?"

Ofer nodded. "All right. Did anybody guard or look after the truck during the night?"

"Apparently not, but Ipekci had taken the keys and kept them himself, strangely enough."

"And then what happened?"

"Nothing as far as Aziz knows." Karaman now wore a completely perplexed expression. "In the morning Ipekci took the driver back to the truck, gave him back his papers and sent him on his way. That was all."

"Odd. How was the driver treated?"

The question elicited an eager string of what was evidently protestations from Aziz.

"He says he was well treated," Karaman translated. "When one of the policemen handled him a little roughly—Aziz says it wasn't him—he was told off by Ipekci."

Ari Ofer thoughtfully stared straight ahead for a moment, then said, "One last question. Did there seem to be an arrangement between this Swedish driver and Ipekci? Or was the driver unaware of the fact that he was going to be stopped and held?"

Karaman translated again, and Aziz responded with many words accompanied by gestures.

"Aziz doesn't think the driver knew anything beforehand. He protested a lot and seemed very angry and also scared, and was very unwilling to go to Ulukisla."

"All right," Ofer said. "This is probably as much as we'll be able to get out of him."

"Would you like a copy of his official statement? We're going to take it down later on."

"No, I don't think that will be necessary. But thanks, anyway."

On a word from Karaman Aziz sat down and at once lit a cigarette with hands that were none too steady.

"Damn it," Ofer said and rose from his chair, "if that thing somehow isn't on that truck. What we have is the name of the driver, his passport number, and the registration number of his truck. The Swedish authorities must have a way of finding out his destination. Who's got the best line to the Swedes?"

O'Neill spoke up. "I think this would be best handled through diplomatic channels." He caught Ofer's sceptical look. "Don't worry, I know the Swedish chargé d'affairs in Ankara well. They'll be jumping in Sweden within hours."

"Very well, could you see if they can supply us with a photograph of the driver, or at least a good description to corroborate and detail the one Aziz gave?"

"Will do. And I'm sure Mr. Karaman will see that the police here try and trace what happened to the truck during the night. If it was touched or moved, the people who lived near to where it was parked might have observed something." O'Neill was being efficient, authoritative in a quiet manner. Karaman nodded.

"In that case," Ofer said, "we'll be getting back to Adana to await the information there. I think we have found what we came for. What remains here is police work." He turned to the under-secretary. "Many thanks,

Mr. Karaman, for your very useful cooperation. I shall particularly include it in my report. You may be certain that our government won't forget it." He offered his hand to the Turk, who shook it with ironic solemnity.

"Yes, you're right, Mr. Ofer, police work. Catching murderers. You wouldn't be interested in that, would you?"

"Actually," Ofer answered with equal solemnity, "I would be very interested in having a word or two with them. Provided only that you catch them, which, you will pardon me, I very much doubt that you will. But what we really want badly, and what we now have a chance to get, is that Swedish driver, and particularly his truck."

*   *   *

The asphalt was a blur beneath him, the white lines an endless series of blips running in beside his left front wheel, the road a ruler-straight grey-black strip that lost itself in the shimmering mirages obscuring the horizon. The sun-baked desert surrounded him on all sides, so vast as to nearly obliterate all sense of motion, as if he were the immovable centre of a slowly shifting universe, the passing kilometres no more registering in his mind than the breaths he drew. A universe unto itself, where the rhythm of the road and the rock-steady drone of the diesel gradually blotted out reality, leaving his thoughts free to wander in ever-widening circles.

To most of the other Saudi pilots this was the most boring stretch of the whole journey, but tens of thousands of kilometres of desert driving had not dulled the subtle exhilaration Leif felt when he looked out.

The *serir*, desert consisting mostly of flat, hard-packed sand, began just south of Halat Ammar and lasted until Tabuk, the first town. He had stopped there to fill his tanks up with diesel, as usual haggling with the station attendant, even though the price was less than one-tenth of the price in Europe. Shortly after Tabuk the *serir* began again, with a hundred and fifty kilometres before the next tree appeared on the left: a single drab, dusty-green, incongruous specimen.

Further south, towards Hafirat al Ayda, the desert changed character, growing hillier until the road curved in gentle turns past the strange mesa formations carved out of the reddish rock by some river long lost in geological history. By sundown he would be driving through little oases, lush with green palms, where he would stop to buy bananas and more bread for his evening meal.

A muted shriek added itself to the sound of the diesel engine and the windstream and Tina Charles, as the thermostat fan cut in. He looked down at the speedometer and saw that the needle had crept up to 120 kph again, with the tach red-lining beside it. He eased his right foot up a little, and the speedo needle crept down below 115, almost reluctantly.

Paradoxically, that was part of the danger of driving in Saudi Arabia. Hour after hour blurred all sense of time and distance and could make you so speed-blind that you blew your engine. And the H4 up north, running down to Dammam along the pipeline, was even more extreme: with turns fifty or a hundred kilometres apart, you could almost set the hand throttle, secure the steering wheel, wind and set your alarm clock, and climb into your bunk.

Little dust devils danced in the shimmering heat, stirring up the grey-brown sand in hazy, shifting columns. A white speck grew ahead, and he pulled out to pass sounding his compressor horn, smiling faintly as he closed in on it. Another one of those flimsy little Japanese pickups. Two Arabs in red-and-white chequered head-dresses were in the cab, one of them turning to gaze at him through the back window, while their wives sat bouncing on the flatbed: two black-clad creatures hud-

dling together against the wind, their flapping dresses
covering their faces, making them anonymous and im-
personal. His Scania dwarfed the pickup, and he watched
it dwindle in his rear-view mirror before he pulled back
in. Hell, a TIR truck could run right through one of
those Dinky Toy things without the pilot noticing anything if he happened to be looking the other way.

You had to watch out all the time, even on the open
road with its sparse traffic. All you had to do in Saudi
Arabia was to pass a simple eye test using symbols to
accommodate the illiterate, and then you could tie your
camel to the nearest parking-meter and buy a Cadillac.
The standard of driving was accordant with this.

Night driving held its own peculiarities. When you
met somebody, it was even money that he would be
on your side, and then you had to flash all the lights
you could raise, including the roof sign, and hope to
make him swerve back over. Sometimes Leif did the
opposite and turned everything off, which as a rule
achieved remarkable results; when some thirty or forty
tons without warning winked out of existence and continued its approach unseen, in complete darkness, Ahmed
usually hastened to make a wide detour out across the
desert before he either got stuck or pulled back onto
the road a safe distance further down. With a driving
style like that, honed to fight Arabs and Turks and
Yugoslavs, small wonder that Annika complained
whenever he drove her Volkswagen back in Sweden.

The thermostat fan turned itself off, leaving Tina
Charles in charge again. The *serir* had changed and given
way to low hills and sparse vegetation. Four camels stood
some distance away from the road, unhurriedly munch-
ing from the dusty green patches. Leif eased off the
throttle as the nearest camel lifted its head, but it made
no other move. It just regarded him with soulful eyes,
as if in a mild way resenting the intrusion in its ter-

ritory. Leif let the Scania pick up speed again as it entered a long, sweeping righthander.

He glanced at the clock. Still a long, long way to go, but that meant little. Time was not of essence, not out here, not in his present mood.

The truck roared on. He caught a glint of white out of the corner of his eye, the sun-bleached bones of a luckless sheep, and then he rushed past, and the dust he had stirred up swirled for a moment over the broken skeleton, while the shadows lengthened imperceptibly ahead of him.

*   *   *

The time was 1645 when the information came through to Adana on the telex. A young lieutenant brought the sheet of paper to the waiting group. Ofer took it and eagerly scanned the text before handing it around with a curiously blank expression on his face.

ATT: ARI OFER
SWEDISH PASSPORT NO DP002670 NAME WALLMAN
LEIF INGVAR SWEDISH CITIZEN MALE BORN 1953-
11-07 CIVIC REGISTRATION NO 491107-3478 PLACE
OF BIRTH KARLSKRONA SWEDEN RESIDENCE
KAEVLINGE SWEDEN HAIR BLOND EYES BLUE
HEIGHT 185 CENTIMETRES
SWEDISH VEHICLE REGISTRATION NO JLS 874
TRACTOR UNIT 1978 SCANIA LBT141 42 SUPER THREE
AXLES BLUE WITH MINOR YELLOW TRIM TEXT ON
DOORS QUOTE BERT NILSSON TRANSPORT AB
LACKALAENGA TEL 046-730386 UNQUOTE
SWEDISH VEHICLE REGISTRATION NO JCK 068 SEMI-
TRAILER 1977 BRIAB TWO AXLES BLUE IRON-GREY
TARPAULIN WITH TEXT QUOTE SPEDITIONS AB JERRE
SWEDEN — MIDDLE EAST TEL 040-936940 TELEX
32804 UNQUOTE LOAD 20.5 TONNES BUILDING

MATERIAL DESTINATION ABV RIYADH SAUDI ARA-
BIA
PHOTOGRAPH OF DRIVER AND COPIES OF LOAD
SHEETS TO FOLLOW THROUGH TEL AVIV STATION
NO OTHER INFORMATION FROM ULUKISLA INTER-
ROGATIONS BUT POLICE HAVE LOCATED GARAGE
WHERE TRUCK WAS TAKEN AND FOUND TRACES
OF WELDING OPERATIONS
WILL NOTIFY ALL FRIENDS ALONG THE ROUTE
RGDS
O'NEILL

"So Hijazi paid off at last," Bill Herman said softly.
"And I bet the poor bastard doesn't even know what
he's carrying."

*   *   *

The lights of Medina glowed in the darkness on his right.
The well-known sign showed up, reflecting the glare
from his floodlights: white letters against a dark blue
background, it looked like any other road sign, but it
carried the additional legend PROHIBITED AREA TO NON-
MUSLIMS. Medina, like Mecca, was a city closed to in-
fidels.

Automatically he turned off his Cibiés and the stereo
and slowed down, flashing his turn indicators. The Scania
swerved ponderously left across the asphalt and onto
the hard-packed sand, and then right in a wide turn,
pulling up alongside five other TIR trucks already parked
for the night with drawn curtains.

He hit the parking brake and switched off all his lights,
then let the diesel idle to cool down while he leaned
back in the darkness and closed his eyes, massaging his
face. God, he was tired. It was almost midnight and he
was a long eight hundred kilometres from the border
with the rhythm of the road still in his mind and body.

He cut the engine and sat still in the silence for a moment, then willed his body into action. He was too tired for supper. He switched on the red ficki-ficki light, grabbed his toilet case and climbed out into the clear, chilly desert night. The water in the can above the trailer tank was ice-cold, and he shivered as he quickly washed his face and brushed his teeth before returning to the warmth of the cab. He drew the curtains and undressed, debated with himself about what time to get up and compromised by setting the alarm for 7:30, then crawled into his sleeping bag. He reached up to switch off the light, then started to take off his wristwatch—and froze in mid-motion.

Almost hypnotized, he stared at the luminous hands and digits. They shone with a furious brilliance, pale green fire. He frowned, uncomprehending and curious. He sat for a long while in the darkness, but the brilliance did not fade. It kept shining steadily as he slipped off the wristwatch and put it down on the seat and turned towards the wall and fell asleep.

*   *   *

"In a truck?" the Director said. There were seven men assembled for an emergency meeting in the small conference room on the fifth floor of the CIA headquarters in the evening of Sunday January 21.

"Yes," Holston replied. He had been quoting from O'Neill's report. "In fact it's brilliant. There are many trucks going down there, and the chances of slipping through—especially for a Scandinavian truck, I would imagine—are virtually one hundred percent."

The personal security adviser to the President leaned back in his chair with a grim face. "But the device couldn't be hidden among the rest of the load," he objected.

Holston smiled without mirth. "Not unless it was on

the load sheet. It isn't. O'Neill's report makes it almost certain that it has been welded to the chassis somewhere."

"But then it would be found if they made a thorough search of the truck," the Director said.

"Maybe, but why should they? And if they did, would they recognize it? The thing is small, gentlemen. It might be disguised to look like anything, an extra LPG tank for instance." He looked at the Director. "Would you recognize all the things that belong or don't belong among the plumbing of a PTB? Those rigs are complicated."

The Director looked thoughtful. Gerald Yager from the Intelligence Resources Advisory Committee and James Cochrane from the State Department started speaking simultaneously, broke off, and then Yager made an "after you" gesture. Cochrane, a tall, thin man with a slight moustache, nodded and took off his glasses before he spoke up.

"I would like to ask, how much does the opposition know? Are they aware of this new development?"

"Tim . . .?" Holston said.

Van Henck leaned forward with his elbows on the table, toying with a pen. "With a probability bordering on certainty, yes. We have approached a number of Middle East countries at the State Department level, asking for information concerning this specific truck and its driver, and the Soviets are known to have a fair degree of penetration in most of them. They know what the Beirut raid was for, and even without knowledge of the Ulukisla incident, they will be able to put two and two together."

"What are they likely to do?"

"Try to grab that truck before us, of course," van Henck said and gave Cochrane a level stare. "Whether they will be able to beat us to it is another matter. We have the advantage of better official contacts, especially with Saudi Arabia and most of the smaller Gulf states."

He coughed and went on. "Incidentally, the hijacking has already had consequences in the Soviet Union. There have been a number of quiet changes in the military hierarchy, the most noteworthy change being the removal of General Dudintsev from the post as Commander of the Transcaucasian Military District."

There was a murmur around the table.

David Griffith, Head of the Directorate of Intelligence within the CIA, straightened up in his chair and spoke: "Have we received any information in reply to the requests?"

"Oh yes." Holston rose, grimacing at the sudden pain from his bad leg, and limped over to the large political world map on the wall. "It was a delicate business getting through to the Syrians, but we managed it."

He took the pointer and started indicating the places on the map as he spoke. "The info concerning the movements of the truck so far is that it left Turkey by way of the border village Cilvegözu around noon on Tuesday the sixteenth and entered Syria. It left Syria again on the following day and crossed over into Jordan via this border station called Ramtha, and left Jordan early in the morning of the eighteenth, following this route here, to another small border station called Muddawa'ara." He turned to face the others. "From then on we know nothing, but the only road out of this place leads into Saudi Arabia. We haven't heard from the Saudis yet, but it's fair to assume that's where the truck is. In any case, I think we can write off Israel as the target."

"You're probably right," the Security Adviser agreed. "But where is that warhead bound? Riyadh?"

Holston shrugged, limped back to his chair and sat down. "Since that's the destination of the truck it would seem so, but who knows? The Arabian Peninsula is a whole subcontinent. The Yemens, Kuwait, Bahrein, Qatar, the Emirates, Oman . . . Your guess is as good as mine. You have little guerrilla movements in lots of places."

He paused, then went on. "With near certainty, whatever happens is going to have consequences for the West. A nuclear charge going off in this area is more likely to have implications of a sinister and long-ranging nature than an extreme but essentially straightforward terrorist action inside Israel. The President might care to make preparations for such an eventuality." The Security Adviser nodded without saying anything. The silence was broken by Yager.

"Now that we have an exact description of the truck and a fair idea of where it is, surely it's just a matter of tracking it down?"

"That's what the Saudis will do for us. We sent another message after we got the information from Jordan, and they're going to stage an all-out search for the truck. But Saudi Arabia is a very large and sparsely populated country." Holston broke off to look at his watch. "It's about dawn over there. The estimate is that by noon, local time, all the cities and towns will be closed and a number of road blocks will have been established at major points."

"Then it should be a matter of hours." The Director nodded to himself.

"I wouldn't be too sure," Holston said. "The terrorists know that their man Hijazi was taken and that we are on their trail, and they're likely to take countermeasures. I have no wish to sound pessimistic, but that's the way it is."

Cochrane from the State Department sighed. "Well, I just hope that we can keep it from the press. They know that something is afoot and they're pressing us, especially since Turkey started searching vehicles at its borders. The official explanation about a narcotics crackdown won't hold water much longer. You've all seen Jack Anderson's latest column, I take it?"

"Oh, that reminds me. One thing I almost forgot." Holston rummaged through his papers until he found what he wanted, and then adjusted his glasses and regarded the text with a sort of ghoulish satisfaction. "As a matter of fact, this truck we're looking for *has* already been searched—admittedly by people who didn't know exactly what they were looking for—along with all other vehicles that have left Turkey since late last Monday. It was right after we had given the Turkish government the first warning. Anyway, the report states that they opened up the semi-trailer and went through the entire load, as well as inspecting the cab and the tanks and everything else. They even crawled under the truck and checked the undercarriage."

There was a sudden hush in the room.

"And?" The Director leaned forward, his elbows on the table.

"They found nothing."

18

THE BANGING ON THE DOOR reverberated through the cab. The driver sat up, dazedly shaking his head before he rolled over to unlock the door. The air inside the curtained cab was stale but not yet hot from the morning sun.

The door was immediately wrenched open. The man who climbed in was dressed in the dark green uniform of the Royal Saudi Defence Forces, had a beret on his head and a revolver in a holster on his wide leather belt.

Cannonball Jack stared at the intruder, squinting at the bright light.

"You come out right away," the military man said in harshly accented English. "Go to outside gate."

Jack's voice was hoarse with sleep. "What for? What do you . . .?"

"No questions! Go to outside gate now."

Jack met the Saudi's dark, unflinching gaze for a moment, then muttered, "OK, OK."

The soldier climbed down and was gone, leaving the door of the F12 open. Jack was suddenly aware of the sounds; the whole of the TIR truck compound in Halat Ammar seemed filled with hands hammering on doors, boots thudding against asphalt, agitated voices.

He was out of his sleeping bag and into his jeans, T-shirt, and sandals with lightning speed. Grabbing his bunch of keys, he jumped down and slammed the door shut.

Slack-jawed, he stared at the surrounding scene. Military personnel were everywhere, chasing pilots out of their bunks, herding them out the main gate. Drivers swore as they tried to button shirts and fasten belts, bleary-eyed and sluggish. He looked at his wrist and swore too. The watch was still inside the cab. He turned back to get it, but a young soldier immediately caught him by the arm and pointed towards the gate. He hesitated, then thought better of it and fell in with the others.

The soldiers were motioning the drivers to line up along the outside of the compound wall. Some others were being marched from trucks parked in the slots by the workers' huts and from trucks that had just arrived and were queueing up before the white-painted iron bar that marked the entrance to Saudi Arabia proper. The whole of Halat Ammar seemed to have turned out from houses and huts to watch; from every doorway, niche, and alley dark eyes peered at them. Jack scowled back. He found himself standing next to Lasse from Trailertransport and muttered, "Man, what do they want?"

"How the hell should I know?" Lasse shot back. "Maybe some kind of search. You got anything aboard?"

For an icy second Jack thought of the whisky, then remembered that the bottle was long since rinsed out and discarded, its label peeled off and burnt. His last two porn mags had been exchanged for a case of beer aboard the ferry to Syria. He relaxed. At least they wouldn't be able to stick anything on him this time . . .

The protests from the disgruntled pilots were petering out and being replaced by a deep hush. An elderly officer, with a white *keffiyeh* instead of a beret, trailed by two orderlies, came across the tarmac from the customs building. He stopped ten metres from the pilots, and at a sign from him one of the orderlies stepped

forward and held up a large paper, on which were printed
letters and figures: JLS 874. JCK 068.

The registration numbers of Leif Wallman's rig. Slowly
the fact sank home in Cannonball Jack's mind.

"Christ," he whispered to himself, oblivious to the
freshness of the morning and the hills on the horizon.
"What is happening?"

*   *   *

The two huge bulldozers that blocked the road were
almost brand new. Where the yellow-and-black paintwork had been accidentally scraped there was no rust,
only the sharp glare of sun on bare metal. They stood
a short distance apart, facing each other, each taking
up more than half the width of the road. The asphalt
had started to give underneath the edges of the massive,
lowered blades, past which vehicles were channelled,
one at a time, in a wide S-curve that made it necessary
to put the outer wheels onto the hard-packed sand.

Major Abdelaziz Faleh of the Royal Saudi Arabian
Army regarded the scene. The sun was two hours above
the horizon, but his troops had laboured since before
dawn, setting up checkpoints, erecting the communications tent and radio mast, unloading the bulldozers
from the low-loading trailers and getting them into position. The barrier they had constructed would stop anything—even a fully loaded TIR truck at 130 kph. There
was a Browning M2HB 12.7 mm machine gun mounted
on a tripod at each end of the roadblock, manned by
alert soldiers.

Major Faleh turned and shaded his eyes as he looked
east, along the road. The town of Al Hanakiyah was
barely visible beyond the hills, and the mounting heat
was already creating mirages in the distance.

The morning traffic to and from Medina, less than a
hundred kilometres to the west, was thin. Only a few

big trucks had passed since dawn, and none of them had been the blue, Swedish-registered Scania they were looking for. He wondered idly where Sweden was; his knowledge of North European geography was hazy. Wasn't it somewhere near England?

Two cars were halted at the hastily erected signpost to the east of the roadblock, a soldier checking the papers of the occupants of the first one, while other soldiers lingered nearby with submachine guns slung over their shoulders. Major Faleh's instructions were straightforward. Should the truck and its driver show up it was to be put under guard, he was to report in, touch nothing, and wait for further orders. In the meantime, all cars were to be searched, and if a man matched the blurred, blown-up photograph that had come with the instructions, he was to be held.

The soldier returned the papers, stepped back, and motioned the car on. Major Faleh eyed it without curiosity, but noticed the dust over the white paintwork, the Lebanese license plates, and the three men inside. He watched it turn and disappear behind the nearest bulldozer, then it reappeared at the signpost on the other side and picked up speed on its way towards Medina.

*   *   *

The diesel engine sang to him again, and for once the cassette player was silent as the Scania rushed along. Leif slouched over the wheel, feeling grumpy as a combined effect of a long day the day before, oversleeping, and no breakfast. Medina was fifty kilometres behind, and he had decided to cover another fifty before stopping to fix up something to eat.

With a sigh he fumbled out another cigarette and lit it. He had another long day before him. It was a consolation of TIR trucking that he only had about half a metre from his bed to his work.

A small speck appeared in the distance, rapidly growing as it approached. It was really going fast. He barely had time to notice that there were three men inside it as the white car flashed by, then, automatically, he looked in his rear-view mirror and saw its brake lights come on.

He kept watching. The white car was dwindling in his mirror, its brake lights still on, then they went out, and he saw the car make a U-turn and disappear in the dead angle behind his semi-trailer.

He felt a tiny ripple of unease. Attracting attention was seldom a good thing in these parts, but evidently that was what he had done. The seconds ticked by while he continued holding his speed and watching his mirrors.

There the white car was again, pulling out to overtake him, turn indicator flashing. It drew alongside the cab of the Scania, and he could see part of the right leg of the Arab occupying the passenger seat; then it was in front of him, flashing right and slowing down.

Leif jammed the brake pedal down, and the truck started losing speed. A frenetically waving arm was extended from the car in front. Leif frowned. Was it a police car? Or was there something wrong with his semi-trailer that he was unaware of?

Both vehicles came to a halt by the roadside. The door of the white Mazda was opened and an Arab unhurriedly got out. He looked up at Leif and motioned him to come down. Leif made a grimace, and stubbing out his cigarette, hit the parking brake. He opened the door and let the diesel idle as he stepped down and closed the door. The Arab before him was unusually tall.

"You speak English, don't you?" the Arab said.

"Yes," Leif replied uncertainly, wondering what it was about. Standing in the shadow of the Scania, he felt cold in his T-shirt.

"Our apologies for stopping you like this, but we have been looking for you all morning. Your name is Leif

Wallmann, yes?'' The Arab lifted his hand and fingered the brand on his cheek.

A wisp of recognition. Leif opened his mouth to speak, and the last thing he remembered as the darkness exploded inside his head was the surprising strength of the tall Arab as he collapsed into his outstretched arms.

* . * *

The knock on the door was barely audible. Dan Morris tiredly lifted his head and said, "Come in, Art."

"How did you know it was me?" Holston asked as he walked over to sink down on the chair before the desk.

"Who else could it be at this goddam hour? Santa Claus with his sack, apologizing for the delay?" Morris leaned forward again, resting his head in his hands. "Besides, I have a pretty good guess as to where you were heading," he muttered.

"Communications. I thought you had left until I saw the light through the crack of your door."

"I'm waiting, same as you. I just came back ten minutes ago."

"You must be as jittery as I am."

"You're telling me. What's the time over there now?"

Holston glanced at his watch. "A little after nine A.M. What's the last word from Com?"

"The word we already have. Roadblocks are up, in most places since dawn, local time."

"Confirmed by our Riyadh Station?"

"Confirmed by our Riyadh Station."

There was silence, and Holston rose and limped over to the window. He stared blindly out into the darkness.

"Any news about this Mahmoud el-Tha'ir the Israelis think is behind it?" Morris asked.

Holston didn't turn, only shook his head. "No," he mumbled after a while, "nothing from the Israelis, nothing from the Russkies, nothing from the Arabs. Nothing from anybody. Just a lost truck with a nuke aboard, somewhere out there.''

*   *   *

Once more there was light and hazy awareness and finally recognition. He was back in his own bunk aboard the Scania, lying face down with his left arm painfully tucked beneath his chest. There was a taste of blood in his mouth as he tried to raise his head.

"Lie still.''

There was no pity in the voice. The back of his neck was stiff and throbbed. Leif blinked; there were tears in his eyes from the pain and the bright light. Slowly the world swam into focus, and he saw the two men who sat regarding him. The man in the driver's seat was the man that had spoken to him.

"Can you hear and understand me?''

Leif managed a nod. He realized that the diesel engine had been cut. He moved to bring the arm out from under him. It felt numb and stung with myriads of tiny needles.

"Then listen. For reasons which we will not discuss with you, we're going to use you and your truck for the next few days. You will drive and do exactly as we say. We will see to it that you get food and sleep. When it is over we will let you go, unharmed. Have you understood?''

Leif stared at him and felt the anger rising inside him. So he was being hijacked. The first time ever down here, and I have to be the victim, he thought. What made them think they could do this to him?

Then he looked at the gun in the hand of the other Arab.

"But my load must be worthless to you, it—''

The Arab's hand shot out and clenched Leif's mouth

and chin in an agonizing grip, twisting his head so that he was forced to look straight into the Arab's eyes.

"Listen again. I don't care about your load. When you were knocked out a few minutes ago it was a demonstration." The sinewy fingers were digging into Leif's face until his vision reddened with pain. "Violence is only a means of achieving ends, Leif Wallmann. I want it understood that should you defy me, we will not hesitate to murder you and take your truck, although that would be inconvenient. But I am offering you a very simple choice. Do you want to live or die?"

The Arab suddenly let go, and Leif fell back on the bunk. He lifted a hand to rub his mouth and chin. His breath rasped in his throat.

"I will do as you say," he said, tasting defeat.

The Arab in the driver's seat made no reply. Instead he turned to the other man for a short talk, of which Leif understood nothing. Then both of them looked at him again.

"Where are we going?" Leif asked.

"Into the desert."

*   *   *

There was a plume of dust and fine desert sand in his mirrors, blocking his rearward view. Another, smaller plume rose before him, thrown up by the Mazda that led the way a hundred metres ahead. The windows were closed to keep the dust out, and the temperature was slowly and steadily rising inside the cab in spite of the busily whining air conditioner. The air filter must be nearly clogged, Leif thought.

His muscles were aching from wrestling with the steering wheel. The bumps and ridges of the uneven desert bed made the entire Scania buck and shake. The heavily laden semi-trailer was pumping the springs of the tractor bogie in a furious way, and not even the hydraulically damped seat could keep the vibrations from being transmitted into his kidneys and spine.

He had thought only one of the Arabs would be riding with him, but there was one on the passenger seat and one sitting cross-legged on the lower bunk, both of them with guns ready. Obviously they were taking no chances. They were hanging on to straps and hand grips, silently and grimly enduring the treatment, not taking their eyes off Leif.

The third Arab, the man with the brand, drove the Mazda. Leif had been told to follow it, no matter what. They had driven along the permanent road for another twenty kilometres, at normal speed, ignored by other traffic. Then the Mazda's blinkers had flashed and it had turned left off the road, heading north into the vastness of the desert.

The driver obviously knew the desert and how to pick his way through it in a car. Several times he had made wide detours around areas that Leif could see, at closer range, were of a different colour: the kind of desert the Arabs call *butte* or *ergh*, looser and more treacherous sand. They also seemed to avoid open areas; the Mazda preferred sticking as closely as conditions allowed to the low desert hills.

Leif wondered where they were taking him. Working the wheel and the gearbox was exhausting, but it was something that could be done with the spinal cord, and he had started to reflect on his situation. The first fears were subsiding, replaced by frantic speculation. Obviously they were not going to harm him as long as he did what he was being told. But he didn't have too much faith in the promise that he would be allowed to go when "it was over"—whatever that meant. He suspected that Saudi Arabian law would be in no way lenient in a case of kidnapping and hijacking. Murder would probably add nothing to that, and they had already declared themselves prepared to commit it. He tried to steer his thoughts in other directions.

He thought of Annika. She would be at work now this Monday morning, maybe thinking forward to his return and feeling happy. And here he was, held at gunpoint, sweating at the controls of his truck as he headed deeper into the unknown desert.

*　　*　　*

The sun was high in the sky, and queues of vehicles had formed on both sides of the roadblock. Soldiers were checking papers, and then letting eight or ten of them crawl past the bulldozers at a time.

A lieutenant came up to Major Faleh, saluted and said, "Major, there is something out there." He pointed, and Faleh turned to look. "Beyond the hills. A large dust cloud, moving east."

Major Faleh saw the thin, grey-brown haze against the blue sky to the northeast, and fixed it. There was no doubt that it was moving. It might be a freak dust storm.

Or it might be something else . . .

Faleh turned back. "Lieutenant, take three men and prepare for a jeep patrol. Report to me when ready."

*　　*　　*

They were not heading north any more, but slowly swinging eastwards, winding their way past the scattered ridges, along the slightly sloping ground. The desert was also becoming more treacherous. Numerous areas of lighter, looser sand necessitated an increasing number of detours, and there were times when Leif felt the rear wheels of the tractor unit slip a little; not enough to make his watchdogs take notice, but Leif was distinctly aware of it.

Here and there was low, sparse vegetation, small,

greyish-green clusters clinging to the ground. The Mazda swung sharply left behind its dust plume, and Leif twisted his steering wheel to follow, downshifting, feeling the tires slipping again on a loose layer of sand. The ground was sloping away to his right, and now he saw the explanation of the vegetation; they were coming to a *wadi*, a dried-up riverbed.

They were driving parallel to it, obviously searching for a suitable point of crossing. Leif looked right, past the guard in the passenger seat. The banks on the other side were gently sloping, but here and there were patches where the topmost, dried layer had ruptured and loose sand had flowed thick like syrup. Hitting one of those spots would mean disaster.

The distance to the Mazda had increased. It swung right, down the bank and onto the dry riverbed, and the dusty plume it trailed almost vanished.

Leif twisted the wheel full lock, feeling the truck skid, and then he pressed the accelerator down as they gained speed down the bank. There was a sharp bump as the front wheels went over the edge and hit the bottom, and a second, stronger thud as the bogie followed. Full power ahead, and an upshift, clutching as fast as the mechanism allowed. The other bank loomed ahead, the Mazda already halfway up, zigzagging, and automatically he shouted, "Hold on!", then the steering wheel was wrenched from his grip as they hit. The Scania slewed right before he got hold of it again and fought back with all his strength, and the revs dropped alarmingly as they started uphill. Leif downshifted, and then a sickening lurch told him that his rightside driving wheels were digging down. Furiously, he declutched, and the Scania almost immediately came to a halt.

Out of the corner of his eyes he saw the Arab in the passenger seat raise his head a little and tighten his grip on the gun.

"*Far åt helvete*," he growled in Swedish. "Go to hell,

I'm doing what I can." He reached out and flicked the differential lock switch to the *on* position. Now at least he would have all driving wheels engaged—and facing uphill, he also stood a good chance of frying his clutch into the bargain.

Leif put the gear in low second with a resounding clunk and slowly let the clutch out, prepared to meet the engagement point with the accelerator. He felt it bite and slowly increased the revs. For a brief moment the Scania crawled forward, then the hard-packed top layer of sand burst, and the tires spun frantically as the bogie sank down, before he had time to declutch and hit the parking brake. He cursed as he pulled the compression release to kill the diesel.

They were stuck.

*   *   *

At the roadblock the lines at the bulldozers had grown with the increasing traffic. Major Faleh's anticipation gradually waned and was replaced by boredom and frustration with every blue truck that rolled up and turned out to be different from the one they were looking for. Twice, blond, bearded foreigners had been told to step outside in order to be subjected to a close comparison with the photograph, but neither was the man they wanted.

A vehicle came rolling in past the line of westbound cars, a staff car from Major Faleh's regiment. He straightened his back and made sure that his beret sat according to regulations.

"Major! The jeep patrol is ready to leave."

Faleh swung around at the sudden intrusion. He had forgotten about the patrol. He lifted his eyes and looked at the hills, but there was no longer any haze obscuring the clear desert sky. He shrugged. It had probably been one of those little freak sandstorms.

"Order countermanded, Lieutenant. Have the men go back to their duties."

The lieutenant saluted and turned on his heels, and Faleh started to walk towards the men who were getting out of the staff car.

*   *   *

The sun relentlessly beating down on his back and the sweat drenching his T-shirt, Leif dropped to his knees to inspect the mess. Despite his quick declutching the wheels had had time to dig down until the bogie axles almost rested on the sand.

A shadow fell across the ground; he looked up and saw that it was the Arab with the brand.

"I assume that you did not do this on purpose." The deep voice was menacingly calm.

"Look," Leif began with an unsteady voice, then cleared his throat. "I promise I couldn't help it, but you had ordered me to follow you, and trying to go up that bank with the truck was—"

The Arab raised his hand to stem the flow of words from Leif. "Can you get it out of here?"

"I—I can try, anyway."

"Then try."

He had been given a reprieve. Now everything would depend on how he was able to use his knowledge and skill during the next few minutes. He took a deep breath and forced himself to be calm.

He got his keys from the dash, and silently followed by the two armed Arabs, unlocked the front lefthand trailer box and took out the heavy snowchains. The Arabs made no move to help him. He hadn't expected it.

He dragged one chain around the front of the truck and positioned it until it lay straight before the outer driving wheel on the right side, the nearest crosslink tight against the warm rubber. Then he repeated the performance on the left side. He locked the trailer box and climbed into the cab, followed by one of his shadows. The other remained standing by the bogie. Good, Leif thought grimly, against his better judgement. He wasn't going to give any warning. If the chain lashed out sideways and chewed off the Arab's leg at the hip it would serve him right.

He started the engine and let it idle for a few seconds. Then he put it in gear, took a deep breath, and slowly started letting the clutch out. The sound of the engine deepened as the truck lurched forward, and with lightning speed he declutched and hit the brakes.

He climbed down to have a look and could not suppress a small feeling of triumph. The wheels had turned half a revolution, enough to pull the snowchains in under them. Quickly, he wrapped the chains around the tires and secured them.

He climbed back into the cab. His hands trembled as he put the Scania in gear again.

Slowly, slowly. Not too much engine speed, or the wheels would spin again, chains or no chains.

The big diesel strained as the driveline and transmission took up the task of freeing nearly forty tons from the grip of the desert sand. A tremor ran through the tractor unit, then the chained tires bit, and slowly the truck crawled forward, out of its hole and up the gentle slope of the river bank. Sweat poured down Leif's brow and dropped from the tip of his nose down into his lap, but he did not dare take his hands off the wheel. Finally they crested the rise, and Leif declutched, letting the vehicle coast to a stop. His body was shaking.

The passenger door opened and the second guard climbed in. None of them said anything. The Mazda came rolling past with the third Arab at the wheel.

Nobody had thanked him or uttered a word.

*   *   *

Twenty minutes later they came to a northbound, badly kept tarmac road, and there Leif stopped to take off the chains and stow them back into the trailer box. Then they continued, the Mazda leading the way over the numerous potholes.

Shortly, houses started appearing. They passed a faded sign that said Al Khalf in Latin letters and presumably the same in Arab script. Leif did not know Al Khalf, but he estimated that it must be situated some twenty or thirty kilometres north of the Medina-Riyadh road.

Al Khalf was a medium-sized village. The Mazda led the Scania east of the main cluster of houses until buildings became more sparse and they stopped in a yard before an unusually large building, probably a warehouse or a garage. The leader came over to the truck. Leif rolled his window down and leaned out.

"Turn your vehicle around and back into the garage!" the Arab ordered in a firm voice over the sound of the engine.

Leif nodded. He made a U-turn until the wide door was lined up in his rear-view mirrors. Slowly the door swung out and up. Leif squinted into his mirrors. The bright light and the white-washed walls of the building made it difficult to pick up details inside the dark garage, but there was no mistaking it; there was another truck already inside, as big as his own. He frowned. There was something vaguely familiar about it.

He put his own truck in reverse and started backing in, checking his mirrors. Slowly the semi-trailer glided in, the grey, dusty tarpaulin barely clearing the top of the door, then the tractor unit, until he was lined up alongside the other truck. He engaged the parking brake and cut the engine.

Then he looked left and knew why the other truck had seemed so familiar, looked into the other cab and saw the blood that had run from the hole in the temple and dried in the thick beard of the friendly giant with whom he would never again share a smoke or a laugh, looked at Preben while the pain inside him was beyond words and tears welled up in his eyes, and then the garage door slowly swung shut, mercifully hiding everything in darkness.

19

ISRAELI INTELLIGENCE HAD CHANGED OBJECTIVES. By the morning of Monday the twenty-second it was no longer a question of finding and intercepting a band of terrorists that might bring a nuclear device into Israel; now it was a matter of watch-keeping, intelligence-gathering, analysis and preparation, politically as well as militarily, for what that device might accomplish elsewhere. The special intelligence coordinating group ceased to exist.

It therefore came as a surprise to Ari Ofer when David Bar-Sharon visited him in his office early in the morning. David was in a glum, fidgety mood, speaking little, prowling about the room, smoking an unending chain of cigarettes which he stubbed out half-smoked. Finally Ofer had had enough.

"Listen, David, haven't you got any *fedayeen* to chase? It's all very well to come here to pass the time of day, but I'm actually rather busy, so sit down, will you, and get whatever it is off your chest, or else get the hell out of here and let me get on with my work."

David stopped, inhaled deeply from the cigarette, then abruptly sat down opposite Ofer and stubbed it out with a violent plume of smoke trailing from his nostrils.

"All right. Ari, can you get me into Saudi Arabia?"

There was a moment of silence during which David defiantly stared at Ofer's expressionless face.

"I can," Ofer said presently. "But I won't."

"Why not?" There was something of a pleading note

in David's voice. Ofer held up his right hand and began ticking off points on his fingers.

"You're not a trained field operative. It would take too long to build a cover for you that would hold up. There's nothing you could do for us in Saudi Arabia even if the device is there. On top of that I would never get the sanction from higher up for sending you in there. Therefore I won't."

"Damn it, I didn't ask you to *send* me in there, I asked if you could *get* me in there, period."

"A wildcat mission? Then it's no ten times over. Don't be a fool, David."

David threw up his hands in an exasperated gesture. "I haven't said a bloody word about any mission. Listen, you know how I feel about the way this country is run. Yesterday I had had enough. I thought hard about it all night and I've decided to quit."

Ofer nodded. "You're still a fool, David. It's your privilege, and I certainly don't hold it against you. I'm not too happy myself about the way they handle some things, but my conclusions aren't your conclusions. Maybe I just have a pedestrian mind. I still don't see why you want to go to Saudi Arabia, unless it is that you're dead set on seeing a nuclear charge go up. And I don't see why I should put my neck out in order to get you in there."

"Look, Ari," David said in a more reasonable tone, "you know that whatever my feelings, I wouldn't want anything to happen to this country."

"Well, nothing will."

David shrugged. "Not with a bang maybe, but whatever happens now is going to influence Israel."

"Sure," Ofer agreed. "And that's what we're preparing to counter. As for chasing terrorists, that seems to be out of our hands now, and I won't pretend I'm not happy that it is."

"But don't you see, we've brought this on ourselves

and others. The frustration and desperation of the Palestinian Arabs in a sense stems from our actions. We're
responsible, damn it."

"All right, all right," Ofer said impatiently. "Fine sentiments, all of them, but bloody impractical. Do you
want to go to Saudi Arabia because you have a bad
conscience, or what?"

David was silent as he debated with himself what his
motives actually were and found that he was quite unclear about them himself. He was aware of Ofer's cool,
dispassionately probing stare.

"No, damn it!" he exclaimed. "I'm not that much of
a fool. I want to go there as a *witness*. I know my
motives aren't all that clear, but most of all I feel that
I don't want to drop this, I want to see the ending of
it. I don't fancy myself being able to do anything, I
know my limitations, but I want to *see* it. Look, Ari,
I'm not asking for any sanction, I'm not asking for any
backing, I'm not even asking you to put your neck out
for my sake—not much, anyway. Will you help me get
into Saudi Arabia?"

Ofer went on staring at David. "Well, David, I don't
know who you're fooling with your rhetoric, and I'm
still not certain it isn't yourself, but—yes—there might
be a way, if you really want to go, that is."

"I do."

"Right, then. There is a guy I know in the Arab Section of the SIS. I've done him a number of good turns
and it's about time he did something for me. You've
studied in England, right?"

"My father was English."

"Good, that'll help a lot. You must realize, though,
that if I can swing this it's going to be handled in such
a way that your cover can't be traced back either to
the British or to us. You will have ceased to work for
the intelligence community. If you're exposed you'll be
disowned. No steps whatever will be taken to get you

out of any tight spot you get yourself into, by us or by them. OK?"

"OK."

"One condition. You'll square this with Saul Shaltiel, or I won't have anything to do with it. Tender your resignation and ask for leave of absence for your period of notice, effective as of today. Don't tell him about what you're going to do, just insist on personal reasons. That way"—Ofer winked at David—"we'll be rid of you, and you won't, for your own sake, go about this being AWOL. Got it?"

"I'll see Saul right away." David shuffled about a little. "And thanks, Ari."

"Ofer shook his head. "For what I wonder. Come back here as soon as you've talked to Saul, and I'll see what I can do in the meantime."

*   *   *

The interview with Saul Shaltiel was briefer, more formal, and much more charged. Shaltiel was clearly suspicious of David's stubborn refusal to give anything but "personal affairs" as a reason for immediate leave of absence.

Shaltiel finally said, frowning, "All right, David. You'll get it. I will just remind you that you're still bound by the Israeli Secrets Act and point out that if you, anywhere or at any time, do anything which is contrary to the security of this country or any of its agencies, you will be brought to task. Understood?"

"Perfectly." For one of the very few times in Saul Shaltiel's presence, David instinctively felt like springing to attention and saluting.

"Good." Shaltiel rose. "In a way I'm sorry to lose you." He reached out his hand. "I don't think I'll say good luck, but take care of yourself, David."

David solemnly shook the proffered hand. "Thanks, Saul. I will."

*   *   *

Night had fallen, but Leif could not sleep. The thin chains
and the padlocks that shackled his left wrist and left
ankle to the short, battered metal bed, were chafing
badly and limited his movement. The meal that had
been brought to him earlier had been unsatisfactory:
bread and a few pieces of stringy chicken in greasy sauce,
but he had greedily wolfed it down. Now he lay on the
two blankets that served as a mattress, staring into the
darkness of the bare room.

He squirmed, trying to find a position that would ease
some of the dull pain in his limbs, and the rusty springs
creaked. Now and then he thought he could hear a faint
rustle from downstairs, and occasionally he caught the
howl of a distant dog, but not a single sound reached
him from the garage, or from the village a little further
off.

They had brought him from the garage, across the
yard and along a narrow lane, to this deserted house
where they had chained him fast. He had offered no
resistance, but stumbled along, mute with shock mixed
with fear. Their warning against crying out for help had
been superfluous.

He remembered another dark cell, and Turkish customs officials searching his truck with ruthless thor-
oughness. Vaguely he realized that those were not
separate, incidental events but parts of a larger pattern.
All the small facts and observations were coming back
to him. He knew that he had seen the white Mazda
before. He had in fact been shadowed by it, at least
since Syria, and maybe longer, and he had not really
noticed it. He had somehow been *used* while phleg-
matically going about his daily routines, seeing nothing.
What a farce that arrest had been. No charges, no bribes.
He should have known that it stunk to high heaven.

And Preben, his smiling, indestructible friend, slouching over the wheel of his rig, the fire inside him put out forever.

All this for—for what?

*   *   *

David returned to Ari Ofer and was told that the British contact had agreed to deliver—but on neutral ground.

Four hours later, after some hasty preparations, David was on a flight to Geneva. His suitcase in the hold of the jetliner was a few years old, without any particular marks or labels except the airline tag. He had bought it in England. The articles of clothing in it were all bought in England or had their origin in some West-European country. There wasn't one thing in the suitcase which would link its owner with Israel. David had even left his toothpaste behind.

In Geneva he registered at the Hotel Jet d'Eau in rue du Simplon under his own name, showing his genuine Israeli passport like a good tourist. From his room he could glimpse a limited expanse of the Lac Leman and the top of the 130-metre pillar of spouting water which gave the hotel its name.

With this tantalizingly incomplete view for a diversion, David Bar-Sharon settled down to await his contact.

*   *   *

Art Holston sank down in the back seat beside Gerald Yager and placed his briefcase in his lap. "We might be late in this kind of weather," he said.

"I've already told the driver to step on it," Yager replied. He seemed morose, drumming his fingers against his knee, and said nothing more until they had passed the gate and were on the road.

"What are you going to tell the meeting?" he asked suddenly.

Holston shrugged. "The truth."

"Which hasn't been amended, I suppose."

"No. The truck has entered Saudi Arabia. The Saudis have had their roadblocks up for twenty-four hours, with negative results. There should have been no way for that truck to avoid being stopped, yet, to all effect, it has vanished off the face of the earth. The simple truth is that somebody has outmanoeuvred us."

Yager frowned. "Still no evidence as to who this somebody may be?"

"Only guesswork."

Yager was thoughtful, and then changed the subject. "The Saudi Arabian ambassador is also going to be there tonight. Looks like we're in for a long meeting at the White House."

Holston nodded wearily, and then turned his head to look out the side window at the trees rushing past in the snow and gathering darkness.

*   *   *

The smell of paint was everywhere, irritating their nostrils, making their eyes water and their breathing difficult despite the masks and goggles, but grimly they kept it up, taking turns with the spray gun. The jet of red fog flowed along the edges of the carefully masked windows, grille, wheel wells and other parts of the cab of the Scania.

Mahmoud el-Tha'ir made a sign and Alawi Kayyal turned off the spray gun. They waited to let most of the particles dancing in the air sink, before they removed their goggles and masks.

Most of the garage was in darkness as there was no fixed lighting, and the one not handling the spray gun had to hold one of the cord lamps so that the other could see. El-Tha'ir made a slow tour around the cab with the lamp held high, inspecting their work. Quite passable, in fact better than he had dared hope when he had conceived this scheme. Only one more coat would be needed.

He wiped off a spot of red where the masking tape had not quite covered a window edge, then let his gaze rove on. The trailer had received a distinct violet hue on the part nearest the cab, but that was of no importance. He looked at the other truck, which was still covered by the tarpaulin from the Swedish trailer.

He coughed, the tang of paint burning in his nasal passages, then said, "Stay here. I will go and see how Fuad's getting on with his work. Won't be long."

"*Na'am.*"

He put the cord lamp down, and carefully made his way in the darkness to the far wall, found the door handle by touch, and opened without knocking.

Fuad Qabali sat bent over papers spread across a battered table. A single lamp cast a feeble light over the scene. He straightened up and acknowledged el-Tha'ir's presence with a slight nod.

"How are you doing with the documents?" el-Tha'ir asked.

Qabali gestured with his right hand, on which the outer joint of the index finger was missing. "Take a look for yourself. Most of them shouldn't pose any problem. If I can only have his photograph tomorrow morning, it shouldn't take more than six or seven hours."

"*Kuwayyis.* Good. You shall have it."

He turned, and stepping into the blackness of the garage, closed the door. In spite of his aching back, in spite of the paint in his hair and clothes, he felt satisfaction.

Renting the garage had been a last-minute suggestion from Markov, who had argued that they might have to spirit the hijacked truck away for a couple of days to correct the timetable if necessary. El-Tha'ir had initially opposed it on the grounds that the fewer connections they had, the better were their chances of success, but had eventually given in and had the garage in Al Khalf rented through his channels in Medina. Now it had turned out to be the solution to the problem of Hijazi being taken. The roadblock this morning had jarred el-Tha'ir, because it clearly told that Hijazi had been broken. But by then the improvised emergency plan had already been set in motion.

In the darkness he permitted himself a tiny smile. The ability to improvise, his Soviet teachers in the Odessa training camp had told him, is the hallmark of the true warrior. What did those Slavs know of improvisation and war? His ancestors had come out of the desert, fighting and conquering, a millenium before those peasants had even looked up from their soil. He was the one who had slipped the truck and its driver out of the net.

He stepped back into the eerie light from the cord lamp on the floor. Kayyal stood impassively regarding the truck. El-Tha'ir glanced at his wrist and remembered that he had taken off his gold watch. Reaching inside his clothes, he got it out and looked at it. Less than sixty hours left.

20

THE MAN WAS ALMOST OFFENSIVELY BRITISH, from the handlebar moustache and the regimental tie to the ruddy distaste with which he regarded the continental breakfast before him as he sat down opposite David.

"Morning," he said and set upon the two pitiful rolls. He sniffed suspiciously at the small pitcher that went with the tea, found it contained cream and called for milk. David suppressed a smile and for a moment toyed with the idea that this man might be his contact before dismissing it as altogether too outrageous.

The continental breakfast was quickly dealt with, and the man wistfully looked around for porridge, whole bran, eggs, bacon, sausages, grilled tomatoes, kippered herring; finding nothing of the sort, he turned to conversation.

"Speak English?"

"I do," David said,

"Oh, good. Thompson. Coutts, Strand branch. English, are you?"

"Might have been. My father was, but he emigrated. I was born in Israel. Bar-Sharon."

"Tough luck. Ever thought about going back?"

The man was indeed his contact. David didn't know what to think. He decided to reserve judgement and answered, correctly, "I might want to do just that."

The man calling himself Thompson nodded thoughtfully and said in a very low voice that barely carried across the table, "What's your room number?"

David told him, in the same low voice.

"Good. Be there in forty-five minutes. Two quick knocks, pause, three quick knocks." He rose and in his brash voice wished David a pleasant day in Geneva before he left the room.

David was duly present forty-five minutes later when the signal came and Thompson invaded his room. That was the only word that described it. The Englishman carried a tattered black briefcase and reached out his hand. "Hullo, again. Stuart Thompson. Call me Stu. Awfully kind of you to wait. Managed to get outside for a spot of proper breakfast in the meantime."

Lord, David thought as they shook hands, he's genuine. Something must have shown in his face, because Thompson went on talking: "Don't worry about the way I go on. It's perfectly all right." He opened his briefcase and rummaged about inside. "Disguise by ostentation. Right, here we are. Your new identity. By the way, I take it that this room is reasonably clean." He handed David four closely typed pages stapled together.

"Went through it last night. Nothing as far as I could find."

"Good. Well, that's who you are. Keep it overnight and learn it. Your accent's good, I've had more difficult cases. Ofer advised me of that, and I've changed a few details to fit in with it. Apart from that all the facts are genuine as far as they can be checked."

Thompson started to search for more things in the briefcase. "Ah, there! Sit down on that chair in front of the mirror please."

He displayed the tools of his trade. David eyed them incredulously: a pair of scissors, a comb, and a barber's sheet of rose-patterned nylon.

"Now, I told you not to worry," Thompson said with patient geniality. "You're quite the type to pass for an Englishman. After all, you might have been one, as you said yourself. But that haircut. We simply have to do something about that."

"Oh," David said and sat down and submitted to having the sheet fastened—expertly enough—around his neck.

"You've no idea how important the haircut is in judging nationalities," Thompson said as he began snipping away around David's ears. "You'll see. I'm jolly glad you're wearing your hair quite long, otherwise it might have been hopeless."

Thompson rambled on, scissors snipping, and fifteen minutes later David inspected, amazed, his new appearance in the mirror. His hair was much shorter, especially at the back, but thick and full above the ears and across the forehead. He *looked* British, suddenly. Thompson, apparently, was a genius in his field.

"Rather good, what? A little *eau de marron* will remove those whitish areas and you'll look quite the *pukka sahib* who spent some time in warmer climes. Now we'll have your photograph taken."

A Polaroid camera was next to emerge from Thompson's bag of tricks, together with a hand-held flash. David was positioned in front of a suitable area of white wall, and Thompson the photographer went into action.

"This is for the passport. You're familiar with the way of getting a genuine false passport in Britain? Yes, I thought you would be. It's in all the thrillers, you know. Nice and lax. So British. Now, we do the same thing now and then, in order to stock up for delicate affairs. That's the sort you'll be getting. I'll doctor it a little, of course, put your picture in it, while the British authorities will have another one, a nonentity, in their files. If you're caught the passport can't be traced back to us. You do understand that you will be very much on your own. Is that clear?"

"Everybody keeps asking me if I understand," David said testily. "I know what I'm doing."

"Delighted to hear that," Thompson said, "since Ofer didn't seem to know. Your driver's license will be genuine forged stuff, by the way, but that doesn't matter much. Right, now let me see what you have in your suitcase."

Thompson went through David's suitcase expertly, examining all labels and other markings on the garments. "Hm, good, good. You used your time in London well, didn't you?" He took a pin-striped suit from the wardrobe and held it up. "Marks & Spencer, eh? Jewish stuff, didn't you know? But that's all right, the Arabs buy it themselves. You've got a good inventory here. Needs only a few additions. I'll see to them tomorrow. Oh, and stop smoking that Israeli stuff. Dunhill, Philip Morris, Pall Mall, that sort of thing will do, even if it doesn't stink as much." He grinned, and David self-consciously put down the cigarette he had been about to light. He had completely revised his opinion of the Englishman. The man was *good*.

"All right, end of today's session," Thompson declared. "See you here tomorrow at ten-thirty. Three quick knocks, pause, one knock. I expect you to know your *curriculum vitae* by then. You'll have the rest of your stuff and final instructions at the same time, which will give you time to catch your flight. And some advice, free and quite deeply felt. Go out tonight and have a couple of quick ones. Once you're on the plane you don't know when you'll be able to get your next drink. Oh, and by the way, you won't see me for breakfast tomorrow. Cheerio, old boy."

*   *   *

He was Peter Feltham, born April 4, 1946, the only son of George and Sarah Feltham of Durham. His entire life was in the abstract, education, girl friends, jobs, etc, in brief, unadorned entries.

Peter Feltham died in 1975 in a car crash on the M1. The fact was included as an inconsequential parenthesis in the abstract, which then blandly went on to state that in 1975 Peter Feltham had changed employment and started to work with a Bristol firm which traded a lot overseas.

Through the unemotional facts, suddenly David could glimpse a hand moving unseen among the records, changing, removing, adjusting information in order to make the fate of the real Peter Feltham as inaccessible as possible, and at the same time prepare for the contingent resurrection it had now fallen on David Bar-Sharon's lot to undertake.

It was in a thoughtful mood that David learned the facts about his new identity. A lot of what was in the abstract he learned by heart, other things he handled more casually.

When he had reached what he deemed a credible mix of immediate and not so immediate knowledge, David carefully folded the abstract and taped it to the back of one of the desk drawers before he went out to follow Stuart Thompson's advice.

*   *   *

They came for him in the morning, but what they did to him was so different from what he had expected that it took him by surprise. His two watchdogs unshackled his fetters, took him downstairs and escorted him to a ramshackle privy at the back of the house, where he was subjected to the humiliation of pulling his trousers down and squatting under their supervision. Then they led him back upstairs and ordered him to sit down on the single chair in the room. Their branded leader did not seem to be present anywhere.

One of the Arabs left the room and returned with a dirty bucket half-filled with water. The other, the one with the mutilated righthand index finger, returned his gun to its holster somewhere under the flowing robe and took out a razor.

The sight of it made Leif stiffen involuntarily, and the reaction brought a smile to the lips of the Arab—not a sardonic smile, but an almost gentle one. Then he dipped the knife in the bucket, took Leif's chin in his free hand, tipped his head back, and started to shave him.

Leif had to repress a sudden, hysterical impulse to laugh. For a second it seemed like some monstrous practical joke, as if all these violent efforts were only to bring him to this improvised barber shop. Then he remembered Preben's face and the dried blood, and quietened down. The Arab worked with swift, economical movements; Leif's sun-bleached beard fell silently in little curls that tickled his bare arms. He was aware of the rhythmic breathing of the Arab and of his own, and then of something else he had not noticed before, a smell of paint. He wrinkled his nose.

The razor was sharp, the Arab dipped it frequently in the water, and soon all of Leif's facial hair was gone. His chin felt suddenly cold, and he grimaced uncertainly.

The razor disappeared and was replaced by scissors and a comb. He closed his eyes and endured the ordeal of the haircut in silence, seeking comfort by thinking of Annika. If she met him now she wouldn't recognize him from ten paces—and very probably laugh if she did. If they ever met again.

"Finish."

He opened his eyes and looked down. His lap was covered with blond hair. They must have taken most of it, he thought, and made a move to rise, but was immediately pushed back. One of the Arabs left the room and returned with a small bottle containing some dark fluid which he started to rub into Leif's chin and around his mouth. It stung a little, and Leif grimaced again, but it was quickly over.

Then they chained him to the bed again and left. Alone, he listened to the impatient rumbles of his stomach and watched the sunlight slowly creep across the floor, turning the latest events over in his mind. The beauty treatment he had undergone could only have been for the purpose of radically changing his looks, which in its turn must mean that sometime soon he would have to pass close scrutiny, scrutiny by people who would have his description and would be looking for him. Maybe that was his hope of escaping, if he could manage to separate himself from his captors.

They were back half an hour later, with a shirt taken from his bag, a Polaroid camera, and food. Leif was made to put the shirt on and pose against a smooth portion of the wall while they shot several portraits. Then he gratefully wolfed down the late breakfast before he was again chained to the bed, where he eventually fell into a restless sleep.

*   *   *

To stand on the brink of certain defeat, and then turn around and discover that victory was still within grasp; to die in the mind and be born again, that is a unique experience.

The man sat back in the high-backed, richly upholstered leather chair, savouring the joy of being born anew, before he straightened up and looked out through the window at the Al Anbariyah district of the city of Medina. Half an hour ago he had debated with himself whether to flee his native soil in ignominy or await the inevitable moment when he would kneel in the public square beyond the mosque of Ali Ibn Abi Talib at the end of Al Manakhan street and sense the anticipation of the silent, waiting crowds as the executioner raised his sword.

Roadblocks, closed cities, rumours, all had told him how close to defeat they were. Then the message had come through that they were still free, that their plan would run its course. It was a sign that the Almighty was with them.

The tall Palestinian was truly a resourceful man. But then, only a very resourceful man would have conceived of such a daring plan and approached him and convinced him that it was actually feasible. And only a very resourceful man could have brought it this far.

Slowly the man rose. The brocaded *aba'a* rustled faintly as he walked over to the window of his spacious office and regarded the tall minarets of the mosque. The age of family strife was not over. Had not the house of Saud itself risen to power on a wave of violence? How fitting, then, that they should strike at the heart of the *dirah* of the al-Saud family. A justice to be lauded by poets, he thought, as his eyes travelled across his own city.

*   *   *

During the afternoon and early evening, the decision and the plan matured in Leif's mind. For the first time since his hijacking and the ugly sight of Preben's corpse he was able to think clearly. He knew that he would play a vital part in the plan of his captors. The trouble they had taken to change his appearance made that clear. He had no doubt that the photos they had taken of him would be used to falsify documents.

But that meant that he was important to them. Before, he had not dared disbelieve the threat of the tall Arab that they would not hesitate to murder him. Now it seemed less certain, and it was this realization that had led to his decision to try and escape. If he succeeded—good. If he failed—well, he had staked his life and could only hope that he had guessed right.

But how could he possibly escape? The bare room

didn't contain a single tool that could be used to break his chains, and although he was bigger, he would still be no match for the two armed Arabs.

He was wrestling with all sorts of impossible schemes when the late afternoon visit provided the clue. This time the Arab with the mutilated finger came alone, unlocked his chains, and escorted him at gunpoint to the privy for a pee before returning him to the bed.

For hours Leif thought feverishly. It was at best a feeble hope, based on the assumption that they thought him cowed and that no one could effectively handle the keys and a gun at the same time. And the provision that the Arab returned alone.

Could he really overpower an armed man? Leif was no stranger to unarmed combat; he had done his mandatory military service in *kustjägarna*, the Royal Swedish Marines. But that was ten years ago. He tried to recall the harsh voice of Captain Mann, his middle-aged but granite-hard instructor. Surprise, that was half the victory; and hit the enemy where it counted, and hit him *hard*. Eyes, kidneys, testicles, where hits made sure a man stayed down.

It had been four years since he had hit another man, in self-defence. He had grown soft, was developing a paunch, and he was not used to brutality.

Darkness fell with near-tropical swiftness, but the minutes seemed to stretch into eternity. He lay on the bed, tense, straining against his fetters, listening. An hour went by, then another, and then he heard footsteps.

His heart leapt into his mouth as he tried to make out whether it was one man or two coming up the stairs. Then the door swung open, and the same Arab stood there with a round metal tray with a bowl of food and a steaming glass of tea. He turned on the single, naked bulb in the ceiling, and inside Leif a very small voice of fear shouted, not now, I'm not ready. The Arab put the tray down on the chair, and Leif managed to croak "toilet" in a half-whisper. The Arab nodded and got the keys out with his left hand while his right went inside his robe as he bent over Leif to undo the shackles. The moment was suddenly there, and mustering all his strength, Leif swung with his right fist.

The Arab must have sensed it, for he started to twist away. The blow connected under the chin and bit deeply, sending him sprawling on the dirty floor. Desperation gave Leif strength. He threw himself sideways and toppled the bed with a rattling, deafening crash, sending the chair and the tray flying in a shower of china and glass splinters. His hip and elbow hit the floor with agonizing pain; he was only inches from the guard. The Arab had risen to one knee, dazed, moving in slow-motion. Leif twisted his body, dug in, then drove his weight with his right leg. The top of his head caught the Arab full in the face and blood gushed and ran and made a little pool beside the prostrate guard.

The sudden silence was awful. Leif had a moment of panic when he looked around and couldn't find the keys, then he saw them nearly hidden under the thigh of the bleeding, unconscious Arab. His fingers trembled so badly that he dropped them twice before he could even insert them in the first padlock, but eventually his chains fell away, and he stood up on shaky legs.

The sound of the fight must have been heard all over the village, and his only thought was to get away. His legs carried him down the narrow stairs and out the door, into the chilly night, and he sprinted through the gate and down the road towards the dark village. He had almost reached the first houses, when he stopped dead.

The gun. He had forgotten to take the gun.

He clenched his fists. How stupid, how unforgivably stupid. He turned and stood looking at the now distant garage, his breath coming in rasping pants. As he watched and hesitated, he saw a door open and a figure step out from the yellow rectangle, and he turned again and ran.

*   *   *

General Yakov Mikhailovich Ladygin stared moodily at the phone while the voice at the other end of the line droned in his ear. The droning ended in challenging silence.

"No, Comrade Chairman," Ladygin said stubbornly, "there is nothing we can do at the moment. Not in that part of the world. Saudi Arabia is one country where our influence is next to negligible, as you know. We have no diplomatic representation, and the regime is virulently anti-communist . . ."

Ladygin was silent for a moment.

"No," he said presently, "I cannot recommend that. Our section V doesn't have the resources for anything of that nature. It would require something more like a task force, much as the Americans have prepared. Such operations couldn't possibly be the responsibility of the First Chief Directorate, Comrade Chairman, more the direct responsibility of the Politburo."

He held his breath.

"Of course I know about Aden. Very good, but I would advise against sending Soviet troops into Saudi Arabia for any but the most inconceivably extreme reasons."

A pause, then:

"No, not even that is extreme enough. Such a thing would be tantamount to war, and would compromise other objectives for a long time. You must realize, Comrade Chairman, the respect with which the other Arab countries view Saudi Arabia. Any interference there might cost us all the goodwill we have in those countries."

Ladygin frowned. "Yes indeed, if the truck should show up in Yemen with our warhead still on board I'm quite confident that our Aden force will be able to cope.

But until it does, and personally I doubt that it will, Comrade Chairman, we'll have to resign ourselves to the fact that the device has passed beyond our normal reach.

"No, the only thing we *can* do is watch. Luckily, we have one very good illegal in Riyadh, and, of course, some sympathizers in high places, but that is hardly sufficient to salvage our warhead. Besides, neither we, nor the Americans, have an inkling as to where it is at this moment."

Viktor Anatoli Chernyshov started droning again, and Ladygin listened with a slightly pained expression. The KGB Chairman, understandably, was not in his best mood.

"Yes," Ladygin finally managed to say. "Well, Comrade Chairman, I'm aware that policy-making is not my responsibility, but as I see it we should be prepared to act politically." So what if he stuck his neck out a little longer. "As I've said previously in my reports, there is the chance that the situation may turn out to be advantageous to us, and we'd do well to be ready to exploit it.

"Yes, of course, military action too, if necessary. Yes, certainly, Comrade Chairman, I'll keep you informed of any new developments as soon as they occur. Very good. Yes. Good night, Comrade Chairman."

Ladygin put the receiver down, relieved. Only the lamp on his desk was lit in the office. He looked up at the dim outline of the Lenin portrait, and permitted himself a thin smile before the stern gaze of the revered leader. If the Soviet Union was indeed able to exploit somehow its wayward warhead, it would mean that not only would it not be a major setback for him personally, but it might even reinforce his position. After all, who had suggested that they should try to keep their nose clean by enlisting the help of the Americans?

Ah yes, the Americans. He didn't envy that man at

the head of the CIA Near East Division, Holston. He must be sweating, knowing that his side stood to lose so much more than the Soviet Union.

Ladygin looked at the papers spread across his desk and thoughtfully studied the features of the man who called himself el-Tha'ir, the man Ladygin by now was convinced was behind the hijacking. Ladygin had sifted through his file again and again, trying to find out his plans and motives, but only coming up with guesswork. The KGB had been on to el-Tha'ir's number two, but the Israelis had moved in before them, and it was only through his American contacts that Ladygin had been able to learn some of what the Israelis had found out.

Maybe he should help Holston and place the file on el-Tha'ir in his hands and increase their chances of stopping him? He toyed with the idea for a moment and then smiled another thin smile and collected the papers, preparing to put them away in the office safe.

No, Ladygin thought, we just watch very closely—and we wait and we see.

* * *

He ran through the streets of the dark, silent village until he was exhausted, and then continued to run, stumbling, bent over with pain from his throbbing lungs and muscles.

Twice he saw Arabs walk under the sparse street lamps in the distance and slunk into the shadows and hid until they were gone, trying to silence his rasping breath. Perhaps they were only villagers on their way home—but he didn't dare take any risks. By now his captors must have found the Arab he had knocked down and were looking for him.

The sweat was drying in his clothes, and he felt cold and dirty. He hadn't changed his underwear since Halat Ammar, and it chafed at his crotch with every step. The

chill crept through his jeans and the thin shirt he had
kept on since the photo session, and he shivered.

He considered knocking on some door and demand
to be let in, then rejected the idea. Who would open
in the night? His banging might even attract his pur-
suers. He had no idea where the police station was, and
with every second he spent in the streets his chances
of remaining alive and well and free lessened.

The fact was that he didn't dare trust anybody here.
There was only one option open to him: to somehow
get back south to the main road and try to be picked
up by a European TIR truck. Then he would be among
friends and could turn to the police and tell them the
whole story.

He looked up at the night sky, trying to get his bear-
ings. He had to step out and peer along a narrow alley.
There was the Big Dipper, and there the North Star.
South was in the opposite direction.

The faint sound of footsteps reached him, and his heart
started to beat violently again. He drew back in the
shadows, found a street leading in a southwesterly direction, and began to run at a jog pace, as noiselessly
as he could. Minutes later he began to grow desperate.
Even though he plodded on due south he didn't seem
to be getting anywhere but lost. The surrounding houses
looked more or less alike, and the streets and small al-
leys seemed to form a bewildering maze.

He picked out the sound of an approaching car, and
fear once more shot through him. He looked around
and spotted a pile of garbage and torn cardboard boxes
outside a house. Nowhere else to go; quickly he dived
behind it and was greeted by a musty stench and flies.
He waved them away and intently watched the street.

The sound of the car grew louder. He drew back and
tried to make himself as inconspicuous as possible.

It was not the white Mazda as he had expected, but
a dusty dark blue Mercedes. Then he saw something

else: the man at the wheel was a European, not an Arab. The light of a street lamp left no doubts about that.

He was out in the street before he had even made a conscious decision, running for the car and frantically waving his arms. The Mercedes driver saw him and braked to a stop. The passenger door was unlocked. Leif tore it open and flung himself into the seat.

"Listen to me, please drive me away from here, I've been kidnapped and I must get . . ." He halted his frantic flow of words, struck by sudden suspicion. "You do speak English, yes?"

The driver looked at Leif with a frown. He was a bearded man of medium height, dressed in a rumpled suit. "Of course I do."

His accent was slightly guttural. German maybe, Leif reflected and launched into his tale again, unaware of the outlandish picture he must present to this stranger he had accosted in the middle of the night. "Please listen, I don't have time to explain everything now, but I've been kidnapped by three Arabs, and I've escaped and now they're looking for me." The driver still stared. A note of desperation crept into Leif's voice. "You must believe me! If they find me again, they'll kill me! You must take me to the highway south, anywhere as long as I can get away from here!" If he doesn't believe me, Leif thought wildly, I'll knock him out and steal his car. "You do believe me, don't you?"

The driver nodded and put the car in gear. Relief washed over Leif as they rolled down the street.

"Yes, I believe you. You must have had a terrible experience. I was just on my way to some friends of mine here. You can call the police from there. Don't worry, we'll keep you safe."

Suddenly the tension seemed to drain out of him; the thought that he had managed to escape and would be safe within a few minutes made him lightheaded, and he prattled on, not really listening to himself.

"I'm a truck driver from Sweden. Those Arabs have been following me for days, and they hijacked me yesterday, I think they're smugglers, they kept me chained in a room and even shaved off my beard . . ." The words ran on and on, the driver listened patiently as he drove, and Leif didn't particularly look where they were going.

He became aware that they had stopped at the back of a house; a small house with a neglected yard and a smaller construction jutting from it. He fell silent as a door opened and a man, a tall Arab, stepped outside and came up to the car. He spoke to the driver of the Mercedes through the rolled-down window.

"Good evening, Sergei Markov. We have been waiting for you."

Leif looked down at the gun in the hand of the driver and knew that the nightmare was about to begin again.

21

MARKOV PUT THE PAPERS DOWN on the engine tunnel and then placed Leif's attaché case in his lap and carefully started to sort through its contents. Most of the stuff was of no interest to him. He glanced over a few pages in the dog-eared address book and scrutinized an old postcard from Sweden. Then he unwrapped the bundle of German D-mark notes. Thoughtfully he riffled through them, then turned to el-Tha'ir in the passenger seat and remarked, "He carries a lot of money."

El-Tha'ir shrugged. "Of no use to us. Besides, it would look suspicious if they searched him and found no money. Apparently all European drivers on this route carry thousands of D-marks."

"I know, I know. It wasn't meant that way," Markov replied testily. He snapped the attaché case shut and put it back on the lower bunk. "You have gone through his belongings?"

"Of course we have." The irritation was plain in el-Tha'ir's voice. "The only thing we had to remove was his camera, otherwise he had no incriminating articles. As for his dressing-case, we simply substituted it with that of the other driver and included a razor."

Both of them spoke in calculatedly cool tones. The quarrel following Leif's attempt to escape had soon blown over, but both of them knew that it was luck, more than anything else, which had saved them this time.

Markov nodded. "Good. Fuad made a good job of the forgeries under the circumstances."

"The best we could do. We were fortunate in planning for such a possibility. I believe they will pass what scrutiny we can expect."

Markov nodded again, and looked at his watch. It was late, and he had a slight headache from the smell of paint and the long drive from Riyadh. He felt tired, drained. It was almost as if he could feel the presence of the cylinder so close to where they sat.

El-Tha'ir broke his train of thought. "We still have to go through the documents you brought from Riyadh."

"I know." Markov sighed. "We'd better fetch them." He reached up and switched off the cab light before they climbed down from the Scania.

*   *   *

The weathered countenance, which had provided so many political cartoonists with their livelihood, did not reflect the characteristic relaxed manner of the man who sat alone at the large desk in the dimly lit Oval Room of the White House. His tailor-made, discreetly grey suit hung loosely on his frame, and the wrinkles in his face seemed to have added years to his features.

He rose, and rubbing his face, did a slow tour of the room to stretch his legs and reflect upon the meeting the previous evening. The Saudi Arabian ambassador and the Israeli chargé d'affaires present at the same time—that was a measure of the out-of-jointness of the times.

Returning to his desk, he sat down in his chair and studied the scattered papers. To his left was a copy of the latest edition of the *Boston Globe*, with the two-column headline FEAR OF TERRORIST STRIKE IN SAUDI ARABIA? and underneath in more modest type, *Government Spokesman Says Road Checkpoints Are to Combat Rising Highway Casualties*. His press secretary could look forward to a busy day tomorrow.

Beside the newspaper was the report that had been

delivered by one of Cochrane's experts in State earlier
in the evening. Its prose was less eye-catching than that
of the newspaper article, but what it said was definitely
more sobering. In convoluted officialese it ultimately
suggested that he, the President of the United States of
America, order a partial mobilization of the American
NATO and Indian Ocean forces in order to be prepared
for the worst, while at the same time cautioning him
that the very act of mobilization could set off the chain
of events.

He was damned if he did, and damned if he didn't.

*   *   *

The cramped toilet-and-shower cubicle adjoining the
garage was cleaner than Leif had expected, and the
needles of cold water from the rusty nozzle stung and
rinsed some of his apathy away. None of the punish-
ments his racing brain had conjured up after his capture
the previous night had materialized. He had simply been
taken to the small room that took up one corner of the
garage, and chained to a sturdy eye-bolt with only a
blanket between himself and the floor. The third Arab
had sat guard with a gun, and through the open door
Leif had now and then glimpsed the leader and the
bearded man moving about in the dark garage. The Arab
he had knocked down in his attempt to escape did not
appear, and the thought that he had after all killed him
fretted on his nerves until he fell asleep from exhaustion. He had been woken only a few hours later to an
early dawn and a sense of urgency in his captors.

They had handed him a dressing-case and ordered
him to shower and shave. With a start he had recognized Preben's dressing-case, but he had no choice. The
mirror had given him his first good look at himself. He
had not liked what he had seen.

He stepped out of the cubicle, towelling himself and

trying to ignore his ever-present guard. He had been allowed to fetch his bag of clothes, and now he put on clean underwear, a clean pair of jeans and a clean T-shirt. The bearded European, Sergei Markov, came into the room. He didn't wear a suit any longer, but faded, baggy jeans, sandals, and a loose-fitting shirt with rolled-up sleeves. He was a bit shorter than Leif, but looked sinewy and in good trim.

Markov fixed Leif with a probing stare. Leif stared back in stony silence.

"I want you to know one thing," Markov finally said. His hand went inside his shirt and came out with a small, black, snub-nosed revolver. "From now on I'm not going to leave your side, and I'm carrying this. I won't hesitate to use it. Understood?"

Leif muttered affirmation. The novelty of being threatened with guns was wearing off by now.

"There is work to be done," Markov went on. "Come." He turned and walked out of the room, with Leif and lastly the Arab in tow. He walked along beside Preben's semi-trailer and reached up to open the door of the cab. For a queasy moment Leif expected the Pirate's corpse to tumble out, then he saw that the seat was empty.

Markov climbed up and slid over to the passenger seat, motioning Leif to follow. Leif slowly climbed up, ill at ease. The feeling that another pilot's cab was his inviolate castle, to be entered on invitation only, was strong in him. And now he had to sit where his friend had died.

Markov had rolled the window down on his side and turned on the ceiling light. "Both trailers have been disconnected," he said. "Now we'll simply switch trucks, so that yours will pull this trailer when we leave. You understand?"

Leif nodded glumly.

A sign from Markov, and the huge garage door slowly started to swing upwards. Blinding dawn soundlessly entered the garage. Leif squinted and pressed the starter button, and the diesel engine turned over, unwilling to fire for several seconds. Finally it did, and he let it idle for a while to warm it up, then he put it in gear. It was a strange sensation to drive another truck that was similar to but not quite like his own; the lower engagement point of the clutch almost took him by surprise, but he caught it and let the Scania roll some twenty metres out into the gravel yard. The Arab followed them.

They left it idling and turned back, and for the first time in days Leif saw his own truck again. It was a startling sight.

Gone was the medium blue paintwork he was used to. It was replaced with a fresh, bright red colour, a shade lighter than that of the Danish Scania 141. Lettering and stripes had been added in close simulation. Beneath the lower left edge of the windshield he could see a patch of grey primer, faked traces of repair. The tractor carried Preben's license plates, and the roof signs had been switched. It was Preben's truck and still not Preben's truck.

Then he saw the large, grey plastic sack under his semi-trailer close to the bogie. Leif stood still, feeling his throat contract.

"Go on," Markov said unfeelingly. "There's no time to waste."

Now he knew where the strong smell of paint had come from. As if in a dream, Leif went through the motions of starting his truck, driving it forward and backing it up so that it was coupled to Preben's semi-trailer. The Danish tractor unit was backed up against Leif's own semi-trailer. Back in Leif's truck, Markov handed him his attaché case. Leif opened it and found Preben's carnet and TIR papers, together with a Danish passport.

"Look through the papers," Markov said. "You're now a Danish citizen. Your name and residence are those of

your former friend, and it's his truck you're driving to
Riyadh. Memorize the facts. Don't bother to look for
your international driver's license in there, we have removed it."

Leif opened the passport. The charade revulsed him.
A photograph of a short-haired, clean-shaven man stared
at him, and it was a moment before he connected it
with himself. He looked closer and saw that the relief
stamp closely matched the original one. His height had
been changed to 182 centimetres and the hair colour
entry now matched his own, but there he thought
he could detect very faint traces from the tampering.
Preben's birthday had been November 14, 1953, only
a week from his own.

And now it didn't matter.

Under Markov's watchful eyes he also scrutinized the
TIR and carnet papers. There was mostly foodstuffs in
the semi he would be pulling, plus a few other odds
and ends for delivery in Riyadh.

"And now for me," Markov said. "My name is Heinz
Sammler, and I'm an Austrian citizen—*Österreich, ver-
standen*? I speak German." He handed a battered passport over for Leif to inspect. "I'm also a truck driver.
At present my truck is at Halat Ammar, and I'm having
a little trouble with the customs clearance. You have
given me a ride to Riyadh where I can go to the proper
authorities and get assistance." Leif opened the passport
for a brief look before he handed it back. To his eyes
it looked genuine enough, but it was no doubt as faked
as the one he had.

Markov pointed to the Arab who sat crosslegged behind them on the lower bunk. "As for him, he is also
armed." The Arab pulled up the left sleeve of his robe,
showing a sheathed throwing knife strapped to the inside of his forearm. "He speaks very good English and
will understand whatever you say in that language. What
you know is that his name is Alawi, and he's a hitch-

a hiker who asked us for a ride outside Medina early this morning. He works as a mechanic there and is on his way to see his brother in Riyadh. OK?"

Leif opened his mouth and asked the single question he had wanted to ask all the time. "Why all this?"

Markov stared at him. "Don't be bloody stupid," he finally said. "But in case you haven't already guessed it, the authorities here are looking for you and your truck. We're going to pass several roadblocks on our way. You may have to step out of the truck and answer questions. Remember that I'll be at your side at all times. Don't be stupid again and do anything suspicious. You'll be of damned little use to yourself as a corpse, right?"

Leif nodded silently.

* * *

At ten thirty-five on the dot, Wednesday morning, there were three quick knocks on David's door followed by a single knock, and Stuart Thompson breezed into the room, threw two briefcases, one thick and battered, one modern and slim, on the bed, and draped himself in the best chair with the satisfied langour of an Englishman who has breakfasted properly.

"Right, old chap," he drawled. "Tell me the story of your life. And do tell it as if you had lived it, not as if you had just learned it by heart, eh?"

David silently pulled out the drawer and pried the abstract of Peter Feltham's life loose. He handed it to Thompson and started. It took him the better part of an hour to satisfy the Englishman, who now and then interrupted the account with brief and to-the-point questions. Finally Thompson rose.

"Top marks, Feltham. Well done. Your diplomas."

He began to rummage about inside the old briefcase, and from its depths came a stream of articles accompanied by Thompson's banter.

"Dress shirt by Stenström's. Swedish, very good. Austin Reed top line. Casual shirts by Cassidy. Two ties by same. Some briefs by Jockey and socks by Wolsey. Conservative, but solid. Good impression. You'll wear your pinstripes most of the time, of course. Soap, shaving soap, deodorant, after shave, all by Yardley. Aquafresh tooth paste. Ghastly stuff in my opinion, but very up to the image. Toothbrush by Wisdom. You don't mind them red, do you? Comb by Kent's. You can keep your Gillette and your shaving brush, but chuck out the rest of your own stuff."

Thompson closed the old briefcase and opened the new, slim one.

"Then the documents. Driver's license, forged. Business cards. Two credit cards, forged. Don't use them, they're only for show. Two is a little on the stingy side, I know, but it was the best we could do. You'll be paying cash for everything. How are you fixed for funds?"

"I'm all right. It's all in pounds sterling. My life savings." David grimaced. He didn't expect Thompson to believe it, but he was telling the truth.

Thompson snorted and held up a small yellow booklet. "Your International Certificates of Vaccination, to show that you're vaccinated against smallpox. Forged, of course. If you aren't, that's just too bad, old chap. You'll simply have to take a chance."

David grinned. Catching smallpox was the least of his worries.

"Then the passport, complete with genuine entry visa to Saudi Arabia. We got it in a hurry, using photos of our nonentity, but that's not your headache. You're free to relish the concluding sentence, 'This visa is considered void if bearer obtains thereafter an Israeli visa.' But I don't think you will eh? Right, Feltham, here you are. Ah yes, you're C of E now, of course. Hope that doesn't cause you any acute religious discomfort."

David shook his head. "What shall I do with my Israeli documents?"

"Manila envelope, here you are. I suggest you put them in there and address the stuff to your British alter ego, Poste Restante, Poste du Mont-Blanc, here in Geneva. Here's the briefcase."

"Eh?" David said. "What do I need that one for?"

Thompson smiled patiently. "Ever see an ambitious young businessman venture abroad without a briefcase? Without this one you'd be a dead duck, old boy. Contains papers relating to your work and your business in Riyadh. Mostly for show, but you'd do well to familiarize yourself with them on the plane. Gives the right touch if you frown occasionally. There are some papers which contain facts about the firm you're working for which you should learn. Otherwise, avoid shop talk, hint at delicate negotiations or something if anybody presses you. God knows they'll have lots of other businessmen to talk to. Your firm isn't represented at the fair, so once you're in Riyadh you won't have anything to worry about. We also managed to get you a reservation at the Hotel Saudia, in spite of everybody pouring into the place. Good hotel on the outskirts of town."

David frowned. "The fair?"

"Yes, didn't you know? The Saudis are having a whopping big industrial fair at Riyadh. Hordes of businessmen going down there."

No, David thought, it can't be the fair. The instinctive jumping of his heart at the mention of the event gave way to sober reasoning. A warhead, and all those risks, only to wreck an industrial fair? There had to be something bigger in it.

"Right," Thompson went on, "that should be it. Just a few words of caution. I want you to realize that this is a rather makeshift cover made a little more solid by the fact that you speak and look the part. It ought to serve to get you into Saudi Arabia and out again within a reasonable period of time, provided you don't get up to anything. If the Saudis get it into their heads to check your cover it's going to crumble within twelve hours on the outside. If anything starts to smell, drop what you're doing at once and get out. Getting out means having to get an exit visa, and that means depositing your passport at the airport the day before you leave. That in its turn means you'll have to lie low for some time after you've dropped off your passport, during which time you'd do well to pray that you *will* be able to get out the next day. Check local exit procedures at once on arrival. Got it?''

"I've got it.''

"Good. Whatever you do, don't go running to the British. They'll show your documents up for the forgeries they are within seconds and hand you over to the Saudis. And I don't suppose your own people will be able to help you much, eh? They may not even care to, even if they could, right?''

David, taken aback, looked into the Englishman's shrewd eyes for a moment and then said, "That's about what it amounts to. I suppose I ought to thank you, Stu, but damn it, your hard-boiled attitude doesn't make it any easier.''

"Then don't bother to try. It's all right. It's my job. As soon as you've recovered your own documents you'll pop those I've given you in the mail to the British Embassy in Switzerland—anonymously, if you please. Photo removed from passport. You're not to keep them, understand?''

David nodded.

"Good. I have a message for you, too. When you've checked in at Cointrin you'll go to the cafeteria in the international departure lounge. You'll see somebody there that you know. You won't recognize him, but at a suitable moment you'll approach him and ask him for a light. OK?''

"OK. Maybe somebody does care for me after all."

"Quite possible. Oh, one more thing, do you speak Arabic?"

"Yes, of course I do," David answered, somewhat puzzled.

"No, you don't," Thompson said with emphasis. "The most that can be expected of an English businessman is that he knows how to maltreat French or possibly German. You'll have to take great care not to react to anything you hear spoken or see written in Arabic, or you'll be under instant suspicion. Don't forget that the Saudis have a very good security service."

"As if I didn't know that," David said a little testily.

"I'm sure you do." Thompson smiled ironically. "Any further questions? No. Well then, Feltham, you're on your own. Best of luck to you."

The Englishman reached out his hand and David solemnly and with considerable respect shook it. "Thanks a lot, Thompson, old boy. Take care."

"You too. Ta-ta."

Then Thompson was out of the door and David was alone, wondering what the devil he had got himself into.

*   *   *

Before he checked out of the Jet d'Eau, David seriously debated with himself which set of documents he ought, if he had any sense, to put into the manila envelope. His almost obsessive urge to see the end of the affair and his curiosity about the rendezvous at the airport got the upper hand. He sealed his Israeli documents into the envelope, addressed it to Peter Feltham, Poste Restante, Poste du Mont-Blanc, Genève, and took a taxi to the airport. Checking in was an uneventful affair, and the Swiss passport police paid little attention to his new travel documents.

As instructed, David made his way to the cafeteria.
His anticipation had been nothing compared to the shock
of seeing the tall, hook-nosed, wild-haired figure of Ari
Ofer looking out across the apron from where he stood
by the far wall.

There was an unoccupied table close to where Ofer
stood. David made his way to it, sat down and ordered
coffee and a Cointreau. He finished his liqueur, got out
a package of Dunhills, put a cigarette in his mouth and
started to pat his pockets. As they seemed to yield neither matches nor lighter, he turned to Ofer, who was
smoking.

"Excuse me, light please?" He held up the unlit cigarette in case the other didn't understand English.

Ofer understood well enough. "Yes," he said casually
and handed David a small matchbook. Inside the flap
was pencilled a name, two words, and a phone number.

Ofer spoke. "Don't ask me how I've found the time
to come here or why I should go to Geneva in order
to stick my neck out for you like this," he said in a
low, barely audible voice, still turned towards the plate-
glass. "I don't even know myself. That's the name, phone
number, and cue words of our contact in Riyadh. Learn
them by heart. I'll hang if it is known that I handed
this info over to you, and I'll tell you one thing. Don't
approach this man unless you have such a damned good
reason as you just can't imagine under normal circumstances. He'll break you in order to protect his own
position, understood?"

David lit his cigarette, puffed smoke and stared blankly
at the name. "I know that name," he finally said. The
person held a very elevated position in the Saudi Ministry of the Interior. "He's *our* contact?" He handed the
matchbook back to Ofer, certain that he would remember the name, the phone number, and the cue words.
"Thanks a lot."

Ofer accepted it and said, "Well, David, or whoever

you are, you've heard about strange bed-fellows politics is supposed to make, haven't you? I tell you, politics is positively chaste compared with spying." Then loudly, "You're welcome." He stared across the field and then moved on, keeping an eye on what was happening on the apron.

The time was a few minutes before two when the PA system chimed.

"Air Saudia, Saudi Arabian Airlines, flight SV 172 for Riyadh, now boarding at Gate 7."

David unhurriedly finished his coffee and rose, and swinging his slim black briefcase made his way towards Gate 7.

* * *

There were moments in Leif's consciousness when the demarcation between reality and fantasy was blurred, as if the deception became what it was only intended to imitate. Perhaps it was the sensation of being back in his own truck, of seeing the black asphalt once more rushing in under his wheels, but at times when he half turned his head to look at the two men with him he found it hard to believe that the bearded European in faded jeans was not a fellow pilot, or that the Arab was not a native who had asked them for a lift and got it, and he had to remind himself that they were both armed and quite prepared to kill him.

His first cigarette for nearly forty-eight hours had an almost dizzying effect. Both of the others smoked, Markov nearly incessantly, Alawi only now and then. Leif did not protest when they helped themselves from his dwindling stock of Prince packets, just as they did not protest when Leif, out of sheer habit, reached for a cassette and plugged it in.

The Mazda ran far ahead of them, carrying the tall leader and the man Leif had knocked down. The Arab had appeared from the house just as they were leaving. Leif had caught a glimpse of bandages under the head-dress, then the Arab had turned and looked at him with such hatred in his eyes that Leif had flinched.

They had not encountered any roadblocks until Al Qurayn, eighty kilometres west of Buraydah. It had been less eventful than Leif had anticipated. Bored soldiers had asked for their passports and taken a hasty look inside the cab. Before them a line of white-and-green oil barrels were placed across the asphalt like a double sine curve. Alawi had not produced any identification. Obviously they were looking for Europeans only.

Or rather, one European in particular—him. That was another unreal thought. As he handed their passports down from the open door and watched the soldier turn the pages, his mind was silently shouting, *Can't you see that they're both forged?* and he had a wild urge to jump out and try to run. Then the soldier handed the passports back and waved them on, and he closed the door and knew that the moment of decision was gone.

Nobody exchanged a word while the music played on and the diesel sang as they drew nearer to Riyadh.

*   *   *

One of the heavy rainstorms which occasionally hit the Nejd in the winter had swept over Riyadh a little before noon and turned the dust into muddy slush. The after-noon sun was at work, drying up; the air was humid, walls still held a well-scrubbed freshness, and plants shone with a lush greenness that was not yet dulled with dust. Beyond the arcade which surrounded the garden of the Royal Palace loomed the modern highrise office build-ings of the city, as if a leap over the wall were also a leap in time, from the medieval peace of the garden with its waterworks, ponds, and little pavilions to the modern bustle of the boom-town outside.

The atmosphere inside the room was cool, serene, heightened by the sparse, wooden furniture, the patches of colour of the round cushions on the floor and the rugs on the walls. Through the window the sun cast a long slash of light across the floor and halfway up one wall. The two men in the room had just been interrupted by a discreet knock on the door and were turning towards it as it opened.

The servant who entered carried a brass tray decorated with a finely traced geometrical pattern. On the tray were two small porcelain cups of black coffee sweetened with honey. The two men accepted their cups and the elder man waved the servant away. The silence continued after the door had been closed, as they sipped their coffee. Both of them wore white, gold-brocaded *aba'as* over their *tobs*, and *keffiyehs*.

Crown Prince Abdullah of Saudi Arabia finished his coffee and with a preoccupied air went on where he had left off. "Indeed, although I can sympathize with those in our family council who are against it, I do feel very strongly that it would be unwise if you—or I—were not present at the opening ceremony tomorrow."

"I am inclined to concur with your reasoning." Abdullah's brother King Fahd Ibn-Abdel-Aziz thoughtfully twiddled the gold ring on his righthand little finger half a turn this way, then half a turn that way. "This is after all an important event in the modernization of our country."

"Yes," Abdullah said. "But there are times when I wonder if our brothers may not be right in the caution they advocate. With this device loose somewhere within our borders you should perhaps consider the risk to your own person."

Fahd smiled a minute smile. "It's in God's hands, and I'm sure you will make an excellent king and prime minister, my dear Abdullah, and have no difficulty in consolidating your position."

"Not if I should be among the victims of nuclear terrorism. At the death of our brother Khaled the transference of power sent smoothly, but the situation today is different. You are familiar with Nayef's reports about unrest among certain powerful families, as well as the rumours among the military and the Palestinian immigrant workers."

Fahd's gold ring made a full turn under his fingers. "This is *Saudi* Arabia, Abdullah, the Arabia of the al-Saud family, we are leading in Islam, and leading in the Arab world. How would it look if the King and the Crown Prince and other leading members of the al-Saud family were to turn tail and hide like cowardly dogs at the mere suspicion of a nuclear warhead somewhere within the Saudi borders? The faithful are looking to us for guidance. To do as they say, feign illness and leave tonight—no, Abdullah, that cannot be."

"I agree that we have to think of our country before anything else," Abdullah said. "But there is a strong possibility that the device is indeed heading for Riyadh."

"I know. But have we not been informed by the Americans as to all particulars regarding this truck? Have we not acted forcefully on that information? And our brother, permit me to remind you, has ordered the National Guard to cordon off Riyadh especially for our protection."

"Yes indeed. But still we have not found it. That worries me."

"The desert is vast, Abdullah. And whether the device is on board it or not, that truck will never reach Riyadh. I suggest that we speak no more of it at present." There was a note of finality and proud confidence in King Fahd's voice.

Abdullah recognized it and threw out his hands. "I agree. *Quisma*. It is written."

Towards evening they stopped for a quick meal in a small village. Leif was made to sit between Markov and Alawi, the other two Arabs facing him across the rickety table where an elderly, surly man served them a mutton stew and hot tea. They were soon off again.

Darkness fell. Now and then they met another TIR truck. The first time Leif flashed his lights in greeting he got a sharp reprimand from Markov; with sullen patience Leif explained that it was expected of him, it would seem odd if he did not greet his colleagues, and Markov reluctantly simmered down and let him go on with his driving. He was beginning to feel the two nights of bad sleep and drove with his inner autopilot, following the red fires of the Mazda's taillights. One cigarette followed another as the hours passed.

Finally new lights grew on the horizon. Pinpricks of bluish white, a denser cluster than the stars in the sky. The lights marked the approach to Riyadh, the beginning of the four-lane highway into the city. The Mazda was slowing down, and Leif also eased back as the cluster expanded and became parallel rows of overhead arclights. He could feel his heart beating faster.

There were flashing red and blue lights ahead, and a tiny red star expanded into a white-glowing nova that bathed the inside of the cab with such a harsh glare that they were forced to shield their eyes against it. They came to a halt within a pool of white light, squinting at the uniformed men that seemed to be everywhere. Heavy concrete blocks had been arranged so as to leave only part of the outside lane free for passage. Ahead of them the other two Arabs were getting out of the Mazda. In the darkness beyond the lit circle the indistinct outlines of armoured cars and gun barrels could be glimpsed.

An officer stepped out in front of the truck, indicating the engine and making slashing motions with his hand,

and Leif pulled the compression release. There was a loud knock on the door. He opened it.

"Everybody inside; take all your papers and get out."

Leif grabbed his attaché case from the bunk and moved to rise from his seat, and Alawi was instantly at his back, following so close that he could feel his breath down his neck. They both jumped down, and Markov followed them in a moment with a sheaf of papers folded under his left arm. They stood close together and shivered a little in the cold night air, glancing back at the men who watched them with weapons at the ready.

The officer frowned as he looked at Alawi, and an exchange in Arabic followed. Alawi reached inside his clothes to produce his papers. The officer inspected them and put questions to Alawi, and presently he shrugged and handed back the papers.

He looked at Leif. "You are the driver of this truck?"

"Yes."

"Your papers, please."

Leif opened his attaché case and got out his forged passport and Preben's carnet and TIR papers. The officer accepted them and pointed at Markov. "You two are driving together?"

"No." Out of the corner of his eye Leif saw Markov lean slightly forward. "He's an Austrian," he added, "another driver, and his truck is in Halat Ammar at the border. I'm only giving him a lift into Riyadh."

"I see." The officer scrutinized Markov. "Your passport too, please."

Markov handed it over. The officer glanced at it and asked, "Why is your truck still at the border? Is anything wrong with it?"

"No, my vehicle is all right." Markov shook his head, seemingly calm. "But the customs people insist that I must pay duties on goods that have been ordered by your Ministry of Agriculture, so now I'm going there to have matters settled."

"I see," the officer said again. "May I have those papers?"

Without a word Markov handed over the thin sheaf of papers under his left arm. The officer thumbed through the papers which were in Arabic, German, and English. "Farming machinery?" he said, and Markov nodded. Finally the officer tucked the papers under his arm and opened Markov's passport.

"Your full name and date of birth?"

"Heinz Adolf Willirud Sammler, sixteenth March 1945," Markov said without hesitation.

The officer put his hand in the breast pocket of his uniform, and got out a photograph the size of his palm which he held beside the passport, looking from one to the other and then at Markov.

My God, it's a picture of me he's holding, Leif thought. *He's going to recognize me and when Markov and Alawi pull out their guns the soldiers will open fire and we'll all die.*

The officer handed the papers back to Markov and turned to Leif, looking at the load sheets. "What is your load?" he asked.

"Canned food, mostly." Leif's teeth were close to chattering from cold and nervousness. "S-some of it powdered milk."

The officer closed the TIR papers and opened the passport. "Your name and date of birth, please."

"Fleming Preben Sørensen, born on—ah—November 14, 1953." No one seemed to have noticed his slight hesitation.

Now the officer held up his photograph beside the passport and looked from them to Leif and back. Leif held his breath and heard his pulse roaring in his ears. The world seemed to have shrunk to this circle of light where they stood waiting. He was aware of Alawi's quick breathing beside him and the soldiers at the edge of the world.

"Turn towards the light."

The words took a moment to sink in, then he did a quarter turn to face the blinding searchlight, almost closing his eyes. Red stars danced behind his eyelids.

"You look young for being born in 1953." The officer's voice reached him from somewhere to his left. Leif could not open his mouth, could only gesture vaguely.

"Very well. Turn back, please. Here are your papers."

He had passed. With an effort he turned and accepted his papers, opening his attaché case with fingers that hardly obeyed him.

The officer barked a series of commands in Arabic and pointed. Two soldiers climbed into the cab. Others brought out flashlights and started to inspect the undercarriage, and at the back of the semi-trailer two were busy unlashing the tarpaulin.

"Stay here." The officer walked along the truck, peering here and there, asking questions, and Leif dared throw a glance at where the Mazda had been. It was gone, together with its passengers. He looked at Markov. The Russian's eyes glittered narrowly as he followed the movements of the soldiers.

The minutes dragged on. Leif shivered in his thin T-shirt. The soldiers in the cab came outside and closed the doors, then, as those who inspected the inside of the semi-trailer and the undercarriage were about to finish their job, another TIR truck came rolling up, and the searchlight moved and left them in the relative dimness of the arc-lights. The officer spoke to some of the soldiers, pointed, gestured, then nodded. With measured steps he returned to Leif and his two passengers and saluted.

"Very well. You can leave."

It was not really his own legs that carried Leif back to the cab. Alawi opened the door and climbed up, then Leif, and finally Markov walked around in front of the

Scania and got into his seat. Leif inserted the key and found the starter button with numb fingers. From down on the road the officer looked up at them as they trundled past the concrete blocks. The checkpoint dwindled in his mirrors and disappeared.

Where the city of Riyadh really began and the high wall with its battlements ran along the street lights, the Mazda waited. It swung out ahead of the truck and accelerated, and Markov said, "Just follow it."

The vehicles turned left into Yamamah Road and headed towards the airport. Only the occasional taxi met them; most of the city seemed dead at this hour of the night.

The airport glided by in the distance to the left, brightly lit. They turned again and were on Al Islam Road, which a little further on joined the main throughway east towards Dammam on the coast. The street lights grew sparser. Leif felt confused. Were they going to leave Riyadh again? That would mean another checkpoint.

New lights appeared on his right, horizontal rows in the darkness, giving the illusion of an ocean liner stranded somewhere on the edge of the desert. For a moment Leif couldn't place it, but then he remembered: it was the exhibition grounds the Saudis had been building during the last year or two. Several of the pilots had hauled materials for it, it had been on the asphalt vine. He himself had not been in that part of Riyadh for a long time.

The Mazda was slowing and turning, heading for a gate on their right. Leif looked at Markov, who motioned him to follow.

The gate was illuminated by twin floodlights mounted on top of the metal fence. Soldiers appeared from the guardhouse, and the tall Arab stepped from the Mazda and went to meet them. He produced some papers and a discussion ensued. The three men in the truck waited, the engine idling.

Presently an agreement seemed to be reached, and the soldiers stepped back to open the gate. The tall Arab returned to the Mazda, Leif put the Scania in gear, and together the two vehicles rolled through the gate and were inside the grounds.

The Mazda led the way, navigating along inadequately lit avenues. There were signs everywhere, industrial brand names from all over the world, as well as several large enclosures where heavy machinery was parked as if on exhibition. Everything gave an impression of readiness.

They came to a halt before a very large, square building of corrugated metal in what seemed the back area behind the main fairgrounds. The building reminded Leif of a hangar. The tall Arab once more stepped out, this time to open the huge doors. Markov leaned over towards Leif and said, "When we have entered, you'll turn sharp right and then left into the far aisle. I'll show you."

The inside of the building was enormous. There were no lights on, but the headlights of the Scania illuminated large shelves full of packing crates and allowed Leif to dimly glimpse the ceiling high above. Another TIR truck, empty and lifeless, stood in one of the aisles. They passed it and turned into the aisle Markov indicated. Leif let the Scania crawl up close to the wall and then hit the parking brake and cut the engine. The silence that followed was cavernous, ghostly.

He reached up and turned on the ficki-ficki light. Markov leaned back in his seat, staring absently ahead. It was as if all energy suddenly had drained out of him. Leif watched him in silence, apprehensively.

Half a minute passed before Markov turned his head. His brown eyes were tired, bloodshot, but there was triumph in them.

"We're here," he said as if Leif were capable of sharing his triumph. "We made it, do you know that? We made it here, and here is where we'll stay."

* * *

Saudia flight SV 172 from Geneva landed at Riyadh airport at 0125 local time Thursday morning, a good ten minutes before schedule due to a strong tail wind at the 10,000-metre level.

For David Bar-Sharon, alias Peter Feltham, the journey was uneventful. The number of western businessmen aboard the plane sometimes made it hard to imagine that he was really aboard a Saudi Arabian flight, and evidently he was accepted at face value as another young British businessman.

Entering Saudi Arabia itself was just as uneventful, except for the well-developed red tape. Nobody in the modern, slightly sterile airport building questioned his being what he appeared to be, and the customs officials were more concerned with the possibility that he might bring alcohol and other prohibited substances into the country than with the possibility that he might be an Israeli agent in disguise.

It was only for a brief moment in the shared taxi on his way to the hotel that the realization that he was actually on "enemy" territory filled his mind, but the realization subsided as soon as he had checked into Hotel Saudia and was in his room.

David had been in a preoccupied mood during the flight. He had gone through his papers, but he had been unable to put the industrial fair out of his mind. The coincidence was simply too great for him to accept that there wasn't any connection between the fair and the wayward warhead. But he was equally unable to reconcile the respective size and importance of the two phenomena. Perhaps there was a missing piece which would render them compatible and confirm that the fair must indeed be the target. But so far he hadn't found it.

He stood by his window, looking out across the sparse lights of the city, feeling that he was about to grasp it; but it never took shape. Still preoccupied and exhausted after the long flight, David decided not to rack his brains any longer. He went to bed, determined to rise early in search for the missing piece.

                              *   *   *

The night was coming to an end, but Mahmoud el-Tha'ir was unable to sleep. He stood outside the warehouse, alone, breathing in the fresh air, full of exhilaration.

They had arrived. How far he had come from the refugee camp. He had managed to get away and keep his dedication, he had not grown fat and contented and contemptuous of his brothers like so many of the others who had got away.

Tomorrow he would have accomplished so much more than they had in twenty years of talking and petty action. That fool in Medina regarded him as a tool, had been encouraged to do so, but he would soon find out who had been the tool and who had not. He was not going to be able, as he thought, to fill the power vacuum that would follow the cataclysm without help, and that help would come from Palestinians and certain high officers.

El-Tha'ir smiled a minute smile. Prince Nayef and his security service knew about them, how could they help not to? That was the divine beauty of it. The key men were few, did not seem all that influential, and in the present situation were not seen as a force to be reckoned with. Prince Nayef was right but for one thing: the warhead. It was going to create such a void, such a revolutionary chaos, that those men, literally in seconds, would become the strongest single cohesive force in Arabia.

He lifted his face and looked east, where the new dawn, the moment when a white thread could not be told from a black, would soon break. Even if Nayef cracked down on them now he would be too late.

The old rage welled up inside el-Tha'ir, nameless and strong. This time he did not shut it out but let it seize him until he shook and whispered to himself the ancestral truth, *dam butlub dam*, blood will claim blood.

22

A CAT WILL GET INTO MOST PLACES it wants to get into. A hungry cat will get in anywhere.

Between the wall and the garage door was a narrow crack. Through the crack the first rays of the morning sun cast a thin bright line across the floor. The brightness stopped just short of the big plastic sack under the towering semi-trailer. Dust particles hovered in the sunlight, flared, and were extinguished.

At the edge of the door, under the crack, grey furry paws had been digging away at the earth for hours, and now the cat's head appeared. Sideways, the cat managed to get its head through the opening and slowly, in rippling, grey undulations, the rest of it seemed to ooze through until all of it was inside.

The cat shook itself back into shape and stood for a moment, its right front paw raised, its tail slowly moving, and regarded the lit dust particles. Then it trotted over and sat on the floor with its tail around its front paws, expectantly looking up at the red Scania. When nothing happened it began to meow, impatiently, and raise itself on its hindlegs as if about to jump up into the cab. Still no reaction, and it sank back, confused.

After a while it grew restless and began to explore the rest of the garage. Presently it reached the plastic sack and sniffed at it, meowing now and again. Then it began experimentally pawing it.

One half-extended claw caught the seam of the plastic, and trying to extricate it, the cat only managed to get it further in, until, in desperation, it tore with all its strength and ripped a long hole in the side of the sack. Through the hole fell a huge, waxy-greenish hand, and with the hand came a thick, cloying smell. The cat sniffed and stroked itself full length against the hand, even tried a hopeful purr.

When there was no reaction at all from the hand the cat sat down again with an incomprehending air and began to meow in earnest.

*   *   *

Markov's back hurt where he crouched low under the Scania to squeeze himself in between the tractor frame members and the massive drive shaft. The magnetic flashlight he had attached overhead was almost useless in the cramped space. From his uncomfortable position he reached in with both hands, feeling his way over the heavy PVC-coated nylon fabric and the thin steel wires. Everything seemed to be intact.

He reached the nearest eyebolt, grabbed the spanner, working by touch alone. The morning sun had not yet significantly warmed the air inside the warehouse, but already the first drops of sweat broke out on his face. The beard he had grown since Turkey itched.

The eyebolt came loose without warning, and his elbow banged against metal. He grimaced and half-strangled a curse, then put down the spanner and undid the bolt by hand. Pushing the now slack steel wire aside, he folded back a corner of the wrapping. Caked dirt fell from it, tickling the back of his hand.

He reached inside, feeling around for the little connection box. The ache in his back was growing, and he shifted as much as space allowed. Dust and grease rubbed against his hair and shirt.

The smooth plastic of the box was a welcome touch.

Carefully he felt around it. The cable was there, still connecting it with the electronics inside the grey steel cylinder after all the road kilometres.

Slowly, carefully, he wriggled it out from the stiff folds of the fabric and brought it over the turned-up edge of the steel plate that hid the warhead. Inspecting it by flashlight, he found it to be in as good a condition as when he had installed it.

"The cable," he muttered.

El-Tha'ir bent down and handed a thin, black cable to Markov. The Russian checked to see that the gleaming copper leads were still intact, then took a slim screwdriver from his shirt pocket. He checked himself for a moment and drew a deep breath.

"No use having the thing start ahead of schedule," he muttered to himself in his own language.

Then, with slow, controlled movements, carefully checking the markings, he connected the four leads to the box, one by one. He inspected it all one last time, put the connection box back and crawled out from under the truck.

*   *   *

Slumping over the steering wheel with both wrists chained to it, Leif had spent a very uncomfortable night. He had dozed, often waking in fits and starts, while Markov and Alawi took turns guarding him and sleeping in the lower bunk. Two watchmen had come by in the morning and had turned on the overhead fluorescent lights among the lattice of roof beams. The tall Arab had turned up and showed them papers and talked while they looked everything over, and then they had left.

On request Leif had been led to a toilet in the far corner, but all other attempts at communication had been met with silence and shrugs. Once more chained to the wheel, he could see in his mirrors that they were doing something to the underside of the Scania, but what he couldn't guess. He felt lonely, confused and scared. Markov had said that this was their goal, but the nature of that goal was still beyond Leif. And after it was over, what would happen to him?

The passenger door opened, and Markov climbed into the seat, carrying a small bag and trailing a thin, black cable. From the bag he brought out a box the size of two cigarette packs on top of each other, with a knob on top. Leif silently looked as Markov with slow movements connected the cable to the box and then carefully laid it on the bottom bunk, looking at his watch. Reflexively Leif looked at the clock on the dash. The time was a little after nine.

"What are you doing?" Leif suddenly asked.

He had not expected an answer, but Markov turned his head and looked at him. "You still have no idea?"

Leif shook his head. Markov shrugged. His red-rimmed eyes were tired, but there was a ghost of a smile around the corners of his mouth.

"I suppose it doesn't matter much if you know or not."

Leif waited.

"Since you were arrested in Turkey—yes, we arranged that—you've been carrying a nuclear bomb in your truck."

"Nuclear . . .?" Leif said. The word meant nothing to him.

Markov shrugged again. "Nuclear bomb, atom bomb— same thing." Leif's mouth fell open. "And do you know why it was brought here to the industrial fair in Riyadh?" Markov went on. "Because in two hours' time the King and most of his ministers will be present at the opening ceremony. Off goes the bomb—no more Riyadh, but most important, no more royal family. Into the chaos will step people who do not bow to the

West . . ." In Markov's tone was a strange mixture of exalted revelation and anger. He lifted up the box and held it up before Leif. "You see this? Press the button and twist, and it feeds the arming signal into the warhead. From then on the process is irreversible, it can't be changed. Forty-five minutes later it feeds the detonating signal into it. That gives us enough time to get out of the city."

He put the little box back, almost tenderly. In the silence Leif whispered, "What about me?"

Markov looked at Leif again. The light was gone from his eyes. When he spoke it was without emotion.

"You stay here."

*　　　*　　　*

In a country where the climate forces you to bury your dead before nightfall if they die during the day, the first thing in the morning if they die during the night, there is no mistaking the thick, cloying, rank-sweetish smell of a decaying corpse.

With the smell came the eerie, continued meowing of a desperate cat.

The two local policemen who had been called by people living close to the Al Khalf garage hesitated only briefly before they ordered the door to be forced. Creaking, the door soon swung up and illuminated the red truck inside, the iron-grey semi-trailer, and the dishevelled cat still sitting by its dead master's hand. At the back of the policemen the assembled locals pushed curiously.

The policemen were also local men who seldom handled anything that wasn't local business, but they had common sense and had been informed about the truck that was looked for along the main roads and around the major cities. Their first interest, therefore, was the vehicle inside the garage and not the corpse.

The tractor unit itself was the wrong colour, but the fact that it was without licence plates made one of them go to the back of the trailer to have a look; agitatedly he came back to the front, spoke rapidly, and then the two policemen started to search the garage more carefully.

Soon they found spots of red paint on the ground alongside the truck. They noted the violet hue on the front of the trailer. Close to the wall, behind the trailer, they then found two licence plates thrown face down, and grew even more excited. They had found both the registration plates of the wanted vehicle, but the question remained, had they found all of the vehicle? One of the policemen tried the cab door, found it unlocked, and entered the cab closely followed by the other. In frantic haste they started to go through the cab in an attempt to find anything that would identify it. It was a stack of round paper discs in the glove compartment that settled it. In the centre of each was written the kilometrage of each seven-day period, plus a combination of two letters followed by a set of figures, the same on each disc, obviously the registration number— and it was not the registration number of the wanted vehicle, not the number on the loose plates they had found.

While one of the policemen stayed in the garage with the unsavoury task of seeing whether the corpse in the plastic sack answered to the description of the wanted driver, the other sprinted through Al Khalf towards the local PTT office.

The call from the district office in Al Khalf was received and registered at the Royal Saudi Arabian Police Headquarters in Riyadh at 0933. The operator who took the message immediately summoned his superior, who took one look at the slip and then hastily retreated to his office to make three calls.

*   *   *

David Bar-Sharon awoke later than he had intended
and found that his subconscious had not, during the
night, synthesized any solution to his problem. Nor did
it come to him during breakfast. It was not until he was
dropping off his key at the porter's desk that it jumped
up and hit him with stunning force.

It came as he glanced at the rack of newspapers on
the desk. It was the headlines of the Arabic papers that
caught him, and for a breathless moment he was on
the verge of reaching out for *Al-Madina Al-Munawara*
or *Al-Riyadh*, then he remembered Thompson's warning and chose a copy of the *Saudi Gazette*. There, too,
but in smaller type, was the news that King Fahd and
Crown Prince Abdullah would be present that morning
at the opening of the fair. David quickly scanned through
the list of other dignitaries to be present and held his
breath. Lord, if those people were wiped out in a nuclear blast, along with a good part of Riyadh, the en-
suing chaos would be so great that there was no telling
who, or what, would come out on top afterwards.

David hesitated, looked around, and then strode across
the foyer to a telephone booth at the other end. He got
out a fifty-halalah piece, inserted it into the phone and
dialled the number Ari Ofer had given him.

A secretary took the call. David introduced himself in
English as Peter Feltham and gave the first cue word
to the secretary to tell the contact. Presently a voice
said warily, "Yes?"

David gave the second cue word and at once went
on. "My name is Feltham, Peter Feltham, businessman
from England. You know about a certain truck that is
being looked for?"

The man at the other end hesitated, then, "Yes."

"Has it been found?"

"No."

"The King and the Crown Prince will be present at the opening of the industrial fair in"—David looked at his watch; the time was a quarter to ten—"just a while. If that truck and its load were to be in that area the consequences might be—ah—far-reaching to say the least."

"Indeed," the contact said, and now there was a supercilious note in his voice. "The possibility has been considered, but I am able to inform you that Riyadh is securely cordoned off, and no such truck has passed into the city."

"But," David insisted, "you can't be sure as long as you haven't found it."

"We're quite sure," the contact said with finality. "Now Mr. Feltham, let me . . ." There was a sudden commotion at the other end of the line, then the contact came back, "Hold on, please."

David hung on, although an uneasy feeling at the back of his neck told him to hang up and get out. The delay might mean that they were trying to trace the call. He was cursing himself for having given his real cover name and not some phony name that would at least have given him a chance to get through at the airport, when the voice of his contact returned.

"We have just received a report," it said almost meekly, "that the wanted trailer and the licence plates of the tractor unit have been found in a garage in a village called Al Khalf. The tractor itself has not been found, but it seems that it has been repainted and disguised with other licence plates."

"Lord," David said, "then it may still . . . Have you got the new registration number?"

"Fortunately," the contact said. *"Alhamdullah.* We are checking right now if it has entered Riyadh."

"You had better check the fairgrounds and the immediate area, too," David said grimly. "And get some crack forces in there."

There was silence for a long time at the other end,
then the contact said, "Where are you staying, Mr. Feltham?"

David hesitated, then, "At the Saudia."

"Good, wait there. I will pick you up. I would prefer
to have you with me during the remainder of your stay
in this country. For your own sake as well as for mine
it would be best if you were to leave Saudi Arabia as
soon as possible."

*   *   *

The phone rang twice, shrilly. With a grimace the man
looked up from his papers and picked up the receiver.

"United States Embassy, Carlton speaking. What? No,
I'm sorry, both the ambassador and the first secretary
have already left for the fair. What . . .? From whom?"
The man was silent, his eyes unfocused. "Oh." Silence
again, only broken by the tinny voice at the other end
of the line. "Changed identity?" Another half minute
of silence. "Yes. Yes, of course." He put the phone down.

"My God," he whispered as he pressed down the intercom button for Com. "Scotty? Carlton. Put me in
touch with State in Washington. And make it snappy,
or we'll all be damned."

*   *   *

The motorcade, made up of Rolls Royces, Mercedes 600's
and American luxury cars, glittered impressively in the
sun as it drew up just inside the main gates to the fairgrounds, the sirens of the motorcycle cops dying down.

The area was bustling with last-minute preparations
before the tour of the King and his ministers and their
retinue. Heavy machinery was being shifted into position accompanied by a fair amount of shouting; people
were hastening in every direction; and to the right, in
the vicinity of the gate, a small, bright yellow helicopter

with American civilian markings was coming in for a landing.

As the noise of the aircraft took over from the motorcycles, police and soldiers in dress uniform and berets kept the spectators at a distance. The motorcade discharged a company no less glittering than the vehicles themselves.

From the first Rolls Royce, resplendent in gold-embroidered black *aba'a*s over sumptuous white *tob*s, King Fahd Ibn-Abdel-Aziz of Saudi Arabia and his brother Crown Prince Abdullah Ibn-Abdel-Aziz. From other vehicles, also in traditional Arab dress, Defence and Aviation Minister Prince Sultan Ibn-Abdel-Aziz; Minister of Finance and Economy Mohammad Ali Abu al-Khail; Information Minister Mohammad Abdou Yamani; Minister of Industry and Power Dr. Ghazi Abdel-Rahman al-Qusaibi; Minister of Commerce Sulaiman Abdel-Aziz al-Salim; Minister of Public Works and Housing Prince Mutaib Ibn-Abdel-Aziz; Minister of Agriculture and Water Abdel-Rahman Ibn-Abdel-Aziz Ibn-Hasan al-Shaikh; PTT Minister Alawi Darwish Kayyal; Prince Salman Ibn-Abdel-Aziz, Governor of Riyadh; a host of lesser officials from the departments concerned; the diplomatic corps of Riyadh represented by a number of ambassadors, chargé d'affaires and first secretaries.

Their Royal Highnesses were met by the director and the secretary of the fair; other officials performed introductions at a less exalted level. Embraces and bows were made, and hands shaken, then efficient bodyguards in civilian dress cleared a path for the King and the Crown Prince, and the preliminary tour, on foot, began.

In other parts of the fair soldiers from the regular security forces on the grounds were silently but hurriedly seeking out gatekeepers, nightwatchmen, guards, and workers in a desperate attempt to locate a red Scania 141 with Danish licence plates which might have entered the area during the night.

At the National Guard barracks near the Royal Palace in Riyadh a platoon of crack Bedouin troops at combat alert were being loaded into trucks for immediate transport to the fair.

*   *   *

The President of the United States had on a bathrobe hastily thrown over his thin pyjamas, and his slippered feet felt cold. He was alone in his private office on the second floor. Around him the White House was partially stirring into life in the small hours of the morning.

A muted buzz came from the phone, and he picked it up and put it to his ear. "Yes?"

"Your Security Adviser here, Mr. President. I'm on my way over. You have read the message?"

"Yes, and I'm about to give all the necessary orders. If that thing has really changed identity, it may have slipped through their roadblocks and can be anywhere. The only thing we can be sure of is that it won't be . . . One moment."

There was a knock on the door, then the President's chief-of-staff poked his head inside the office and said, "Just wanted to let you know that Cochrane has already arrived, and the Director will be here any moment. We're trying to reach the Secretary of State."

The President nodded, and the door shut. "I was saying," he went on into the phone, "that one thing is for certain, and that is that we'll see the end of it soon, this time. We've got to be able to *move*, so the orders will include full mobilization of our Middle East and Indian Ocean-based forces and putting the Strategic Air Command on Red Alert Status. You'll get the full picture as soon as the meeting here can start."

The Security Adviser's voice reached him, thin and quiet. "The Soviets will reply in kind within the hour. Let's just hope we won't have a full-scale war on our hands."

*   *   *

They were getting ready to leave. From the Scania's cab
Leif could see them putting the last things into the boot
of the Mazda, toolbox, some clothes, nothing much.
Markov and the bandaged Arab did the carrying while
the tall leader paced back and forth a little way off,
every so often looking at his watch. His steps on the
concrete echoed inside the huge warehouse. He had
removed his headgear and nervously fingered the brand
on his cheek. The fourth Arab, Alawi, was nowhere to
be seen.

Leif watched them with a kind of numb dread mixed
with strange anticipation. Half-consciously he wished
that it would be over soon, that Alawi would return
and all of them leave, but he knew the dark terror he
was going to feel the moment one of them climbed into
the cab for the last time and started the mechanism that
would irrevocably mete out the final forty-five minutes
of his life. But until that happened he couldn't rid himself of a feeling of unreality in spite of it all, and he
was surprised at his own calm.

Earlier there had been movement at the far end of
the warehouse, but now it was uncannily silent. Everybody must be outside, waiting for the opening and perhaps a glimpse of the royalty. Only occasionally the sound
of engines in huge vehicles rumbling by penetrated the
walls.

Leif's thoughts were a curious mixture of the trivial
and the profound. Lars Persson at the Jerre head office
who would probably never see that load, left behind in
the Al-Khalf garage, delivered to ABV. Bert Nilsson,
whose best truck would soon be vaporized along with
a city. His friends, his parents, Ellen in Odense—would
they ever know the truth?

And Annika; he had promised to come back to her,
and now he never . . . He wished he could reach up

and fold down the sun visor and look at the photograph of her, but he couldn't even get that comfort—if it would after all be a comfort. He wasn't really certain.

The cold steel links around his wrists chafed.

He had faced Preben's death. Soon, alone, he would face his own.

*   *   *

The man stood unmoving before the large window, hands on his back, looking out over Medina and the mosque of Ali Ibn Abi Talib, and wished that his window faced a little more east. Would he then have been able to witness the end of the house of al-Saud with his own eyes? Perhaps.

In dozens of places the allies he had so carefully enlisted were ready to move; in one hour Allah would make him ruler or traitor, the man on the throne or the man before the executioner. Hypnotized, his mind oscillated between the two like a pendulum while he looked out over the city with unseeing eyes.

*   *   *

The green jeep crawled through the thronging crowds; the driver frenziedly honked his horn, shouted and gesticulated. Reluctantly people made way for it, shouting and gesticulating back.

The fat Arab officer in the back mopped his face with his sleeve, looked at his watch, and wondered resignedly if he might not make better progress on foot. Then the crowds thinned out, and the driver gunned the jeep towards the gate. The man in the back had to grab hold of the side of the jeep. His face was pale under the *keffiyeh*.

They reached the gate just as two dark green, medium-sized trucks drove up from the other direction, and the three vehicles braked to a halt. A small, wiry man stepped down from the first truck and approached the jeep at an easy half-trot, a submachine gun slung over his shoulder. He was in greenish-yellow and brown desert combat fatigues. The man in the jeep glanced at the trucks as he with some effort stepped down from his own vehicle. In them were more men dressed in the same speckled fatigues, all fully armed.

Prince Abdullah's crack Bedouin troops had arrived.

They quickly introduced themselves. The fat head of fair security was outranked by the Bedouin commander, a major whose scarred face was so darkened by the sun that his expression was difficult to read. When he spoke it was with the *Badawi* accent of the desert tribes.

"Their Royal Highnesses, have they been informed?" The loyalty of the Bedouin to the ruling family was legendary.

"Yes, most certainly," the security head panted. He wiped his face again. "I have just sent a reliable man to beg them to leave the fair, for the sake of their own safety. But I also have important news! *Alhandullah!*" He touched his heart with his right hand. "A truck answering to the new description is here at the fair. Two of my men saw it this morning."

The major bared his teeth. "Are they absolutely sure? Do they know where it is now?"

"Why yes, I just . . ." The security head didn't have time to finish the sentence.

"Take us there at once!" The Bedouin major swung around and beckoned to the trucks. "For Allah and for the King!"

23

THE MAN bowled two more spectators over and reached the outer security line around the royal retinue. He was stopped by a soldier, and an agitated palaver followed as the man showed his identification. Then he was let through and ended up against one of the personal bodyguards of the dignitaries. The entire retinue stopped as much the same scene repeated itself, and ministers, diplomats, officials began to talk among themselves in undertones.

The bodyguard, after listening to the security man's story, approached the King's personal aide, who finally spoke to the King itself. Fahd listened impassively, then uttered a single word, turned, and calmly led the procession back the way it had come. Runners made for the gate, and soon the motorcade came driving up to meet the company.

Talking baffledly, the foreign diplomats, the officials, the ministers, entered their cars. Last into his car, having said nothing further, was King Fahd of Saudi Arabia.

Moments later the motorcade, accompanied by wailing police motorcycles, had left the fairgrounds and was heading at high speed towards the centre of Riyadh.

*   *   *

Alone in his office in the Kremlin, Yuri Vladimirovich Andropov knew that it was going to be a stormy meeting with the Politburo. He cursed the other members for being old men, at times exasperatingly slow in taking action, before he picked up his phone.

Things must have gone seriously wrong in Saudi Arabia for the Americans to partially mobilize the way they had. He wondered a bit why the KGB knew nothing about the reasons for it. There would be no quiet weekend at the *dacha* now, at any rate. The situation was getting unpleasantly unstable. The Soviet mobilization he was forced to order in answer to it might lead to war or to nothing more serious than mild diplomatic altercations.

Then there was a click in the phone, and the Premier of the Soviet Union was connected with the Soviet commander-in-chief, Marshal Dmitri Ustinov.

* * *

As the jeep braked to a halt, the head of security touched the arm of the Bedouin major and pointed to the warehouse that loomed large some hundred metres ahead of them. "There, inside that building! My men said it was closest to these doors and parked along the wall to the right," he said eagerly. "There are three or four men, and the truck itself is red with . . ."

The major silenced him with a movement of his hand. "The description is known to me." He jumped over the side of the jeep and ran towards the two trucks. They had stopped some distance back, and the soldiers were streaming out in a disciplined, practiced fashion, four of them going into cover fire position close by the trucks while the rest sheltered behind. They carried Ingram MAC10 submachine guns, light and compact close-combat weapons, and hand grenades and spare ammo clips in their belts. Three of them, in addition, had Colt M79 grenade launchers.

The major unslung his own weapon as he slipped behind the trucks. He gave brief orders regarding the approach to the building, blowing the doors open, and finished with, "I want the greatest speed and accuracy when we go in. Those men must not be given time to act. Shoot on sight, and shoot to kill. Questions?"

There were no questions.

The major cast a glance around the nearest corner of the trucks. The jeep had moved away, out of the line of action. Other people were scurrying to safety among buildings and machinery on display.

The voice of the major carried clearly to his men.

"Regroup! Ready to attack!"

*   *   *

David Bar-Sharon was waiting just inside the entrance of the hotel when the black limousine drew up outside and the driver got out. He stopped just inside the door, looked at David and said, "Feltham?"

David nodded, and without a word the driver went outside again and opened the rear door of the car. Inside was a slim youngish Arab in western clothes and with aristocratic features. He did not look at David or offer his hand as he got in beside him and the driver closed the door. As soon as the driver was in place the limousine drew away.

"My driver doesn't speak English," the Arab said with an unmistakeable public school accent.

David said nothing.

"I can't say that your being here pleases me," the Arab went on. "And I shall be relieved to see you on the plane out of the country. That way we will both be able to forget that you ever came here."

David still said nothing.

The Arab suddenly turned and regarded David. "What puzzles me is why you were sent here in the first place, Mr. Feltham."

"I wasn't sent," David said. "I came on my own."

"With my name in your book?"

"It was given me by a friend."

"A friend of whom, I wonder. But I'm still puzzled. Did you come here just to warn us of the obvious?"

"I came," David said quietly, "to see."

"So," the Arab said in an odd tone of voice. "That we can arrange."

"Where are we going?" David asked.

"To the fairgrounds."

* * *

From the cab Leif could see Alawi talking to the tall Arab, but he had difficulty catching any sounds at all.

The tall Arab looked at his watch and turned to Markov, pointing to the Scania, and Leif felt his pulse race and almost drown everything. It was actually going to happen; they would start the countdown and leave him.

The explosion rocked the air inside the warehouse with such a loud fury that the entire truck trembled. A second later it was followed by two more in quick succession, a massive thunder that echoed and rolled along the aisles. The lights overhead went out, and there was only harsh daylight through the gaping holes in the huge doors that cast long, eerie shadows from the latticework supports across the concrete floor.

Blurred shapes swarmed past the twisted sheets of corrugated steel and fanned out, dodging for cover behind crates and shelves, advancing in rushes or stopping to fire.

Alawi had fallen on his hands and knees from the first blast and was struggling to get up as the first bullets slammed home in his legs and back, spinning him screaming half sideways. El-Tha'ir had turned and was sprinting for the Scania when a blast sent him tumbling by the right front wheel. Leif saw Markov, who had flung himself to the ground and was desperately trying to crawl away, get a shot off from his revolver before a soldier emptied most of his clip from close range and nearly took Markov's face away. Suddenly the paralysis was gone and Leif ducked, sliding forward with his head wedged between the door and the back of his seat, out of sight below the side window. He felt small, sharp vibrations and dully realized that they were bullets tearing into the coachwork of the cab. The chains bit into his wrists, but he was hardly conscious of the pain.

Outside there was more gunfire, reverberating between the walls, and the sound of tearing metal and breaking glass. That must be the man in the Mazda, Leif thought and could imagine the bullet-riddled white car with the bandaged Arab slumped inside.

Something moved in the corner of his eye, and he managed to turn his head a little to see the passenger door open a crack and a bloodied hand grasp at the edge of the seat.

Slowly, his brand flaming liverish, the tall Arab heaved himself into the cab. His face was scraped and contorted with pain, the front of his robe a dark red sticky mess. Half lying across the seat, he felt with sluggish movements for something on the lower bunk. He found what he wanted, and while Leif watched, aghast, unable to move, managed to push in the large knob although his fingers were slippery with blood, and then twist it with what must have been his last strength.

The volley of bullets almost shattered the right half of the windshield and made the Arab jerk upright with an obscene movement before he slipped and fell, bouncing against the edge of the dash and against the seat before he slid out, hitting the ground with a dull, clearly audible thud as the shooting ceased. The door on Leif's side was wrenched open. In grotesque slow-motion, hanging with his face upside down, he saw a soldier lift his submachine gun and aim it straight into his face.

"Gif!"

The soldier hesitated and lowered his weapon. An older man with a dark, scarred face came running from behind the soldier, and strong bony hands reached up and pushed Leif back into an upright position. Leif emptily looked at the bloodstains on the seat and on the small box and breathed, "*Herregud, han startade den.*"

Somebody pulled at his arm, talking in a language Leif didn't understand. With eyes that were glazed with terror he turned and looked at the man outside the cab, silhouetted against the light from the doors.

"My God." His voice barely rose above a whisper. "He started the bomb."

The echoes of voices and shots died in the warehouse and were replaced by an uncanny quiet. The major once more tugged at Leif's sleeve before he realized that they had no language in common. He shouted for one of his squad leaders, who came running up. The other squad leaders took their men and started searching around the truck and among the aisles.

The major looked at Leif's chains and said, "Ask him how many men there were and why he is chained."

The squad leader put the question to Leif in broken English, but had to repeat it twice before he got any reaction.

"They kidnapped me and brought me here," Leif presently mumbled and shook his head.

The fat head of security warily entered the warehouse, tiptoeing past the soldiers. The major barely glanced at him. "Where are the keys?" he asked and indicated the chains.

The squad leader translated, and Leif mutely nodded in the direction of Markov. One of the soldiers callously rolled the corpse over and dug through the pockets until he found the keys. They unchained Leif, and the security head tried to say something, but was silenced by the major who went on with his interrogation. Leif listened with an air of deathly tiredness.

"But don't you understand?!" he finally exclaimed in desperation, staring at the major. "He started the bomb!"

"What does he say?" the major demanded.

"*Yigul she antashghil ilqunbula*. He says something about starting the bomb."

"*What*? Make him explain."

Leif's apathy was suddenly gone, and assisted by the bewildered squad leader, he finally made the major understand. There was stunned silence.

The security head wiped his forehead and whispered, "*Wa'allah*, their Royal Highnesses . . . the city . . . all the people, we cannot possibly evacuate . . ."

The major glanced at his watch in horror. Four, maybe five, precious minutes had already slipped by. He grabbed Leif's arm and shook it, opening his mouth before he realized once more that he could not make himself understood directly. He yelled at the squad leader, but the security head was faster.

"Listen," he translated. His jowls quivered and glistened with sweat. "You must drive the truck away from here, out of the city to the east, where there are fewer villages." He stopped and the major provided him with more words. "If you don't, thousands and thousands of innocent people will die, the city will die, it will be murder . . . We implore you . . ."

"And what about me, then?" Leif croaked, on the verge of hysterical laughter.

"We will try every way to save you. Please, in the name of God . . ."

He pleaded while the major went on shaking Leif, his face twisted with rage and grief. The soldiers had assembled around the truck and stood motionless, weapons lowered as they silently regarded the driver in his truck.

Something broke inside Leif. *Screw you!* he thought vehemently as he pushed the major back and slammed the door. *I don't care about your king or about your* city. *I'll get rid of the thing because I'm tired of being screwed. If I stay here and die with your lousy lot I'll still be screwed. Hell, I'll die on the road where nobody's screwing me!* He turned the ignition key and pressed the starter button, and the sound of the diesel roared along the aisles of the warehouse. He slammed the gear lever into reverse and backed out of the slot. Soldiers scampered to the side as the truck rolled forward again. It accelerated towards the wide doors askew on broken hinges and with a rending crash broke into the sunlight, sending bent metal bars and crumpled sheets of corrugated iron flying.

In the silence inside the warehouse, the head of security turned his ashen face to the major.

"We have condemned him to death."

"What else could we do?" The major's voice was flat as he quietly went on, "To each, the fate that God bestows upon him."

* * *

The red truck pushed through the gates like a crazed mastodon, and was out in Al Islam Road. The driver of the black limousine it came near to crushing cursed and hit the brakes. Then the guards came running out among the remains of the gates, and David Bar-Sharon and his Arab contact instinctively crouched in the back seat of the limousine as they raised their guns and opened fire.

The semi-trailer keeled over momentarily and slewed right, then recovered partially before it was swallowed by the traffic.

"It is the truck we've been looking for!" the Arab cried and looked up at the fleeing Scania. "Wait here. I'll find out what has happened." He was out of the car and talking to the agitated guards before David had time to answer. He could see one of the guards shake his head and then point to some vague place inside the fairgrounds.

The Arab came back and ordered the driver to drive into the area in the direction indicated by the guard before he sank down again beside David.

"They didn't know," he said, with a puzzled air. "They only knew that there had been explosions and shooting in another area, and then the truck came crashing through. Let's hope we can find out. I'm worried."

David nodded silently as the car with difficulty made its way among the excited crowds. Presently they reached a place where soldiers in combat dress were embarking from two green trucks. A bit off to the left was a large corrugated metal building with torn and mangled doors. Curious spectators were gazing at the wreck, and the more adventurous ones were even trying to peek inside, but were driven off by other soldiers.

"*Wa'allah*," David's contact said softly and was out of the car once more.

*   *   *

The Scania braked and swerved over into the left lane as it cut across the intersection with blaring compressor horns. People on the pavement scattered like chickens as the careening truck picked up speed again.

"*Quss ummak . . .*" The driver of the police car outside the shop cursed as he gunned the engine and swung out, accelerating across the intersection in pursuit of the truck. The other policeman reached for the radio microphone and shouted into it above the roar of the Chevrolet's engine and the wild blasts of the truck.

Once more it swung over to the left, squeezing past a small pickup. In the gap an oncoming brown car showed for a moment, then it was on the left side of the truck, on the pavement, hitting a house wall with a loud, grating sound before it bounced back into the street, front badly crumpled. The police driver yelped as he twisted the wheel. The brown car slammed into their rear fender and sent them skidding before he could recover and set off in renewed pursuit. The driver cursed once more and grimly turned on the sirens and the rotating red and blue lights.

The rear of the semi-trailer lurched crazily with every change of direction, and as the policemen drew closer they could see that two of the trailer's right-side tires were punctured, and large, uneven strips of rubber flapped frantically against the asphalt and the carriage. There were small holes in the tarpaulin, and larger rips in the backside of the trailer.

"He's a madman!" the policeman in the passenger seat shouted.

Houses were thinning out at the outskirts of Riyadh. Ahead was another intersection with traffic in all directions, but the truck only kept on gathering speed, and in the police car the speedo was creeping past 100 kph. There were new long blasts from the compressor horns, and drivers ahead saw and heard and braked in panic to avoid the onrushing juggernaut; all but a small moped to which two robed men clung, looking neither right nor left as they neared the intersection. Their lives they had placed in the hands of Allah.

The truck swerved, its horns blaring again, and the riders on the moped finally looked up, with astonished and horrified faces. Then it was over and something red and white and shapeless swirled and bounced on the tarmac by the huge tires.

The road levelled out and straightened and for a moment was clear of traffic from the other direction. As both the truck and the pursuing police car accelerated the policeman in the passenger seat reached behind to unstrap the submachine gun. As the police car pulled out he rolled down the window and lifted the weapon, taking careful aim at the truck driver as the car drew up alongside.

*   *   *

David was beginning to fidget where he sat in the black limousine and think that maybe it hadn't been such a great idea to approach their contact in Riyadh. His eyes restlessly roved over the scene and registered pavilions and stands, signs and trademarks for agricultural machinery, aviation industries, electronics, all the technology of the western world. His contact stood by the mutilated doors of the warehouse, talking to a fat man in traditional dress and an officer in battle dress while soldiers kept back the gathering crowds.

Presently the contact returned to the limousine. David reached across and opened the door for him, and the Arab sank down in the seat, staring straight ahead as if unaware of David's presence.

"Bad news, Mr. Feltham," he said with unnatural calm. "Your premonition was right. The truck and the terrorists managed to get into the fairgrounds last night. Our troops went in to eliminate them, but unfortunately they weren't fast enough. The truck we saw crashing through the gates has the warhead on board, and the countdown, which is said to be irreversible, has started."

David sank back in the seat, his mind reeling. "He's saving Riyadh by driving it away," he said weakly. Suddenly he realized why there had been no vehicles in pursuit of the truck.

"*In'ish Allah,*" the Arab said.

"What made him do it? The thing is going to blow up."

"Yes. It's difficult to say. Maybe a promise that they would try to save him. He did it." He shrugged fatalistically.

"He isn't going to be saved?"

"How could we save him? I'm sorry, but all we could

do was get on the police and military radio channels and order them to clear the road out of Riyadh for him."

The murmur outside of the excited crowds continued. In the relative silence of the car David looked past his contact.

"Perhaps," he said, "perhaps there is a chance after all."

*   *   *

Leif looked left and found himself staring into the muzzle of a submachine gun. "*Bastards!*" he growled and twisted the wheel left. The semi-trailer swung out and nearly crashed into the police car which swerved and braked. The volley from the submachine gun went wide and shattered the left mirror and the roof sign. Shards of glass and plastic rained around the cab. The police driver cursed and wrenched at the wheel as the outside wheels went off the tarmac and threw up a plume of brownish dust. The car lurched back onto the road and started to close the distance to the truck.

The police radio crackled the code for a general alarm, then: "Attention all units. Attention all units. Red European TIR truck heading through the eastern suburbs of the city at high speed. Registration number at rear of semi-trailer D-V-1-1-5-8-2, visible signs of gunfire damage. Truck must not be interfered with regardless of its actions, repeat, truck must not be interfered with regardless of its actions."

The police driver slowed down and dropped behind the truck as his colleague pulled the submachine gun inside. They looked at each other blankly as the message was repeated twice on the radio.

Ahead was the roadblock that barred the eastern route to Riyadh, and even at that distance there was no mistaking the frantic action as soldiers and military vehicles tried to clear a path for the approaching truck. The last jeep jerked backwards from the road and stalled the second before the truck thundered through, swaying, weaving, groaning, barely clearing the concrete blocks.

The police car braked to a stop just before the road-block, and silently, together with the soldiers, the policemen watched the red truck dwindle in the distance.

24

DYING IS BASIC. Consequently, your reactions to dying are basic.

The engine, thermostat fan, and hurricane through the broken windshield screamed together. The cab shook as the speedometer needle hovered above 125 kph. Leif strained at the wheel, fighting the damaged truck that was trying to pull itself off the road. In the single remaining mirror loose pieces of black rubber spun from the wheels of the semi-trailer bogie. On the dash the water temperature had long since climbed into the danger zone.

So what if the engine seized now? Death for him would come in the same way anyway.

There were fragmented sensations of fear, rage, and desperation in his mind, and yet he was strangely calm. His heart was hammering furiously, his body was being driven to its limits, his T-shirt was drenched with sweat, but the realization that he was actually going to die was drowned in the stream of adrenaline in his veins.

Death was something that happened to others, and while the thing in the chassis of his truck meted out the remainder of his life, he was more alive than at anytime. The bomb, the future, his death, were as unreal as the minutes on the clock on the dash.

His lips drew back as he looked at it again. Even allowing for the margin of error in those first, frantic moments, nearly forty minutes had slipped by.

Five minutes left.

He lifted his mute face and looked at the empty strip of asphalt that cut a straight slash across the expanse of arid desert. There had been no other traffic for some time. Perhaps they had stopped all traffic at some road-block ahead.

For a moment he was overcome with a feeling of unbearable desolation. God. I never wanted to die alone like this. Damn them!

He had five minutes left before he would die and nothing but the empty road ahead of him.

Habit made him glance in his mirrors and he saw something that hadn't been there before. He stared un-comprehendingly at the fuzzy, yellow dot in the vibrating mirror. It trailed him some distance above the ground, steadily growing.

The lurch as the right-side wheels went over the edge of the road jarred him out of his stupefaction, and he tugged at the steering wheel and wrestled the recalcitrant Scania back onto the road. When he looked in his mirror again the yellow dot was gone from it.

Furiously he turned the window handle, which caught badly from time to time. Then he had the window down and stuck his head out, looking back along the trailer. As if in a dream he saw a small yellow helicopter come gliding up alongside almost level with the tarpaulin top. A bright sun blazed at him from the dark canopy of the craft, and its thunder drowned the roar from the diesel and the screaming gale that tore at his face and hair.

The pilot leaned forward as far as the shoulder harness would allow, craning his neck to look past David Bar-Sharon at the red truck below. Its cab filled the lower right half of the smoke-coloured canopy. The driver was still poking his head out through the window, staring at them.

"Sure looks beat-up to me," he shouted into his helmet microphone with an unmistakable Deep South accent. "You really mean that thing's carrying a goddam live nuke?"

"Believe me, it is," David shouted back. "And it's going to go up any minute now!"

"Well," the pilot said, "I reckon we won't feel it much when it does."

"Not if we're still around," David said grimly. "Can you get a little closer, Wade?"

"Sure can." The Hughes 500M-D dropped a little sideways. Below the driver pulled his head in. "Can't get too close, though. These 'copters get awful skittery from rotor blast deflection. Besides, if that rig hit my skid we'd take one hell of a drop."

"Do what you can. I'm going back." David unbuckled his harness and the helmet connections, and steadying himself against the back of the seat, squeezed past to the aft part of the cramped cabin. He unhooked the harness from the bulkhead and put it on. He had discarded his jacket and tie and wore only his pale blue shirt and his pin-striped trousers. The straps of the harness, designed for fitting over uniforms and thick coveralls, cut and chafed badly as he tightened them. He looked at his watch again, acutely aware of how close to the time limit they were and knowing that they might be off by as much as five minutes. Yet he felt a strangely fatalistic calm and determination.

He plugged in his helmet and adjusted the length of the wire that joined him to the opposite bulkhead, then he pushed the safety interlocks back and slid the aft cabin door open. The blast of air almost tore his fingers from the grab bar and knocked him down, but he managed to hang on, blinking to clear his watering eyes. "Can you get her forward a little more?" he screamed into the mic. "I want him to be able to reach the skid from the cab roof!"

"Gonna try, Pete." The helicopter crept forward until David shouted, "Try to hold her there!"

He could see into the cab, could see the driver wrestling with the wheel, and had a vision of a huge, wounded beast in its death throes. It sluggishly weaved over the road; the distance between it and the helicopter grew wide, then shrank until David involuntarily stiffened expecting a collision. The driver looked up, his eyes met David's and David frenziedly motioned at the cab roof and the helicopter skid, trying to make himself understood.

Leif looked once again at the yellow helicopter, which hovered so near and yet seemed so unreachable, then his passivity suddenly vanished.

The incongruously clad man in the helicopter doorway was beckoning at him once more, pointing to the cab roof and the nearest skid, and finally Leif understood. He had no idea of who the man was, why he was dressed the way he was, or whatever it was that drove him, but suddenly he was not alone any longer.

He couldn't let go of the wheel, or the damaged Scania would immediately veer away from the helicopter, off the road and onto the uneven gravel. Wildly he looked around inside the cab.

He needed something to lock the wheel with, a rope, anything. Wildly he cursed the Scania engineers for not having included a steering wheel lock in the design, then he found the solution. He reached down, steering with one hand, and unbuckled his leather belt and pulled it from his jeans. Trying as best he could to offset the wheel to the left, he wound it around the wheel spokes and the steering column before he tightened and buckled it. He pulled the hand throttle out against the stop to its maximum setting, then cast a last glance around the cab and with a cry pushed the door open into the howling wind.

Flying sand and dust raked his skin like sharp needles. He looked down at the blurred asphalt that rushed in under the wheels, and the taste of animal fear was like ink in his mouth. The helicopter hung suspended above him with the skid out of reach, its engine and rotor thundering.

Almost blinded by the wind, he hung on to the door frame and groped, unseeing, for the metal ladder outside the cab; finding it, he gripped it with a strength that fed upon his fear. He transferred his right foot to the ladder and could feel his sweaty fingers slipping on the rung. He swung out from the cab, for a moment hanging in the buffeting air, before his other hand found the ladder and grasped it.

Clinging so tight that the sharp edges of the ladder cut through his clothes into his skin, he hung on and tried to catch his breath. He looked up, squinted, and started to climb. The climb was agony, and suddenly he had a very real feeling that he was trying to climb away from the thing below while knowing fully the futility of it all. Then his left hand found the single metal rail around the roof, and he heaved himself up, panting from exhaustion and panic.

Holding onto the metal frame of the roof sign, he raised himself in a half crouch. The helicopter swung in over him in what seemed excruciating slow-motion, and he let go of the roof sign and reached for the skid overhead.

The jar as the wheels went over onto the gravel made the truck shake and caught him off-balance. The skid swept by inches from his outstretched hands as he twisted and fell over the sharp edges of the roof sign, catching it with his chest in a shock of agonizing pain. He could feel his T-shirt get thickly sticky as he looked down the windshield and grille at the brownish blur beneath. Only a desperate handhold kept him from toppling over. Groaning, as the truck shook across the gravel, he managed to regain his balance and pull himself back up.

The helicopter was coming in again, lower this time. He threw up an arm and got off his knees. The skid hit him in the chest with numbing force and carried him off the roof. His heels hit the metal rail and one of his sandals was knocked off. Then he was free of the truck, clinging wildly with his legs swinging in the air. The man in the door shouted something, and the helicopter banked and turned with a dizzying, sickening movement. Terror gave Leif the necessary strength to force his left leg over the skid.

The helicopter was accelerating as it came out of the turn, straightening up and skimming away low above the ground. Leif felt a hand gripping his jeans at the hip and looked up. The man inside the helicopter was down on his stomach. Leif threw up his left hand and grasped the harness over his shoulder, and they both pulled. The skid bruised his thigh and knee as he let go of it, then his chest was on the metal floor, and he pulled himself in.

The helicopter banked again, dropping even lower as it accelerated towards a range of low hills north of the road. On his hands and knees close by the helicopter door, Leif had a last glimpse of his truck. The Scania looked incongruously small in the distance and shrinking with every moment. Obscured by a plume of brown dust, it rushed on alone while the last seconds ticked away before the blinding light and searing heat of near doomsday.

FREE!!
BOOKS BY MAIL
CATALOGUE

BOOKS BY MAIL will share with you our current bestselling books as well as hard to find specialty titles in areas that will match your interests. You will be updated on what's new in books at no cost to you. Just fill in the coupon below and discover the convenience of having books delivered to your home.

BOOKS BY MAIL
P.O. Box 901, 517 Lorne Avenue
Stratford, Ontario N5A 6W3

Please send Books By Mail catalogue to:

Name_____
           (please print)

Address_____

City_____

Prov._____ Postal Code _____
                                    (BBM1)

FREE
SUBSCRIPTION_____

Books By Mail will send you our free newsletter.
We will share with you current bestselling titles,
as well as hard to find specialty titles in areas that
will match your interests. Just fill in this coupon
and mail it to us today. You will be updated on
what's new in books . . . from time to time . . . at
no cost to you.

Below is a list of specific book categories. Check
the ones you're interested in. This will help us keep
you better informed about areas that you've indicated.

A ____ Bestsellers	J ____ Health/
B ____ Cooking/		Psychology
	Gourmet	K ____ Consumerism
C ____ Sports	L ____ Home/Garden
D ____ Children	M ____ Crafts/Hobbies
E ____ Arts/Photography	N ____ Money/Careers
F ____ Reference/	O ____ Pets/Nature
	Science	P ____ Family/Child
G ____ Romance		Care
H ____ Travel	Q ____ Beauty/Dieting
I ____ Current Affairs/	R ____ Automotive
	History	

Write to:
BOOKS BY MAIL
Box 901, 517 Lorne Ave., Stratford, Ontario N5A 6W3

Name_____

Address_____Apt.____

City_____

Prov._____Postal Code_____

(BBM3)